WINTER OF THE WHITE SEAL
by Marie Herbert

In a great bestselling tradition, yet entirely original,
Winter of the White Seal is the journal of young
Jonathan Horn, stranded in the Antarctic in 1819 by
a sealing expedition. His battles against nature at its
cruellest, his vivid description of the changing
seasons and wildlife and how he survives in the face
of incredible odds are only part of this enthralling
adventure. For at the centre of this truly unusual
novel is Scruff, the orphaned white seal whom
Jonathan adopts and raises and who is his sole
companion. Not since *Ring of Bright Water* has such
a memorable animal appeared in literature.

WINTER
OF THE
WHITE SEAL

Marie Herbert

Marie Herbert

Blessings & joy,

Marie

COLLINS
St James's Place, London
1982

For Wally

William Collins Sons & Co. Ltd.
London · Glasgow · Sydney · Auckland
Toronto · Johannesburg

First Published in Great Britain by William Collins in 1982
ISBN 0 00 222132 2

Made and printed in
the United States of America

Foreword

Winter of the White Seal, while essentially a product of the imagination, is nevertheless set against the background of the Southern sealing industry, which witnessed the ruthless and indiscriminate slaughter of millions of fur seals in the nineteenth century. In the South Shetland Islands alone in 1821 and 1822 an estimated 320,000 fur seals were killed and 100,000 pups were left to die, resulting in the near extinction of the species in that group (*Antarctic Pilot*). Similar drastic carnage was reported at various times in South Georgia and elsewhere. While the numbers recovered to some extent in the half century following the first slaughter, further hunting again reduced them to a pitiful few. Happily, today fur seals are reemerging where for years they had been nonexistent—and the vulnerability and beauty of these marvelous creatures is what partly prompted the writing of the *Winter of the White Seal.*

One cannot read the history of the early sealers without being impressed by the extraordinary courage and hardiness of some of the men involved in the industry, especially some of the skippers, who were in every sense explorers. Taken a step further, the history of exploration in the Antarctic uncovers even more of those rare and special qualities of bravery and endurance which characterized so many of its men. I am brought to the second motive for writing the novel—an attempt to avow man's incredible instinct for survival and the amazingly deep wells of strength within him.

A fascination for the history of exploration and a great deal of reading, especially of polar literature, provided the inspiration from which the book evolved. This story could actually have happened—sealers were frequently shipwrecked and even marooned on desolate, uninhabited shores. The latter was the penalty for "blabbing"—divulging the whereabouts of the sealing beaches to a rival crew. Competition was bitterly keen for possession of the beaches, and bloody battles were fought to protect one's catch.

The island chosen for my hero's marooning is Livingstone Island, one of the South Shetlands, which was discovered by William Smith on February 18, 1819, although when the British claimed the discovery of the South Shetlands in 1820, articles appeared in the U.S. newspapers claiming that American sealers had been going there for years but had kept their voyages secret. In view of this element of doubt I consider it quite proper for the purposes of my story that the hero be allowed the privilege of discovering the island a year ahead of Smith. By coincidence, my husband, Wally Herbert, while working for the Falkland Islands Dependencies Survey, was amongst the first group of young explorers to map the interior of the island in 1958.

I could not have tackled a book of this character without having drawn on the knowledge and experience I gained in living for two years with the Eskimos of northwest Greenland. Nor could I have written it without drawing on the experience and films and field notes of many of the people at the British Antarctic Survey who were unbelievably generous with their advice and time. In particular, I should like to thank Nigel Bonner for his invaluable advice and for the loan of his films on South Georgia; Mike Payne for the loan of his marvelous colour transparencies and for answering many an involved question; Geoff Renner for unearthing facts and figures and photographs on many and varied subjects to do with seals and sealing, geography and geology; and Mike Thomson and Pete Clarkson, whose descriptions and colour slides of the Byers Peninsula inspired the last chapter in the book.

To Harry King, the Librarian of the Scott Polar Research Institute, I owe a deep sense of gratitude for the countless logs of sealing ships and precious manuscripts he put at my disposal. Finally, a very big thank-you to Wally, my husband, who was a constant source of inspiration and encouragement over the five years it took to write the book and without whom my hero might have lacked a soul.

—MARIE HERBERT

WELFORD-ON-AVON
June 10, 1981

Contents

Foreword 7

1. South Georgia 15
2. The Screaming Sixties 33
3. Tranquility 42
4. Alone! 53
5. To Light a Fire 72
6. Coming to Terms 90
7. Midsummer 100
8. Household Chores 110
9. The Moult 120
10. The Fighting Penguin 130
11. Lost in the Blizzard 139
12. The Approach of Winter 149
13. The Big Storm 160
14. Aftermath 168
15. Winter Routine 174

16. The Intruder   180
17. Desperation   184
18. Sacrilege   190
19. The Return of Life   198
20. No Latitude for Error   202
21. Methuselah   213
22. Killer Whales   224
23. Scruff's Choice   238
24. The Ice Cap   253
25. The Last Decision   270

WINTER OF THE WHITE SEAL

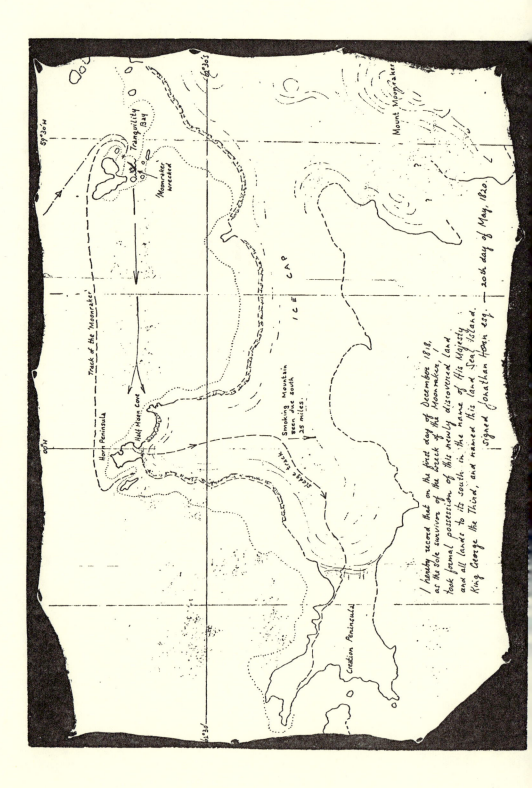

1

South Georgia

The men cheered spontaneously as a great wave of excitement spread through the ship. For a moment I held back, thrilled with the glorious expectation of it all, until I could no longer endure the suspense, then I leapt for the shrouds to get a better view, and what I saw made me hold my breath, for I had never seen any place more wild or more beautiful.

Before us was an island, snow-capped and sparkling, which rose like a diamond out of the sea. Huge towering peaks were separated by great flowing rivers of ice, and it was all so fiercely grand and unexpected that I was quite beside myself with joy. Why had my shipmates not told me about it before? It would have made the whole journey seem worthwhile.

Several weeks had elapsed since that night in the sweet-scented summer of 1818 when I had made that fateful decision to leave home and make my own way in the world, and not a night had passed since then without my regretting it. Any romantic notion of life at sea had been dashed long ago by the squalid and overcrowded conditions in the fo'c'sle. Whereas my crew mates were inured to hardship, having been spawned in that teeming cesspool of humanity that swamped the back-street gutters of most cities, I had come from a comfortable home and a family that enjoyed a privileged social position.

I was born in Liverpool in 1798 to a prosperous merchant, whose business interests were multifarious but were mostly concerned with ships and shipping. As my father's only son and heir to his considerable fortune, I am told that my arrival was welcomed not only as a blessing upon my parents' happy union but as yet another extension of my father's personal empire and his formidable ambition.

My mother—morbidly solicitous of my welfare, having lost her only other child when he was three—was inclined to pamper me, her fears for my well-being taking the form of denying me any kind of strenuous physical exercise in case I should hurt myself. Worried by what might happen if I strayed beyond the reach of her protective influence, she sought to keep me indoors and offered vicarious excitement in the form of books of travel and adventure. Far from curbing my adventurous spirit, however, the books heightened my imagination and curiosity, so that I developed a passionate desire to go out and see the world for myself.

At the boarding school that I attended later, in company with the sons of the English aristocracy and a few like myself whose fathers had earned their fortunes by their enterprise and skill, my curiosity was further whetted. I worked hard and attained my grades without effort, which prompted my tutors to comment to my delighted parents that I was destined for a distinguished career in whatever profession I chose to enter. In the light of this, my declared intention to go to sea must have been a shock. My mother fainted, and my father became quite violent. The two of us argued for several days, during which time my mother refused to speak to either of us. And although I claimed that I had a right to follow my own ambitions, my father insisted that I had a duty to continue my education at university, qualifying in some subject such as law so that I could take a useful place in the family firm.

The deadlock remained until my father produced a compromise which he knew no lover of ships could refuse. "See here,

Jonathan!" he had growled with a hint of triumph in his voice as he carried into the room the most exquisite model of a ship. "This model is yours the day you go to university. AND!"—he forestalled my interruption—"the day you graduate, my boy, the ship of which this is merely a model will be yours by my word and deed!"

I doubt any student had more incentive to complete his studies. After I had graduated and taken possession of my ship I thought I was the happiest man alive. Pride and elation mingled with an almost indescribable kind of caring. I wanted to be a good shipowner whatever onerous duties such a title involved. And with the extravagance born of this new sense of duty I resolved that my vessel should carry only such cargoes as would be deemed worthy of this queen of three-masted ships, while her crew would be the finest ever to man the yards of a barque and sail a seaman's course.

How short-lived was my elation. Owner I might be in name, but there was not one item concerning the manning or running of the ship that my father intended to entrust to my stewardship. True, I lacked experience in commerce and seamanship and had no money to fit her out, but in my youthful excitement I had imagined that enthusiasm would make up for such lack and felt cheated and humiliated to be denied the chance to prove it. For a month I withstood the dreariness of the countinghouse, where I had been sent to acquaint myself with the books, and although several times I tried to approach my father to impress on him my need for independence, he refused to discuss it.

When things finally came to a head he stormed at me that no other son could have had more done for him, going on to jibe, "Why, if you never worked as much as a single day in your life, thanks to me and my efforts you could retire a rich and influential man!" I hated him at that moment, and yet I should have thanked him for exposing the futility of the life he offered me based on inherited wealth and privilege. I knew then that I had to leave home. I would be my own man, and I would make my own name in the world.

I left that night, slipping away while my parents were asleep.

London attracted me as a stepping-stone to the life of adventure I had planned for myself, but like most greenhorns I fell easy prey to the land sharks that crowded its streets, and within minutes of my arrival had been robbed of most of the money I possessed. By nightfall the city had lost much of its enchantment, although my attitude was coloured by the prospect of eating meagerly and sleeping rough. So when a voice enquired amicably, not five minutes after my arrival at the docks, "Lookin' fer a berth, sonny?" I could hardly believe my luck. After signing on I was escorted aboard the *Moonraker*, whose appearance, unlike her beautiful name, filled me with dread. Too late I realized that I had been duped into joining a sealer, which, like the whaler, was one of the most loathsome vessels known to man. Living conditions were notoriously squalid and the discipline so barbaric that only a fool would join of his own accord. I had cursed my decision often enough since then and wished to reverse it—until now. And gazing out from my perch in the rigging, with our destination like some sparkling jewel rising out of the sea on our southern horizon, I felt my heart ready to burst with excitement. Bounding down the shrouds again, I reached out to shake hands with my crew mates, full of an uncontrollable need to share my delight. They responded irritably to my gesture, going so far as to ask if I had gone soft in the head. Already they had begun to fear that rival crews might have got to the sealing beaches ahead of us, leaving precious little on which to stake our claim.

The sight of several ships farther along the coast made the crew even more edgy. I, on the other hand, did not give a fig for our sealing prospects, since I was on 1/120 of a lay, as against their 1/90, which meant that I would get only the price of one sealskin out of every 120 sold. Apart from this, I did not enjoy the prospect of butchering animals and felt sure that when it came down to it, the sealers would be rather lacking in finesse. So, ignoring the growing tenseness of my crew mates, I stood by to take directions while marvelling at each new aspect of the island and at the fantastic variety of birds and sea creatures. Among the most engaging of these were the penguins and the Southern fur seals with their enormous, lugubrious eyes, who occasionally would pop their heads out of the water to look at us before darting away out of sight.

Of the two kinds of seal that we had sailed over 8,000 miles to harvest, it was from the prime pelts of the fur seal that every man on board, with the certain exception of myself, hoped to make his fortune. From the much larger and rather obnoxious-looking elephant seal we hoped to obtain a goodly supply of blubber. This would be melted down into train oil—a commodity which was in great demand in the manufacture of candles and paints and which was also used in ships for caulking, preserving ropes, sails and timbers, and as a lubricant for various mechanical devices. Since the numbers of ships involved in the sealing trade had increased dramatically, the numbers of both fur seals and elephant seals had been correspondingly reduced, which meant that there was usually a race to get to the sealing grounds as early as possible in the season. This way a crew might get a head start on the other—although even if a ship did arrive early it could soon expect to find some competition turning up. Very often there was bitter fighting and loss of life before the rights to a sealing beach were established and the killing of seals could begin.

Now, arriving three weeks later than we had anticipated, the crew were only too aware of the difficulties of getting a good beach to ourselves and, as they sharpened their flensing knives, I could detect that they had a mind to use them in a situation for which they were not originally intended.

There were numerous indentations in the coast that would have afforded us shelter had we been able to negotiate the rocky obstacles at their entrance, but safe harbours near the sealing beaches were infrequent. And since the island, according to the old hands, was a place of violent and sudden squalls, in spite of its benign appearance, it made it all the more imperative to chose a harbour carefully.

Our hope of success in this respect soon wore thin, for all along the coast there were ships at anchor and, rounding a promontory, we saw a veritable fleet. Many of these were from foreign ports whose crews were all engaged in sealing. The sight of these vessels excited me but drew a gasp of consternation from my mates. The skipper, hearing this, growled, "We'll get a beach if we have to take on the whole bloody lot of them, but we'll scour the coast before we waste time and energy getting rid of the competition."

For the rest of the day we followed the coast round in a northerly direction and passed many ships at anchor, most of them brigs, although there were several three-masted vessels boasting as much as four or five hundred tons that were forced to anchor a mile or so from shore. Their crews, however, patrolled close to the coast in shallops or cutters, either searching for new beaches or acting as deterrents to those likely to challenge their comrades, who had already started sealing.

On account of these early arrivals we were forced to travel way beyond the well-known grounds in the hope of finding an unworked but well-stocked stretch of coast on which to stake our claim. And since the depth was too shallow to allow for the passage of the ship in many places, we were obliged to stand off from the shore and send in the longboats to reconnoiter a beach or to look for a suitable sheltering place.

It was several days before the longboats' crews had any success, for the beaches were either too dangerous to approach, accessible but devoid of seals, or loaded and occupied by larger crews than we could hope to shift. Eventually, however, a signal was hoisted from one of the longboats that signified the discovery of a harbour, and we made haste to reach it before any other ship might see us going in. With a longboat leading the way to sound, we stood cautiously in to land, and finding that the entrance was rather narrow, we were obliged to warp our way into the cove.

We had no sooner dropped anchor and got the ship under snug canvas when the weather thickened, and we were plastered by great masses of sleet that drove blindingly into our eyes and sneaked inside our collars. We brought the longboats aboard for fear they would get damaged, for even in this little haven the surface was whipped into peaks that could have dashed the boats against each other till they eventually broke up.

The storm ended as abruptly as it had begun, and we were

away at first light to look for seals. The nights were short now at this latitude, and although cold, it was midsummer, the seasons being the opposite of those in our part of the world. The fact that this was so intrigued me, for it served to emphasize the distance we had come from home.

The longboats left the harbour surreptitiously, and our orders were clear: we were to go in search of sealing beaches and, on returning, to draw off any competition that might approach, for the skipper wanted no one but his own men to know of his harbour and no ship to block his passage to the open sea. The longboats were loaded up with sealing gear, and we had to take great care to avoid sunken rocks and large pieces of ice which crept up on us without warning, being low in the water and difficult to distinguish until we were upon them. We narrowly missed driving straight on to one of these "growlers," as they are called, which would surely have holed us had we done so, for it had great pointed fronds projecting just below the waterline; but at the last minute we managed to turn the boat's head aside, almost capsizing the craft as we did so. I would not have counted much on our chances of survival had we fallen in, for in such freezing waters a fellow could hardly last more than a minute, even supposing him to be a strong swimmer, and, strange to say, very few sailors are able to swim.

We had taken a few days' provisions with us and some sailcloth to make a shelter, the idea being to camp on a good beach if it promised a fair catch. The cooper was in one of the longboats, surrounded by staves and barrel hoops with which to make casks to contain the blubber—although I could not see how he was going to make use of any of his expertise with these, since he was in such poor shape. It was only two days since he had had his leg crushed in an accident in the hold, and this was not time enough for the limb to set properly or for the pain to be relieved. As compensation for his injury and also as some kind of palliative, he had been allowed an unlimited amount of rum, which, of course, only perpetuated his stupor, so that he had to be lowered into the boat alongside his professional accoutrements. How much he was aware of, I did not know, but on occasions the air above him cracked with the heat of his profanities, which

21

he released like gunfire when an unexpected jolt to his wounded limb triggered off fresh pain.

We had been rowing for hours before we saw any kind of promising landing place, and I was chilled to the bone by the frequent blasts of offshore wind and beginning to tire of our exertion when, without warning, we rounded a point to find the tip of a concealed beach just visible through a cluster of tall rocks. Despite the fearsomeness of the surrounding waters, caused by the pressure of the ocean currents forcing their volume through the narrow passages of the upturned fangs, we attempted a landing, for we could see that the beach was alive with elephant seals.

A stench stronger than farmyards assailed us as we neared the shore, together with a clamour that defies description, being made up of the screaming and bickering of a horde of birds which mingled with the squeals and barks of young seals and the retching roars of their elders. I was not put off by this, however, for I had an uncontrollable urge to tread land, and without giving a thought for the boat or for any of the others, I leapt into the foaming water, which reached my knees, and made a dash up the beach. I made for the hinterland, which was green and hummocky and tufted with high grass. On the way I zigzagged through a herd of females, jumped over a heap of pups, hopped up several mounds and did not stop running till I was hidden from view and very out of breath, whereupon I threw myself, whooping abandonedly, into the shoulder-high tussock. A moment later I was on my feet, springing up even faster than I had lain down, for I had found myself face to face with the ugliest animal I had ever seen, and most definitely the largest I had seen at such close quarters. I had landed beside a bull elephant, full twenty times my own weight if he was an ounce. On being disturbed from his sleep, he had made such a roaring sound in my direction that I nearly jumped out of my skin with fright. As I stumbled and slipped as fast as my legs would take me back the way I had come, that terror increased with each lurching step, for, concealed amongst the tussocks, what passed for mounds of earth beneath my feet were more often than not the wobbling, upturned stomachs of sleeping animals, each of which started up and, roaring indignantly at my intrusion, threatened my retreat. My reception from the crew when eventually I returned to the beach was scarcely more welcoming. I was cautioned that I would go to feed the try-pots—the iron cauldrons in which we boiled the blubber—if I did not jump to and pull my weight, a threat I respected enough not to put to the test.

The beach we had come to was small, bounded a little way inland by a coastal hill on which scores of penguins were to be seen. Some stood wistfully to attention, while others came and went in waddling relays that proceeded endlessly back and forth from the hill to the beach, their faces marked by such thoughtful expressions that they might have been searching their minds for a reason to be there at all. Occasionally one or two of the sealers who got in the way of this continuous motion were treated to a peck on the leg. This not unreasonable reaction of the birds the sealers returned with indiscriminate favour, catapulting half a dozen of the nearest creatures into the air at the end of a stout boot and putting an end to the birds' solemn dignity for a while, besides inflicting no doubt a certain amount of undeserved pain.

At either end of the beach there was a rocky outcrop which blocked the view of the rest of the island. On climbing the southerly one, a sailor came rushing back to announce that there was a colony of fur seals on the other side. It did not take me long to realize that our beach was divided up between families of elephant seals, which consisted of a male bull and maybe ten or more females comprising his harem.

Here and there were "mounds" of pups who, being removed from parental authority, seemed quite content to lie in heaps, with those on top clearly unconcerned by the cries of those who were surely suffocating or being crushed somewhere deep down below. The cows seemed amazingly docile, appearing not to be alarmed by anything and content on the whole to lie about like great fat slugs. The claylike mud had been churned into a quagmire in some places, caking them all over. The bulls, on the other hand, were singularly bad-tempered, and constantly rampaging around and bellowing as they challenged each other to fight. They filled the air with a cacophony of the most awful noises, which varied from a full-bellied roar to a strangled gargling, which turned one's stomach inside out. They reared themselves up, balancing on their hindquarters. Seeing the deep gashes and scars of ancient fights on their hides made by their strong canines, I decided to keep them at a respectful distance. Not only were they vicious but when they pulled themselves up to their fullest height they towered above the tallest of us by as much as two or three feet.

The crew were feverishly excited to have found such an assembly, and they lost no time going in to the kill. They worked with a zeal that could not have been more urgent. At the back of everyone's mind was the fear that they might be discovered and have to fight or share the beach with another crew. And each knew that he would have to work doubly hard and fast if they were to recoup lost time and harvest anything like the quota of seals that would make the voyage worthwhile. At a rough guess, there were probably about ninety mature animals to be taken on the beach, not to mention those hidden in the tussocks; but we needed several hundred elephant seals, in addition to several thousand fur seals, before the voyage was ended if we were to make a decent lay.

While the carpenter and another fellow, under the doubtful supervision of the poor cooper, set up the tryworks, which was the stone or brickwork that supported the iron pots, I was detailed to tussock up the boats to make a shelter. This meant turning them upside down, with one gunwale resting on the ground and the other raised three or four feet on a bank of stones and tussock, leaving an opening for a doorway sufficient for men to creep in and out of. Despite our impatience and willingness to work, we might all have to take refuge under them to escape a particularly violent storm. Even if we did not use the boats as shelter, they had still to be secured by filling them with stones or sand so that in the event of a storm they would not be blown away. There was no lack of stories of sailors who had been stranded on a beach when they had been too careless to bother weighting down their boats. These had been either smashed against the nearby rocks or else blown out to sea.

The boats secured, I was directed to attach myself to the business of stoking the tryworks while at the same time keeping my eyes open for any situation in which I could give a hand. I felt relieved to be absolved of the gory duty of slaughtering. I was loath to kill, however repellent the animal, although I was to find that by the end of the day I was as exhausted as my crew mates and as soaked with blood and slime. The events that followed were horrible, but, for all my reluctance to be a part of this slaughter, I found it exerted a dreadfully hypnotic influence that kept me watching.

The great bulls were the first to be attacked. With them disposed of, the crew could get at the cows and pups that would otherwise have been tirelessly defended. While censoring the crew for a good deal of unnecessary brutality, I could not help admiring the cool nerve with which one or two of them approached the fearsome custodians of the beach. They advanced to within a few paces directly in front of each bull, which, when it became aroused, drew itself up to the full extent of its enormous height, inflating its nose to such grotesque proportions that it looked positively monstrous. At the same time the animal made such a conglomeration of awful noises that I thought it would burst a blood vessel.

The sealer had to position himself so that he could drive the bull backwards towards the sea; for, before the blubber was boiled, it had to be washed at the water's edge to remove as much blood from it as possible. It took several men with much shouting and brandishing of pikes to force some of the bulls to retreat. Once or twice a few of the crew came very near to suffering a most gruesome fate when they slipped in the mud in front of an oncoming animal, whose sheer weight alone, if it had thrown itself on them, would have burst their bodies like squashed tomatoes and whose teeth, if they had made contact, would not have parted till they had torn away a lump of flesh. Fortunately, others of the crew were courageous enough to lay in against the bull with all their might, jabbing their pikes into his nose and neck so that he stopped in his tracks and retreated before inflicting any harm. Once up, although shaken and covered in slime and liquid excrement, the crew advanced again towards the attack, and in a short time the bull was killed.

The method of dispatch varied according to the size of the

animal, the young ones being stunned with a stout blow upon the head before being finished off with a quick thrust in the side by the lance. Cows were slaughtered in much the same way; but the bulls required great skill to kill, since their enormous bulk made them virtually immune to a blow with a club. They had to be approached carefully, with the lance held in a horizontal position in both hands by one man. The shaft was grasped near the end, and the left foot had to be placed slightly in advance of the right, not only to give the body a firm stance but to enable the striker to make a quick retreat. The lance itself was overall eight feet in length. A sharp pointed cutting blade about a foot long was attached to a two-foot shank, and this was riveted to the handle, which was of a convenient diameter to be grasped firmly by a man's hand. Having been roused to an elevated position—a touch on the nose with a lance raised the head of the animal as much as eight feet off the ground—the bull exposed the most vulnerable part of his chest. Nonetheless, the sealer still needed courage and not a little strength to effect a fatal thrust to the heart. Care had to be taken that the animal did not seize the lance with his teeth and snap it in two, or even run amok with it, flailing its head about with the shaft protruding from either side of the mouth. And even if one did strike a fatal blow, one had then to be agile enough to get out of the dying creature's way.

Only as many animals as could be dealt with conveniently were dispatched at one time. It was essential, especially in the case of the bulls, that the blubber be flayed off them quickly before the cold touch of death made them too stiff to skin effectively. My first shock came when I was sprayed from head to foot by a jet of blood that burst out of the dying animal as it was lanced. It spurted into my face, covering my hair and running down my clothes. The crew laughed at my surprise and discomfort, saying that now that I had been baptized I had only to make my first kill to be confirmed as a sealer. Horrible as it was, I was more disturbed by the significance of the dousing. I saw in it a token that I too shared the guilt for the unholy sacrifice.

Each sealer had a wooden scabbard hanging from his belt. It contained his curved sealing knife—ten inches long, his steel and a sealing club for stunning fur seals. Small hooks were used to grip the blubber and larger hooks to haul the carcass over. There was another useful piece of equipment in the shape of a three-pronged hook used for hauling carcasses of fur seals out of crevices in the rocks where they might have fallen but these were not always carried on the sealer's person, since they were awkward and inclined to get in the way. I had managed to obtain a set of sealing weapons from the slop chest—a well-used set marked with the initials W. W. on the scabbard. This hung alongside a specially made sailcloth pocket attached to my belt that housed my diary—the only item I had brought away from home and which I never took off my person.

It took four men to handle a carcass. To remove the skin, they first made incisions round the flippers and then lengthwise down the middle of the back before following this up with several transverse incisions across the back that allowed for the flaps of hide to be flayed off each side. When this was done, the white fat, or blubber as it was called, which amounted in some animals to a good eight inches or more in depth, could then be removed with comparative ease. It was cut away from the muscle in large, square "horse" pieces about a foot and a half long and one foot wide—so called from its being cut to fit the "horse," which was a contraption employed to cut the blubber into slices. After the dorsal area had been flensed, the animal was then rolled over and the process repeated on the ventral side. Afterwards, the pieces were hooked onto long poles and carried by several men to the sea to be washed. To give an idea of the weight involved in handling these animals, I can tell you that it would take two men to carry the skin of a large animal, and this with a bit of a struggle. The head would similarly require two men to carry it, which only goes to show how strenuous was our exertion.

Once the first animal had been killed, there arose a frantic hubbub from the birds encircling us as they dodged and dived to feed on the carcasses. My job was to cut up the horse pieces as they arrived at the tryworks into strips about two inches wide. I then had to score or "mince" them at intervals of about an inch, ready for boiling. This way, the heat could penetrate every portion of the fat, and the oil would be extracted faster, leaving only scraps of crisp and shrivelled matter which floated on the top. These were then removed and pressed to extract the remainder of the oil before being thrown onto the fire beneath the cauldrons to feed the flames. Usually the blubber was left to soak for twenty-four hours to remove the blood; but in view of our haste to get the job done and move on to the next beach, we could not afford any delay. The resulting oil would not be as pure as was desirable, but if we were to reap the maximum harvest we would have to work nonstop till all the seals available to us were slaughtered and the blubber casked, or, sure as heaven, some other ship's company would come cruising by and challenge us to our catch.

The nauseating stench of the blubber reached an even greater foulness when some of the crew began slaughtering penguins so that their skins could be used as fuel. These had a layer of fat on them which burned well, although I was soon coughing, my eyes streaming, from the fumes. The air around the tryworks was laden with great greasy globules that settled on our skin and clothes, layering them with fat. I could only guess at the dreadfulness of my appearance—certainly it would be no better than that of my mates, who too were layered with blood and filth.

Hour upon hour we toiled with barely any break. I had never seen such carnage. Carcasses were strewn everywhere, and the beach had become a quagmire where we had trampled around in the sea of blood. Slaughtering, butchering, hauling and trying out—the process seemed endless, and all the while the oil was accumulating and being run off from the two cauldrons into the barrels. Whether the cooper had been any help I do not know, but so far the casks appeared to have been put together adequately. The invalid, meanwhile, was ensconced near the tryworks with his back against one of the upturned boats, punctuating his recommendations with snatches of indecipherable song.

Since we had eaten nothing except ship's biscuits and cold salt horse all day, a halt was called around midnight for a hot meal. After our exertions, our bodies had become sapped of strength. Shivering, we huddled together near the heat from the try-pots, waiting for the meal of boiled elephants' tongues which had been thrown into a pot over a small fire and which tasted surprisingly good. The day had been marked by frequent short squalls which had driven blinding snow off the mountains down into our faces, but we had worked systematically through them as though this were the only way of keeping alive. There was no doubt that this was the hardest work I had yet been put to. Whatever the motives of the crew for tackling the job, I could not help feeling a sneaking regard for their hardiness. Tired as we all were, there was no delaying over the meal, and in no time at all we were back at our duties.

Although the glare from the try-pots cast a reasonable wide glow, we had still to use oil lamps to give us enough light in which to work, and the resulting effect was macabre. The great bloody carcasses of the seals looked gross and obscenely naked. More often now there were great tirades of abuse from those who had slipped in the mess surrounding them and landed up to their necks in a slush of slime and blood. The normally docile cows had become quite fretful, and more and more a howl of pained surprise cut through the slish-slashing knives to mark the seamen who had been bitten by a frightened animal. The sealer's revenge was always immediate—a savage blow into the upturned face, followed by another for sheer spite. Afterwards, the creature was left to suffer a lingering and painful death if the two blows had not already killed it.

The deadly seriousness of the scene was quite frightening, and I could not help thinking how it dehumanized my crew mates. But then I reasoned that this was their livelihood; when all the unpredictabilities of it were taken into account, maybe it was only natural that they should act thus. I dreaded, however, that I should become like them and wondered how I should be able to avoid it.

That night was the hardest I had experienced since leaving home. Although we were frozen to the very marrow and weak-kneed with exhaustion, there was little or no letup of our task. We worked at the try-pots in rotation so as to let each man benefit from its heat, and this meant that I was detailed to join in the flensing. Although the wind had moderated, the cold was intense, and from time to time we had to work under a barrage of hail. Our caps were not sufficient to cover our ears, and the sides of our heads began aching as though our ears had been removed with knives. Even though we tried pulling our collars up to protect our necks, there was little we could do with clothing that was inadequate, and our beards were soon masked with ice. Our hands suffered most of all, becoming in time so numb we could barely hold a knife; but the process of skinning was not allowed to stop. One was, however, permitted the brief relief of thawing one's numbed extremities by shoving them beneath the steaming flaps of blubber for a while so that they could be warmed by the heat of the animal itself.

Daybreak saw us still struggling on, fortified by the odd ration of grog. Work had slowed to a less than frantic pace, but we continued all that day and through another night with only an occasional rest. By late evening of the third day, just as we were contemplating driving the rest of the seals from out of the tussock, it happened. Quite unexpectedly, we were attacked! To our surprise it did not come from the sea, where we had kept a lookout, or even from the rocks on either side—for which we were prepared. It came from inland, from a hill, where we had obviously been observed for some time.

Before we knew it we were engulfed. A horde of howling seamen rushed us, brandishing knives and flourishing steel hooks, which they launched abandonedly against our persons. I recognized a few of their shouted words and realized that they were Hollanders. Without a qualm or hint of hesitation, the leader ran a spike straight through the slumbering cooper's heart while shouting lustily to his companions. They roared exultantly and pressed us harder, hoping no doubt to intimidate and catch us off our guard and expecting to mow us down in seconds and steal our catch. In truth we had a job to dodge and parry, for long exposure had dulled our wits and put a drag on our responses. But sometimes nature acts in curious ways. When we saw how they had killed the injured cooper, our anger at their cowardice fired our courage, igniting at the same time that rare surge of strength reserved for moments of great danger. A voice emerged from our ranks, exhorting us to keep together. Forming a tight-knit group, surrounded by dead carcasses of seal, we lunged and thrust at our attackers.

It was a most unreal scene. The sky was drained of light by now, and the air was thick with scores of birds that shrieked and squabbled for bits of meat. They swooped and fluttered about our heads and hopped between our feet, emitting enraged squawks when we trod on them. Above their noise the grunts of men mingled with the clash of steel as knives met in opposition. Threats and oaths accompanied the dull thud of bodies; men knocked each other to the ground and rolled on top of one another in the gory mess. We fought with no set pattern, sweating and straining to beat off the men who hacked and stabbed at us. Faced with the threat of being killed or maimed, I found myself responding to a primitive instinct which overrode my acquired manners. I would have done anything to stay alive, but I was hopelessly unversatile in fighting such desperate battles and no match in strength or cunning for my opponent.

When finally I had failed to touch him, his reach being greater than my own, I felt a sudden burning pain along my arm and knew his hook had ripped my sleeve and scored a channel along my limb. The blood poured down my wrist, and seeing it made me angry. Grabbing a sealing club from the ground, I swung it wide before smashing it hard against the knees of my assailant. He fell to the ground beside the try-pots, and immediately I jumped on him. Astride his chest, I grabbed his ears to beat his head against the ground and stun him. The result would have been ludicrous had my life not been at stake. The surface being like a marsh, his head made slurping noises in the mud, while he was given a chance to rest. He grinned, baring black, broken teeth, and jabbed his outstretched fingers in my face. They jammed my nostrils as he shoved me back. His boot followed, slanting off my chin. He scrambled up, drawing his knife, which he pointed at me as he lunged. Dazed with pain, I was too mesmerized to move. I lay there gasping, waiting for the inevitable blow, when suddenly his body seemed to trace an arc away from me as he was caught sideways by one of his own men. There was a thud, followed by a crunch of heads, as the two of them fell against the stone works which supported the cauldrons of boiling oil. Even as they fell, I knew what had to happen. Shouting a warning as I scrambled clear, I watched the bubbling cauldron begin to tip. Seconds later boiling oil poured out of it onto the two upturned, screaming faces; and as it poured the oil caught fire. Within a moment, there was a mighty conflagration, and those nearby who had been spattered with burning oil went rushing to throw themselves in the sea. I darted forwards to drag back the men whose top halves flared like burning torches, but I could do nothing to relieve their pain.

The sudden fire, together with the hideous screams of the injured men, stopped the fighting. Despite the layers of filth that covered all of us, the bearing of each man showed his horror, and the eyes of everyone were rimmed with fright. I had thrown mud over the burning men to douse the flames, but they continued to writhe in agony. Unable to contain the sight of their comrades in such dire extremities, the Dutch crew fell back in blind and stumbling confusion until caught by panic, they began to run. We let them go without murmur, too stunned to watch them leave. The fight was over without a victory, and we stood around or sat on carcasses to nurse our wounds. My injury was not as serious as I had expected, but it hurt more now that I had time to think. If this was not a dream, I mused, we must surely have crossed beyond the bounds of sanity.

2

The Screaming Sixties

We were altogether eighteen days in South Georgia, during which we were beset by rain and snow and fog, which visited us in varying order between spells of limpid calm and brightness. Of fur seals we took only fifty, but we were fortunate enough to find another small colony of elephant seals which made up in oil for the amount we had lost. Our attempts to find more seal had proved fruitless, and our skipper decided we should leave South Georgia while there was still some time left in the season to explore the possibilities of finding seals elsewhere. He had been beside himself with rage on hearing how the cooper had been killed and the rest of us attacked and would have insisted on searching for the crew and exacting further vengeance had not the pressure of time made him decide otherwise. Once the decision to leave the island had been made, however, he was anxious to weigh anchor just as soon as we had loaded our cargo.

Although our approach to South Georgia had been inviting, nothing in the island's southern countenance made us want to stay. Where the northern coast had shown a smiling, though rugged, aspect, that of the south was bleak and hostile, with bare cliffs for a sea front and mountain ranges behind, whose ice-fanged watchdogs, guarding the interior, had muzzles frozen in a perpetual snarl. I had liked the island despite its tempests, and though smarting from the wound received during the skirmish fought on it, I felt renewed in strength from the fresh meat its beaches had provided. Eating seal meat had reduced the signs of scurvy which had begun to appear in most of us; and while there were newer scars to show beside the old ones on the persons of my crew mates, not one of the crew did not boast of having given better in return. Their concern was more for their sealing prospects than their injuries, however, and I could only assume that prolonged exposure to hardship had added several thicknesses to their hide.

Being at sea again was accompanied by a degree of uncertainty. The odds were as heavy against the discovery of virgin sealing grounds as they were against finding seals in those places where a few years ago they were thought to have become extinct. But the sealer has an extraordinary streak of optimism that encourages him to believe stories of islands still uncharted where the seals are so numerous that they block the way ashore. Whatever the chance of finding such a place, it was a pleasing notion which encouraged the sealers to take a gamble in the hope of a big reward.

No one doubted that the skipper would try to round the Horn, making for the sealing beaches on the west coast of Tierra del Fuego, the "land of fire." This southern tip of the continent is so called because of the constant fires kept burning by the Indians who inhabit it to ward off the bitter cold. I listened enthralled to descriptions of the Horn—a place, the crew said, where sea and land came together in such fearsome opposition that spray was shot several hundreds of feet into the air by the force of the sea's impact against the rocks. These, they continued, were so constantly hacked and slashed by waves that they had been fretted into the most weird and jagged shapes. For a ship to have tried to approach this tip of land through its outlying maze of rocky islands would have been suicidal. Along every narrow, turbulent waterway were hidden sunken reefs with splintered profiles whose razor edges could lacerate even the stoutest ships.

When we left South Georgia on November 5 the day had begun dull, with dirty patches of wind-torn cloud smudging an even murkier sky. Towards midmorning, the sun had emerged in dazzling splendour, colouring the sea a deepening green. Wherever the eye looked, playful, frothy-crested wavelets ran nimbly across the tops of the swells, so that the whole ocean seemed to dance and sing. Such a rare opportunity to refurbish the gear could not be ignored. We spent several hours oiling and tarring the standing rigging and bousing it taut where it had slackened. After several other essential jobs had been done, such as setting and overhauling the blocks, the brig looked ready for any seas that the Horn might throw at us.

That evening the weather turned quite bitter. Jagged waves leapt up towards a carmine sun, which finally exploded like a ball of fire, releasing jets of brilliant colour that flared across the sky. I had never seen a sunset so beautiful. I was so enraptured by it that I forgot what I was about. Suddenly a shout, directed towards the helmsman, announced a mighty growler bearing down on us, which, as we narrowly avoided it, showed up the size of a house. Fortunately, no one had noticed my lack of concentration, but this timely sighting was in itself reproof enough, a warning that we were in waters that required the greatest vigilance.

To seasoned sailors' eyes, the evening colours signified more the prospect of worsening weather than a spectacle to be admired. All hands were kept aloft most of the watch, passing extra gaskets round the sails they furled and lashing with rovings the heads of those still set. The low whine in the rigging grew more strident as the wind increased until it reached a scream. The ship's lurchings became more violent, and we began to reel and stagger as we fought with silent concentration to retain our balance. While the night rolled down on us, a heavy sea got up which beat against our bows and sent spray flying over the deck to drench us through. We tacked ship at midnight. All hands were ordered to stand by in preparation for a big blow, and throughout the night the storm increased, with rain and hail and snow and sleet doing their damnedest to embalm us.

To our surprise that blow abated and for the next three days we made good progress, advancing in a northwesterly direction before tacking west for two more days. Then again we altered course, passing to leeward of the Falkland Islands and heading southwest on our run for the Horn. Although such a course might seem circuitous, it was the only way we could approach that notorious and awesome cape of storms. To have tried to run directly for it would have been to court disaster, for a square-rigger's masts are set and stayed only to accept a strong wind from behind. Put a square-rigger into a head wind while she is still carrying sail and her masts are likely to be jumped out or snapped off like brittle twigs. Our only means, therefore, was to beat to windward, which meant making progress in a zigzag manner—taking the wind first on one bow and then, after a difficult tacking maneuver, taking the wind on the other. The normal way of doing this was to bring her head up into the wind and brace the yards round so that our sails could be filled from a different quarter. This maneuver, it need hardly be said, could only be used in moderate winds. The alternative was to wear ship. This meant bringing her round stern to wind and running before it with the minimum of sail set while hauling the yards as far as they would go from one side to the other; then using great care to bring her up to the wind again, ahead of her other beam. Running off like this and coming up again lost miles and could be dangerous, but either way demanded skill and a great deal of concentration. The Horn is a malicious opponent of seamen with its momentary lulls, its quick shifts of wind and its sudden lethal gusts. If a skipper is daring and quick enough he might employ them to make good his passage, but every mile made is one mile nearer to that mistake that will cost him and his crew their lives.

As we closed on the Horn a sudden blast of wind rocked the ship from gunwale to gunwale, sending wraiths of fog scurrying into the rigging as if to take possession of the craft. Gallantly she kept her head as the waves with startling rapidity began to gain in height. Soon a big sea was ripping across our bows and crashing and foaming across the deck. Those few who had been below rushed on deck in time to see an enormous wave about to break on us. We had hardly time to grab the lifelines before we were buried under an avalanche of freezing water and fighting an urge to take a breath. When our heads lifted clear for a few moments, there was just time enough to spit the water from nose and mouth and gulp some air before another wave overwhelmed us in a rush and squeezed the breath from our lungs.

From now on we became subject to more and more dangerous situations, and I can remember moments of wild exhilaration. Such raptures were quickly over, however, ended as often as not by a shrieking hailstorm that would swoop out of nowhere, stinging our eyes, blinding our vision, and forcing us to cling on with every ounce of strength or be toppled off our swaying perches into the heaving sea. Despite the obvious dangers, I felt an odd satisfaction in mastering the difficulties and was aware of a deep companionship, born perhaps out of communal fear, perhaps out of communal courage. Either way it expressed a mutual dependence in the face of danger which, being embraced resolutely, seemed to satisfy a deep and personal need in each of us for physical fulfillment and proof that we were men.

Indeed, the conditions facing us were almost insurmountable. Large black clouds rolled down on us from the southwest, blackening the whole heavens and bringing with them winds of such piercing, cutting keenness that they penetrated even the thickest layers of our clothing and inflicted the pain of stab wounds across every inch of flesh. Aloft, battling with the sails, now stiff and heavy and hard as boards, we had to beat our numbed fingers to make them bend—almost crying with the pain as the blood began to flow again and feeling reasserted itself in the form of an intense and burning agony. Along the yardarm it was as black as pitch, and had a soul gone overboard no one would have known. We crawled aloft through merciless buffeting and had to turn away from the force of the wind before we could breathe at all. It took ten times as long as usual to furl and reef and several minutes of unceasing struggle to descend the rigging. And even then a murderously destructive wave could appear out of nowhere and fall sweeping across the deck, forcing all hands to jump for the shrouds or the lifelines or be thrown off their feet and washed into the scuppers or even overboard.

It was so difficult to keep the ship steady on her course that only the best helmsmen were allowed at the wheel—and it was impossible for them to handle her without assistance. Perspiring, in the cold weather, the helmsmen had to heave together on the wheel's spokes—now coaxing, now forcing it to where they wanted it—to prevent the ship from broaching to. Sometimes it took three men merely to hold the wheel. When they were relieved, they came off flapping their arms or blowing into their frozen fingers, their faces strained and livid.

Conditions worsened so much that the watch had to be divided into three, a different group going below every half hour to get some rest. There was the danger that without this break we would not survive the constant hardship and exposure. We were glad to lower ourselves into the fo'c'sle's sanctuary, where the blue fug of tobacco smoke had a comforting effect. But the bravado of the seamen's quips could not disguise the hint of unease in their eyes as the ship leaned. Many is the time that we had barely grabbed a slice of cold salt beef before there was a rap on the scuttle and a red, wind-chaffed face, streaming with salt water, shouted down the companionway, "Hurry up, lads—give us a smart relief!"

The tenth day out of South Georgia began disturbingly. On coming down from an hour and a half aloft, I heard an urgent yell. "All hands on deck, the main hatch has lifted." No one needed further urging, for it was the hazard we most feared. Big seas were pouring over us, and there was the danger if they broached the hatches that water would pour down the hold and sink us in a few minutes. The captain himself was at the helm. Some of the crew made a dive for the tarpaulin cover, which they clung to doggedly, though water swirled around and on top of them, fairly burying them beneath. We were battered and bleeding and half drowned before we could be certain the hatches would remain secure; but just as we were reaching for the safety of the lifelines another wave broke angrily over the bulwarks, knocking us flying across the deck.

The few who had seen it coming gripped the handrail, while

the rest of us rolled around in heaps, grabbing frantically for the capstan or belaying pins—anything to which to cling to as the sea yanked and tugged to drag us overboard. I clawed desperately with my nails through the seething water to try to reach a ring bolt. I had barely managed to get a grip on it when a figure went slithering past me, face downwards across the deck. I saw it hit the lee rail, out of control, and I scrambled towards the belaying pins to grab some rope to throw just as another wave broke over us. Though the man stretched out his arm to catch it, I watched with frozen horror as it fell short of his grasp. A moment later he had vanished without a murmur, leaving me chilled to the heart with the ease with which the sea takes life.

The drowned sailor was a Portugee from the starboard fo'c'sle. Maybe it was because of this that his death did not affect our watch. I felt horror at his loss, finding that his disappearance created for me an awful sense of mystery; but the others in our fo'c'sle chatted in a way that made me wonder if they were really so indifferent to death or if this was just their way of coming to terms with it.

The following day conditions were no better. All light was drained from the sky and replaced by clouds of grey, which deepened into blackness. The deck was constantly awash with icy waves that swirled around our waists and filled our boots. While it was impossible to get a sight, we could sense well enough we were making little headway despite the endless round of work that kept us labouring day and night. We were exhausted, bruised in body, sick in spirit, so wet that when we came below we had to strip our soaking garments off and ring them out before we dressed in them again. We had long ago run out of dry clothes. For comfort we emptied the water out of our boots before turning in. Hot food was little more than a memory, the stove having ceased to function in the galley. Were it not for the issue of revitalizing grog, we should have long before succumbed to the cold and the hardship.

Even so, our weakening bodies could stand only so much strain, and the skipper must have known it. To give him credit, he had tried his best to drive the ship when others would have hove her to; but his valiance or daring, whichever it was that had made him act, had not paid off, and we were losing miles faster than we were gaining. At this rate, we could remain forever in the path of storms until we were too weak to control the ship, in which case we no doubt would sink with her. We could turn about and return to South Georgia, with all the uncertainties that that entailed, or we could try to find a route *around* that stormy belt of ocean. The skipper had to make a quick decision. And he did so now with confidence and courage. We would head south and make a wide detour, hoping thereby to catch better weather. As if rewarding him for his daring, the wind gradually lessened until, towards midday, we felt secure enough to pile the canvas on again. It was an extraordinary good feeling not to have to battle with the wind but instead to use it as a partner. The Old Man took the opportunity to get some sleep while the rest of us took alternative hours below, turning in fully clothed to enjoy the blissful luxury of unconsciousness.

The temperature had been falling steadily as we began moving southwards. It was now so cold that spray dashed into the rigging promptly froze. The ropes became caked with ice, and the sails so stiff with it they could not be furled. So serious was the situation that we were ordered to use hand pikes to break off the ice lest it overload the ship. Already its weight on one side made her lean to windward. To counteract this tendency, the Old Man ordered us to lay her on the other tack so that as the ship heeled sharply, dipping her ice-laden side into the waves and spray, the water-softened ice could be scraped away. From then on we were kept constantly on deck chipping and scraping at the ship and rigging. As fast as ice was cleared from the lee side, a mass of it would have accumulated on the weather side, so that every few hours we were obliged to wear ship—the only way to keep her from foundering. More and more now we were so enclosed in fog that we could barely see the length of the ship.

Our position was impossible to guess. After days of sailing without sight of the sun, navigation was very difficult. And it was this, I think, that prompted fear, together with a sort of uncanny certainty that we had strayed beyond the boundaries of the chartered oceans into an area of monstrous seas where we could only guess the dangers.

It was a northwest wind that finally brought about an unexpected and dramatic change in our circumstances. It came bringing waves of such mountainous proportions that their crests loomed higher than the masthead. More terrifying were the hollows between the waves into which the ship plunged headlong as if she would never rise. Occasionally a giant wave even bigger than the others would charge out of nowhere—a freak wave—with little or no warning. Dazed, battered and barely able to move after one such assault, we became aware of an extraordinary sensation. The hurricane clamoured furiously, deafening our ears with its piercing wail, but for some inexplicable reason it passed right over us and left us huddling together on the watch, feeling alone and unprotected, weighed down by a sense of foreboding without knowing what exactly would be the nature of our fate.

We wondered if the skipper felt it also. If he did, he gave no sign. Grim and grey-faced, his eyelids red and swollen from too many hours on duty relieved by barely any rest, he kept his station by the weather rigging and never spoke except to give an order. How long we would have suffered with him is a question we might all have asked had not a sudden strangled cry stopped the heart of every man. The third mate stood white-faced, pointing overboard. There, bearing down on us, was the blurred shape of what appeared to be a truly enormous wave. It was as though the sea had been building up somewhere out there in the fog, that one great wave that would crush the ship and suck the soul out of every man. Even as we watched, the shape grew so big and black that it threatened to obscure the sky and swallow us completely. So transfixed were we all that several minutes passed before we realized that we had been the witnesses of a miraculous mutation—for the specter of that monstrous wave had gradually transformed itself into a solid mass of land!

3

Tranquility

At 4 A.M. on November 22, 1818, we dropped anchor in Tranquility Bay. When daylight seeped into the places that the night had vacated and revealed an island of high rugged rocks intersected by many great snow-filled chasms which swept down from an icy dome, there was not a man among us who could believe his eyes. To the east were numerous islands and islets, while to the south was an island of much greater mass than the one we had approached, with a mantle of ice truly awesome to behold. The sight swelled the pride of every man whose fate had led him to that place. We had survived a barrier range of mountainous seas that no one would have thought navigable and discovered land where, according to the charts, nothing but sea existed. There could never have been a more glorious reward after all the hardships we had suffered than to realize that what we could see before us no man had ever seen.

Not two cables beyond where we lay, a fearful hurricane was still blowing. Yet where the ship was anchored the water was as smooth as glass. Ironically we owed our safety to that final gigantic wave which, as it hit us, had made the ship drop from under us as the whole world reared on top. In rolling us so violently from side to side, it had shunted us out of the main track of the galloping seas and into a wonderful natural harbour that was protected by a sweep of land. Nevertheless we took a while to become convinced of the safety of our sanctuary so that the sounds of the wind no longer tore at our nerves.

When we did go below to rest we did not sleep at first, in spite of our weariness. With the fire lit in the stove, where for the last two weeks there had been none, a new spirit invaded the fo'c'sle. We crushed around the fire to soak in its warmth while drawing on pipes that seldom if ever had tasted so good.

The storm continued throughout that day, and had it not been for the shriek of the wind we would not have been aware of it, so tranquil was the water in which our ship lay sheltered. Some claimed a miracle at work. Others shrugged in disbelief; but no man was fool enough to provoke the wrath of God by ridiculing those who were convinced that He had saved them. So the day passed peacefully. We arose at various times to walk on deck or to find something to eat. Seeing plenty of seals and finbacks sporting in the bay around us, the mate decided that evening to take a party ashore to look for seals. He returned to report that he had found nothing except the skeletons of whales and fragments of marine animals scattered on the beaches. Far from being disappointed by what he had seen, he was strengthened in his conviction that there must be other beaches in the vicinity where the seals would congregate. This belief greatly pleased the crew. The atmosphere on board was also enlivened by the discovery that the bay was rich with a fine rock cod, and for once the cook needed no persuasion to prepare a hot meal for us.

In the first watch the following day, the carpenter recruited a party to assemble two longboats to replace those that had been stove, while the rest of us settled down to making spare oars and boat hooks. A grindstone was broken out, and on this we whetted our knives and lances. By the time we turned in at midnight we had all the equipment ready for sealing. We were only too glad to go below, for we were to be called at first light to get ready to sail. Although the storm had blown itself out by the time we awoke, we did not weigh anchor and head out to sea until about 9 A.M. on November 23.

In the lee of the island the breeze was barely sufficient to give us steerage. On clearing the rocks at the entrance of the bay, every man among us breathed a sigh of thanks for the hand that had delivered us safely into that haven we called Tranquility Bay. Yet the heavy sea left no man free to contemplate the meaning or the warnings of our reprieve, for every ounce of strength and skill was called on to sail west along that rugged coast at a distance close enough to keep a good lookout for the seal beaches.

When they saw us, close-packed masses of penguins abandoned the rafts of ice on which they had been huddling together in the hundreds and came porpoising and squawking towards the ship. Try as I would, I could not disguise my delight and longed for a chance to commit all my impressions to my journal. The latter was already half full—the writing accompanied by many drawings, but much had to be done from memory in the dogwatches, since my duties did not allow for such pastimes. I suffered many a curse from the crew when I allowed my interest in the scenery and animal life to distract me, and the mate more than once threatened to confiscate my journal. Seals sported in abundance in the sea all around, but the beaches were too narrow to warrant the effort of going ashore. Nevertheless, the sight of so many encouraged us and augured well.

A sighting having been taken soon after we had set sail, much speculation ensued as to the result. But the skipper, in the tradition of all sealing skippers, made no effort to divulge this information. To discover new land is like blundering upon the enactment of the most sacred ritual. The excitement of knowing you are witnessing something meant only for the very few is heightened by the fear that a terrible price might be demanded for the privilege. Already one seaman had been sacrificed to the Horn. Was this enough to satisfy the gods? Suddenly a dreadful premonition began to grow within me—a premonition which was cut short by a call from the masthead of "Seal on the port bow."

Four hours' sailing had brought us close to a peninsula on

whose beaches we could see seals basking in the thousands. As we came abreast of the cape, the waters were so thick with seal that not a single man could contain his eagerness to get ashore and begin this massive harvest of fur.

Lacking a shallop to ferry us to the more difficult areas, we were limited in the places we could work. Since we could not transport barrels full of oil and a large quantity of skins any distance from the shore, we had to find a safe roadstead near the sealing beaches for the ship. Over a short distance, horse pieces could be transferred from the beach to the ship by means of a raft rope some three fathoms long with an eye splice at one end. To this raft rope would be attached the pieces of blubber and a line that would be thrown to a boat offshore and beyond the breakers. The raft of blubber could then be towed out to the ship—and this, it seemed, was the only way that we could operate.

On rounding the cape to the west we saw the sort of cove we were hoping to find. It promised shelter from all winds except from the northwest, and since the last northwester had only a few hours earlier blown itself out, the skipper decided that we should stand in. By now the, wind had slackened to an almost deathly calm, although a big swell was still running strong. With the soundings finding a rocky bottom, we had to exercise the utmost caution as we took the ship in. Boats were sent ahead to scout a route, and we ended up by towing the ship through an entrance with barely enough sea room. This course the skipper charted by taking a bearing on a large flat-topped and perpendicular rock in case we should need to repeat or reverse this same awkward maneuver. By 9 P.M., as the light was fading, we found a place well over on the west side of the cove where we were protected by an island. Here, just about two cables from some rocks to our southeast, we anchored.

The lookouts were ordered to keep a sharp watch for any hint of a northwest wind, for with a wind from that quarter we would surely drag anchor and be smashed up against the cliffs on the opposite side of the cove. We also feared a southwesterly gale, and such a wind blew all that night, rolling us from gunwale to gunwale. Fortunately that fear was unfounded, for the incoming swell, rebounding against the rocks to our southeast, created a vicious undercurrent that kept the brig from straining her cables. Even so, sleep was impossible with memories of our recent hardships still too fresh to have lost their terror. We arose with the sun at 3 A.M. and, finding that the wind had dropped, made ready for the slaughter that was the purpose of our voyage.

We split into two parties. The mate's, in which I was included, comprised the larger number of men, and we were detailed to take two boats and look for both elephant and fur seals on the beaches to the east of the cove, the second mate's group was to land on the nearby island to our west and concentrate on fur seals. That party was the first away, being unencumbered with tryworks and all the heavy paraphernalia necessary for elephant sealing. In fact, we were still loading our boats when two of their number were seen rowing frantically back to the ship.

From their manner we feared some misadventure ashore, and I could see that the skipper and the mate were expecting the worst. No sooner were the two sailors within hailing distance of the ship when both began yelling and gesticulating. We could not distinguish a single word, and even when they had clambered aboard they seemed so overcome with what they had seen that they were incapable of making themselves understood. The Old Man's brows beetled as he began to lose patience. Grabbing the two of them by their necks, he brought their heads together with a sickening crack, threatening them with worse if they did not calm down and give a good account of themselves.

"We come back to get salt," the less dizzy of the two sealers managed to splutter through the blood streaming from his nose.

"Salt!" the skipper bawled—and they might well have suffered a further clash of heads had they not blurted out quickly that they would need at least half the ship's store to take care of all the skins they expected to get on one beach alone. The seals were so numerous that there was not a square inch of beach that was not "lined with fur."

In spite of the distaste with which I regarded this gory occupation of sealing, I could not help being caught up in the excitement that their news aroused. Fur-lined beaches had a sumptuous ring to them in keeping with the notion, put into my head as a child by various sailors that I had met, that there were lands where the beaches were strewn with pearls and rivers where the beds were paved with gold. An island where the beaches were lined with fur was no less exotic. On the contrary, the statement added a lush and breathtaking new dimension to our discovery, which, for me at least, was nothing less than magic.

With much shouting and laughing we loaded extra salt into the boats, and with a final reminder from the skipper to watch out for his signal from the ship's masthead should the threat of bad weather necessitate our immediate recall, we pulled away from the ship. A swift high swell carried us effortlessly for a good way towards the west side of the peninsula, where bands of ruffled white water gave sign of sunken reefs. We looked for a gap where the sea boiled less violently, but as we approached we saw that landing the boats would not be easy. Not only was there a heavy surf cannonading against the rocks that guarded most stretches of the shore, but, true to the description we had heard not half an hour before, there were so many fur seals on the part of the shore we were approaching that we would have to maneuver the craft so that two men could clamber out into the shallows to clear a beachhead before we could run the boats in and make our landing.

With a horrifying lurch we almost toppled as a wave took charge and lifted the boat high. "Now!" bellowed the mate, and we all jumped out of her, grabbing hold of the gunwale in preparation to run her in. We were not prepared for the shock of the icy water. As it swirled around our waists, the boat escaped our fingers shooting forward to crunch onto the beach before being sucked back almost instantly and bowling us over. Spluttering and gasping, we grabbed for the side again and tried our damnedest to keep a hold. The load was heavy and the boat cumbersome, and another wave tore the craft once again from our grasp. Up, higher, the wave now lifted it; then *whoosh!* it flung it down again, sucking it back in an instant just a bit nearer to the rocks. We must have made six attempts before the boat was finally borne on the crest of a foaming breaker high onto the beach.

A good hour passed before sufficient space had been cleared of seals to allow the boats to be hauled above high water mark. When this was done, the mate ordered me and another hand to be quick and light a fire. This we accomplished with the aid of a tinderbox and a few bits of timber we had brought ashore. Once we had some blubber, however, it burned loquaciously—babbling and spitting—and we all stood around it for a few minutes enjoying its company and the delicious sensation of its warmth. I stayed with the tryworks to feed in the blubber and had a good opportunity, because of this, to absorb the atmosphere around.

One thing I could not help noticing was the ammoniacal stench of the place, which was as repellent to its accordant sense as was the unbelievable clamour to the ear. To our left, fur seals sent up a chorus of yaps and squeals with an occasional angry and deep-throated roar while, to our right, penguins and other birds chattered and squawked incessantly to the accompaniment of loathsome snorts from the bull elephant seals who had territory to protect.

The beach was about three hundred yards in length and maybe fifty yards across at its widest point. It was equally favoured by both elephant and fur seals, although the latter kept to the north of the beach and the elephants to the south. I could see no obvious access inland, except possibly by way of a steep snow-covered rise on the southern end of the beach. Countless penguins kept a constant traffic up and down the slope from the beach to their breeding ground on the flattened crest of the cliff and made it stained and slippery with their droppings. Elsewhere, the beach was protected inland by black splintered cliffs, except for the table-topped rock on its northwestern limit, which had provided a good landmark when we were looking for a place to anchor. The female sea elephants lay in heaps, quite indifferent to their pups, their ponderous bodies covered with ordure, while occasionally a bull lifted its head wearily and belched a slothful warning to keep away from him and from the precious collection of females that he regarded as his. Over the lot of them hung such an air of indolence and boredom that it seemed nothing short of a miracle that the species could procreate.

Elsewhere, the beach was already slippery with a slimy trail of blood. Fifty fur seals lay dead—bludgeoned when a space had to be cleared to haul the boats ashore. Those whose skins were wanted were flayed on the spot, while the others were just chucked aside and piled in a heap. With so many seals available, the crew could afford to be selective, and they were unperturbed if a few unwanted animals got killed or mangled on the way.

The procedure, when the beaches were not so cramped for space, was for the sealers to form a lane, facing each other two abreast, through which they would drive the fur seals with much noise and gesticulating to the water's edge. Stunning them with a blow from their clubs, they would then rip the skin down the belly from jaw to tail before stabbing the animal in the breast to kill it. Since the water's edge was so thick with seals, they dispensed with routine and just lay about them indiscriminately.

Seeing how trustingly those fur seals looked at the sealers was heartrending; never having encountered men before, they had no reason to fear them. Like the elephant seals, they gathered in harems presided over by a single bull; but in all other respects, they could not have been more different. Whereas the elephant seal was gross, clumsy and extraordinarily ugly, affecting a kind of slothful consciousness, the fur seal was sleek and graceful and possessed a far keener intelligence.

They lay in close-packed groups, with barely a space anywhere to walk between them. Here and there their guardians, or "wigs," as the male fur seal was called because of the thick shaggy mane which adorned his shoulders, challenged another bull to do battle, and the skins of many of these animals were badly scarred. The wigs inflicted most of the wounds which the sealers sported, for they were brave and fast and exceedingly possessive.

I had assumed that the sealers would kill the wigs first, as they had the male elephant seals, to avoid the bother of having to dodge them, but this the sealers were loath do, for the bulls, by guarding their harems and preventing the cows from escaping, actually helped the sealer to accomplish his task. For this service, the creatures were cruelly rewarded. The sealers, not wishing to have the bother of constantly dodging these irate bulls, would blind them in one eye and creep past them on their blind side. Far from feeling remorse from such barbarity, the sealers actually enjoyed the spectacle that such cruelty created. The poor animal was forced to tilt his head at a tragic angle to see where he was going and frequently charged straight into another seal or some obstruction. One or two of the men were not above tormenting the poor animal further by giving him a prod on his blind side and watching him race around in demented circles. When I felt sick at this awful savagery and called out that they should have a heart, the mate fairly bellowed at me to mind my own business or he would have to give me a few lessons in how to behave like a sealer.

Half the crew were now culling the fur seals, the others were slaughtering elephant seals. Meanwhile I was kept busy shifting blubber, cutting it up into horse pieces, mincing it and feeding it to the try-pot. The work was back-breaking, and my muscles soon ached. While the carpenter set up some barrels, not only for oil but for some of the skins, the majority of them would have to be towed on a line to the ship and salted when they were brought aboard. The skins were taken off the seal with the fat and even some of the lean still adhering; the greater the weight of fatty tissue the easier, evidently, they would be to "beam." "Beaming" was another word for the scraping process. A rounded knife was used and the skin laid across the curved side of a barrel so as not to nick the valuable pelt. After being scraped and washed, the skins were packed on top of one another into a stack, or "book," with heavy stones on the top to press out the water. A day or two of this treatment, if the weather was fine, and the skins should be ready for salting. Then they would be restacked in the same manner until the salt penetrated, or "stuck." After this they could be packed away in casks or in pounds located in the hold.

I had never seen the crew so excited. Not only were there more seals than they had ever seen together in one place even in their wildest dreams, but the quality of the furs and the plumpness of the elephant seals promised an opportunity to get the choicest yield. From the look of things, we could spend several days sealing on this beach alone. No sooner would the crew clear the beach than more seals would haul themselves out of the sea to sun alongside, and even occasionally on top of, the steaming carcasses of those already flensed. The scene represented an extraordinary example of nature's bounty, and the crew were absolutely astounded by the sheer magnitude of it all.

With the excitement of sealing, no one bothered about the time except to glance occasionally towards the ship to make sure that all was well.

Now and then a short sharp wind brought the colour to our hands and faces, as though they had been lashed by whips. During the worst of these blasts we were allowed to take a break and gather round the fire, where we quieted our hunger with biscuit and the tongues of elephant seals until one of the crew struck on the idea of collecting penguin eggs. These some of the men ate raw with molasses, while others with more patience boiled them in the water in which we had cooked the tongues.

For water we had been obliged to use snow, since there were no running streams near our beachhead. For shelter we had brought some canvas ashore to wedge round the barrels. We could not tell how long at a stretch we could stay on the beach, since at any hint of a northwester we would have to return to the ship immediately. We had come prepared for at least three days and could leave some of the stuff ashore should we be called back. No one could predict what the island held in store for us, but the sky was so clear and the dome of the ice cap so dazzling white that the least we feared was the weather.

During the afternoon the mate detailed everyone to concentrate on elephant seals. It was my job to drive the elephant seals down to the sea. What could not be tried was to be put into barrels, and what was left over was to be buried under rocks to keep it from the scavenging beaks of the birds which descended in the hundreds to devour it.

The work was grueling, and by early evening our backs were lame from the constant strain of hauling and bending. I was sent off to fetch a quantity of snow for my thirsty companions; and as I made my way towards the northern part of the beach, I stopped by an odd outcrop of rocks that rose into the air like two obelisks. Other smaller rocks nearby formed a kind of broken circle in which a fur seal had his harem. This in itself was nothing remarkable, and I should have given it only a momentary glance had I not been stopped in my tracks by a sight that I shall never forget for its sheer tenderness and beauty. There, surrounded by a crowd of other seals, was a gorgeous white fur seal suckling her pup, which was also white and soft and silky. As the mother turned on me her large brown eyes, which looked as beautiful as any woman's, I felt some urgent premonition directing me to walk away so as not to draw the attention of my crew mates. Somehow even the presence of men defiled such a beautiful wild creature, let alone men as brutal as sealers. I hurried off, changing direction abruptly in the hope that none of the sealers would see me staring and wander over.

So preoccupied was I by the unexpectedness of such an exotic creature that I did not hear the shot demanding our recall to the ship. I did not even look seawards as I pressed my way through the thick barrier of seals to the snowbank beyond. Only as I returned did I notice the tremendous activity in the camp ahead and the urgent signs directed at me to hurry and make a cache of the remaining blubber. But far more alarming than the recall signal on the ship's masthead and the line of black cloud building on the northwestern horizon was the sight of the mate hurrying towards the stacks of rock where the white seal lay hidden. No doubt he imagined it a good place to cache the blubber. However, on seeing that beautiful creature as she broke cover to make her way towards the sea, he quickened his stride to intercept and kill her.

Breaking into a run, I tried to head him off. As he saw me coming, he snarled a warning to keep away. The seal was his, he growled. I supposed that a white seal meant a bonus, and he imagined that I wanted the skin for myself. I had no time to explain my motive. As I lunged at him he swung his fist. I cannot recall if I felt pain. All I remember is a haunting vision—a blurred glimpse of the mate's face contorted in a grimace of hate —before my world turned black.

4

Alone!

I came to, I do not know how many hours later, with a dreadful ache in my head and a feeling of great weight across my chest and legs. For a minute or two I could not tell where I was. I could see nothing, and on attempting to move my arms I found them pinioned against my sides. I could not decide whether I was tightly bound or whether I had lost the ability to move my limbs at all. Whatever the reason, I was wedged firmly into a tight space that allowed me room to move only my head. This, I avoided as much as possible, since the slightest inclination set it throbbing madly. I was confused; I felt warm about my body, but I was aware of a bitterly cold wind against my face. My hearing, however, keen as ever, made out the sounds of a terrific storm and other noises nearby that I could not identify. I was aware too of an odour of such foulness that I was filled with a feeling of total revulsion; yet I could still see nothing and began to grow afraid that I had lost my sight.

I heard a strange sound then just a few feet away from me. It was followed by a tremendous upheaval all around, and in an instant my limbs were freed from their invisible fetters. The sound was the male fur seal's curiously deceptive whimper, which disguised the fierceness of its urge to mate. I knew immediately then that I was in a harem—an unwelcome intruder in a reserve dominated by a wild animal who would be at his fiercest and most unpredictable while his females were in season and he was in rut. The thought was enough to freeze the blood in me. I lay paralyzed with fright, not knowing what on earth to do. All of a sudden I was aware of another sense of urgency as the seal beside me began responding rhythmically to an inward imperative. I sensed a dramatic quickening of its movement, recognizing it intuitively to be the final spasm that preceded the emergence of life. The poignant cry of a newborn animal floated on the air, followed by the rasping reassurance of its triumphant mother. I could feel a tiny body against my chest, together with an extraordinary sensation of inadequacy. The little creature was crawling over me, nibbling and nuzzling me to locate a teat.

My breath came heavily while I sweated, not knowing if the seals ignored me because they were unaware of my presence or if I could expect that any minute they would discover my intrusion and attack. As I pondered the awfulness of my dilemma, I found I could just make out the dim outline of the surrounding figures. My joy at discovering that I still had my sight was almost my undoing. My shout of relief set the whole herd heaving, nearly suffocating me in the process. Fortunately, I had female seals all around me, forming a living barrier between me and the bull. I would have to remain unobtrusive if I were not to distract the latter, however, for I had seen evidence enough of how possessive the bulls could be and how vicious their attacks. I had also the problem of how the cows might react if they became too nervous. One or two already seemed restless and snapped irritably at their neighbours when they turned their way.

Close by I could make out a bull seal sniffing the air while guarding the harem in lionlike stance. He had positioned himself to overlook his harem and at the same time keep an alert ear for any intruders that might dare approach. At intervals he would lunge at his group and growl imperiously, as if to warn the cows of the penalty should they try to stray. I wriggled lower amongst them to be less conspicuous; otherwise, he would surely spot me when the light returned. I had seen enough disfigured sealers to know the savagery of bulls and did not count much for my chances if he should charge and sink his teeth into my neck.

How to get past him would be a problem. At the slightest movement, he became suspicious and his mane became erect, making him look twice his normal size. Even if I should be able to escape, however, with such a blizzard blowing I would be overcome by the cold unless I could find an immediate shelter. I had not noticed any cave near the beach that would afford protection, and I could easily stumble into another irate bull while looking for an empty barrel in which to sit out the storm. Most probably all the empty barrels would have been blown away by now—a thought that left me with the strange conclusion that if the fur seals did not maul me, I would be better off remaining where I was. At least if I waited till daybreak I would be able to see where I was going and avoid the obvious dangers.

Meanwhile two choices lay open to me: I could lie on top of the seals, exposed to the fury of the elements, or I could snuggle down further amongst them, where I could benefit from the shelter afforded by their bodies. I chose the latter, even though I ran the risk of being savaged if I were not suffocated by the combined strength of weight and smell. This course at least promised a chance of survival, whereas the alternative offered none. And so, using the utmost care, I wriggled my way down amongst the bodies, cautious to do nothing that would seem tantamount to a threat. As long as I kept my body horizonal, none of the seals took too much notice, but one or two of the cows with young made rapid darting movements towards my face every time I raised my head. I had the devil of a fright the first time one of them did this, its teeth snapping shut on the very ends of my whiskers. From then on I was extremely careful to keep my head low and lie with it protectively buried in my arms, trying not to breathe too deeply in the steaming stench.

Not surprisingly, with all the immediate problems of my condition I had little time to think about anything else; but once I had established myself in a reasonably suitable position I let my mind wander back to the events that had brought me to such an incredible situation. Presumably the mate had been in such a hurry to skin the white seal and to get to the boats that he had forgotten about me. He may even have decided to leave me behind to teach me a lesson, although he must surely have realized there was a good chance that I might not survive. I was sure now, as the storm raged over me, that I could easily have died of exposure had I not fallen amongst the harem, where I had been protected from the wind. And what of the crew? I wondered. Had they been too busy with the boats to notice what was happening between me and the mate, or had they in fact connived in this prank to leave me ashore as their answer to my enthusiasm to set foot on uncharted land? Perhaps no joke was intended and they actually meant to abandon me there. The thought was so awful I jumped with the fright of it, immediately setting off a bout of snapping and jostling that lasted long enough to make me concentrate on the danger and the horror of my predicament.

The fur of the seals was good protection against the wind, but nothing could alleviate the dampness of my bed or the discomfort of feeling my limbs tightening into a cramp. On top of this, the stench of the animals was so acrid that my head felt ready to explode. Towards daylight the bull became so restless and aggressive that even if I had not begun to feel chilled and hungry, his disposition would have urged me to make my bid to escape. How odd that I should have to talk in terms of escape when just the day before I was walking quite casually among the various harems unhurt. Either I had been mistaken about the docility of these fur seals, or else I had fallen in with a particularly aggressive bull. I was beginning to think that the latter might be the case.

Significantly, our bull had about twenty cows besides the various pups in his harem, whereas the others boasted only about ten or twelve. Of course this meant that I was well protected. Although the bull made frequent charges towards any female that appeared likely to stray, they kept him from entering the heart of the harem by snapping at him viciously. Observing this, I made quite sure I kept to the very center of the seraglio, taking comfort from the fact that I had a ring of females around me who were better capable of defending me than I was myself.

I did not hurry to make my escape once the light returned and the wind abated. Instead I used my time to observe the guardian of the harem and judge his reactions. I took advantage of the sleeping cows on either side of me to raise the front part of my body in an attempt to assess my chance of success should I dare to make a dash for it. Each time, the old bull came charging round the side nearest me, bristling with anger. Terrified, I dropped my head, not knowing I had reacted perfectly. After several repetitions of the exercise, I came to the conclusion that by lying flat I had cancelled my "threat" and assumed, by chance, the submissive posture of the cow and the coward. With this intelligence in mind, I dared lay plans for my escape.

I had observed enough of the antics of the nearby bulls to get a good idea of what harem life was all about. The beach was divided up into territories, each of which was presided over by a bull. In general, a bull had to fight to keep what he regarded as his territory, for the impulse to extend the harem exerted a strong influence on every male. My bull, because of his large harem, had an unusually large area to guard against usurpers. In his continual excursions round the limits of his territory, challenging other bulls to stand and fight, he always left one side of his harem unprotected from intruders or unguarded as a route of a potential though risky escape.

From my perilous position I had seen at close hand some of these territorial fights. Strangely enough they were not preceded by an elaborate display. After the initial challenge the two opponents would make a powerful lunge at each other's throats, using their teeth to stab each other rather than to bite. If the blow stuck, they would then wrench and worry at the opponent's hide till it tore or until the aggressor lost his grip. Most of the blows were aimed at the neck or chest, but occasionally a nasty wound would be delivered to the unprotected extremities or across the rump or back. Although hardened to some extent by all the slaughtering I had witnessed, nothing I had seen prepared me for the sickening sight of some of these fights.

I could not help admiring the fighting prowess of that great bull whose harem I had joined. Now that the cows were waking up, he was quicker to investigate any movement or hint of insurrection and more aggressive than ever with the neighbouring bulls. I took advantage of this growing confusion to look round for a suitable route.

Newcomers making their way inland from the sea received rough treatment from some of the established bulls. If I wormed my way to the water's edge, however, I could make my way along the shoreline to where I would have an easier passage towards the try-pots. Thankfully they were still there. If nothing else could reassure me, the presence of these was an indication that the ship would have to return—and the thought of this was a truly profound relief.

Only under cover of a great confusion could I hope to disguise my flight. Therefore I must enlist the services of the female seals in the creation of a disturbance. Unsheathing my knife and choosing four females bunched together whom I hoped to frighten out of the harem by an unexpected jab, I set the plan in motion. The result was more dramatic than I had intended. In fact, when the first few seals moved away with a frightened cry, several others followed, causing considerable alarm. Seizing my chance amidst the pandemonium, I burrowed out of the harem on the side farthest from the bull and dragged myself along on my belly, stopping whenever I sensed the approach of an irate bull. In this way I escaped and crawled several yards through other bulls' territories with only a few scratches and abrasions that I got from dragging myself over the knife-edged rocks. Once up, I made a dash towards the sea, running the gauntlet of several males till I reached the water's edge, where I felt safe enough to stop and pause for breath. I had survived an ordeal in the company of those seals that the creative imagination of man would have been incapable of contriving. Although shaken by the experience, I could not at that time fully comprehend how close I had been to death.

The wind, which had died off during the early morning, already was blowing up again. Just as vicious as formerly, this time it came from another direction. Several empty barrels had been blown away, as I had expected, but those that had been filled with blubber had stood their ground. These formed a good windbreak for me to shelter behind until my hunger drove me in search of supplies. The supply cask was missing, and for a nasty moment I thought it might have been returned to the ship. After a good deal of rummaging around I found it wedged between some rocks farther down the beach.

The cove itself presented a dramatic picture. The high wind had whipped up a tremendous foaming sea that broke with violence over the entrance, sending clouds of spindrift racing towards the land. No way could a ship have been safe in such a roadstead, and little reason was needed to conclude where the Old Man must have taken the vessel. Tranquility Bay was the obvious harbour, since it had provided refuge in the previous northwesterly storm.

No doubt the crew would be discussing my predicament. I could imagine a few of them chuckling at how I would have to fend for myself. Well, I would not give them a chance to scoff at me. I would have everything squared away before they returned. Strangely enough, I felt no loneliness at their absence, revelling rather, in spite of the obvious discomforts, in the luxury of being alone. I would soon make some sort of makeshift shelter, and provided I could find the tinderbox, I should soon be enjoying the warmth of a fire. Nor did it worry me how long I might have to wait for their return. I could not imagine a gale blowing at this force for more than a couple of days. Even if by some chance it should blow for a week, a look in the provisions cask happily confirmed that I had enough salt beef and ship's biscuit to last me for about ten days.

Oddly enough, I hoped the ship would be delayed. I liked the feeling of pioneering. After all, I had been the first person ever, in the whole history of the world, to sleep on this icy island. That was something to be proud of. I knew that the crew would joke about it, but I knew also that they would admire me for having done it. They might even feel a touch of envy. And for all the teasing, they would acknowledge it secretly as an achievement. When I thought more about it, I felt no particular resentment towards the mate—after all, he must have reckoned that there were provisions enough for me to live on during the time the ship must be away. Only then did I remember the cause of my predicament—the white seal. The chance was hopeless that she had evaded the mate; but what, I wondered, had become of the pup? As soon as my priorities allowed, I would go and look for it. In the meantime, I had to build a shelter before I succumbed to the numbing wind and cold.

The most obvious place for a shelter was in the lee of the barrels, where I could take advantage of their solidness and position to make a semicircular wall. With this as the base of my structure, I should be able to top it with barrel lids supported on a lattice of staves and barrel hoops that I would then cover with some of the sealskins and hold down against the wind with rocks. I could afford a few skins for the base and another couple as a kind of curtain instead of a door. In this way I managed to construct a small but serviceable shelter that would do for however many days the bad weather lasted. The wind was now blowing down from the cliff tops, suggesting it had swung round to the east. The effect on the cove was to make it look rougher than ever, with a confused pattern of waves thrown up in the cross swell.

My immediate necessity was a fire. When a search in the cask revealed no tinderbox, my confidence received a nasty shock. Could it have been returned to the ship by mistake, or had it been lost amongst the shingle on the beach? Without it I certainly could not light the fire, and without fire I would be unable to cook or melt snow. The lack introduced a serious discomfort to my otherwise welcome experience, besides providing the crew with further grounds for amusement at my expense. Which of these considerations was the more important, I could not say. Whichever it was, it spurred me to keep looking for the tinderbox.

I might have tried looking for a bead in a mountain of sand for all the success I had. And really, it was not surprising. So small were these objects that, even if one had been left, it could have rolled just a few yards from the tryworks and been lost forever. The ground was soft beneath the seals where their warm bodies had melted it, and the tinderbox could well have sunk into any one of a score of soggy depressions in the area we had been working. Disconsolate, I returned to the barrel site, and what I would have done had not a sudden impulse made me examine the hearth beneath the try-pots I do not know; but to my utter amazement, not to say delight, I found that a tiny trickle of blubber had kept the fire aglow.

Wasting not a second, I painstakingly shredded some more strips of blubber, which I added cautiously to the embers until the whole thing was aflame. In no time at all I had a good fire going, which I could keep burning indefinitely if I took some care. However, I could not help reflecting how near I had come to being without it, and how very many things there are in the world which the civilized man takes for granted.

My shelter was positioned with the try-pots just inside the entrance of the den. In this way I could feed the cauldrons with blubber while enjoying the panorama of embattled nature outside. The heat from the tryworks soon warmed me, and noticing some large chunks of crystal-clear ice washed up onto the beach, I collected the biggest of these and chipped it into pieces to fit into the kettle that had been left behind by my shipmates, along with a lance and a few other items. Sucking a tiny piece of this ice, I discovered it to be quite fresh, although the larger chunk had been covered with a thin salty layer. I could only assume therefore that this had broken off an ice cliff or an iceberg, where the water is always sweet, and that it had been immersed in the sea for some time. Ice of this kind was a great bonus, for it would be a much better source of fresh water than collecting snow. With some ship's biscuits and some salt beef inside me, my sense of well-being was soon restored. As I relaxed, I kept my eye open for the ship, in case it should venture back now that the wind came from a different quarter. Not that I desired her speedy return—far from it—but I did not want to be surprised with precious sealskins adorning the walls and floor of my den. I would need to return the borrowed skins to their stacks before the crew arrived, so that the mate would have no excuse to discipline me.

For a while I set to, chopping up the pieces of blubber that were still not minced and going on from this to scrape one of the skins that made up the pile that had been left on the beach when the crew departed. Weeks under the tyranny of a sadistic mate had rooted out any tendency to be idle, but I convinced myself that I deserved some rest and spent a couple of hours, after this, absorbing the marvellous spectacle of the world around. Of course, I could imagine the reaction of the mate should he see me and could foresee how he would stride up the beach when he returned to demand that I give an account of the work I had done while he had been away. I would be ready for him, however, with my answer, for overnight I had begun to see him for the petty bully he really was. Carried away by a sudden feeling of self-righteousness, I proceeded to compose aloud the harangue with which I should like to greet the mate, if only I had the courage, startling as I did so a few wandering penguins who replied to my provocative outburst with a barrage of loud and indignant squawks.

The day passed leisurely, with enough activity in the wildlife around to engross my attention. I was not once bored. Toward evening, feeling a drowsiness come over me, I imagined there would be nothing to stop me from falling soundly asleep. Oddly enough, however, this was not the case. I found I actually missed the sounds of the ship, the hum of companionable chatter and the thud of sailors walking on the decks above. For so long now I had become accustomed to the creak of the spars and the groan of the ship's joints as she rolled from side to side that without these familiar sounds I was unable to sleep. Of course, from my pitch on the beach I could still hear the sea, but its sound was violent as it crashed against the boulders and lacked the soporific and rhythmic swish and trickle as the waves slid past the hull.

Restless, I left the den for a stroll along the sea edge. The fading light of day warned of the approach of night. The crunch of pebbles underfoot had a reassuring, familiar, quality; and I responded to a boyish urge to flip handfuls of them into the water, listening pleasurably for their predictable flop. The seals were more restful than earlier, and their sounds were muted by the thickening weight of wind, whose swirling patterns were stippled and filled out with snow. My hair lifted on my head, and I noticed too that the manes of the bull seals stood out sharply like ruffs, making them look coiffed and regal.

Occasionally against the hisses and swishes that filled the air, a seal bleated, its sound far away and strangely poignant like a lamb's. Pricking up my ears to isolate one in particular that seemed more stressful, I found myself drawn as if by a thread towards the stacks of rock where I had last seen the mate. As I neared it, I quickened in response to the urgency of a cry which, for a wild moment, as it seemed so human, I thought must be a baby's. There were several seals with pups that were all now bleating for attention, but in none of them could I distinguish the searing, lonely quality of the cry that dug uncomfortably, spurlike, into the tenderest of my emotions. I could not find its origin, but, as if conscious of my presence, the crying became more frantic and insistent, combining with its infinite sadness and despair a demand that it be recognized and answered. Had I tried to turn away I am sure I could not have done so. At any rate, I indulged the instinct that urged me to persevere till I had located what was causing such obvious distress.

The fur seals were fairly thickly distributed around this area. A little way to one side of the place in which earlier I had been entrapped. I pinpointed the disturbing cry in a cleft between a group of rocks whose only exit was barred by a fat and pregnant sleeping female. I was amazed that any creature could sleep through such a clamour, but I was to find that the fur seals could be extraordinarily indifferent to the sufferings of their fellows while displaying a remarkable affection to their own young, whose particular cry they could recognize and isolate amongst a thousand others.

Anxious to end such piteous squalling, I scrambled up the needle-pointed rocks to raise myself above the seals and look down into the cleft. At first I could not see a thing. As my eyes grew accustomed to the gloom, I could just make out what seemed to be a living ball of creamy fluff whose tiny frame, jammed within a narrow fissure, trembled so much with the gigantic effort to attract some sympathy that I feared it would fall apart. Luckily for both of us, there was a hole wide enough for my arm to slip through to allow me to reach it. If the jagged perimeter of the opening was most uncomfortable against my chest and shoulder, it saved me the problem of trying to move the sleeping seal.

"Steady on there, little fellow," I said aloud. "We'll have you out of there in no time." And I slipped my hand underneath its belly so that I could lift it backwards and ease it out. The second it felt my touch it stopped complaining and gave a kind of grateful whimper; but the next second it had begun its crying all over again.

Its back was to me as I held it up. When I turned it round, I was startled to see just how large and beautiful were its eyes. They looked like two deep luminous pools of brown behind a haze of blue, yet rippled with a dark bewilderment. It was quite the liveliest creature I had ever seen, and I was certain it was the same white pup I had discovered the day before, since there was not another white seal on the beach amongst all that throng of black and silver. It shivered as I held it up, and I could feel the warmth of its inner self and the great turmoil of its little heart as it pressed its belly into my hands, where it wriggled slightly before wetting them. It was not unlike a fluffy puppy, although larger and a good deal heavier, its head more rounded. As it opened wide its tiny mouth, its petal pink tongue quivered behind a row of miniature sharp-edged teeth, and I was prompted to place my finger against its tip to soothe it. The squealing stopped that instant, and the little mouth closed around the finger, sucking madly at it in the hope of milk. Its eyes closed expectantly, and its face was suffused momentarily with a look of bliss. While I was greatly relieved to have stopped its bleating, I winced with the realization that my finger might be sawn in two before it discovered the deception.

What I should do with it now that I had extricated it from its rocky prison was a problem. The seals around us were as indifferent to its bleating as if it did not exist. One thing was certain: if I put it back in the harem and did not keep a watch on it, it would be suffocated if it did not starve to death. Obviously it was hungry—just the sheer effort that it put into sucking my finger was proof of that—and I could predict that any minute the look of bliss was going to vanish to be replaced by temper when it realized that the effort to suck milk was to no avail. The best thing, for the moment, was to keep it warm till I could find some food for it. Snuggling it against my chest, I made towards the den again, hoping to find the answer over another brew.

I had hardly reached the den before my well-sucked finger began to lose its magic as a soother. A complaint more terrible than before started from the little creature. This time the overtones were distinctly irritable and chiding. Nothing I could do would silence it, and I wondered at the amazing cunning of nature to have invested in the cry of the young an ability to manipulate the affections of those sensitive enough to respond to it. I must obviously be one of the more sensitive ones, for I could feel myself actually cringing with the sense of guilt that my failure to provide nourishment had induced. Once I was in the den, I hoped it would settle down, and I prepared a nest from sealskin in which to make it cozy. I need hardly mention how exasperating it was when it prolonged its yelping. In fact, so painful was the noise to my ear that I was almost tempted to go straight out with it to some distant part of the beach where I would not be able to hear it and abandon it there. Fortunately, I had enough self-control to ignore this impulse while I made some soup for both of us, judging that for want of anything better it would have to suffice.

I used some of the meat from the fur seal carcasses that strewed the beach, together with some elephant tongue and blubber. Combined, they made a good thick stock that smelled quite appetizing. My new companion did not share my enthusiasm for my cooking, however, and I had the devil of a job trying to get it to swallow anything. Its tongue seemed too short to lap the soup up, even if it had wanted to. The steadfastness with which it tried to avoid my offering left me in no doubt as to the measure of its disgust. I was determined that I should feed it somehow. I was afraid that without some immediate nourishment it might shortly die, although, from its caterwauling, it was nowhere near the point of death.

Lord knows why I should have been so concerned to keep such a bawling bundle of baby beast alive. I did have some success, after a very long and patient effort, in feeding the infant by dipping the edge of my shirt in the rich-blooded stock and persuading it to suck that. Naturally I expected that, with its tummy filled, drowsiness, if not a sense of gratitude, would have induced a sense of tranquility in my companion; but not a hope. The nourishment only stimulated it the more, so that, throughout the night, despite my cosseting it and stroking it, it bleated piercingly—worse than the colic-stricken crying of any infant. I was driven nearly mad with exasperation. That I could get no sleep understates the case; indeed, I can say honestly that I felt more frail and nerve-wracked after this night of "baby-minding" than I had felt at any time during the worst of the voyage. When morning came and the wind seemed spent, I determined I would bear it no longer. I made it my intention to find a seal mother who had lost her pup and use all my persuasion to make her suckle my foundling before I was driven crazy by its demands.

To my astonishment, by the time the sun had reached her peak, I had not succeeded in this. Discouraged by attempt after attempt to introduce my pup, as I hesitantly refer to it, to a seal mother whose own pup lay for some reason dead or crushed beside it, I found that they all rejected it, snapping viciously when it tried to suckle. Disturbed and worried that my good intentions seemed to be causing it unnecessary distress, I was on the point of returning with it to the den when I saw a seal give birth to a pup that I knew immediately to be stillborn. In an instant I had snatched it up and smeared its wet afterbirth about my foundling, remembering how on a farm as a child I had seen a farmer use this method to introduce a foundling lamb to its foster mother. Whether it was this that formed a bond between the two seals I do not know; but as I placed the white pup down, the female allowed her teat to be sucked into the eager and demanding mouth.

For several hours, at least long enough for the ship to make a journey to Tranquility Bay and back, the weather had been quite moderate. When I had become so involved with the seal, I had not concerned myself with the passage of time. By midafternoon, however, feeling just a little uneasy, I scanned the coastline to the north for the sight of a sail. When by late evening the brig still had not appeared, I began to grow restless and started pacing up and down the beach rather than sitting cramped in my den. The fire I kept fuelled, although more blubber went in to feeding it than should have, since it should all have gone into the try-pot. Loath to kill the penguins to use their skins as fuel as the other sealers had done, I reflected that what the mate did not see he would not miss.

When night fell, with the weather calm and still but without any sign of the ship, I realized ruefully that I would have to spend a third night alone on shore—an experience which was beginning to lose its appeal. I was even tempted to go and look for the white seal pup before turning in for the night in an odd sort of hope that it would need my company. It had, however, seemed well satisfied with its foster mother, and I had not the heart to disturb it.

Try as I would, I could not sleep. My thoughts kept returning to the ship. By first light I was up and had a brew going, and I decided that if midday arrived without the ship showing I would try to make my way inland to a point high enough to get an unrestricted view.

I could not imagine that the skipper would delay his return unnecessarily and wondered if, during the storm, the ship had incurred some damage that made it imperative for her to lay up while the crew did repairs. They surely would not start harvesting seals on another beach without first clearing the ones they had culled on my own, unless of course they had found a beach that would allow the ship to anchor closer in to shore. In this case they would take the opportunity to clear that beach first so as not to waste time sailing to and fro. At any rate, I still had provisions for a week, which they must have taken into account when deciding where to hunt. In spite of these considerations, however, I had a nagging worry and felt a strong urge to climb the steep slope to the penguin rookery and try to make my way to the opposite side of the peninsula from there.

The white seal was sucking blissfully when I departed, and its new mother appeared none the worse for its foundling's voracious appetite. Remembering my own healthy love of food, I took a good thick slice of salt beef with me, together with half an elephant tongue and some ship's biscuits. I should have liked a container full of tea; but, lacking the luxury of a flask, settled for drinking as much of the morning's brew as my distended stomach would allow. Unencumbered with any bag—I had managed to stuff the food into my pockets—I skirted the elephant seal colony and began the ascent of the penguin cliff.

I had no idea what I was letting myself in for. It was a good two hours at least before I stood at the top of the low rise, sweating and muck-covered, with clothes torn and a wealth of scratches and bruises to show for my efforts—not to mention a seriously ruffled temper. Being a bird colony, the cliff was so thick with droppings that it was almost impossible to keep a footing. Stopped by an overhanging rock, I was obliged to try the steepest route, which was up a very slippery snow slope. This I managed to scramble up after a great deal of frustration and exertion, only to lose my footing on reaching the top and to go sliding down, ending up in a heap at the bottom. I was immediately overwhelmed by a horde of penguins who, following my example, had launched themselves on their bellies down the chute. These landed in a squawking pile on top of me and proceeded to peck and buffet me for getting in the way.

After several repetitions of this experience, I managed to surmount the obstacle by using my knife to gouge handholds and footholds in the hard-packed snow. Even then, I had another steep stretch of cliff to mount, flanked by scores of brooding penguins, who, regarding me with wary eyes, waited till I was poised most vulnerably before they attacked. Without warning, they pecked and stabbed at me, causing me sometimes to lose my grip and slip and bang myself against the rocks. Nothing I could do would restrain them, and the air around was thick with my threats and involuntary imprecations as each sharp beak jabbed home. When, on finally reaching the summit, I was confronted by a rather large and self-important bird who struck me with his flippers, screeching and ruffling its feathers as it tried to bar my way, I did the first thing that occurred to me. Swinging my boot underneath its backside, I lifted it high into the air before sending it slithering and squawking down the way I had come. That done, I felt distinctly mollified. Finding that in the meantime the rest of the colony had stopped its chatter, I took credit for this effect and was encouraged enough to announce imperiously to those birds squinting up at me that I would do the same to each and every one of them if I so much as heard another squawk.

Quite how preposterous my threat was I did not care; there were hundreds of the birds on the cliff top, and they would have taken me forever to shift. The practicality of the threat, however, did not matter. What mattered was that I had a brief moment of snatched triumph while quite miraculously the birds kept silent. I glared at them briefly before hobbling a few yards to a butt of rock, where I stopped just out of sight to examine my numerous and painful bruises. My disappearance set off an immediate clamour, as if the whole rookery had been simultaneously unmuzzled, and for all the soreness of my wounds I could not help laughing at their shrieks of outrage.

Once beyond the penguins I found a narrow passage leading roughly eastwards through a steep gorge bounded by dark, ice-encrusted rocks. Underfoot the ground was distinctly icy, although in parts I made my way along snow-free slopes of scree. I must have travelled half a mile between towering walls of weirdly shaped rock before I came to an open space that shelved steeply northeastwards, with precipitous drops to the beaches below. My intention had been to explore northwards and to find a route down to the headland beaches, hoping in this way to be able to spot the ship when she was approaching and to have time still to return to my own beach before the crew could get ashore. But since the descent looked too slippery and dangerous at this location, I was obliged to follow the easier route that lay southeast towards a cove shaped like a half-moon. I sank up to my knees in places in deep snow, but here and there I could follow bare rocky ground across the broad sweep to the beach. Below the snow line were several meandering melt streams, and channels nearby showed evidence that these would increase as the summer wore on.

I was so busy trying to avoid wrenching my ankle on the uneven ground that I was actually on the beach before I noticed the longboat. So spontaneous was my joy that I did not have time to feel angry that the mate had landed a party on another beach without first coming to look for me. At first glance not a soul could be seen, and I presumed that the party had gone exploring towards a rocky outcrop that gave access to another beach beyond. Why they should do this when there were so many seals on the present beach was a mystery.

As I dodged my way through some of the harems towards the boat, I saw that it had been beached in a very casual manner near some stranded ice and that no thought had been given to weighting it down. I might have regarded this as very ominous had not the discovery of some empty liquor bottles in the boat and another nearby on the sand not suggested a simple reason for its casual abandonment. The crew had no doubt been a good deal intoxicated by the time of their arrival, probably not even knowing which beach they were on. Like as not, they had slumped off to find some little glory hole of their own where they could imbibe with the necessary privacy and secrecy. Obviously the sheer glut of seals had gone to their heads and taken the urgency out of the usually chancy sealing business.

As if to bear this out, I caught a flutter of some garment along the beach and could make out two figures sitting side by side against some rocks, heads touching, as if they had nothing more pressing to do in life. I thought they might be looking for the ship, the island that had first given us haven being in the direct line of their vision not thirteen miles away. But the ship was nowhere to be seen, which suggested that it was already rounding the northern part of the peninsula if it was not already about to anchor in some other cove.

Although I could see the two figures, I could not identify them. Any chance of attracting them by shouting was out of the question. Even if the seals had not been so loud in their protestations, the wind would have carried the sound away. I set off towards them, thinking at first I might creep up and surprise them. However, since I would have hated anyone to do this to me in similar circumstances, I called out as I drew nearer, waving my arm to attract their attention. Their heads were still inclined, one towards the other, as though they were exchanging confidences. Only when I was about twenty yards away did I delightedly recognize one of them. For the life of me I could not think what celebration would make that particular crew member so friendly with the cook, for there was no mistaking the bald pate of the second figure. Normally neither of them had a good word for the other, which made it strange that they should be found together—unless of course the cook had provided liquor for a party. I was prepared to believe this was the case when, without warning, a chill ran down the length of my spine, and I found myself questioning why the cook should be ashore at all.

I had to approach the last few feet from behind because of a large harem of seals blocking any other route. As I neared them, I tripped over a boot, and my heart began to race alarmingly. In a couple of strides I stood before them with my back turned towards the incoming sea. They sat slouched against the rocks, their eyes unseeing, their whiskered faces blue and bloated beneath whitish streaks of salt. Not a word would either of them ever utter again. They were frozen stiff in the posture that the tide had left them in, their shoulders leaning against each other in an intimacy they would never have suffered in life. In that moment I had a premonition that I would never see the ship again, nor any of her seamen unless they, like the two tragic figures in front of me, were washed ashore on the back of a wave, forlorn and lonely and unutterably dead.

5

To Light a Fire

I staggered back, and as I did so stumbled over a mound of seals from beneath which protruded the arm of a corpse I knew intuitively to be the mate's. A few yards farther along the beach two other bodies lay facedown with their arms outstretched as in silent supplication. The very fact that they were starboard hands and separated from the other members of their watch was proof enough, if I should doubt it, that a calamity had struck the ship in a sudden and most vicious way. How else could it be explained that five such souls be found together? Feeling my knees buckling beneath me, I leaned against a rock to support my weight.

For a moment, I could not think at all, and the scene seemed to blur around me. Gradually my senses returned; but even when everything around me had regained its shape, I could only sit on a rock and grieve while the full import of the tragedy sank in. I was alone on this deserted island—the first human to inhabit this desolate place. That in itself was frightening enough without the realization that I might never be rescued, for I had strayed with the crew beyond the boundary of the world which was then known to mortal men.

They, for their temerity, had lost their lives. I, on the other hand, had been spared, perhaps to suffer a longer, lonelier, lingering death. The thought was overwhelming. I could feel my senses reeling with the awful threat of it when, noticing the returning tide stretching out stealthy fingers towards the bodies, I was seized by an upsurge of intense anger. It started as a tingling sensation in the tips of my fingers and toes and spread out along my limbs like a red-hot stream of lava till, shooting upwards it exploded like a volcano when it reached my throat, into a howl of pent-up bitterness and fury.

That I was demented temporarily, I will acknowledge. I began stamping my feet at the water's edge, as if by doing this I could drive it back. When this had no effect, I snatched up stones and began hurling them into the sea in an attempt to beat the life out of the malevolent element that had destroyed my friends. My heart was racing faster and my anger rising with each second. I screamed at the sea and pelted it harder, rushing inshore to fetch larger rocks to hurl without any thought of how irrational or futile was my behaviour. With all the nearby stones used up, I turned my raging madness upon a large boulder embedded deeply in the shore. When it refused to yield to my efforts to uproot it, I became crazed with a maniacal hatred and frustration, tearing at it till my hands were bleeding. I was sobbing like a child, my strength flowing from me until I finally collapsed.

I do not know for how long I lay drowning in my misery and bitter self-pity, my cheek against that lifeless rock. Not until I finally lay empty of all human emotion did my soul rekindle in me that instinct of survival.

I began to take a more rational note of the state of the tide. Already it was swirling around my ankles and shifting the bodies of my mates. I must move quickly, I told myself, if I was to retrieve them. Hitching my arms underneath those bodies, I proceeded to drag them one by one beyond the reach of the sea which had destroyed them, through the colony of seals to a space beyond where there was no chance that a seal would lie upon them. The task was tiring and gruesome, the bodies too heavy and too awkward to lift. Gulls and other birds flocked in, newly excited by the smell of death. They hovered around with predatory eyes, sometimes even darting in to peck at the corpse I was dragging. I shouted at them till I was hoarse and was so sickened by the sacrilege that I would have killed every one of them if I had been able.

Burial was impractical. Even if I had possessed a spade, the ground was too hard to excavate. The only alternative was to build a mound around the bodies from loose materials I found nearby or to go in search of a rock formation that would act as a partial sarcophagus cutting down the number of rocks that would be required to cover them. Eventually, I was forced by both fatigue and expedience to inter each body above the storm beach, using whatever materials came most readily to hand. But although I was conscious of a need for reverence in the presence of the dead, the effort of beating off scavenging birds had left little room for sanctity. Added to this was the practical problem that the bodies had frozen into weird shapes, that made it impossible to compose them into postures symbolic of heavenly peace without resorting to butchery. It took an age to erect the mounds of stone over them and to fill in all the gaps with smaller stones and sand. I was exhausted when I was finished with all the heavy labour, only to be faced with an unforeseen dilemma.

The burial service! Should I not perform some sort of ceremony for the repose of the souls of the dead? I was at first loath to do so, not because I had a desire to be irreverent or sacrilegious but out of a sudden conviction, however misguided, of the total impracticality of prayer. Having decided that God was to blame, or at least that He must take the responsibility, since everything was supposed to happen by His great design, I did not see any point or need to prepare Him for their arrival in His heavenly kingdom. Obviously He would be expecting them.

Despite these intensely impious feelings, a natural inhibition made it difficult for me to walk away without at least a token valediction. My words got started along several avenues of thought, but each effort petered out before I managed to say anything suitable. Finally I abandoned my attempt to eulogize my crew mates, deciding on the simple alternative of asking the Almighty to take the souls of the departed into His celestial kingdom—adding involuntarily that I hoped He would treat them better there than He had on earth. The remark was out before I realized its irreverence. Half expecting to be struck dead for this blasphemy, I was surprised several minutes later to find that I was still very much alive. Not that I had very much to lose, I reflected, whatever I said. A day or two's grace would not make much difference to my peace of mind. I even wondered whether there was any point at all in trying to survive in such an inhospitable place, not realizing how irrepressible the instinct was in every sane man to keep his grip on life.

I had been so busy burying the dead that I had not noticed how very quickly the tide had come in. When I looked for the boat I found it was in water well out of my depth and already being slammed against the tips of some submerging rocks. There went any hopes of salvaging it. By the next morning I knew it would have been broken up and its contents, whatever they were, scattered on the seabed. I cursed at my folly for not having anchored it, while also cursing the time that it had taken to make the graves. Evening was already well advanced, and I would have to hurry if I was to get back to the other beach before dark. Much as I needed to look for salvage, I could not afford to be caught out during the night without the protection of some sort of shelter. Already I had seen enough examples of the weather's treachery to know how carelessness in this respect could cause disaster.

The wind was chill and the sweat had begun to freeze on me, making the clothes feel most unpleasant against my skin. I had on two jerseys and a jacket. These were pretty torn and worn now and were not going to be enough, I warned myself, when the weather worsened. Then, as if the implication of my predicament hit me for the first time, I was unable to move for a few moments with the awful dread of what my future offered. Finally recovering my equanimity and remembering the need for haste, I scrambled up the hill a bit farther, only to be shocked to a complete standstill when my thoughts took a new hold. In this manner, with many stops and starts, I reached the penguin rookery near the other beach and slithered down its decline among the startled birds.

I felt hungry, but it did not dawn on me to grab any eggs till I was at the bottom of the ice chute. I wondered how it was possible that I could feel so hungry in the face of death and with the awful knowledge that I was a castaway. But hungry I definitely was, and, what is more, I was determined to do something about it. Probably nature was using this way of encouraging me, in the face of all my worries and grief, to believe that I had the basic grit to be a survivor. The thought was comforting, and I should have held on to it had not the idea been cruelly dashed the next minute when I returned to find my den in ruins. Not only had the fire gone out in spite of all my preparation, but some clumsy elephant seals had obviously barged right through my shack, knocking over the barrels that supported the roof as well as the try-pots, whose oil had run all over and swamped the place.

Cursing was useless; but if it could not clear the mess away or rebuild the den, at least it gave some release to my nerves, which were beginning to coil tightly. I used every possible expression I could muster, including some of the worst I had heard aboard the ship. Next, I set out to repair the damage. My first job, before trying to upend the barrels, was to remove the saturated skins that had absorbed the oil. This back-breaking task took me a good while. The ground around the skins had been trampled into a quagmire which tended to imprison them. By the time I had it done, I was desperately chilled, and my teeth were chattering from the raw wind which found its way easily through my thin clothes. Since I could not afford to take long rebuilding the den, in case I became too numb with cold even to crawl into it, I threw down a few stones as a kind of base over which I put a couple of barrel lids to form a floor. This done, I hurried off to the stack of furs to fetch some fresh ones for a roof and covering.

I was very dispirited and tired by this time. On the way, however, I passed the little white seal, which seemed well established with its adoptive mother and for once was not bleating in complaint. "It is all right for you," I thought ungraciously. "I would not be here if I had not tried to protect your mother." And then, as I hurried past it to the stack of skins that miraculously was still intact, the sober thought suddenly occurred to me that, were it not for the seal whom I had tried to protect, I would sure as anything be dead.

The idea was startling, and one I was to mull over for some time after I had crawled into my miserably inadequate hovel to pass the night. Prompted by it, I had to ask myself whether it was by chance alone I still existed, or whether there was some greater reason that I had been preserved. The answer would play a vital role in my expectations of survival, if by virtue of chance alone I was alive, it could follow equally that the chance was slim of my continuing to survive. Not only had I been marooned on an island that no one knew about, but it was far beyond the limits of the normal shipping routes. If this in itself did not preclude the hope of rescue, the fact remained that the island was further isolated by a belt of winds and monster seas that would deter even the bravest seamen. Add to that the fact that it was an icebound island which boasted nothing growing on it that could support my life except for a few miserable patches of moss and lichen.

If, on the other hand, my continued existence was by the design of the Almighty, He would no doubt provide the necessary means to ensure my welfare. The latter concept I preferred to entertain. Not only did it pander to my self-esteem, but it suggested an element of concern on the part of some Being greater than myself that I found comforting. Unless!—a horrible suspicion wormed its way into the corners of my mind—unless the Almighty had spared me only to make a mockery of me because He intended to snatch my life away from me, in any case, within a few days!

The thought was terrible! I can hardly describe the nameless terrors to which it gave rise. Suffice it to say that an awful dark vacuum formed around me in which I drifted weightless and helpless, terrified and desperate for something familiar to which I could cling for comfort. When I found my voice, I started upbraiding God hysterically for teasing me, ranting on in this manner for I do not know how long between intervals of racking grief when I could do nothing but bury my head on my knees.

77

I tried persuading myself that God could not be so cruel; yet had I not seen just hours before ample evidence that he permitted a great deal of cruelty to go unchecked? What was it, therefore, but an ironic joke that we should have been the discoverers of this island and yet wrecked within a few days of arriving on its shores? By virtue of precedence, I was ruler of this new country no one knew about, ruler of a place where nothing grew, king of the seals and the birds and the penguins, of a sterile worthless land.

Once I even challenged God to finish me off immediately. I actually lay down and struck a suitably pious posture, since there would be no one around to straighten my limbs and bury me when I was dead. Of course, nothing happened that could be termed miraculous, and I turned myself at last to more practical matters.

All the little unexpected physical problems I had to contend with were, in fact, salutary. They prevented me from dwelling too long on the apparent hopelessness of my condition. The only course to avoid despair was to isolate the difficulties and try calmly to make out an order of priorities. What with battling against the cold, trying to locate some food for myself amidst the shambles, restoring the den and making occasional sallies outside to drive off the frequently intrusive animals, I kept my mind absorbed enough in immediate physical concerns to allow me eventually to succumb to fitful sleep.

I awoke at first light, which must have been around 2:30 A.M. in those latitudes, cramped and cold. Thinking I heard voices, I dashed out of my makeshift shelter to investigate, my heart pounding. The beach, however, was as deserted of people as when we had first arrived, and I realized miserably that what I had heard must have been the morning chorus of the animal world greeting the light of day. The penguins had already started their empty chatter, which was interrupted now and then by the human cry of the fur seals and the complaint of the seal elephants that, through the morning mist, sounded as dismal and distant as a foghorn. Disappointed, I felt more alone now than ever, conscious that I was a misfit in this world of animals whom nature had equipped in her own special way to meet the vigors of this seemingly sterile land. Even a casual look at the seals was enough to see how devoid I was, by comparison, of the elementary requirements for survival. Where they were not covered with layers of blubber as were the elephant seals, they had been given a thick warm fur to insulate them against the cold. I, in contrast, had only a few miserable thread-worn clothes to protect me. The season was summer, the warmest time of the year. How I should cope when the weather became really cold, I did not know, and I was without the basic means of even starting a fire.

If no other cause could have made me melancholy, the thought of being fireless would have been reason enough. Along with food and adequate clothing, it was one of the three essentials that I could not do without. Fortunately, amidst the melancholy, it did occur to me that I at least had food that should never run out. I was surrounded by more birds and seals than I could count. There were eggs in plenty and fish, no doubt, that I could catch if I had a mind to. Come to that, with a little bit of practice and ingenuity, I might even be able to make some clothes for myself out of the seals' skins, although I could imagine what a problem making these would be. However, heartened by the practical solution to at least two of my worries, I searched for a bit of salt beef to chew on while I pondered the urgent problem of lighting a fire. Significantly, my attitude to the animals had changed enough to make me consider slaughtering them now that they featured in my system of survival. Maybe, after all, I was no different at heart from any of the sealers.

The weather was cold and overcast that day; but I was too restless to stay where I was. Soon after rising, I decided I would make a trip inland to the half-moon beach in order to salvage anything brought in by the tide before it had the chance of grabbing it back. At the same time I might find something that would be useful in lighting a fire, perhaps a tinberbox from one of the longboats, where one was always carried. Scrambling about in the oiled mess around my hut to find what was left of the few days' rations, I stuffed some of the salted beef down my shirt before hiding the rest in a crevice in some nearby rocks to retrieve when I returned.

Remembering the trouble I had had climbing the penguin slope the day before, I took a length of hemp which I discovered near the barrels, intending to fasten it to a suitable rock above the slope so that I could use it in the future to draw myself up. The penguins seemed less irritated by my approach this time, being too busy huddling from the wind to bother about me. The result was that I got up fairly quickly and unmolested. Once beyond them, I put my mind to the methods of creating a fire should I find nothing suitable on the beach. I tried to recall what I had heard of rubbing sticks together. I concluded, however, that it would be simpler if I found some flint or other rocks to strike together to make a spark.

By keeping my eyes open for something that I might use as tinder, I was surprised to notice what I had missed the day before. There was a variety of lichen about, which, if I scraped it off the rocks and kept it in my pocket, might dry out sufficiently to become tinder. Some of it was hard and funguslike —orange in colour or else a greyish-yellow—but there were other kinds, some fibrous, some fleshy, which grew in patches on the northeast-facing slopes. The orange sort, I observed as I neared the coast again, grew in great profusion on the cliff's seaward face. Strange that I had not seen it earlier! I wondered if there were other features that I might have missed. Obviously, if my life was in the balance, even the most insignificant factors could tip the scales. I resolved to be a good deal more observant and to try not to take for granted even the most ordinary things.

As I approached the half-moon beach, a certain dread built up in me lest I find something horrible; but this time the sea was more merciful. Although no tinderbox or flint appeared, I did find a strange mixture of ship's paraphernalia which confirmed to my mind that she had been completely wrecked. I wandered up and down the beach several times, combing its shoreline for spare bits of clothing and odd-shaped bits of wreckage mixed amongst other items of more personal nature. Food casks, strangely enough, were nonexistent, except for a small cask of molasses and another full of bread. The latter was mouldy and sodden with seawater, but I prized open the molasses and scooped up a handful. Everything I saw I collected, whether or not I could think of a use for it, foreseeing a day when I would find a desperate need for something I might have thrown away. I spent a good few hours carrying up all the bric-a-brac that lined the beach and a further hour or so caching the odd assortment beneath some rocks. I had half expected to discover more bodies and was greatly relieved when nothing as gruesome as my previous day's discovery came my way.

By the time I left the beach I was feeling much more confident. By chance I had come upon some white and yellow pebbles that I was sure were quartz. If this was so, I could almost certainly rely on finding some larger pieces with which I should be able to strike a spark. For the moment, though, the beach around was so thick with the murky effluent that always surrounded the elephant seals that I could have come across a diamond and not have noticed it under the slime.

Deciding that I would be better off returning to the other beach, where at least I had a bit of timber and blubber should I be able to find something there that would enable me to start a fire, I set off up the hill, mulling over in my mind the possible run of events that had led to the ship's destruction. The skipper was an excellent seaman, which made it all the more difficult for me to find a plausible explanation for the wreck of the ship. Like all men of exceptional courage, he was a cautious man. I therefore concluded he must have been struck by some freak condition—something totally unexpected, for which he would have had no possible reason to prepare.

Upon further reflection, I decided that the east wind must have been the cause of the ship's destruction. Had not someone remarked, even as we left Tranquility Bay, that there were too many lee shores around for safety in the event of an east wind? That would account for the bodies and the wreckage I had found on the east-facing half-moon beach, which was in a direct line from the rocky islets that must have taken the full impact of the stricken ship.

If I was right in my surmise, I would have to try to reach some of the other beaches on the northeast coast of the peninsula to salvage more of the ship. For that matter, I might even find someone alive, although I did not really believe I would. Even if anyone had been able to drag himself ashore after the calamity, I knew that wet and shocked as he would be he would soon have succumbed to exposure.

In less time than I had expected, I had reached the uplands from where I could look down on the beaches. They were swarming with seals and penguins, and there was no way of knowing if these animals concealed any bodies or any wreckage. As yet, conditions did not favour a safe descent. I would have to wait till the snow melted before I would be able to pick my way down the precipitous decline.

Being accustomed to a civilized and, to be truthful, a privileged way of living, I knew it would take quite a while to adjust to the problems of surviving in the wild. Already I had ample warning that my progress would be dogged by a series of trials and errors. Having always been able to strike a light at a moment's notice with a flint and steel, I was totally unprepared when faced with the need to contemplate an alternative to this form of ignition. Civilization teaches us to take so many things for granted and buries the instincts with which the savage is born. My only hope was to hang on until my "primitive" intuition had time to assert itself. With no way of knowing how long that might be, I was deeply worried. Fire meant more than just a means to warm my body and cook my food; it meant the element of life itself. Light was the only thing that could tame the darkness, the companionable spirit that could keep at bay the primeval terrors of the night.

My makeshift shack had so repeatedly been flattened by the insensitive elephant seals that I decided to find a new place for my den, one that would not only be out of the way of the general traffic but that would offer more protection from the winds, which rarely fell to below twenty knots. I eventually settled upon a site near the northern end of the beach, sheltered by two sides of a rock, and laboriously transported my belongings to it.

As for my fire, I reasoned four agents were necessary. First I had to have a spark or other light to start with; secondly, I needed some tinder or smouldering substance to receive the spark and keep it glowing; thirdly, I needed some form of kindling to create a flame which I could then augment by adding the fourth element, fuel. A spark being useless without some tinder, I went in search of the latter, which I supposed could be made from anything dry and ground down enough to support a glow. A systematic search of the beach and surrounding rocks produced some dried bird droppings and old bits of bone. After scraping the latter with my knife to fine white fragments, I added it to the collection of lichens and crumbs and odd bits of dried tobacco lying in my pocket.

This done, I collected a pile of kindling from an odd assortment of barrel shavings, splinters of wood, feathers and dried moss, together with any bits of thread or patches of clothing that I thought I could do without. Since I was not going to let sartorial vanity stand in the way of my ultimate safety, odd strips of cloth or even one or two pocket flaps went towards my intended pyre. Digging my fingers into the barrel of blubber, I extracted some pieces of this highly flammable stuff and wove them into the kindling, while nearby I arranged a pile of larger pieces to burn as fuel.

Once this was collected, and having arranged a heap of tinder in the center of three flat stones around which I had partly circled the kindling, I addressed my mind to the ultimate problem of creating the spark. Several methods of trying to use the pebbles of quartz I had found on the beach the day before proved of no avail. If I did not succeed in producing sparks, I was soon nursing raw knuckles that had been stripped of skin. No other choice was open but to go in search of larger pieces of quartz or some other suitable rock; yet after a long and fruitless search I returned disconsolate.

It was much colder now. Huddled beneath a fur skin in the angle of the rocks, I faced the beach and its swarming mass of somnolent seals. What was the point in struggling to exist at all, I wondered, when all the company I had were birds and seals. Before I could answer my own desperate question, the cold set its icy hands on me, and I felt compelled to get up and jog around to get warm.

Thirsty after all my efforts I remembered I had no water. There were no melt streams yet on this stretch of beach because the cliffs were kept in morning shadow. Unwilling to go to the other beach for a drink, I made a raid on the penguin colony so that I could benefit from the moisture available in the raw eggs. These I gulped till I had downed a dozen rather than torment myself by eating snow, which only aggravated the thirst and left my insides feeling chill. More than anything in the world at that moment I would have liked a brew of tea. With this additional reminder that I needed a fire, my mind started grappling with that problem again.

I had no alternative but to try fire sticks, but I could not recall how they worked. I had read once that, if one rubbed one stick vigorously against another and sustained the friction for a while, one of the pieces would spontaneously light, enabling one, with the judicious addition of some tinder and a certain amount of gentle fanning, to create a substantial fire. Obviously there must be a knack to it, if in fact it did not require a certain type of wood; but there being nothing else for the time being that I could think of to experiment with, I set about trying to fashion some sort of contrivance with which I could obtain the necessary friction.

I took a while to reason out that there must be one stationary piece of wood against which friction would be created by a moving or spinning stick. With this in mind, I got a barrel top and prized it apart so that I had two pieces of wood, one fairly thick, in which I hacked out a notch, and the other just thin enough to fit in the notch. I then proceeded to draw the thin length of wood through the larger piece as quickly as I could in a sawing motion, continuing for about ten minutes till my muscles were aching and my body was dripping with sweat. I had to stop for want of energy, but hard as I had been rubbing the wood there was no sign of scorching, just a shiny mark where the two surfaces had begun to polish each other.

I did not count how many times I tried the experiment. At the end, my arms were weak and trembling, the sweat had turned into ice and I was almost fainting from fatigue. I had to pile skins on me to stop from freezing while I tried to revitalize myself with a cold meal. Attempt followed attempt until I was nearly desperate. Then I hit on the notion of notching the stationary piece of wood in a different way, so that I could actually put a tiny amount of tinder inside it, which would give me more of a chance of starting a glow.

This time, instead of holding one piece with one hand, I anchored it against a rock with my feet while I sat on a small boulder and tried setting the tinder alight with a rapid drilling kind of motion, twirling the working stick, which I had smoothed, between both palms so that it spun rapidly in the notch at the base. How the devil fire could be created by this method was beyond me. All that happened was that the tinder spun out of the hole, and once again my sticks took to polishing each other.

Sitting with the sweat in thick frozen clumps against my body, I felt an uncontrollable ague take hold of me. My teeth chattered, and the wind was getting up, whistling and cutting the edges off my ears. Already it was late evening, and the sun was very low. I was hungry again and had a raging thirst. I might as well turn in. First I had to rebuild my shack; but that done, I hoped that the elephant seals would leave me in peace.

What an utter waste of time and effort the day had been. Exhausted, cold, lonely and frustrated, I was convinced that I had reached the limit. I was worn down, frightened suddenly and petulantly anxious—terrified to allow myself to fall asleep in case this time the numbing cold would lay its icy fingers on me and I would never wake. Maybe to stop myself from sleeping or maybe as a result of my anxiety, I started screaming at the Almighty again, threatening that if He persisted I would forswear His existence and profess the Devil. In this childlike, rambling way, from time to time during that night I addressed, argued and tried to reason with the Creator until, silenced by sheer exhaustion, I fell asleep—to dream of climbing mountains towards some bright and beckoning light.

When I awoke many hours later, the sun was high enough to have scaled the cliffs and scattered the gloom beneath. Seeking out the chinks in my den, it pierced the darkness inside with rays so powerful that for a moment I was blinded by its brilliance. On venturing outside I was uplifted to see that the beach had been transformed by snowfall into a scene of dazzling beauty. All the dross was hidden by layers of gems, while the ice cliffs to the south looked like cliffs of turquoise encrusted with clusters

85

of pearls. A penguin greeted me formally, bowing in a rather courteous gesture. Feeling unusually cheered by the day's enchantments, I returned the greeting in a similar way.

Without any wind to chill or irritate me, I felt remarkably light-spirited, observing nothing in nature to induce fear or foreboding. As I strolled along the beach I remarked how many icebergs of various size had been caught by the tide and washed ashore. Some were milky white in hue, others greenish-blue with streaks of grey where earth or rock had been embedded. Then I saw one that made me stop short. It was a thing of incredible beauty and glistened like a boulder of the purest crystal. The sun, catching it at a certain angle, sent millions of sparkling rays shooting in my direction to pierce the very center of my brain. I stood mesmerized as its brilliance leapt out at me with all the colours of fire.

At that instant I recalled a childhood moment when I had been given a crystal lens whose powers of magic could make things look larger than they really were. But more than anything else I had been astounded by the fact that it could concentrate the rays of light to produce enough heat to cause a fire. I remembered the keen thrill of this amazing discovery and the sense of power that the possession of such an object inspired. I had spent the good part of a week setting fire to countless experimental objects, and much to my mother's displeasure I had burnt several holes in my clothes. Why should the sight of this berg bring alive such memories—unless, of course, it was intuition commanding me to experiment. Was it suggesting that I should try to sculpt a lens out of this piece of ice and, if successful, use it to ignite some tinder? If so, then surely my biggest problem would be solved. Before I knew it, I was walking towards the crystal boulder, drawing my knife to strike it a brisk clean blow. All I required was a palm-sized chunk to work on; but I had no idea what would be the knife's effect.

I heard a loud crack, followed by a million bell-like tinklings as the block fell away into a heap of sharp-edged chips. I gasped in horror, totally unprepared for such a dramatic mishap, which, had I known it then, was the surest proof that the ice was pure.

Faced with the destruction of the beautiful object, I felt sick at heart, grieving at the unforeseen mischief of the act. Not only had I destroyed the beautiful ice boulder, but I had scuppered my chances of trying the experiment that might save my life. I was about to drag myself back to the den when I felt prompted to spread the ice mound with my foot. As I did so, I uncovered about five sizable chunks that had been lost in the heap of chippings. I now knew, however, that I would have to be exceptionally careful with these, for there was not another clear piece of ice on the beach. Although the interior of the island was a gigantic mass of it, in order to collect another sizable chunk I would have to climb a hazardous cliff, with the prospect, if I fell, of breaking my neck.

I took a while to compose myself before attempting to shape the first piece of ice crystal to the required form. Indeed, when I began the task, I approached it as though I were a jeweller about to cut the rarest diamond, so fragile was the material I had to sculpt. I gauged the strength with which I chipped around the edges with special caution. The least slip or misdirected blow could destroy it completely or spoil its effectiveness with an ugly flaw. Difficult as the task was and requiring the greatest concentration and patience, I had achieved practically the rough shape required before the process of smoothing or polishing when the last slight tap shattered it into countless splinters. Aghast, I hardly dared try again. And, indeed, the next two shattered the same way after only a few slight taps. Despairing, I contemplated the two pieces left. What if they should shatter also? Returning to the hopelessly exhausting labour of the fire sticks was an alternative I could not bear. A person can take only so much disappointment, and I knew that another day of rubbing sticks together without a satisfactory result would break my spirit.

And so I picked up one of the two remaining pieces of ice and, wishing to speed up the process of melting, placed it carefully in the pit of my arm. I had of course decided that I must treat this piece of ice as though it were my last. Only in this way would I take that extra-special care necessary to succeed. The discomfort was at least proof that my body heat was beginning to have an effect on the ice. Sure enough, when I examined it before paring it down, I saw that it was already smoother and becoming slightly rounder—although I had to pare much away before it could be finally shaped. I was loath to attempt this with the knife's tip after the previous failures, but, plucking up courage, I used the blade of the knife to scrape very gently at the flaws and knobbles, all the while holding my breath until I had a shape that seemed perfect in every respect except for the scratches that marred its surface. The only thing remaining to do was to polish it. Holding the ice gently between the palms of both hands, I rubbed it in an almost circular motion till my hands were freezing and it began to shine. I was now highly excited. Indeed, I had reason to be, for when I had finished with my handiwork, I had a palm-sized lens of perfect proportions whose convex sides glistened in the rays of the sun.

Looking at it lying there in the center of my palm, I wondered if this was the answer to my search for fire. So anxious did I suddenly become to test its magical properties that there and then I held it over the back of my hand as I had done as a child to see if I could achieve that intense and caustic ring of light that would prove the principle and convince me that I had made my lens correctly. The sun seemed hotter now than ever—smiling down on me in anticipation of my great experiment. Gazing with bated breath, I saw a bright circle of white light appear, almost iridescent and with coloured edges, which flitted across the surface of my hand as I altered its angle beneath the lens of ice. Indeed, so intent was I on proving the principle that I gave no thought to how this proof would be manifest. OUCH! I jerked my hand away and sucked the back where it hurt. The principle was indeed accurate. There was a bright scorch mark where my hand had begun to burn!

Hardly daring to hope that I could extend the principle, I rushed to the northern end of the beach where I had left my firing things the day before. Chucked to one side were the sticks I had abandoned; but the pile of blubber had been demolished by birds except for a few strips of skin and other scraps. Struggling with one hand to gather some of the tinder together, I built up a little wall of kindling around it, which I tried to thread with the blubber that the birds had left.

For a moment or two nothing happened. Suddenly a little puff of powder came from the tinder, and the kindling moved slightly with the warning of a breeze. "Curse it!" The wind would have to start blowing at this vital moment! I cupped my hand to try to shut out the draught. Another breath of wind fanned my cheek. And then, without warning, a miniature circling movement appeared in the tinder and in an instant developed into a suspicion of a glow. With another puff of wind it spread outwards, and the kindling round it burst into flame.

At that instant I heard a cry, like the wild spontaneous cry of a savage. Although it issued from within me, it seemed not of me but derived from another age, another place. A strange sensation of oneness with another being swept over me, as though by this simple act of creation I had reenacted that moment of triumph when man, the primitive, had spread his fingers for the very first time to warm them by heat of fire. Like him, I felt my heart almost bursting with awe and jubilation as I prostrated myself in adoration before the sun. I had drawn fire. that divine element, from the heavens. What now would the heavens, in return, expect or demand of me?

6

Coming to Terms

With all the anxiety of the recent days I had not taken too much notice of the many changes that were taking place in the animal world around me. Each day a shifting pattern of birth and death was affirming the order of the natural law. The peninsula was the breeding ground for thousands of birds and seals —the former represented by several species, each dependent somehow on the other life around them, which suggested some inexorably practical if pitiless design. Here, as in the world I had left, beauty and ugliness seemed to go hand in hand, which, I supposed, was the way life had always been.

I had now been nine full days on the island. It was already December, and once I had come to terms with the fact that I was marooned and that I was unlikely to be rescued I felt a much greater interest in my surroundings. The discovery that I had the means to create fire out of the most unlikely substance had affected me deeply, as would a miracle, and I could not help but regard the fire as something sacred, to be tended with all the respect afforded some religious rite. I was aware too of a new respect for that supernatural Influence that seemed always pres-

90

ent but that I could not see. At times I was imbued with a feeling of its essential goodness, and then again I would be tortured by a conviction that it bore me ill. I could not afford to dwell upon it, for my imagination had a way of conjuring up manifestations of unearthly terror which at times almost frightened me to death. Initially I explained them to myself as simply a condition of loneliness, worse when the weather was bad or overcast. At these times I was convinced the island was inhabited by malevolent spirits and, terrified to be alone, I would rush to keep some sort of company with the seals. As a result, we began to get used to each other, and I noticed fascinating things about them that I had not observed before.

Every day more fur seals came ashore to have their young. Surprisingly, they made no elaborate preparation for this event. Often the only indication of an impending birth was a sudden restlessness in one of the cows, followed by the appearance a few minutes later by a wonderfully streamlined object which, since it was still wrapped in membranes, the mother would draw towards her, nibbling carefully at the veil surrounding it as though unwrapping some beautiful gift. And beautiful the new arrivals were. The pups were endowed at birth with a gorgeously sumptuous dark brown fur, shading in some to deepest black, which later would moult and expose a lovely silver-grey pelt. Almost immediately after the pup was born a horde of screaming birds would descend, scrapping and squabbling for the afterbirth, and the poor mother would be driven to distraction for fear they might molest the pup.

I was not surprised that she should be so concerned. Two of the birds, the skuas and the giant petrels—nellies, or stinkers, as they were also called—had viciously destructive beaks which could have torn the pups apart. These were quite large birds, and the latter was especially obnoxious. The sheathbill, on the other hand, which was the first to grace the scene when, in its intuitive way, it anticipated a birth, was really quite pretty, being white and dovelike, although no less a scavenger.

The rookeries, as the sealing camps were known, were constantly filled these days with the sound of duets between the cows and pups. Almost as soon as it is born the young fur seal greets the light of day with its plaintive and insistent bleat for food. Before she responded to this demand, however, I noticed that the cow would answer the pup with a protracted demonstration of her vocal powers, as if to impress on it the essential uniqueness of her voice. Sensing that her call fell on rather deaf ears, and maybe making allowances for her young one's unpracticed memory, she went over and over her particular call while presumably making mental note herself of her own pup's cry. This duet would last for a miserably long time in view of the young seal's obvious hunger, and I could sympathize when the baby seal's unrequited yaps for food degenerated into a desperate howl. The mother was not to be rushed, however, and she would not concede the welcome teat until she was sure that the ritual had been satisfactorily concluded. I could never witness the transformation from pained hunger to blissful satiety without a chuckle, for the fur seal, as much as any dog and perhaps even more so, seemed to have the capacity for instantly recognizable expression. And I have seen the young seals so determined to continue sucking that they could manage to change the entire position of their body without once releasing their grip on the nipple—a maneuver, needless to say, which was not without its disadvantages for the mother, who would invariably demonstrate displeasure at such antics by a sharp, reproving nip.

It would be some time before I could identify the general pattern of behaviour amongst the various animals and birds, and I suspected their practices would take varying forms thoughout the year. I was somewhat concerned, therefore, when, passing fairly close to where I had established the white seal pup with its new relation, I saw it apparently abandoned by its foster parent. It had grown in the space of a week to remarkably chubby proportions, and I guessed it weighed about fourteen pounds at least, which said much for the richness of the milk it must have guzzled. Now, however, left once again to its own resources, it wandered round pestering all the females nearby for food, and on being turned away by them, it gave way to such an awful caterwauling that I had not the heart to ignore it. Its cry must have been indelibly fixed upon my brain when I first rescued it, since I can say quite honestly that I could distinguish it from any number of others.

Reluctantly I had to admit that I was beginning to feel a certain responsibility towards the yelping creature who seemed to bring nothing but care and trouble. Had I been longer on the island I would have realized that there was nothing ominous in its being left on its own. All cows deserted their pups after the first eight days or so in order to feed for a while at sea. The white seal had been fostered by its new mother on the day her own pup had been stillborn, which would account for the mother's disappearance now; but I had still not grasped all the intricacies of the natural cycle. The cows stayed away for about three days. When they returned they were replenished and fit again for the gruelling fast they were obliged to endure during the many days that their hungry pups sucked. Like the young of any species, the fur seal pups seemed blessed with inexhaustible appetites. Observing the pup's rapid growth, I could imagine what a drain it must be on a cow's reserves, and I could sympathize with her irritability when a stranger's pup solicited her for milk.

However, I had seen so many dead pups which had been suffocated in the close-packed throng, trampled by a bull and crushed or starved to death when they had lost their mother that I could not in good conscience take the risk of leaving the white pup to fend for itself. I therefore decided to take it with me when I left to make my camp on the other side, having concluded that I would fare better if I established myself on Half-Moon Beach, as I now called it. For one thing, it contained many fresh-water streams; secondly, the rocks there were more suitable for building a house; and thirdly, it had an uninterrupted view of the sea. I imagined that should another ship be blown off course, or if another captain took the same decision as our skipper and sailed south to avoid the cape of storms, it might approach the islands on the same course that we had done ourselves, in which case Half-Moon Beach would be the best location from which to see it. I had, as you may judge from these remarks, not totally given up the idea of my being rescued, and I did not want to miss an opportunity to escape should such a lucky chance arise. On top of this, Half-Moon Beach was the receiving beach for a great deal of flotsam. After an easterly storm, the tide line was usually ankle-deep in shrimplike creatures, which would be a welcome addition to my diet. Yet another reason why I liked Half-Moon Beach was the fact that it seemed generally warmer and less gloomy than where I now was —having the benefit of receiving the full glory of the rising sun.

Unlike the fur seals for whom December meant the month for parturition before the act of mating, the elephant seals—now that I took the time to notice them—seemed a stage farther on in their cycle. Their young were already exploring the hidden pleasures of the shallow water. Some floated with their bodies crescent-shaped beneath the surface and only their heads and hind flippers showing, while others paddled around with rapid uncoordinated movements, getting nowhere slowly but with a great deal of splashing and flapping. These pups, unlike their gross and rather ugly elders, were quite engaging, and their attempts to swim were unexpectedly amusing. How vulnerable life was in this latitude, even for those whose habitat it was naturally, was borne in on me when the bodies of two tiny pups were washed up. Maybe they had panicked on finding themselves amongst the ice pans in deep water and had either been crushed when the pans came together or had tired themselves out floundering around instead of paddling calmly or floating. This discovery had convinced me that it was my duty to accept responsibility for my orphan seal. Strangely enough, as soon as I reached this decision, I became absorbed into the atmosphere of the animal life around me, as though the self-imposed duty I had taken on made me automatically a participant in the island's life instead of some kind of alien voyeur. I felt drawn towards the seals with much less fear than formerly, and this change of attitude was reflected in the animals' response to me as well.

The days that the white seal had been lying around in the ordure of the beach had done nothing to enhance its beauty. On the contrary, its fleecy coat, which had been a golden white when I first found it, was now distinctly matted and mucky. Along with this, the random growth of facial hairs that had appeared all of a sudden contributed to giving it a grizzled look.

"You little scruff!" I accused it critically as it hollered loudly at my feet. "You noisy, mucky little scruff—you are a disgrace —do you hear me?" He did not hear me. Having decided apparently that he was once again a foundling, he was devoting himself to the rowdiest demonstrations of self-pity, all the while closing his ears to the world around him and forming such a barrier of noise that it would have deterred the angels of mercy from approaching him had they not been as foolishly softhearted as I was. Open-mouthed, he bellowed, yelping and screaming in the most uncouth fashion. And although I ran the gamut of vocal sounds I could not find a noise to stop him. Mouth agape still and with eyes close-lidded, he continued squeezing and labouring his lungs to extract every ounce of noisy breath from them. I hissed and shouted to shut him up; but he did not falter. Finally, exasperated, I clapped impatiently—more as an alternative to thumping him than in expectation of any dramatic effect. The result was startling. Jumping up in mid-yap and nearly turning a somersault in the air, he landed mute in frightened silence. The mouth closed slowly as the eyes unveiled, and two beautiful brown orbs—hugely timorous—stared at me. The seals nearby seemed startled, and my young seal remained equally apprehensive.

"That's better," I addressed it firmly. "Don't you dare bellyache again." And although there was no response from my little listener as I hoisted him up to chest level to take him through the rookery, I got the distinct impression that he sighed serenely.

Because the pup was too young to climb the slope that led to the penguin rookery, I was obliged to make a harness for it from my jacket and haul him up the hill behind me. Even then I had to carry it the rest of the way, for the distance was too far for it to waddle. I arrived at the other beach out of breath and sweating.

I had too many things to do immediately to afford the time to look for a foster mother. My priority was to establish some sort of sturdy shelter for myself, but I was loath to abandon the pup amongst the throng of other seals in case it got hurt or got up to some mischief. When I saw a little group of pups of various sizes had formed a pod away from the harems at the landward fringes of the beach, I decided this would be a good place to deposit Scruff—as I had definitely made up my mind to call him. This way he would have companionship while I went about my various tasks. I was to learn that the pups frequently formed themselves into these small companies while they awaited the return of their mothers from feeding at sea and that they slept together quite contentedly. I was half expecting Scruff to start up his wretched wailing again when I walked away. Surprisingly, he seemed not to mind being left with his fellows, which made me wonder if it was not hunger that had made him cry but a feeling of utter loneliness. Whatever the reason, the group of pups seemed to sleep contentedly for the next two days, Scruff included, which gave me ample time to erect a shelter.

Starting with a few large boulders and some salvaged wood, I found a place, set back from the beach, with an overhanging jut of rock where I could build a temporary lean-to. I had decided on a place nearby for a larger, more permanent dwelling, but I knew that it would take a long time to get this built. With a bit of careful thought and attention I had kept the fire going on the other beach; and using a spare kettle without the lid, I had devised a means of transporting a small conflagration with which I could start a larger fire on this beach. I was determined that I would never again let it go out.

Scrutinizing every weird piece of flotsam and jetsam, I had built up a store of worthless bric-a-brac which I could not throw away, not just because I might find some use for it but because it was the only link with the world I had left. Occasional pieces of timber or bits of clothing or other items would be useful but, more often than not, I saw pathos in the sort of article the sea gave back. A bird cage had been washed up amongst some bits of knotting, together with a hempen skirt one of the hands had worn during the ceremony of crossing the line. The odd shoe suggested one of the crew members, while a dog-eared drawing of a woman indicated some dream of love.

With each new tide, I spent hours combing the waterline to make sure nothing was lost. There was no cave near the beach to store the salvage, so I had to make a cache of it inside a circle of rocks. Half-Moon Beach, like White Seal Beach—as I had named the other one—was populated by both fur and elephant seals, although the former seemed to prefer that part of the beach that was covered with rocks.

I suppose it was natural, although I could hardly expect to see a ship, that I should scan the seascape every day for a sail. Maybe the fact that I did this was therapeutic, for it meant that I retained some hope instead of lapsing into despair. As might be apparent, the cataclysmic significance of my isolation had not totally sunk in, which was just as well, since with all the difficulties of my way of life this extra burden might at that time have been too much for me to suffer. However, as the thought of being marooned became slightly less unbearable, I glanced less and less out to sea and began applying my thoughts to finding a viable way to exist on the island. Eventually, it became a relief to forget about being rescued. I could put my whole mind to the business of surviving without any outside distraction, and I began to be much more inventive and relaxed.

The greatest bonus of Half-Moon Beach was definitely the abundance of tiny shrimps which were washed up on the beach whenever there had been a storm. These provided the basis of much of the seal's diet, as I discovered when I opened up the stomachs of some of those that had died. They were also very good added to seal broth.

It cost me a good deal of time and labour to salvage the gear and carry it up the beach where I could secure it against the wind and the tide. But what did it matter how long it took me. I had all the time in the world to call my own. Occasionally, the very limitlessness of that time frightened me, and I would feel overwhelmed by the scale of nature and the power of its manifestations. I was conscious, too, of my own insignificance in the world around me. I often talked aloud spontaneously and gained some consolation not only in hearing myself speak but also in freeing myself of the fear that I might lose the power of speech altogether. I would talk about any subject that came to mind, racking my brains for topics to discuss that had no bearing on my present circumstances. I racked my brains also for words that had slipped my memory and took to scratching some of these down on bits of timber. I had dreams of a ship appearing one day and of being unable to attract her crew as they sailed past the beach in their longboat because I could no longer communicate.

I was naturally curious about the size of the island and whether there was any other part of it similar to my peninsula or supporting a different kind of life. I was deterred from exploring to the south, however, by the great mass of ice which apparently covered the whole of the interior. I had not at that time shoes or clothing to cope with this, quite apart from which I considered it would be foolish to go exploring without first having established myself on the peninsula and given some thought to how I could survive the winter. Besides, I had much to observe and enough work to keep me occupied for several months.

One curious reaction to my isolation was the feeling of having trespassed. My need to treat the island and its creatures with respect was somehow based on the belief that if God had intended man to be there He would have put him there some time ago. As part of this self-deprecating line of thought, I would wonder if I was guilty of some gross presumption in even trying to survive and if maybe the fact that we had trespassed beyond the limits of the natural world was what had angered the Almighty. In spite of these fears, however, my curiosity was hard to fetter. I longed to know if I had been marooned on an island or if my peninsula was in fact the most northerly projection of a huge and undiscovered continent to the south.

At times when searching for an explanation of why I had been saved, I wondered if my quest for manhood was only now beginning. If I had been chosen specially to represent mankind on this island, a tremendous burden was upon me. While on the one hand I might look upon this "calling" to provide a sense of purpose to my existence, I wondered if I were capable of accepting—or even whether I wanted—such an onerous responsibility.

I reflected that it was a piece of good fortune, if not kind design, that my marooning had happened at the start of summer. I had the unfolding wonder of nature to look forward to and time to acclimatize myself before the winter's desperate cold. Now that I had fire, I was really well furnished for my subsistence. Food and fuel were to be had in plenty, and with some ingenuity I could use the animal skins for clothing. All I needed was to build a more serviceable hut and I should have all the physical requirements for living.

Of course there was more to surviving than this. I knew that it would also require a radically positive approach to the value of life itself if I were to combat the fierce opposition to the spirit that loneliness, hardship and constant setbacks breed. Therefore, before I could control the physical part of me, I would first have to be able to control my will. Since I was convinced that it was better to be alive than dead, however miserable the conditions, I sought some way of putting joy into my life, convinced as I was that without a conscious effort to lighten my load, the burden would eventually crush me. I decided I would make a point of observing in fine detail the natural environment of the area, including the habits of the birds and animals. I would keep a record of the weather, and I would even make a study of the tides, having already noted that they seemed irregular. And I would make some kind of calendar, not only to keep track of time for my own interest, but to be able to relate the study of the wildlife to each season of the year. And who knows but maybe one day I should appease the Spirit whose territory I had violated, and He would suffer me to be released and returned to my own kind.

7

Midsummer

Not long after I had run out of the rations with which I had been marooned I was compelled to face the unwelcome fact that in order to procure more food I would have to kill. Of course penguin eggs were plentiful, as were the shrimps that were washed up on the beach; but I had reached the limit of how much of either of these I could bear as a staple diet, and I began to crave a stew made from fresh seal meat. I was, however, still somewhat afraid of the elephant seals; and, in any case, apart from the tongue and heart, the flippers and the brains, this seal was not good eating. The fur seals, although they offered a variety of meat that was appetizing, I still hesitated in killing, for the now impractical reason that they were such beautiful creatures. Not until hunger had eroded some of these fine sensibilities could I come to terms with the wildlife all around me and my need to kill to survive. God, I then argued, must have meant me to sustain myself on animal flesh, or He would surely have marooned me where there was no animal life. While in this frame of mind, I conveniently ignored the fact that at times I actually refused to believe in the existence of the Deity. On reflection I am bound to admit that signs were developing in my character to suggest that I was becoming something of an opportunist.

In defense, I must say that I did make certain resolutions governing the slaughter of animals. I like to think these arose out of my genuine remorse and concern. The most important of them was that no animal should be killed heedlessly or cruelly—that I should be as humane as possible and kill only what was essential to my survival. I further decided, in spite of its impracticability, that I should do my slaughtering on the other side of the peninsula. Even though this meant transporting the carcass a considerable distance over difficult terrain, I thereby ensured the inviolability of the life on my own beach—a fact I felt to be important for a reason I cannot explain.

On the day I decided to kill my first seal I set out for the distant beach with an unpleasant fluttering in my breast. It had less the touch of fear about it than the awful sensation of guilt. Since I also had the uncanny feeling that the seals on my beach knew what I intended, I was an uncomfortably furtive figure as I crept away to perform my nefarious deed. The penguins seemed noisier than ever and pecked me more than usual, and my conscience was so sensitive that I actually imagined I heard them squawking, "Murderer!" I even hesitated before penetrating the colony of seals in case they had interpreted the warning of those noisy birds and decided to attack me all at once. But they showed no concern, and I could move amongst them, provided I kept away from the bulls, as freely as on those other occasions when I had intended them no harm.

I avoided those animals that were awake, being too distressed to confront the gentle creatures who looked up at me with their disturbingly human and trusting eyes. Instead, I chose to creep up on those females that were sleeping, timing my attack to coincide with the bull's engagement elsewhere so that I had time to complete the deed unhampered. To my shame, I could devise no satisfactory alternative to the sealer's method of killing, which involved a quick stunning blow to the head with a baton, followed by slitting the throat or a quick stab to the heart. I was not adept at this initially and suffered agonies of remorse when my first careless blow maimed the seal before the final blow extinguished its life.

I was afraid that I had committed sacrilege and more than ever expected to be punished by the hand of fate. To salve my conscience, I made up my mind to refrain from killing any females that were in pup and would refrain also from doing anything to the dead animal that would deprive it of its dignity.

The sight of my hands covered with the dark red blood of the seal I had killed was disturbing, and I performed an elaborate washing-of-hands ceremony before dragging the butchered carcass inland. I cached the larger part of it under rocks so that the birds could not get at it before hauling the smaller pieces to Half-Moon Beach. In time, however, I became so accustomed to my new role as predator that I was no longer distressed by the sight of my prey. On some occasions, when I was really hungry, my craving for flesh was so strong that I would cut a slice from the still-steaming liver and eat it raw, savouring the warm, sweet, blood-rich taste it brought to my mouth.

As expected, my clothes had become impregnated with grease and filth and were torn and thin from the constant effort of scrambling over the jagged rocks. Although I was sure that eventually I could clothe myself from the skins of the seals, I had not the time right then to sit down and experiment with that difficult task. Therefore I decided, not without some misgivings, that I would have to remove the clothes from my dead companions in order to have a reserve till I could make my own.

Shifting the stones that covered the dead bodies was quite tiring, and my skin began to creep with horror as I got down nearer to them. The cold had preserved the corpses so that they looked no different from when I had buried them. Even so, I was startled at being again confronted with the dead and hurried with my gruesome task for fear of letting loose some malignant presence. I had to cut the clothes from those frozen corpses, there being no other way I could have removed them. But trying to avoid any unnecessary disturbance, I removed only their jackets and trousers, leaving the underclothes for the sake of decency. After covering the bodies again, I set up a cross made from what little wood I could spare at the head of those two burial mounds and offered a kind of formal thanks to the dead for the clothes they had provided. The boots I left, since they were too stiff to remove, although my own were barely holding together and I could see that within a day or two I would be forced to find some alternative kind of footwear. Meanwhile a group of penguins had formed a circle around me. Squawking and peering inquisitively at me, they so added to the shame and embarrassment I felt that for a long time I was unable to overcome my feeling of guilt and, by way of compensation, bowed reverently every time I passed the graves.

Between my various tasks I often rested and ate my food near some of the young seal pups. These were a delight to watch when they were not sleeping, and they showed signs of being extremely lively and adventurous the bigger they grew. As for Scruff, he was still without a foster mother. While there were probably females who had lost their young who would willingly have nursed him, they were not easy to locate without a great deal of searching, and I did not want to spend too much time away from my work. The result of this neglect was a seal pup that barked frantically upon seeing his small companions paired off with their returning mothers.

The sum total of my knowledge of seal pups was that they required enormous quantities of milk—in this way resembling the young of so many other species; but I knew also that babies could be weaned quite early and wondered if the same would apply to a seal. The only answer was to have a try. Discovering a dead yearling seal's stomach to be full of partially digested shrimps, I removed the whole of this organ, which I kept as a food bank till I had fed its entire contents to my starving foundling. As might be expected, the first attempts were not entirely successful, and on several occasions I had to dodge a spray of food particles that my white seal coughed up. Hunger was a stern persuader, however, and before long I was spooning this naturally prepared mash by the mouthful down the little pup's throat.

Once in a while, taking advantage of a particularly docile cow, I would remove her sucking pup and substitute my own charge at the oozing teat. This way I could be sure Scruff was getting some milk and, at the same time, the comfort inherent, as I imagined, in the sucking action. Needless to say, by doing this I merely substituted one problem for another. No sooner had I removed the pup from its mother by tickling it with a piece of wood than it would set up a caterwauling almost as bad as that produced by Scruff. On these occasions, when I thought Scruff had drunk enough to satisfy the ordinary demands of thirst and before he could outstay his welcome, I would tickle him in the same way as I had done the other, expecting of course the same reaction. But he would cling on to the teat, squirming with discomfort, till the poor cow was goaded into snapping at him to relieve her distress. I could believe that Scruff knew that such opportunities would not come often and he was seeing to it that he made the most of them. With his teeth clamped around the teat, he would suck with a look of rapture spread over his features which disintegrated, on the instant he was removed, into a look of indignation. Immediately he would go into a kind of tantrum, his hysterical resentment taking the form of snapping between high-pitched yaps and screams. Occasionally he would even make an hilarious attempt at a growl, his face then wearing an expression of such pained concentration for a little babe that it never failed to amuse me. In spite of the peeved disposition of my charge, I would roll him over and over on the ground and tickle him mercilessly. The one irritation having been replaced by the other, he would have forgotten the former by the time I had released him.

I must admit I felt sorry for the little thing, bereft of mother, warmth, security and comfort, and frequently I would take him in my arms. He would respond immediately to my caresses. "Poor old Scruff," I would say as I stroked him fondly, "poor ol' orphan—life's tough on little seals like you." He would look up, nuzzling me while bleating faintly in agreement, with a voice like a little lamb's. After a while I noticed a remarkable docility in him in spite of his obvious high spirits. He took to eating directly out of my hand, and I suppose it was only natural that eventually he should look on me as some kind of substitute parent. His attentions proved a blessing for me in my loneliness; for, apart from Scruff and a few of the other pups nearby, all the other seals on that beach were inclined to retreat hastily if I came too near. And if disturbed while sleeping, they showed a most petulant reaction.

As Scruff grew, he, like the pups around him, became more mobile, and frequently he would follow me. Many is the time when, halfway towards the camp on the other beach to collect some blubber or food, I would look around on the suspicion that I was being watched. Then I would find Scruff leading a troop of other pups who were all shuffling and humping along in my footsteps. When I stopped, they did the same, feigning rocklike immobility, only to start up again as I moved off, in the manner of children playing a game of grandmother's footsteps. No amount of shooing or shouting would get rid of them, although they all dived behind the nearest boulder whenever I began to clap. A minute later they would reemerge, reminding me of a bunch of naughty children, and would proceed to follow, their faces alive with mischief.

The pups created total confusion in the penguin rookery, romping through the penguins and then whizzing down the chute. But having once got down, there was no way they could get up again unless I helped them. Although agile in most circumstances, they were stopped by the overhanging rock. Meanwhile I was obliged to let them follow me through the colony, where we were joined by a few more hangers-on. By the time I was ready to climb the penguin slope I had twice as many seals behind me as when I had arrived. The problem now was that I could not identify which seal pups belonged to which beach.

Scruff, of course, being white, was easily recognizable and was the first I carried up unwillingly to the top of the rise. I do not know how many pounds he weighed, but he and the others were heavy, and so exhausted was I with the effort of carrying all those seal pups up that slope that I was exasperated when several of them joyfully descended the chute again. I was half inclined to forget about them, reasoning that they had brought the trouble upon themselves; yet some ridiculously soft instinct made me go down to retrieve them after first shooing those still at the top far enough inland to give me time to return. Even so, when finally I got home, I had a collection of seals in tow that could not possibly all belong to Half-Moon Beach. Once again I was inclined to wash my hands of all responsibility for them while I got on with my own affairs. But a niggling sense of guilt kept bothering me, and within a few hours I was quite aware of which pups were the strangers in our midst, and these I finally shepherded across the peninsula to the other side. I made sure this time I would not be followed by pelting would-be followers with pebbles which I had collected for that purpose. The two lost pups forlornly waiting where we had left them on the beach at the bottom of the penguin chute I brought back to Half-Moon Beach.

As the young pups grew in size, I observed that water had an irresistible appeal for them. There was not a puddle or streamlet without its share of pups wallowing or romping about therein, and the young seals of both species loved to lie at the edge of the shore and let the incoming waves roll over them. By the beginning of January, only the older ones ventured into the sea. I was to discover that fur seals suckle their young for about three months, and not until they are past this stage do they tend to spend more time in the water and forage for themselves.

With all the exercise of walking and climbing, my legs by now were developing muscles that I had never had reason to notice before, but all the foot-slogging over the sharp stones that strewed the hills played havoc with my boots. The soles were worn through and had loosened from the uppers, and I was constantly tripping over the flap caused by the gaping hole in the front. My toes had long worn through my socks; and as an alternative footwear I skinned any dead penguins I found lying around, turning their skins inside out after I had dried them so as to have the feathers on the inside. These I then wrapped around my foot beneath a covering of sealskin, which I attached round my ankles with strands of rope. After this footwear wore through in a day, I thought of the expedient of tying beneath them a flat piece of wood to act as a sole. This style was not too practical, and I determined to improve on the model when I had the time.

As regards my morale, for the most part I did very well in fighting off the melancholy which occasionally threatened to overwhelm me; yet for all my good intentions I could not possibly plan ahead—the weather being so unpredictable. Suddenly out of blue skies a squall would shriek and the cove would turn leaden, slashed with streaks of white. My world would be blotted out by a pall of fog, and a dreadful gloom would descend upon me. More often than not I would experience at such times a terrible sense of foreboding. Occasionally, though I was able to turn a storm to my advantage by claiming it as an achievement that I had stuck to my task in the face of the most inclement weather that the gods could throw at me.

Early on I resolved that good spirits, or at least a sense of optimism, would be my most useful asset. Out of this came strength and inventiveness as against the misery of the pessimist's debilitating apathy. I determined not to miss any opportunity of a celebration, and Christmas was to be no exception. I had prepared a meal of seal meat which I had fried in seal oil and which I was to follow with penguin egg beaten up and lightly fried into a sort of pancake that I spread with molasses. The latter I used sparingly for treats and still had a good half-cask left. I had set three places in my den to give at least the pretence that I had company, but who my companions were to be my subconscious mind had not dared to inform me.

For several days now gales had arrived at midday and raged until evening, leaving a hard frost to remind me not to take summer lightly. Snow fell, driving in hissing sheets across the surface of the sea, burying the seals and sifting through the cracks in my makeshift den. More than ever, I missed England, the softness of its countryside and the innocence of its little birds. Only a few days before I had found that the stack of sealskins had vanished, with only a few pieces left to suggest that they had been ripped to pieces and eaten by the birds. To compare a robin with a skua was like comparing a child with a rapacious killer. Yet life in its natural state was the same all over the world, being the plundering of the weak by the strong and the killing of fellow creatures for survival.

Reflecting on such sentiments made it hard to be merry, and I fought hard to drive off the depression that blew in with the weather. The idea occurred to me that I should sing as a way of raising my spirits. Starting with the simplest songs I could remember, I finished up those carols that had been my favourites as a child, toasting my feet the meanwhile over the blubber fire till the soles were very nearly scorched. I must admit that I was beginning to get pretty maudlin, and I might well have lapsed into another bout of self-pity had not my solo turned unexpectedly into a duet. For Scruff, creeping inside my shelter without my knowing it, launched suddenly into a vocal accompaniment of his own. Swaying, his head raised ecstatically, he took up a sort of tuneless wailing, his eyes turned inwards as he crooned his refrain. The more I sang, the more varied and intense became the accompaniment and the more droll became the expression on the young pup's face. Outclassed, I was forced to abandon my efforts, Scruff showing his disapproval of my irreverent laughter by a snort and a flurry of his front flippers.

One of the jollities of Christmas being the surprise of receiving presents, I was not to be done out of this enjoyment. Having found a cask washed up a few days before which I had not been able to identify, I decided to keep it as a treat to be opened on Christmas Day. All morning it stood untouched while I waited for the right moment to explore its contents. My mind went over all the possible delicacies it could contain, since its size suggested it was reserved for the captain's table. Several times I thought to broach it but stopped myself at the last minute, relishing in some subtle way the anticipation of its enjoyment. At last, my curiosity having reached fever pitch, I simply had to open it. One whiff was enough to destroy my illusions—putrid was the only word to describe its smell—and it was only because I thought I might need the cask that I did not hurl it seawards.

I was as much peeved as disappointed. Nevertheless, my mood took a dramatic plunge. Of a sudden I was overcome by a desperate feeling of homesickness, and the memory of past Christmases spent with my family flared inside me, making me ache for the good-fellowship and festive gaiety of it all. I had a vision of my mother, frail yet beautiful, gracing a table bedecked with holly and candles and laid with all manner of delicious fare; while my father, who was rather large of figure, beamed on the two of us and called for a toast. Christmas was an occasion to indulge our pride in family—a time to drink to our successes and aspirations—and at the memory another wave of emotion swept over me as I contemplated the contrast between my present circumstances and what I had lost. I knew now for whom I had laid the two extra places; and conscious of the misery I must have inflicted on my parents by my hasty decision to leave home, I was overcome by a crushing sense of guilt.

8

Household Chores

After much to-ing and fro-ing and pacing out and repacing I eventually laid the cornerstone of my permanent dwelling. The location was set back on a raised terrace some thirty feet from the landward extremity of the beach and protected on its northern side by a bluff of rock which would shelter it from much of the prevailing wind. This position also had the advantage of being not too far from a melt stream, which for the next few weeks at least would save me the bother of melting snow.

The stone walls needed to be two feet thick—solid enough to resist the strongest winds besides acting as sufficient insulation against the winter cold—and man height to avoid the irksome business of having to stoop or the irritation of banging one's head. The rafters of the roof were to be made from a collection of timber salvaged from the beach, and over the top I intended to spread some bits of sailcloth that I had found blown inland from the wreck, together with the skins of young sea elephants that I had not as yet been able to obtain.

In my early plans for the hut I had been wildly extravagant, envisioning a dwelling that was impracticably large and complicated. I had told myself that I had no reason to build a hovel just because I was a castaway. I soon changed my ideas once I started to work. Although there was no shortage of suitably slablike rocks and stones, these were about fifty yards away from the hut site. They were heavy and extremely difficult to prize out of the frozen ground.

Only after I had started the foundations did I realize that the base of the walls would have to be thicker if they were to support the full weight of the hut. Consequently I further reduced the size of my dwelling until it was only about twelve feet by ten. The building I estimated would take two or three weeks to complete if I worked on it full-time but I knew I could not possibly maintain the pace set on the first day. Not only had my back given a slight twinge at times as a warning not to overtax it but I had not taken into account the bad weather that might delay me. January had already arrived before I managed to get the roof on the hut, and I had still the task of filling in with pebbles and moss the millions of holes and tiny crannies. So frequent and violent had been the storms, however, that I was seldom able to work for more than an hour without having to thaw some of the numbness out of my wind-chaffed hands. The wind was a most persistent misery, and everything became more difficult as a result of it. I would complain loudly and accusingly at the impossibility of doing things without adequate tools and materials. And I was becoming anxious to get the hut finished, since my lean-to was showing scars of exposure to the storms. Even when I had the roof anchored down, with ropes thrown over the top and secured firmly to large stones on the ground, I still had not safeguarded the interior against getting drifted up with snow. The wind seemed to ferret out the smallest crevices and drive a remarkable quantity of snow through them. Worse still was the discovery, on my return from the other beach one evening, that my door had been blown open and that at least a ton of snow had been deposited inside. I saw then that what was needed was a tunnel built out from the doorway, angled to protect the entrance from the prevailing winds.

I had at one time entertained the notion of building passages and tunnels out from two of the walls to be used as storage space for food or clothes or for anything else that I needed to keep handy, but bad weather had delayed my progress. I realized that to get the hut finished quickly I must make the shell as simple and functional as possible or I might be overtaken by the winter. Now with my errors confronting me and compounding themselves against me, I had no alternative but to go back to work.

Fortunately the animals at this time provided me with an absorbing interest, which relieved some of the frustration and heartaches of the hut. Every day I added something new to my knowledge of them, and I felt enriched by the discoveries that I stored in my mind. I could recognize the fur seal cows newly returned from feeding and observed that they usually hauled out very close to the area where they had left their pups. Some of them did not wait till they got ashore before announcing their presence and would start calling to their pups while they were still in the shallows. Slowly the mother would advance up the beach, stopping every few feet or so to call her pup, and frequently she would be approached by strange pups soliciting milk. These she would drive away or just ignore, saving her nourishment for the owner of that unique yap she could identify amongst a million others. Even then, however, she would often subject the pup to an investigative sniffing, in order to make sure that she had made no mistake.

I was glad to see that a mother had enough good sense not to feed her pup on the beach, where the bulls were always jousting and where even some of the other cows seemed jealous and aggressive. Instead, she would lead her pup to the back of the beach, where she carefully selected a site before lying down and letting the pup feed. This gradual shift of the population inland meant that I had more company than I had anticipated while I was building the hut, with the fur seals keeping to one side of the beach and the elephant seals to the other.

The night that the hut was finally finished I felt enormously satisfied at a job well done. Admittedly there were still shelves to build and hooks to be made for odds and ends and some sort of table and stool to be put together, but they could be done at any time. The fact was that I had a home at last—a sturdy, reasonably spacious, solid shelter which I had designed myself and built with my own hands. I can really not describe the joy of that except to say that it must be one of the most satisfying things a man can do. My one regret was that I had no other human being to admire my work and applaud my great success.

I had given much thought to the business of heating my new home. Blubber having proved to be an excellent fuel which gave off a good deal more warmth than a coal fire, albeit with a rather powerful odour, I was happy that I had an unlimited quantity of this resource and could therefore be generous with it. Another advantage was that it would burn on its own, although small amounts, such as you would use in a lamp, required a wick of some sort. The oil that had been left in the try-pots had, alas, been lost when the elephant seals knocked them over; but there were still two barrels filled with blubber and one full of oil on the other beach that I could ferry over as needed. When this was finished, I could replenish my supplies from the many elephant seals on Half-Moon Beach.

I had not as yet taken note of the fact that these animals were already beginning to use up their store of fat as a result of their long fast ashore. Had this occurred to me I might have been a bit more anxious to obtain a supply in reserve; as it was, however, I believed that I had fuel enough to last me for months, and I was not anxious to bring forward the time when I would have to tackle these enormous animals single-handed.

I had kept a fire going all the time I was in the lean-to. Using the kettle as before, I transported some of the burning blubber to my new home, where I installed it in a specially hollowed-out hearth in the floor that I had lined completely with small flat stones. The diameter of the "bowl" was about ten inches. Across the top of this, I laid a grate made from a twisted barrel hoop, on which I put a small piece of blubber. This, gradually melting with the heat below, dripped its oil onto the fire and kept it going. Should I require a larger blaze, I could put more blubber on the grate so that eventually the whole of it caught light, providing ample heat both to cook with and warm my shelter.

Around the hearth I had placed three heavy stones that I used as a support for my kettle. By a stroke of luck I came upon an empty pitch pot which somehow had not been slung overboard

113

with the other gash and which I converted into a frying pan. Being without a window—since for the moment I could think of no suitable material with which to make it—I had to depend on the fire to provide both heat and light. Later I contrived a lamp by making a shallow bowl from the remainder of the hacked-off pitch pot, and I put a small amount of oil and a rope yarn in it to act as wick. This I lighted from the fire, although not without difficulty. The gentle flame created was easily doused by any sudden or violent movement of air. Once established, however, it gave off a soft, friendly glow that I could regulate as I chose on the same principle as with the fire. When the oil in the dish became low and more wick was exposed, heightening the flame, the piece of blubber I hung over it would start dripping its tried-out fat into the dish. This in turn would raise the oil level, covering the wick. As a result the flame would lower and of course the blubber would drip more slowly. For the most part, however, I just topped up the dish with oil from the barrel, replacing the wick when necessary with bits of dried-up moss or lichen in preference to the strands of rope, which I felt I ought to conserve for emergencies.

What I would have done without the barrel hoops I do not know, for they could be used for all sorts of things, from pot holders to hooks of various sizes. I even contrived a saw from one of them by hacking at the edge to produce a row of rather jagged teeth. This, together with a hammer and shovel that I was lucky enough to salvage, was one of my most useful possessions.

Although I understood, or so I thought, the principles of making fire with blubber, it would be wrong of me to give the impression that I did not make any mistakes. Indeed, to begin with, when I first experimented, I thought my whole shelter would go up in a smoking mass of soot and flames. Starting off sluggishly, the fire's burning power would accelerate so suddenly and dramatically that often I was driven out into the air, coughing violently, my eyes smarting and watering.

Even with my present arrangement I found that a certain amount of melted fat ran over the bars of the grate to form a sticky patch around the fire which was difficult to clean and impossible to remove from my boots once it was trodden in. In spite of my care, the blubber always gave off a bit of soot, and my hair was soon a thick mat of greasy fibers. My clothes and skin were equally impregnated; but I discovered an answer to this problem almost by accident one day when, washing off the blood from my oil-ingrained hands after killing a seal, I noticed that my skin appeared remarkably clean and free from grease where the blood had been. Wondering then if the blood contained some cleansing element, I decided to experiment by soaking a piece of oily rag in blood before washing it out thoroughly in the sea. The result was quite spectacular. The blood seemed almost to dissolve the grease, and from then on I used it as a detergent for both my skin and clothes. Finding that much blood collected in the intestinal cavity of dead animals once these organs had been removed, I employed this natural receptacle as a basin on hot days, soaking my tattered garments in the gore before rinsing them at the water's edge. All this must sound horrific; but to me at the time it seemed perfectly natural, since it was, after all, my only substitute for soap.

In the beginning I slept at floor level on several skins. Finding this rather draughty, I decided to build up my bed so that in the day it could become a seat. With this in mind, I achieved a fairly substantial sleeping platform against one of the walls, and I built it up with stone. Over the top I placed some moss to smooth down the rough edges, and on top of this I placed the skins to serve as a mattress. The pelts of male fur seals being thicker, especially around the head and neck, than those of the other seals, I adopted these for bedding and found them very warm and comfortable.

Scraping so many skins would have been a time-consuming job had I not got help from a most unexpected source. Having removed the skin from a seal and put it to one side out of the way, with the intention of scraping it later, I was alarmed while cutting up the carcass to suddenly see a flock of skuas descend on it and, with their razor-sharp bills, attack the skin like vultures. I ran and assailed them, hoping to disperse them with shouts and gestures. When this had no effect I pelted them with stones to drive them off. This eventually I succeeded in doing, but not before the skin had actually risen in the air as though they were trying to carry it away. Indeed, had they all been flying in the same direction and not each been pulling separately they would no doubt have done so. When it dropped, however, to my astonishment I found it was pecked almost clean of blubber. The skin was torn in places, but I could hardly complain, since those skuas' appetite for blubber had made my job of scraping the skin almost unnecessary.

Finishing the job they had started was easy. I rubbed sand over the inside of the skin with a stone to remove most of the remaining grease. With the skin thus treated I could stretch it and dry it before putting it aside in my hut to be softened for use. By the time I had returned to the carcass I had been cutting up the skuas had already devoured a good portion, and I had again to beat them off. The lesson I had learned, however, was an invaluable one. From that day on I made good use of those otherwise obnoxious birds.

When I speculated on how to make a sleeping bag, I realized that I had no materials to sew the skin nor any idea of the technique of sewing it. Suddenly all my work seemed pointless. Without the ability to sew suitable clothing I had no hope that I could survive. Only a moment before I had been reflecting on how well I had been adapting to my new circumstances, and yet I could fail for want of the very simplest resources. Was it really too much to expect one person to be able to sustain himself in such impoverished surroundings? Such a question I knew from past experiences was to be avoided. It posed a greater threat of defeat through self-pity than ever it might through the weakness which the question itself had exposed. As it happened, a temporary expedient did occur to me that enabled me to make a good large "blanket" by making small nicks in the edges of the pelts and tying these together with strips of sealskin. The first night I used it happened to be the first night I slept in my new dwelling. It was a night to remember for various reasons, and one in which I got very little sleep.

I had only just finished a meal and settled down on my bed of skins when I was distracted by a strange snuffling noise at the entrance. The next moment a woolly head appeared through the doorway, sniffing the air enquiringly before the rest of it sidled in. It was Scruff, as I might have expected, who these days was taking a great deal of notice of me in particular, as well as a lot more interest in his surroundings in general. In the last few weeks he had grown considerably and appeared much surer of his ground than a human infant at the same stage of growth. He was also extremely active and capable of climbing over some pretty difficult obstacles. On this occasion, insinuating himself into the hut in a rather furtive manner, he nosed inquisitively into every corner before turning towards my bed. This he approached inch by inch with great caution, his eyes bright and his woolly, doglike face advancing towards my own by minute stages while his body remained posed, alert, as if ready to jump back immediately should the need arise.

I had grown fond of the creature, despite the trouble he tended to generate, and although tired-out and ready for sleep, I could not help watching him, fascinated, through half-closed lids. I lay quite still, pretending to be asleep while he sneaked closer, and allowed him to explore my face with his nose, suffering the fishy smell on his breath and the sudden hot blasts of humid air as he huffed and sneezed around my mouth and nose. I expected him to go out then, but being Scruff he had other intentions and began pattering around quite confidently now, sniffing and snorting and giving everything the closest inspection. When he had finished examining the hut, he humped back over to my sleeping couch. Before I knew it his head was under the covers, and the next moment I was being nudged and jostled aside as my visitor made himself comfortable beneath the skins. Within seconds I was plastered with squalls of hot breath as the intruder began a systematic exploration of my person. Between bouts of snuffling and sneezing, he butted me with his snout without any regard to comfort or decency. Naturally there was a limit to how long I could stand such irrepressible activity. Once forced out of the covers, I proceeded to unburden them of the demon beneath them who already had my bedding in a hopeless mess. There then began a chase around the hut, with me after the intruder until I eventually managed to evict him with a great deal of noise and clapping. Exhausted, I had hardly tidied up my bed and settled into its welcome coziness before there was another snuffle at the entrance announcing the return of my visitor.

If I had already recognized the fur seals' predilection for play, I had not as yet realized the extent to which his inventiveness could be put. That evening Scruff left me in no doubt of the inexhaustibility of his high spirits. Not satisfied with being evicted twice, he went on to repeat the exercise several times more, in spite of all sorts of obstruction put at the entrance of the lockless door. What is more, in place of the startled expression he had shown the first time I had ejected him, I thought I now detected a look of gleefulness as he scampered out. This look was confirmed the next time and became set in an attitude of unadulterated mischief by his seventh return. My patience was wearing thin. Exasperated but still not wishing to harm the creature whose playfulness, had I not been so tired, I should have found quite charming, I decided to ignore his presence in the hope that he would become bored with my indifference and go away.

I covered my head with my furs when I settled down, leaving only a small hole for me to breathe through. But Scruff had no intention of abandoning me that evening. Going straight to the end of the bed, he began worming his way up under the covers. Naturally I was just about to yell and push him out, maybe even strike him, when I noticed that this time he was being much more discreet than earlier, wanting no more than to curl up quietly against my belly. I was too tired to go through the whole business of chasing him outside again, and so I let him stay there, judging that sooner or later he would feel quite suffocated and escape. But Scruff was to have a way of always confounding me, and when I woke a few hours later he was curled up in the same place with his nose uncovered by a gap in the skins.

The following night he repeated the whole exercise, responding to my threats and chasing with gusto as though he thought I was at last entering into the spirit of the game. For game it came

118

to be, and in time it was a nightly occurrence, ending always with him settling down against my belly when I wanted to sleep. During the day Scruff attached himself to me for longer periods until gradually I realized that I had not just a foundling whom it was my duty to protect but a very lively and likable companion as well.

9

The Moult

Unlike the other fur seals, Scruff had no maternal bonds to sustain him and had therefore adopted me. Almost without my realizing it, he had become the pivot around which I now arranged my life. This is not to say that his special inclination for human company had robbed him of the natural joys of romping with the other pups. Our relationship at this stage was by no means possessive. But he was, I realized, beginning to cultivate certain habits that were incompatible with the other seals'—such as following me when I left the beach and inventing games that he insisted only he and I should play. He was by this time responding readily to his name and demanding that each day I allot a certain amount of time for fun. No matter how busy I was, he would not be pacified until I had indulged him. Sometimes when I tried to snooze he would nose and romp about, biting me playfully, and sometimes he would brush and tickle my face with his flippers, nipping at my head and neck as he frisked and teased. He would regard me closely, and from the extraordinary antics he performed on occasions I began to suspect that he was trying to mimic me. He would spend ages grooming himself, giving his snout particular attention, and when I petted him he almost purred with delight. But it was my voice and its range of expression that, more than anything else, fascinated the creature, and I had the impression he understood everything I tried to convey.

For my part I considered his face as engaging as that of any animal I had ever seen, while being infinitely more expressive. I had only to see his whiskers lift and his eyes open wide to know he was planning some activity. In truth, since the first time his eyes had focused their attention on me and I had watched his little face relax from that of tense and anxious enquiry into an expression of grateful recognition, I had become his slave. No mother hearing that whooplike sound that babes use to express their uncontainable joy and their need for communication could feel more sympathy than I had felt at that first corresponding and unexpected bark from Scruff. And Scruff had responded in a way that indicated that the healthy balance of his being was as much dependent on my affection as it was on the air he breathed. Like a true parent, I could recognize those changes of expression and sound that signified each subtle shift or surge of emotion, and I was as pleased as any parent at Scruff's superior intelligence and undeniable charm.

His favourite game when we were out walking was a kind of hide-and-seek-and-chase-me. He would peer round from behind a rock to face me and then dart back with a kind of exaggerated buffoonery as though to say, "Uhh! What a shock you gave me!" After he first repeated this several times, it dawned on me that this was a kind of invitation to come and play. Making a swift lunge towards him, I almost made him leave his skin as he jumped, quite genuinely this time, to escape me.

From then on began a chase that nearly crippled me. Scruff took off like a firecracker exploding from a lighted torch. Leaping up and down rocks, whizzing around me and darting past my legs, he spun circles round me, daring or maybe imploring me to catch him. I would begin in earnest, struck by the irresistible clownish charm of his appeal, and would spare no effort to lay hands on him, chasing him around rocks and down inclines till I was breathless and worn-out or stopped by some minor hurt. I could have hardly chosen a more treacherous terrain on which to sport, so slippery were the slopes and so rocky and uneven was the surface of that playing field of ours. At the end of those games, when I lay prostrate to catch my breath, Scruff would bound up and blow squally kisses into my face and neck to show his gratitude and affection.

Sometimes, when inclined towards solitary entertainment, he would spend hours playing with a feather, snuffing and blowing it along the ground and bounding after it when it ascended into the air. Or he would sit for ages daydreaming, with his nose pointed at the sky. From that position he would squint at me drolly along the length of his curving back. Like the other pups he would play with and chew anything and, suspecting him of having swallowed pebbles, I took care to put all small and precious items out of his reach.

Scruff was not the only pup with an adventurous spirit. The other seals were just as agile at climbing rocks and reaching apparently inaccessible places. Unfortunately, a summit achieved did not necessarily ensure the skill that was needed to descend, and I had frequently to rescue pups that had got themselves stuck. A sad occurrence, which I suspect happened frequently every year, was for very young pups to explore and fall into crevices in the rocks that were uncovered when the tide ebbed. Invariable these were narrow with sheer walls, offering little chance for the pup to escape, and as a result they drowned when the tide came in. Each day I took it as a duty to inspect the rocky area of the beach and saved many a young fur seal from an untimely death, without any reward or even the certainty that they had learnt a lesson.

Initially I devoted most of my time to observing the fur seals, rather than the elephant seals or any of the other wildlife on the peninsula. They really were the most endearing of creatures to be with, and as beautiful as they were intelligent. Not only were they perfectly proportioned, but in size they were about a quarter of that of the elephant seal, whose distinguishing characteristic was a kind of shapeless bulk that was gross to the point of being almost obscene. The fur seal was at ease on land or in water, displaying a remarkable agility on the one and a sinuous gracefulness in the other, whereas the elephant seal humped along laboriously, caterpillarlike on land, and, although masterly in the water, was too ugly to be a delight to observe. In one sense, I suppose, they were to be pitied, for they seemed cursed with an inability to get any joy out of life. If they were not fighting or being thoroughly irascible, they were sleeping, belly side up, while their bodies twitched as though they were having some terrible nightmare. Whether awake or asleep they seemed afflicted by some discomfort or itch and were constantly flinging mud or sand over themselves and their neighbours, scratching their heads and chest with their handlike fore flippers.

As far as I could gather, since I had been too busy with my own affairs in the early days to make accurate observations of the wildlife around me, elephant seal pups were weaned within a month of birth and lived for another month on the reserves of blubber acquired during suckling. Towards the end of this time they took to the water. After they learned to swim properly, they began to forage for themselves; and on examining the stomach of a dead pup, I found it contained some small crustaceans. Naturally, after weaning her pup, the mother elephant seal went to sea to feed, having lost several hundred pounds in weight during nursing. When she returned to land to breed she would have to rely on the food acquired during these trips to sustain her for the month or so she would remain ashore before her next excursion into the water. The male elephant seals, on the other hand, would spend two whole months ashore during the breeding season, unlike the male fur seals, which enjoyed more frequent feeding bouts at sea. Since they were bulky and ugly and condemned to fast most of the summer, no wonder the elephant seals were lethargic and irritable.

I was not long established in my hut when I was made very much aware of the elephant seal's further cause for distress. Like the fur seals and the birds, they had begun their annual moult, which for them lasted a period of several weeks. In the baby seals the moult had begun shortly after birth, the lovely silky black pelt being gradually replaced by a sturdier grey variety after about a month. No doubt this new pelt afforded them better protection, but it deprived them of their engaging gamine look. I do not think moulting in any creature is a pretty sight, but in elephant seals it is a thoroughly loathsome-looking process. The poor animals appear positively diseased. Not only does the hair shed, as with many other animals, but the skin itself peels, starting on the head and spreading through the whole of the body. At such a time the colony is transformed not only in sight but also in sound, with seals whining and groaning as if in great pain, like the victims of some dreadful disaster. Their skin hangs in tatters, revealing pink patches that look really sore; yet the seals cannot refrain from scratching them. The young ones rolled and rubbed themselves against the rocks, no doubt speeding up the shedding process; but the older animals appeared shocked by the painful transformation in themselves and looked as if they might be ill.

Gradually they would leave the lower beaches, making their way inland some considerable distance, which suggested that they could not bear the proximity of other seals. The sexes segregated, and the favourite retreats of all were those near a stream where they could wallow in the cooling mud. I was amazed by the steepness of the climbs which some of the bulls forced upon themselves and the enormous physical exertion that these pitiful creatures were obliged to expend for no other reason, apparently, than to change the site of suffering.

During this I was awaked one night by a sort of tremor that ran through my bunk and the walls of the hut. Suddenly the stones built up round the entrance passage caved inwards, and on the other side of the wall of rubble I heard the most pitiful moans, which sounded like a person trapped or hurt. For a moment I was totally confused; then, guessing what was happening, I expected the whole structure to cave in and bury us at any second. Although the main structure of the hut remained intact, the tremors were increasing so in strenth and frequency that I could feel them throughout my body. The rubble began to rain down upon me, and in a state approaching panic I tore at the debris that was blocking my way to the exit tunnel, only to find the exit closed by what looked like a solid wall of flesh.

I had no doubt the obstacle was Methuselah—a truly enormous bull elephant seal, quite the largest I had seen. He normally occupied a territory bordering the fur seal colony, and it would have been a most unobservant and foolish castaway that failed to take note of how aggressive this creature was. It appeared that he had either taken a dislike to my hut or else chosen it as a convenient edifice against which to rub himself. In spite of the dim light of that passage I could see that his sides were covered with bare patches of flesh, red and bleeding and extremely sore. I had hardly time to register this fact before the tremors began again. He lifted the whole front portion of his body and slammed it down upon the wall, which immediately began to crumble. I scrambled back inside the the hut, pressing myself up against the rear as the whole front of the hut collapsed. Left unmolested, he would probably continue battering himself against the hut until he had demolished it. Yet if I tried to drive him away by jabbing him with a knife, he would most probably attack. What I needed was some subtle method of repelling him, though for the life of me I could not think what.

Fortunately, temporarily relieved of his itching, he settled down for a while. Sensing the danger was over, Scruff amused himself by nosing into all the spare junk I had collected along the beach and stored at the back of the hut. While snuffling through this, he found an item which, ridiculous though it may seem, I thought might be the answer. It was a quill. Snatching it from under the nose of the startled Scruff, I crawled cautiously towards the brute that was blocking our route of escape. At close quarters, the red, exposed flesh of the enormous animal looked very sore. Choosing the largest patch of rawness, I gently ran the feathered end of the quill all over it, repeating this on other patches so that the whole side nearest me became a mass of irritating itchiness. The old bull started as though he had been stabbed by several knife blades simultaneously. With a grunt he hauled himself up, gathering his strength to hump his massive body out of the way and down the hill towards the beach, roaring in a strange mixture of anger and distress.

After a few days I had repaired the damage and built a further wall beyond the existing one to protect the hut. Although I had obviously erected my abode on a desirable moulting location, I had no further visitors of such dramatic proportions. I discovered that I could frighten the others away by rattling stones in my kettle.

My little stream, on the other hand, which I had intended as a ready supply of fresh water, was a location to which both the seals and I laid claim. Not only did the fur seal pups enjoy the facility it offered for fun-making, but the elephant seals looked for suitable places along its length in which to roll themselves and wallow. Soon they had several feet on either side of it churned into a morass in which they sank themselves gratefully to suffer out the moult. These wallows became places of utter revulsion to me. In no time at all the animals had turned them into cesspools of green slime. What was worse, the stench from them was overpowering, the more so when the weather was balmy and the sun released the odours that the cold normally held fast. With so much competition for the little streamlets, I was forced to climb some way into the hills to get any fresh water. When this new source ran dry, I had to collect ice that was washed up on the beach, although it was often salty, necessitating an even farther walk to collect fresh ice from the icefall that blocked my route to the ice cap of that desolate island.

Scruff, meanwhile, appeared more than aptly named. His moulting fur gave the impression that he had contracted the mange. The process was accompanied by such a deal of fidgeting and scratching that you would have thought him to be alive with fleas. Because I could never see him balanced on three flippers and scratching away with the nails of the fourth without feeling a great urge to scratch myself, soon my skin too was raw from rubbing.

But the day came when Scruff and the other young fur seals had nearly all completed their moult. In place of their fluffy baby fur they now had a silkier, sleeker look. And with their transformation came an awareness of their surroundings, as if they had newly found the gift of life itself. From seeking safety in the shallows, they set out to explore the water's greener depths, where they plunged and rolled in joyful and wild abandon. Taking my cue from the female seals, I had been in the habit of leading Scruff to the water's edge, letting him gambol

with the other pups and delight in the frothy feel of the surf as it
drove him up onto the beach. But now he, too, was bent on testing his swimming skills, and he left me waiting on the beach as
anxious as any parent whose youngster takes the plunge for the
first time.

Almost immediately I wished I had put him on some kind of
leash. Like all youngsters he was impetuous, and I could not
expect him to have the sense not to go out too far. Within seconds he was making for the rockier part of the coast where the
older pups usually sported, revelling in the rough-and-tumble of
the seething waters there. Such an area was dangerous for the
small pups. The rocks were sharply fretted, and I went cold with
fright as I watched Scruff. Already I could see one tiny casualty.
I yelled to him, but either he did not hear or he did not care.
Certainly he did not falter from the direct line he made towards
the reefs. I could track him easily for a while, his tiny white head
conspicuous amongst the hundreds of silvery black ones, but
when he reached white water, his head disappeared in a cloudy
froth of whirling spray. *Whoosh!* Sea dashed against the rocks,
and a wall of spray was hurled high into the air. It fell just as
another wave slammed against the reef with savage and spectacular explosions.

No pup at all could survive such power. Their tiny bodies
were as yet too weak and uncoordinated to pierce it cleanly like
an arrow, which was the only way. So if they chanced to stray
within this boundary, they were immediately swept up, knocked
back and rolled over sideways until, halted by some rocky reef,
their tiny bodies were dashed to pieces. This was simply another
example of nature's harshness, of which already I had had so
much experience, and I could do nothing about it. I froze where
I stood, torn between the urge to watch and the dread of discovering his bloodied and mangled body. When eventually I did
move my leaden feet I was already sick with the horror of what
I imagined must have happened. Poor little Scruff. Poor, plucky
little blighter! Why the hell did he have to be so daring!
Couldn't he have played with all the others? Why did he always
have to be the odd one out? It seemed he was almost cursed for
being different. Hot tears crept into my eyes, brought on partly

by rage and partly by the sudden loss of a life I cared for. But though I scanned the turbulent waters, not a sign appeared of my former pet.

Overcome by melancholy, I almost ignored the snuffling, snortlike summons of a seal in difficulty which came from behind some nearby rocks. Usually I was only too anxious to retrieve some casualty, but the loss of my little companion had left me wondering what was the use of caring for life when nature itself seemed so cavalier. And yet, as I had to pass nearby the desperate sounds of the labouring creature on my way from the beach, some instinct I could not stop made me investigate. What I saw forced me to smile in spite of my melancholy. On a partially submerged ledge was a largish ruffled piece of sailcloth flopping about like a thing possessed. That there was a seal caught beneath it I had no doubt, for the sailcloth was caught on the rocks like a snare for anything leaping out of the water onto the ledge. Desperate as the predicament could be for the poor trapped animal, the sight of the inanimate sailcloth humping and jumping about was comical, especially with the accompaniment of the creature's snufflings and snortings. Droll as the moment was, however, the future would not have been so funny. When the tide came in, the trapped seal would surely have been drowned; so, in spite of my earlier feeling of hopelessness, I really had no choice but to save the poor thing. Imagine my surprise when the head appearing through the folds proved to be that of none other than Scruff himself. Relieved, and yet angry at having been caused so much anxiety by his disappearance, I cuffed him round the snout, haranguing him sternly, but so pathetic and bewildered did he look, crouched uneasily and gazing up at me with his beautiful big eyes, that I had to forgive him and hug him.

My fears for his safety were groundless, for Scruff was born with an instinct for survival that clearly was much keener than in his fellow pups. And he developed such a mastery of his watery surroundings that his skill was incredible and its display seldom less than spectacular. Water for Scruff was essentially an element created for his delight and amusement. When he moved in it he combined the gracefulness of flight with all the variety of dance, and I never tired of watching him clowning in the shallows or sporting with the waves. In all my life I had never seen a creature with such a gift for enjoyment. He rejoiced in water, ecstatic when it was tranquil and fearless when it was wild; and I, made partner to his joyousness by his soft barks of affection and his faculty for sharing his adventures with a man, began to feel a peacefulness and oneness with the environment that convinced me it was wonderful to be alive and well.

10

The Fighting Penguin

I experimented with food; but when I cut the flesh of seal into thin strips to dry on the rocks, the whole lot was pilfered by birds. As an alternative, I hung the strips from racks inside the hut near the fire to smoke. The treatment was not one I would repeat by choice. The meat turned out reasonably palatable but lacked the flavour and texture that I could have expected with the right condiments and utensils.

To vary the diet I fished, but my bait of blubber invariably disappeared. Only once did I actually manage to hook a fish, and this after several hours of effort. The catch was a dragon-headed creature, which I fried in seal oil and which tasted quite pleasant. I had avoided killing penguins for the sentimental and irrational reason that they seemed so "human" in many ways and I had enjoyed watching them so much during the summer. I little knew then how soon I would be forced to reconsider my attitude, or how soon my whole way of living would have to be reexamined.

Towards the end of summer, the days grew noticeably shorter and the nights colder, with longer periods of twilight. The sunsets were more glorious than ever—the dying sun firing the heavens with riotous colour in order to keep the approaching winter dark at bay.

I became aware about this time of a certain unease amongst the wildlife of the peninsula. It communicated itself even to Scruff, who appeared strangely disturbed for no apparent reason, his face animated at times with an expression of disquiet—hinting at the presence of deep currents of conflict within himself. For a while I did not worry, making note as a matter of course that the rookeries were beginning to thin out as large numbers of seals and birds left them for longer periods to feed farther and farther out to sea. Then, gradually, it began to dawn on me that, as the weather became colder, the wildlife was leaving the island.

More and more seals and birds were making for warmer places northwards—to kinder shores or even to some warmer areas of sea, and the implications of the exodus created a panic in me. Once again I started searching the horizon earnestly for a ship and racking my brains to hopeless effect for some practical means of making my escape.

I could probably have accepted my fate more easily had the weather been less inclement, but where it had been erratic before it was now totally unpredictable. Often a damp and all-obliterating fog would sweep down from the mass of inland ice and give a ghostly appearance to the icebergs that haunted the waters beyond the cove. An air of gloom would descend, too, with sleet or heavy snow, and I would be forced to remain indoors for periods of as much as several days. I would emerge to find more seals had vacated the beaches and more birds their nesting grounds.

To emphasize the agitation in nature, large masses of ice would break away with ominous sounds from the nearby ice cliffs, while from the sea, thunderous booms reported icebergs breaking up or turning over. The whole world was undergoing an upheaval, a sudden dramatic change for the worse.

With the assault of nature came the realization of the need to kill and store enough food to last me the winter. For a while, overcome by panic, I began laying about me as the sealers had done till I had a score of carcasses—their dark blood pouring out of them to stain the new-laid snow. In time, I saw the sense of limiting the number of animals I killed to the number with which I could cope efficiently. If I did not skin and cut the carcass into manageable pieces immediately, it would freeze solid or be devoured by the marauding birds. I was not without guilt at my merciless mission. Embarrassed that Scruff should witness my felony, I barricaded him in the hut, sneaking off to the sound of his pitiful cries, which went through me like a knife—as much as his squeals of welcome on my return made me feel like some kind of Judas. At these times my clothes and boots were soaked in gore, and I would remove them in the passageway, replacing them with fresher garments in order not to be reminded of my work. Even so, my mind could not rid itself of the image of the frozen streams of dark red blood, or of the sad look in the glazed eyes of the seals that I had killed.

With the fear of running short of food, I was forced to brave the severest weather. Frequently my hands were so benumbed from the blood freezing on them and forming a complete case of ice that I had to plunge them into the still-quivering and steaming entrails of the dead animal, as I had seen the sealers do, until blood in turn became cold and clammy. After flensing the animals as rapidly as my stiffening and complaining fingers would allow, I would remove the liver to take home and cut up the carcass, dragging the flesh piecemeal to the nearest cache. Even as I was doing this, a company of rapacious birds would descend from the rocky headlands to attack the carcass, clawing and tearing at their booty with bloody beak and claw. Several of them would often scoop up the same piece of carrion, tugging at it with hoarse cries of rage. Bespattered with the contents of the bursting gut, one of them would seize the advantage and fly off, with several others in pursuit, screeching and snatching at the flailing innards. When gorged, these birds would waddle to the water's edge and float there so bloated and heavy that they could not rise however much they flapped their outspread wings. Eventually, some of them had to vomit up part of what they had eaten before they could take to the air and soar majestically out of sight.

Slaughtering seals was long and laborious work. What is more, they were becoming so difficult to catch that I was tempted to consider penguins as an alternative source of food. These, I argued, should be easier to kill and would also provide an essential addition to my footwear. I had already run through several pairs of my homemade boots and could foresee that I would be kept busy replenishing my clothes through the winter. A few young elephant seals had by now fallen victim to my blows. Their pelts were strong enough for the soles of boots, and I could cut their skins spirally to make a good rope that had a natural strength and stretch to it. Penguins would provide warm stockings, and who knows what other comforts I might devise.

Two kinds of penguins were accessible to me. In physical appearance there was not much difference between them, but in temperament I detected a lot. I liked the birds of one kind in particular for the way they waddled about upright with a certain donnish air. They had only to feel threatened or at risk to transform themselves immediately into pugilists, yammering and ruffling their head feathers as they struck hammer blows with their strong flippers. Even if rebuffed, these Adélies would return bristling to the attack. Their cousins, the Gentoos, on the other hand, were no less likeable but lacked the Adélies' dashing recklessness.

As to how I should kill the birds, I was in some doubt, having seen only one method used by the sealers, which was as repugnant as it was brutal. They would sweep up the poor birds by the legs, swinging them into the air before bashing their heads against a rock. To me there was something grossly obscene in this method of killing. It showed a lack of respect for the creature, and I resolved to be much more humane in my butchering. But I had no idea how difficult killing these plucky little fellows would be, or how close I should be driven to dispatching them in the same way as the sealers.

On my first encounters with the penguins, I had been subjected to a great deal of unpleasant pummelling and mauling. I had experienced more of their pugilism during my many excursions to their rookery in search of eggs. Without warning, several would charge at me from various directions and sink their beaks into my scantily protected flesh while striking me violently with their flippers. I had soon learned to pad myself for protection, but with all my padding my legs had suffered from their attacks, and I had felt the pain for ages.

With the memory of these skirmishes still clearly in mind, I bandaged myself about the arms and legs with sealskin to dull the blows. I decided to choose a victim on the perimeter of the rookery, so as not to be set upon unexpectedly by any others. In my ignorance, I thought that the quickest method, and possibly the least painful, would be to throttle the birds. With this intention I sneaked up on my prey from behind, moving in the manner of a seal in case any of his shortsighted companions should spot me. I was quite surprised by how easily I managed to creep undetected right up to my victim and seize it by the neck.

If I had grasped an eel with a greasy hand, I could not have held on with more difficulty, nor could I have been more ill-prepared for the bird's aggressive and galvanic strength. Kicking and flapping, pecking and jabbing, it struggled to resist me, screeching at the same time in such a bloodcurdling manner that the whole rookery was instantly alerted and turned in unison to where we fought. At the call of alarm my hair went rigid, for in a concerted assault I knew its fellows could make short work of me. Already my victim had stabbed me so viciously with his powerful beak that my body felt sore all over. I had to move fast if I was to escape. Clutching that writhing bundle to my chest, I rolled sideways several times in order to put some distance between us and the rookery while I perfomed my grizzly task. Fortunately, penguins are shortsighted creatures, and this ruse succeeded in keeping off the horde. In their confusion they went rushing in all directions, peering blindly for some sign of an assailant.

In no time at all I regretted ever laying hands on the penguin. It was so strong and agile I had the impression I was grappling with six penguins and a donkey rolled into one. Bristling with fury, it kicked and thwacked at me, striking randomly with feet and flippers but inflicting always the most telling and painful blows with its beak. When I squeezed its neck to try to choke the creature, it performed the most extraordinary antics while

134

continuing such an assault on me as it squirmed and wriggled that I thought I might have to give up the fight. My arms were trembling and I felt weak all over, and I was not a little vexed and embarrassed at my lack of success. The creature's neck seemed as tough as a hempen cable and as difficult to compress.

This way and that I twisted and pulled in an effort to stifle the life out of the bird and end what was becoming for me a crippling affair. But it was as impossible to break the creature's neck as it was to throttle it. I rolled on top of the bird in an attempt to smother it, and I shook it violently up and down to subdue it. But neither tactic was the least bit effective, and I had to dodge its beak repeatedly so as not to be jabbed in the face.

Feeling desperate at last and very much weaker, I determined on one last gigantic effort to strangle the bird. My hands were trembling and bleeding from beak wounds and my heart was beating wildly. Tightening my grip, I dug my nails in, squeezing for all I was worth till I heard the bird croak. How long it would take to die I could not imagine, but it was gasping, with its tiny button eyes nearly popping out of its head.

The satisfaction I felt now the battle was closing had less triumph in it than a sense of relief. There was no doubt the creature had fought me bravely, and I could not help viewing the bird with a deep sense of respect and sympathy. I must have slightly eased my grip as I thought this, for the next moment the penguin's head shot upwards. Snapping viciously, just missing my eye, it dug its beak into the fleshy part of my ear and gripped with such savagery that I danced and howled in agony, clawing and punching the bird to try to make it let go.

It would not. Crazed with pain and anger I screamed and stabbed and hacked with my knife to make it give up; but it seemed only to tighten its hold on me, forcing me to bend double as the weight of its body pulled on my ear with its viselike grip, until I began to fear all of a sudden for my very life in case the bird should manage to take hold of me by the neck.

How dramatically the issue had altered and how suddenly the roles had become reversed. Now it was I who was the victim, while the penguin in turn was the oppressor. Terrified, I fought the bird with all the ferocity and desperation that it had earlier brought to the tussle. It would not release its hold on my ear, and the blood from both of us was gushing out and bloodying the other. In my flurry of fear I had no idea where I had stabbed the bird or how much injury I had inflicted; but, in what seemed at the time a miraculous moment, it released its grip and dropped to the ground to stagger off towards the sea, swaying and squawking valiantly, blood pouring from the knife wounds I had inflicted. Within moments it was surrounded by a flock of skuas and other scavengers, and when I next returned to the beach only a few bones and feathers marked the place where it had finally succumbed.

I had meantime returned to the hut, humiliated and utterly weary. There I sank onto the bunk to nurse my wounds. When I felt my ear, I discovered that the penguin had actually severed the lobe. After much reflection, I decided it would be prudent to stun future victims before cutting their throats with a knife; but this remained, in fact, a bloody business until one day a post mortem on a bird revealed a soft patch at the base of the skull through which I could insert a knife to kill the stunned creature without very much fuss. From then on I used this method of dispatching them, which was quick and painless for both of us.

I imagined that I would suffer from scruples as the prospect of a barren winter urged me to build up my store of animal meat. While the next three weeks were sickening because of the great number of animals I was forced to slaughter, my basic instinct for survival soon overcame my feelings of guilt. I was not absolved completely of any retribution, however. Where my hands had been pecked by the penguin, my wounds swelled up to the size of eggs. They were very painful and inconvenient and severely hampered me in my task. I could not afford to wait till they had healed, however, or I should have been deprived of any further supplies of food.

I chose several sites to cache the carcasses, after removing the skin and feathers intact from most of the penguins and dumping these at one end of the hut. As it happened, most of the natural well-shaped rock formations that I used as caches were along the beach; but I made sure that they were all above high water mark.

I filled them with meat or penguin carcasses and covered the lot with various-sized stones. It was not easy work, since the stones were heavy and sometimes had to carried from quite a way.

I had meat now on both sides of the peninsula and a cache that I had built on the high ground, halfway between the two beaches. The reason I had back-packed so much to my side of the peninsula and cached it in the rocky outcrops on my beach was for fear of bad weather preventing me from travelling inland. I did not want to bring all the food over, however, thinking that the exercise would be healthy for me during the winter and that it would serve a double function by also getting me out of the hut. No doubt the urge would be strong on occasions to idle my time away in its warmth rather than face the rigours of the cold outside. I had an intuitive feeling that to hibernate in the hut would be a danger to my morale, making me soft and weak-willed, demoralized and easily depressed.

I had replenished the emptying barrels with more horse pieces. These were taken from young elephant seals, who were less endowed with blubber than their elders had been when we first arrived. One particular expedient of which I was quite proud was a sack made from a very young elephant skin. This I had filled with pieces of blubber and hung in the hut so that I would have a ready supply. It was not an easy container to make in spite of being simple in design. It involved removing the whole of the skin intact by making incisions around the head and extremities, and then inserting a knife to cut away the pelt, which was attached to the flesh by a layer of blubber. The latter was simple enough to do, but removing the carcass from inside the pelt, or rather removing the pelt from off the carcass, required a great deal of strength and the application of every ounce of my ingenuity.

I had previously extricated the back flippers, and I eventually hit on the idea of tying them to a projection of rock while I tugged on the skin with all my might. At first the two seemed unwilling to part company, coming together again after each pull with seemingly greater cohesion than before. Gradually, though, the naked carcass emerged. Finally, after one gigantic

137

tussle, in which the posterior edge of the pelt had to stretch to its utmost to get over the bulge in the middle, I hurtled backwards onto the snow with the heavy skin on my lap.

I had entertained thoughts of sewing the ends together but, having as yet still not mastered the technique of sewing skins, I made do by tying up all the openings with thongs made from other skins. The extraordinary shape of the sack when full made it look something like a punching bag, although its smell would have offended the nose of even the toughest boxer. I was, however, by now used to all manner of natural smells that a few months earlier I would have found offensive. It was, in fact, extraordinary to think that only seven months had passed since I had been with my family. But memories of home were so distressing that I made no attempt to lower the wall that had begun to grow up between me and my past.

Each day I became more aware of a drop in temperature, and the valleys of the peninsula became more filled with snow. Even the beach took on a different aspect. The receding tide left an almost continuous wall of fresh-water ice boulders where earlier it had deposited only a scattered few. I collected a considerable number and built a store for them outside the hut. They produced, when melted, the most wonderfully pure drink and gave excellent value for the effort involved in carrying them to the hut. Around this same time I was also given warning of what winter might bring and learned not to be complacent about anything and always to treat nature with the utmost respect.

11

Lost in the Blizzard

I had risen to a particularly fine morning which gave promise of a windless day. Being in an active and lighthearted mood, no doubt evoked by the fairness of the weather, I decided to take advantage of it to go for a longer walk than usual. I had recently noticed on one of the more inaccessible beaches near the headland a broken section of longboat that I wanted to secure and had resolved to try to reach it before heavy winter snows made the descent impossible. With the prospect of a fair day ahead of me I decided that now would be the best time to retrieve the timber and therefore equipped myself with various lengths of line that I had made from sealskin. With this I intended to form a link between the beach and high ground by attaching the line at certain intervals to suitably projecting rocks to facilitate both the descent to the beach and the returning climb. I left Scruff behind, fearing he might hinder me by sliding down a descent too steep for him to ascend later without my assistance; but since I had no wish to barricade him in the hut, I was obliged to wait till he had dived into the ocean for his daily swim before setting off secretively on my errand.

I need hardly describe my joyfulness when, almost on the beach, I glanced down and confirmed that there was indeed a goodly-sized piece of boat's wreckage washed up, together with several items of sealing gear with which a longboat was always equipped. On examining the wreckage, I found not only a tinderbox, which was the greatest gift, but also a pickax, hammer and some nails—the latter being as much a part of the longboat's equipment as were the oars, by reason of the frequent damage that had to be repaired when the boats accidentally struck some submerged reef or rock. Nearby, buried in the shingle, was a large fragment of broken grindstone, and here and there, scattered haphazardly, were bits of wood and various bric-a-brac of ship's property that were as exciting a find as buried treasure.

So intent was I on gathering all the fragments of wreckage that I did not notice the clouds piling up. Even when drifting snow made the change in weather all too obvious, I was reluctant to abandon my beachcombing. Accordingly, I delayed as long as I could. I piled most of the flotsam in a heap near the cliff foot to be collected later and backpacked the tools and various oddments after first wrapping them in sealskin to make a parcel. The climb to the top of the cliff was wind-lashed, and I congratulated myself on my forethought in having secured the line on my way down, or I should never have been able to get back up.

When I reached the top, the whirling snow had obliterated the track and curtained every view. The air was so thick with flying snow that I could not see farther than a couple of feet; and when I peered into the wind, it pelted my eyes with hard stinging pellets. Soon I was obliged to creep on all fours. The wind, funnelling through one of the nearby passes, was so strong that it would have swept me away like a leaf if I had been upright. Already it barred my way like a solid wall in certain directions, and in no time at all I had lost my bearings.

I had to move slowly and cautiously to avoid stumbling headfirst over one of the many sheer drops to the beach. Being warned by experience that in such circumstances there is always a chance of panicking, I cautioned myself to be still. And so I waited, my ears straining for sounds that might give me a clue to the right direction; but the roar of surf was lost somewhere in the overall roar of wind. Then I remembered that the wind had been on my left cheek as I had climbed the cliff. This thought momentarily raised my hopes. If I positioned myself so that the wind was on my left again I should have a good indication of the correct direction. But, as if to confute my sense of logic, there came immediately a stronger blow, and I was assailed at once by gusts from several directions.

Confused, I paused and listened, trying to form in my mind a picture of the ground that would help me regain my bearings. Finally, I chose a route and set off, crawling cautiously to keep from blundering into some hazard from which I might not be able to make my escape. I have no idea how much terrain I covered or in what direction. The snow was now filling the air in a flying, whirling, blinding mass, and there was no way of distinguishing land from sky. I was further confused by the strange illusion of seeing hummocks where there were only depressions and dips where the ground rose steeply before me. As a result, I plunged into snowdrifts several feet deep and slammed into boulders that were, I swear, invisible.

I had no way of calculating my direction, and yet I had to keep trying. Already the snow was caking my beard, and with my breath now freezing on top of this it was beginning to form a thick mask of ice. Snow settled on my brows and eyelashes, and the latter began to stick together in small clumps of ice that I had to warm and squeeze off with my fingers lest they accumulate and completely seal my eyes. As I stopped on these occasions, bending my head into my chest, the blizzard continued its assault on me, slapping snow into every crevice and pocket of my clothing. I became afraid. What if the mask should completely cover my face? Responding to a feeling of urgency, I stood up to try to see some landmark. The sudden movement together with the weight on my back took me off balance, and, caught by the wind, I was knocked back a couple of steps before being spun round. Blown off my feet, I went slithering and tumbling down a steep slope of ice. Fearing that I was on one of those slippery slopes that ended abruptly over jagged rocks or the sea, I clawed desperately at its icy surface, slithering faster every second until, still unable to get a grip, I fetched up suddenly and unexpectedly with jarring impact against a rock.

Winded and badly shaken but with only a few minor hurts, I thanked heaven that I had not gone plumeting down to the bottom, from which direction there came occasional upsurges of snow mingled with the salty taste of sea spray. My instinct screamed at me to climb, for every minute the mask was building on my face and very soon would cover my nose. Unstrapping the bundle from my back, I took out the pickax and some long nails, which I put in my pocket. Using the pickax to cut out hand holds and footholds in the slope, I began with a will to climb. But the wind had become even more violent, and time and again I slipped out of my footholds and was blown slantwise like a feather, to end up slamming against some rock or boulder.

I was grateful that there were boulders to break my fall, however painful the collisions. By the very fact that I was brought up so many times against these obstacles I confirmed what I had begun to fear, that I was on a most dangerous slope which, in better visibility, I had previously observed shelved in two steep tiers before plunging some hundred feet or so to the sea. Luck had intervened when fate seemed set to destroy me by setting some obstacle in my way to break my fall; but soon my luck might run out, and with the next slip I might plummet the full length of the drop into the furious sea, which I could hear pounding the rocks below me. I was continuing to have difficulty keeping my eyelids from being frozen together, and already the mask had crept down the lower part of my face and over my mouth. I could not part my lips, and one nostril was blocked. If I did not find cover immediately, my face would soon be completely covered with ice, and I would suffocate.

My fear-tortured mind was desperately trying to work out some solution. If I could find a cave, I might survive, but I had neither the time nor the energy to go in search of one. In any case, there was no route which in my condition I could safely climb. It was then, as I was crouched beside a snowdrift to the lee of a rock, that an extraordinary impulse made me dig at it. I had at first intended to make some sort of simple windbreak behind which to shelter while I tried to de-ice my face. But as I dug deeper it occurred to me that the snowdrift was large enough to serve as a cave. Cheered by this, I at once set to, digging frantically to enlarge the hole, and crept into it not a minute too soon, for my mask had almost closed the last vent through which I was able to breathe. At that moment I think I came nearest to panicking. I do believe that if I had done so I would have lost my life. However, a voice from deep inside me, of some other, wiser self, demanded that I should keep calm.

My heart was pumping erratically, and my chest, aching from the double pain of constriction and assault, felt as though some wild and desperate creature was clawing and tearing at it in a hopeless struggle to escape. Again, I wanted to thrash out. Again, a voice within cautioned me not to panic. My will and my nerves, locked in mortal battle, were demanding more breath than I could draw through that last minute hole in my mask. Only after a terrible struggle was I finally able to subdue the screaming man within me and to inhale more slowly. As I did so, I noticed that my heart began to pound less violently and that my fear began to dissipate, leaving me calmer and better able to help myself.

With my nose clear, I did not feel nearly so anxious. My mouth was still sealed by the ice, and I was cold and cramped in that tiny snow burrow, but I knew that I was past the worst—that somehow I would survive.

I reasoned that if I were to be any length of time in the cave I should be better off making myself as comfortable as possible. So, taking the bundle from my back, I removed the sealskin and put it to good use as a mat. I loosened the bindings on my boots and wriggled and rubbed my frozen toes to restore the flow of blood. When this happened, it was like being stuck with hundreds of tiny red-hot needles, and I squirmed with the agony of the treatment until the pain finally eased. After that, I returned to the task of removing my heavy mask of ice and gave some well-deserved attention to my freezing hands. The best thing I could do to conserve heat was to find some way of cocooning myself. Drawing my arms through the sleeves of my jacket, I held them against my body, with the hands snug in the

143

warmth of my armpits. This way I sat, banging my feet together at frequent intervals while the storm raged outside just inches away.

The hours dragged by with painful slowness. Steadily I got colder. From time to time I thought I detected a drop in the wind's force, but it eased slightly only to increase in violence again. The whole of that afternoon it raged on an on, and throughout the whole of the night. Meanwhile I twisted and turned my shivering body every few minutes, trying to relieve the cramp and to keep from freezing to the walls of that tiny burrow. After several cramped hours, I was no longer aware of any benefit that the sealskin afforded as insulation. My joints had begun to ache, my body temperature to fall and my fears to creep back like a tide that might this time overwhelm me. My back suffered the worst agony, pressed up against the cold of that snow cave in such an unnatural position. Even when I knelt to take the pressure off my buttocks my body could hardly bear the contortions. I must have changed from sitting to kneeling a thousand times during that terrible night without anything more than a momentary relief from the crippling effects of the cold.

Daylight came as a sort of drab greyness. Although facing sea-wards, I could see nothing. The storm had drawn a veil across the entrance to my burrow which, as I grew hungrier and colder, I feared might become a tomb. My enforced restlessness had exhuasted me, as had the shivers that racked my frame. These lasted sometimes for several minutes, and once I thought my back must break, so violent had been the spasm. My feet had finally lost all feeling, despite my banging them together to try to restore the flow of blood. Remembering that a condition called frostbite was likely to occur when a limb had lost its feeling, I worried that my feet might be frostbitten and fumbled to remove my boots so that I could take a look. Apparently frostbite, if severe, resulted in the blood ceasing to circulate in a particular area, which might become gangrenous. If that happened, the dead area of flesh would have to be amputated in order to halt the spread of the gangrene.

Dreading what might have happened during the night, I had barely the courage to take a look at my feet. When I did, they appeared none too healthy in colour, being a yellowish-white all over that merged into a mottled blue at the toes. It was a good while before my poor hands could bring any warmth to them. Obviously I had caught them just in time, but if I were to prevent frostbite during the remainder of the time I was holed up I would have to find some way of keeping the circulation going. I concluded that the best remedy would be to wrap both feet in the sealskin I had been sitting on. This way they would draw some warmth from each other, and I could rub them against one another to restore the circulation when they grew numb. The boots meanwhile could double as a cushion in place of the sealskin.

Twilight was returning on the second day before the wind dropped. Although I was convinced it was merely a lull, I could see the shapes of rocks at least ten yards away and decided that it might be worth a scramble to reach more familiar ground before it got dark and the wind once again forced me to seek a shelter. If I could get to the area in which I had my cache, I should be able to find my way to the hut—even if the storm struck again —for I had travelled the distance between those two points many times in the past few months.

I had, however, become so weak through cold and lack of food that several times my legs collapsed before I was finally able to stand. Even when they could take my weight I had to drag my feet to move them at all and could only move them slowly. To make matters worse, the wind had polished the slope to such a degree that I slipped back almost every time I took a step. I count the moment of inspiration almost divine when I remembered the nails that I had in my pocket. Using a small rock, I knocked several of them at intervals into the ice as aids to haul myself up. This I managed at the expense of much effort. My ordeal had greatly weakened my muscles, and at first I was unable to coordinate my movements.

Once at the top again, I felt much better. I trod carefully, since I still could not get my bearings with the contours of the ground changed so much as a result of the newly formed drifts. A couple of times I jarred my ankle in holes surrounding the rocks and boulders, and several times I fell heavily on the wind-polished surface of the iron-hard snow. But finally I did reach the cache, which was about halfway between the two beaches. Darkness was already descending, and the wind had begun to blow again. This time, however, I did not fear it. I was on home ground and knew my way. I thanked heaven that I had been forced to come this route so many times. Every inch of it was imprinted firmly and clearly on my mind. "Blow your hardest, wind!" I shouted into the teeth of it. "You will not catch me out again so soon!" And I smiled to myself as I set off determinedly, feeling an almost reckless desire to show whoever it was that had conjured up such weather that I was in control, whatever it might care to throw my way. For a few minutes I felt confident enough not to slow my pace; but quite abruptly I was brought to halt by an obstacle I could not recognize.

It was dark now and completely overcast, and I could not see even the black profile of the land against the usually starry sky. I would have to retrace my steps till I could pick up the familiar track. For the life of me I could not think how I had gone wrong. I backtracked a short distance toward a place I recognized and altered my heading to a slightly different route. A few yards farther on I was completely foxed again, coming on a rock formation I could not recall having seen before. I was not only frustrated but also alarmed, I was once again hopelessly lost, and I was also beginning to develop another heavy mask of ice.

Growing more and more anxious, I started exploring in random directions, hoping to come across a feature I could recognize. What I had foolishly not allowed for was the change in the appearance of this area resulting from all the new drifts of snow—a confusion which was greatly increased by the darkness and my fatigue. Admittedly I was nearer home; but the situation was hardly less dangerous than it had been two days before. What an idiot I was for having left the snow burrow. I upbraided myself aloud. At least there I had been protected from the fearsome impact of the wind.

I had to lean into that wind now, with my head well down. A few minutes later, I was knocked backwards by a sudden and unexpected blow. The next moment a furry body was on top of me, and hot fishy breath fanned my face. It was Scruff! I could hardly believe it. How long he had been looking for me I could not even guess, but a more welcome creature I could not possibly have met. With his arrival my spirits lifted instantly, not only for his company but for the value of him as a guide. I did not doubt that he was as capable of leading me home as any faithful dog could have done in the same near-tragic circumstances. What I had not been prepared for, however, was his own irrepressible high spirits, which resulted in his haring off the next second to race me home; frequently at the end of an excursion somewhere we used to race the last few hundred yards to the hut. Now, left suddenly alone again, I felt angry and despondent and full of invective at what I unfairly considered the stupidity of the pup. And when he did return in answer to my despairing whistles and supplications, he jumped up and gave me another squally demonstration of affection before bounding off once more.

Cold and frustrated, I screamed at him, but all of my frantic calls were shredded and drowned by the roaring of the wind. Several minutes went by before he returned, by which time I was furious at him and almost embalmed by the cold. I had no easy task persuading him to stay still while I attached a piece of cordage round his body in an attempt to make some sort of harness. And there then developed a most hair-raising scramble when I tried to follow the creature who, I could only trust, would have the good sense to take me home. Scruff's vocabulary of recognized words included the word *home*, and I said it firmly several times into his ear. Unfortunately Scruff's favourite paths were more fit for a seal to scramble along than a man, with the result that I tumbled over the ground more often than I walked. Finally, having stumbled, slipped, fallen and crawled, we came to the door of the hut. Frozen and frostbitten as I was, its warmth and its security was like the bosom of a mother to a hurt and frightened child.

For several days my face was raw with burning sores, and my hands and feet were blistered and swollen. Restoring the blood to the affected areas had to be done by applying warmth gradually and my massaging them very gently. Such treatment, however, was excruciating, and many were the times that I almost gave up.

The experience, when I had healed enough to reflect upon it, made me realize just how vulnerable I was. If I were to survive the winter, I would have to treat the elements with a good deal more respect. I would have to obey their first warning signs of danger and make sure that I was equipped with adequate clothing to meet the weather's various demands. I should also have to consider making some sort of markers that I could use to stake out various routes, and to these I should attach a line. This way I might save myself from getting lost in the future. If the storms I had seen were anything to go by, I could lose sight of home within a very short distance of the hut. I wondered, too, what other lessons nature had in store for me and whether it was presumptuous even to hope to survive.

12

The Approach
of Winter

It may seem extraordinary that I had known Scruff for eighteen weeks, during which time we had shared so many new experiences together, and that I had not until now realized the most important thing about my charge—namely that *he*, as I had thought of him, was in fact a *she*. Yes, Scruff was female, there was no doubt of it. That I could have been blind to this fact for so long only shows how preoccupied I must have been with other matters. Of course, after the moult, I had been impressed with her pelt's new richness, but Scruff was too much of an urchin then in her habits for her good looks to be obvious. Over the last few days, however, I had detected a sort of languid grace in the creature which seemed out of keeping with her previous boisterousness and which prompted me to question my assumption of the pup's maleness.

This particular day, being near the beach as Scruff emerged from the sea in a glaze of water, I was struck by the extraordinary beauty of the animal, noticing for the first time a sinuous and silky sleekness. She shook the water off her fur and bounded gracefully to meet me—a gorgeous creature, her body stream-lined and covered with a pelt of white over which there was a warm and gentle tinge of gold. Dark-flippered and dark-nosed, she had eyes that were large and lovely—brown, but framed exotically with a thin line of black. Her ears were tiny and scroll-shaped, while the pretty touch of russet on her face was enhanced by delicately sensitive silver whiskers.

She nuzzled up to me as I stooped in greeting and rolled on her back for me to pet her, squirming pleasurably as I touched her belly, which was round and firm and warmly responsive to my kneading. While she wriggled appreciatively, I allowed my fingers to explore her body for some indication of her gender. It was not as obvious as one would imagine, for nature has a way of concealing the sex of some animals for her own peculiar reasons; but I was able to confirm what had become a suspicion—that the pup I had adopted was a female. "Scruff!" How truly inapt the name now sounded, and yet, as I laughed and teased her, she responded so affectionately to it that I knew I could never call her by another.

To a certain extent the fact that Scruff was feminine made a difference to our relationship, although in exactly what way it is difficult to say. All I know is that I felt a subtle if illogical ten-derness towards her all of a sudden which prompted me to be less rough when we played together, almost as though her femaleness should make a difference to her natural strength! From then on I noticed all sorts of subtle charms in her which were probably as much the seal in her as any distinct difference from the male; but I chose to see them as only greater proof of the feminine side of her nature. In most ways, however, the discovery made no actual difference to how I treated her. Male or female, Scruff and I continued to draw pleasure from each other sleeping side by side in order to draw mutual warmth and comfort—a warmth without which perhaps neither of us would have been able to survive. We were both unsuited by nature to live on this island throughout the winter, and only by a symbiotic union of man and animal were we able to accept the challenge.

The past few days, during which the last of the wildlife had deserted the peninsula, had been dispiriting. Where before there had been thousands of birds, now there was only desolation and foul, slimy earth and rocks caked brown and white with the accumulation of a season's droppings. Storms had already blown away the millions of feathers that had formed a thick carpet over everything, and what few were left Scruff had romped through with all the abandon and delight of an infant scattering a carpet of crisp autumn leaves. She had tossed and snuffed them, sneezing and leaping into the air as she chased and caught them. Then snow had settled, covering the bare ground and rock, and there was soon no sign that there had been any life there at all.

Every day I was made more and more aware of the harshening conditions, and I reflected that Scruff and I were the only two creatures left on the peninsula. Sobering as the thought was, I could not help realizing how terrifying the prospect would have been had Scruff obeyed that call to migrate and left me totally alone. I could not help wondering whether there was some natural explanation for why Scruff had stayed or whether fate had played some part in it. Either way, the fact bound us closer together. Scruff shadowed me because she knew no better, while I encouraged her affection, knowing that we were partners sharing a common destiny in a struggle against nature which could be equally destructive to man or animal.

Fortunately, there is a remarkable strength in the human spirit which shows as an ability to adapt to the most stressful circumstances. While at first I was alarmed and despondent to discover that we had been left to battle what promised to be a fearsome winter by ourselves, I soon convinced myself that this was no cause for despair. Where there was a limit to how much an animal could adapt if thrown into an intolerable situation, I, on the other hand, could draw on the unique attributes of human foresight and reason, with which endowments I should be able to anticipate problems and also work out, in advance, a solution.

Cheered with the thought of this, I applied my mind directly to drawing up a list of things I should do in the winter to ensure our well-being—a list which involved not only a timetable of physical pursuits to fill out the day but also a set of mental disciplines to engage the mind. I was intuitive enough to realize that there would come moments of intense depression or weakness of will when only strict adherence to an established habit might pull me through. There was no reason, I reassured myself, why I should not survive—and Scruff too, for that matter. I had cached food in plenty, enough to last several months, and I had a shelter that was solid, with enough blubber to heat it. In other words, I was well set up to provide for any material demands. On the abstract or intellectual level, however, there might be inadequacies. Therefore, in spite of having a companion who would to some extent relieve my loneliness and offset the monotony that would be inevitable, I decided I should divide up each day into periods of work and exercise, mealtimes and play. In this way I would benefit from different pursuits, besides imposing some shape on an otherwise featureless future.

My most pressing need was for some good cold-weather clothing. Even so, I refused to confine myself solely to domestic requirements. It was important for my morale that I do something other than just look after my survival. Some sort of study was necessary—some alternative to the recording of my observations on the wildlife which had previously taken up so much of my time. I had a morbid dread of becoming purposeless and believed life without purpose to be itself a form of death. I decided to make a log of the weather, together with a measurement of the tides, which would become of use one day to mariners when these islands were rediscovered. I had no doubt that ultimately other sealers would follow where our own ship had led the way. My fear was that I might not be alive to see the day.

The hut left several things to be desired before it would be proof against the weather—draughts from practically every angle being a constant source of irritation. However finely I stopped up the crevices, the snow still filtered its way through the crannies. I eventually hit on the expedient of building a wall of snow around the hut and plastering it with seawater slush, which froze to a solid crust. But even this had to be repaired on occasions because of the scouring affect of the blizzards. By midwinter, however, snowdrifts had formed high banks of hard-packed snow around the hut, and the insulation of the shelter, for a while at least, required no further attention.

This is not to say that the drifts of snow were an irreproachable ally. There were many days when I had to dig myself out of the hut, and I was glad then that I had made an entrance passage long enough to contain the snow I excavated and that I had had the good sense to make a door which opened inwards. This door, in fact, was a simple arrangement made out of a barrel top. It could be held fast to a frame by wooden clamps on the inside and could be lifted into the passage when I wanted to get out. To close it from the outside I used a second barrel top, which was held in place by the same principle—thus dispensing with the need for hinges.

Normally, the blubber fire provided ample heat to warm the hut, but early in the winter, before the drifts had formed and when the wind blew from a certain quarter, I could pile the blubber onto the fire and the place would still be cold. The wind sucked out every scrap of warmth. There were different temperatures in the hut at different levels, and my legs could be freezing while my head and shoulders were pleasantly warm. Building another layer onto my bunk went some way towards solving the problem, but living at a higher level had its disadvantages. The fumes from the blubber fire were very bad at times; so much so in fact that I was frequently driven out into the air coughing and spluttering from the suffocating smoke. As an answer, I made a chimney and knocked out a hole in the top of one of the walls as a sort of ventilator which I could block up when the wind came whistling in from that direction. Another disadvantage was that the fire gave off an oily soot that coated my skin and clothes. Scruff became so dirty that at times I could hardly distinguish her in the shadows. Afraid that this might reduce the natural insulating qualities of her pelt, I would remove it with urine which I would rub liberally over her before a swim so she could cleanse it off in the sea. Always after such a treatment her pelt would be more lustrous than ever, and I eventually used the same treatment on the greasy mop that was my hair.

As an extra comfort as the winter closed in, I made a carpet of penguin skins and hung a few sealskins from the ceiling around my bunk to keep off the draught. They also deflected the heat onto the bunk, which was a good thing, especially at night when the fire got low. Outside, the winds blew more violently and the waves broke on the rocks of the northern beaches, covering them with spume, which froze instantly and built up into a thick cover of ice with each successive dousing. Sea ice formed in the coves in streaky patches, and as these jostled against each other their edges grew rounded and turned up until there were thousands of discs with raised rims floating on the surface of the sea like icy pancakes. Many of these, caught by the waves, piled on top of each other till several layers froze together, joining with others of their kind and small broken-off pieces of iceberg to form a continuous though rough skin of ice that extended in places far out to sea. Not every cove was similarly icebound. The thick sheets of ice only formed in the bays, which were better protected from the wind. In those bays and coves where there were strong currents, ice seldom formed; and when it did, it seldom stayed for more than a day before being torn away.

Every day darkness crept in a little nearer and stayed a little longer. It was not easy moving about outside now. In places the wind had so furrowed the snow that it had the appearance of frozen waves which were hard at the crest and soft in the troughs, making walking difficult. Sometimes I could not go outside at all because of the wind; and when I did I floundered into deep snow or skidded on the wind-polished slopes—wrenching my back more than once. Where I had not expected it, walls of drift were building up, so changing the land's appearance that on days of fog, when there was no wind, I could easily lose my way even in the immediate vicinity of the hut.

The patience to sit out bad weather did not come naturally, but I used these occasions to get on with my domestic pursuits. Till now I had managed to get by without any sewing by covering the deficiencies in my threadbare ship's clothing with skins of fur crudely attached by thongs of skin to form a kind of protective cloak, which I held in at the waist with my belt. This, however, was not protection enough against the bitter winds of winter, which pierced the gaps like saber thrusts. I therefore set myself the task of designing a better-fashioned and closer-fitting garment in which the seams would be well enough sewn to exclude the draught.

Necessity demanding that I put my mind to the problem of making a needle, I examined a collection of various bones I had picked up to see if there was one that might suit my purpose. I was delighted to find several wing bones of some large bird amongst various other natural debris, and I tried to whittle them into a suitable needle shape with my knife. My first efforts to make the eye were failures, the bone splitting when I tried to pierce it; but when I experimented with heating the knife first, it cauterized the bone sufficiently to make a hole.

Yarn was the next problem I had to solve. Although I could unravel strands of hemp or even pull threads from my already worn-out garments, I felt sure there must be some natural substance I could use, if only I had sense enough to realize it. For a long time I thought about it without results, and I might have continued to remain in ignorance had not my natural curiosity pointed the way.

Intrigued by the discovery that the tides were irregular, being sometimes high water for twenty-four hours at a time and at other times flowing tide and half tide—remaining high water for three or four hours before ebbing again—I had taken special interest in their measurement. In general there appeared to be one flood and one ebb every twenty-four hours, but after a gale the wind sometimes raised the level of the tide as much as twelve or fourteen feet above high water mark. After one such gale, going to the head of the peninsula to gauge the effect, I saw that it was strewn with the partly picked skeletons of some unidentifiable marine animals. They were not seals, being much larger in size, but were probably the remains of some type of whale or porpoise which had either been washed up and stranded on the shore by the abnormally high tide or else had been chased ashore by some fearful marine predator. Either way, they were to be a boon to me. On examining their carcasses with an eye that was mildly clinical, I detected long tendinous fibers near the fin and tail which were still partly covered by some of the muscle. Fascinated, I began extracting these tendons without any definite purpose, when I realized suddenly that they might serve as yarn. Closer scrutiny reinforced the idea, and hurrying back to the hut, I washed and split the tendons, stretching the fibers out so they could dry into fine strands. To my delight they made excellent sewing thread—strong and stretchy—and I had probably collected enough to last the winter. The discovery made me think hard about other possible sources of the commodity, and I decided that the elephant seals would be a certain provider when they returned.

The skins for clothing would need to be as supple as possible for comfort. I therefore took to stretching them hair side downwards on the floor of the hut after scraping the blubber from them and rubbing them over with sand and grit, using a flattish stone to avoid rubbing the skin off my hands. This process was highly efficient in cleaning the skins; but breaking down the fibers was a difficult and tedious task. I had stored a pile of skins in the hut without drying them properly first, and to my horror they had all rotted. I was obliged to work extra hard after this to save those that were still intact. I learnt the error of rushing a job without due care and reminded myself I could not afford any similar mistakes. Some of the skins I stretched across the ceiling of the hut to dry; but others I stretched out in the crisp frosty air outside whenever it was not damp or snowing. This had a desiccating effect and proved satisfactory, bleaching their undersides to a remarkable pale colour.

Once they were treated this way I could cut the skins up with reasonable ease before sewing them. I was thankful I had spent so much time sewing the sails aboard the ship. I was now able, with moderate skill, to work an overstitch across the seam that did nicely. The style and cut of the finished product left much to be desired, but I produced a pair of breeches and jacket that were at least functional. These I topped with a kind of bonnet made from the mane of the bull fur seal. It proved most serviceable, extending over the neck of my jacket to a good way down my shoulders. A more barbarous getup I could scarcely fashion; but I had nobody to impress with my appearance and only myself and Scruff to impress with my ingenuity.

One great advantage of the fur seal for clothing was its waterproof quality. I had, however, to remember to beat all the snow off before entering the hut, or it would have melted on the skins and made them wet—and wet skins take a long time to dry.

I soon realized that I needed two suits of clothing, since the skins could get wet inside with sweat, even in the cold weather, if I had been working strenuously or doing a lot of climbing. This sweat would later freeze, forming a layer of ice inside the fur that was both dangerous and uncomfortable. I would leave the clothes to dry in the entrance passage to the hut, fearing that too much heat might spoil them, but they always dried out like suits of armour and required a good deal of kneading and jumping on to make them manageable enough to put on. If some article of clothing got really wet, I would hang it near the fire over a drying rack, taking special care that it did not get too warm or too dry. While the care of clothes was a chore, I could not afford to ignore the discipline without running the risk of freezing to death.

I tried to make it a daily habit to spend some time out of the hut, not only for the purpose of replenishing my stocks of ice for water or bringing in more meat or blubber but also for the purpose of exercising Scruff, whose unused energy after too long indoors was in danger of erupting. Fortunately, she had a marvelous capacity to amuse herself by inventing games with a sealskin ball that I had made for her. Favourite among these games was anything that involved a pursuit. These she would join in with so much gusto that in no time at all the orderliness of our den was transformed into chaos. I would hide the ball or else she would hide it herself before pretending to go in search of it, dashing around the place while she pulled things out of corners and scattered them everywhere. Often she would come upon the ball and ignore it, pretending she had not seen it before suddenly pouncing upon it. I do believe she invested the ball with a life of its own. She frequently shook it and then dropped it, waiting and watching it intently, poised to pounce, half hoping it would run away. On some occasions I suspended it from a point in the celing to see what she would do, and she would leap delightedly at it, butting it with her nose in all directions. Even without these games I am sure she could have found something to amuse her. She was constantly exploring, rolling or shaking everything in the hope that it might respond.

She was quick to learn, even to the extent of recognizing several words, but in one matter Scruff insisted on doing things her own way, in spite of my encouragement to the contrary. I had hoped to train her to perform her natural functions outside or even in one corner of the hut set aside specially as a privy during bad weather. I am sure Scruff understood my intention, but she would not go along with this seemingly pointless rule of etiquette, preferring to relieve herself whenever she pleased. Not infrequently she chose different locations round the floor of the hut by way of letting me know that she had as much right to mark her territory as I did mine. Fortunately, the floor was constantly cold and these territorial claims froze solidly; but it was one bone of contention between us that was never resolved.

Most mornings I woke to see the walls glittering with frost. This melted and ran down the walls during the day to accumulate as icy stalagmites. These built up from the floor into a considerable cake of ice if left several days, engulfing any objects which lay in their way. I tried not to let the ice get too thick before I cleared it. Not only did it encroach on my penguin carpet, but it gave the hut a depressing effect, suggesting that the world outside was creeping in to encase me—and such morbid thoughts came more often now as the winter closed in upon us.

I was very worried that Scruff might succumb to the weather, it being an unnatural thing for her to be so far south during the coldest part of the year. I feared that her fur might not be warm enough for her to go outdoors, and I was anxious too that I might not be able to provide her with enough food. During the summer I had taken the precaution of drying the contents of several seals' stomachs to feed her on in the winter months. She liked and even thrived on this, but she had also grown accustomed to foraging for herself in her natural element, the sea. At first this presented no problem, and I expected she would still be able to fish for herself throughout the winter. What I had not counted on was there being so much ice in the bays, nor on there being days on end when we could barely move a few paces from the hut. Another serious cause for concern was the lack of shrimps to be found on the beaches in the wake of a northeaster or an easterly. Formerly the shore had been ankle-deep in them after a gale, and I could only assume it was the ice that was to blame. After a while I could not help wondering whether the colder weather had affected the concentration of these tiny sea creatures around the island, and whether they and the fish besides had migrated to warmer climes.

For the time being, however, we had food in plenty, and whenever the weather permitted I would take Scruff down to one of the beaches nearer the headland, which was not so ice-bound, due to the fast currents running there, and wait for her while she went in for her swim. I could wait as much as an hour or more for her to return, while I walked briskly up and down to keep warm, stamping my feet and flapping my arms as if I was doing some wild dance. Always when Scruff came ashore, I would roll her in the snow to absorb the water from her fur and prevent its freezing on the way home. This activity Scruff grew to accept as an essential part of some ritual, even rolling voluntarily of her own accord. Most days the activity developed into a game of rough-and-tumble, with me chasing her to make sure she kept warm. In this way she seemed to be adapting to the harshening weather, and I began to be more confident in her strength to survive.

13

The Big Storm

A month into winter Scruff and I were learning to cope with the restrictions and uncertainties of our lives, and I was proud of our achievement. There were odd moments when I became despondent and fearful for the future, but these moments rarely lasted. Scruff, sensing something amiss, would go out of her way to cheer me up, nuzzling me and rubbing her head against mine between bouts of affectionate nibbling and snuffling. Often, without even knowing what she did, she transformed my mood, and I never ceased to be amazed at her vitality. Joyfulness bubbled out of her, spilling over me, and frequently I laughed out loud at her unconscious humour and spontaneity.

The night of May 5, however, I could not shake off my unease. The sky was as black as the very devil, and a tension in the wind reminded me of the buildup to our worst storm at sea, when we had been almost devastated. The air had grown colder and colder. Though I felt warm enough initially, swaddled with furs, with Scruff snuggled as usual against my belly, my breath froze in droplets on the edge of the sleeping bag, and I had to draw it tightly around my head to prevent the latter from freezing completely. Usually I let the fire die down a bit overnight, but this time I heaped the crackling lumps of blubber onto it. Even so, the warmth was whipped away as if the hut were a meeting place for a thousand currents.

The noise of the elements was almost deafening, increasing in violence as the night wore on. What had begun as spasmodic rumblings grew until it became a roar which burst upon my ears with all the ferocity of attacking beasts, savaging and snarling. From the ice dome came staccato sounds like ice cracking and exploding; and the ground shook with the impact of masses of falling matter, suggesting avalanches of gigantic proportions. From all around sounds bombarded us—violent and destructive —until it seemed the world itself was being wrenched apart.

Despite my efforts to calm her, Scruff was in a high state of excitability. I myself was too disturbed by the unusual ferocity of the elements to relax enough to sleep, but she would not permit me to hide myself in the comforting protectiveness of my sleeping bag, butting me constantly with her nose to rouse me. Then she jumped from the platform where we lay, her whole body assuming an attitude of tense expectancy—almost alarm— and she whimpered constantly as a kind of challenge. This unnerved me in a subtle way, because it suggested a perception more heightened than my own, which was already terrified with so many strange imaginings.

What made it worse was that I thought I could hear the pounding roar of surf close at hand; yet the beach was icebound and three hundred yards away. Another thing I could not explain was the urgency of an inner voice prompting me to go outside, while common sense and my natural inclination would have me curl up near the fire, burying my head against the dreadful fantasies that were now filling it. Something malignant was unleashed about the place and had as its intention our destruction. In my imagination this phantom grew until I was quaking with fear. I could not help thinking how closely the world about me resembled some primeval age, and with that came imaginings of monsters that defied description. Terrified, I buried my head to try to forget the storm; but the muffled din, penetrating my sleeping bag, carried with it an even subtler menace than before.

With morning the storm had not let up; but at least some of my more wild imaginings had vanished with the darkness. Worn out with tiredness, I felt a blissful lassitude creep slowly over me, drowning my fear and making me indifferent to the elements. Having survived the night, I thought myself secure from anything the storm might threaten and confident enough to sleep, if Scruff would only let me. But, strangely, Scruff acted more uneasy than before and was more determined than ever to make me share her anxiety. She continued to whimper and run around, insensitive to commands or cajolings, pulling at the sleeping bag and butting me. Finally she bit my ear, making me jump with pain and rage. It was at that moment, when I scrambled from my bag to hit her, that there came a WHOOSH! Suddenly the entrance hatch blew out; part of the roof collapsed, and I fell to the ground beneath a heap of snow and rocks. Precious items, caught by the wind, vanished completely. Millions of whirling snow pellets stung my eyes, and I could not breathe because of the density of the incoming snow that clogged my mouth and nostrils.

I managed to form a protective canopy about my head while I tried to assess the damage. Fortunately my head and torso had been spared the brunt of falling stuff, but when I tried to move my legs an intense pain shot through one of them, making me cry out. At the same time Scruff, who had managed to avoid the cave-in, nuzzled up to me, pushing beneath the canopy of skins to blow steamy caresses into my face.

I was in a bad way. The fire was out—extinguished in a hissing flurry—and the roof gaped, letting in a smother of snow that settled thickly. Somehow I had to keep myself warm and relieve my legs from the crushing weight I realized was entrapping them. Without Scruff's help I doubt if I could have survived that ordeal. The difficulties of extricating my trapped limbs from the debris and dragging myself to what seemed like a safer place in the den were really quite beyond me. Scruff, sensing my helplessness, added her weight to my efforts and, in so doing, for the second time that winter saved my life. Even so I managed the operation with dangerous slowness, almost sobbing at times with the pain of my injury and the unbearable feeling of rawness, equivalent to being skinned alive, from the cold. At what stage I collapsed, I do not know; but Scruff must have lain on top of me keeping me warm for some time—all the while breathing near my face and keeping it clear of snow. When I woke I found the storm had abated and that the lower part of me was cocooned in a thick layer of drift.

I believe now that if Scruff had not been my companion—if I had been alone—I would quite possibly have given up the struggle. I could have just lain there in my sleeping bag until, too numb to worry about the cold, I could peacefully nod off into a permanent sleep. Death at times is strangely attractive compared with the painful effort necessary to survive. Now, with my habitation in shambles, my leg crushed, my toes probably all frostbitten, the fire out, half my gear blown away and what was left of the hut smothered in drift, I had little incentive to stay alive. And even if I wanted to, where should I start? Build a fire? I would have to clear the debris off it first, and chop fresh blubber. And how should I light it? I would be lucky if the tinderbox had not been sucked out along with other of my valuable possessions. And even if it was still in the hut, I would have to dig for it in the snowdrift. Meanwhile, what was I to do about my leg? Any movement sent pain shooting through my body to lodge in my brain like a quivering arrow. I felt sick and near to retching. My toes had long since lost any feeling, and I could not even tell whether they were moving when I tried to wriggle them. I had deep fears that they might be past saving as a result of being frozen for so long, and I could not bear to think of the consequence. And when, on top of all that, I considered what needed to be done to the hut, the whole enormity of my predicament struck me, and I sank back dejectedly.

Minutes passed while I lay inactive. One part of my mind toyed with the idea of death as the only relief from my misery and suffering, but another part of my intellect, or maybe even of my spirit, demanded that I justify any decision to die against the duty that I had to live to prove that I was a man. To give in now would be nothing short of betrayal and would make a mockery of everything I believed. And so, naggingly, the voice continued while my poor body lay inert, too weak to protest.

Bitterly I yelled that I was finished, that I had endured enough and that I deserved the right to die. I became aware then of Scruff crying and pressing her body against my own half-dead one as if in need of reassurance. Suddenly my one and only duty was clear. Scruff! How could I forget her? There flashed before my mind the vision of the lonely, desolate orphan seal I would be abandoning if I were to die. And it was this thought rather than any other that I nurtured and that gave me the sense of obligation I needed at that moment in order to live.

I still wonder from where I drew the strength to cope with the many difficulties and hardships of the next few days, but somehow I mobilized my slender physical resources. Much of what I did remains a blank in my memory, presumably because my injuries and weakness induced some kind of daze in me. I do remember that every act was done slowly and with great deliberation. At first, my priorities were confused, because they were all so vital. I confirmed, at least, that my leg was not broken, although it was badly bruised and sprained. The frost had killed three of the toes. They looked horribly black and would probably soon be gangrenous; yet I decided to worry about them later, for mercifully they had no feeling. As long as the leg was kept in motion, it would heal, albeit painfully, but if, for any reason, the flow of blood should cease and the whole limb turn gangrenous, I would have to amputate the leg, and I doubted very much my capacity to perform this grizzly act, let alone to live through it. Faintness seized me several times before I had a chance to make enough bandages to wrap the painful swelling around the ankle; but once it was supported in this fashion, the leg movement was less of a torture.

To describe all the misery of the next few days would be too harrowing, if not too self-indulgent. A thousand times I had to make a special act of will, and they were all agonizing. Providence, however, did grant me one favour in the discovery of the tinderbox. I could have wept with gratitude. It still took an age to light the fire, for my hands were frozen solid. With the neces-

sity of putting some form of roof on my shelter before the
weather worsened again, I set about clearing a way before literally dragging myself outside to make my repairs. Fortunately the
snowdrifts around the hut had reached roof level, and it required
only the excavation of a few broad steps in the slope to make a
natural stairway. But why had the roof caved in? It was a mystery. I was in no state of mind to answer that at the time, but on
reflection it seemed to me that the way I had built the roof had
been correct. It had not collapsed but had been lifted by the
strong vacuum created when the door was broached.

In spite of my resolve to defy my difficulties, I was many
times tempted to give in. Every little act required the most enormous physical and mental effort. The heavy burden of work fell
on my hands, which were pitifully swollen and covered with
enormous blisters. Worse still, the matter inside the blisters had
frozen and turned to ice. Rubbing against the raw flesh underneath like sandpaper, it caused the most awful agony. There was
a jarring pain every time I moved my leg, and every minute in
the cold added to the torment of my swollen and frostbitten feet.
At times I collapsed and howled from the sheer unremitting
weight of suffering.

Although reduced to a crawling, whimpering parody of a
human, I struggled to retain a sense of decency. In my worst
moments, Scruff showed herself most attentive, making me
believe she understood completely. At all times she offered her
body and her affection as warmth and comfort. Though dumb,
the creature was wonderfully expressive, and I was uplifted to
know that such a beautiful, intelligent creature cared for me. In
all the darkness of my isolation she was the one constant ray of
light.

Repairing the roof was a herculean task, the more so since my
injuries had left me uncoordinated. Balancing myself while at the
same time hauling up and setting the skins back in place was an
almost impossible strain. I retrieved a large skin which I managed
with great difficulty to throw over the hole, and this I anchored
with stones at the edges. However, I could not build up the roof
towards the middle as I had done previously, and the stones that
I put in place fell through repeatedly. Depressed beyond measure

at my successive failures, I was reduced to crying and shouting with frustration. Only when my eye caught sight of the wedges of snow I had cut from the drift to make steps did it occur to me that they could be used for building.

Experimenting with a model first, I became convinced of their practicality. From the far reaches of my memory, I recalled the knowledge that there was a race of people, living on the northern boundaries of the world, who lived in snow houses. It is extraordinary how in the depths of despondency a single achievement can be uplifting. The realization that the hard-packed snow could be cut into suitable slablike pieces gave me the strength to transcend the pain that I was finding so crippling.

I discovered through error in cutting one of the slabs, making it lopsided, that if I put the snow blocks together in a certain way they formed a natural dome. And if I filled the cracks with loose snow, packed firmly, I could seal them by covering the joinings with water which then froze. With the roof completed satisfactorily, I put my mind to how I would deal with the entrance passage. After some consideration I concluded that instead of rebuilding it I should block most of it off, excavating a tunnel instead through one of the deep drifts that ran at right angles to it. This tunnel would serve to deflect the wind from rushing into the main part of the hut; and, by hanging a skin at the juncture of the two passages, I could not only exclude the draught but provide an easy exit and entrance for Scruff without my having to get up to open a door. In stormy or windy weather I could use a slab of snow to act as a temporary door, which I could seal at the edges with loose snow and cut through when we wanted to get out.

These tasks took me well into the next day, with only occasional rests to eat and get warm. I was exhausted by the time they were finished. Yet tired as I was, I dared not sleep before I had seen to my leg. The left foot was now swollen badly—so much in fact that I had to take off my boot and wrap the foot with loose sealskin to keep it warm. The bandage was satisfactory, but I had to remove it from time to time to massage life into the limb. Such action was always painful, but it was as nothing compared to the treatment necessary on my foot. The frostbitten toes were a revolting sight at the extremity of my puffy limb, being black and putrid-looking where the skin had been rubbed off the flesh. The fact gradually registered on my tired and distressed mind that sooner or later I would have to take the knife to them and cut them away from the still-living flesh. How to get the courage to do this, though, I could not answer, yet every moment I wasted threatened the health of the rest.

I spent a miserable few hours trying to gather my strength for the ordeal. I kept my feet away from the heat of the fire, for any intense heat drew the blood to them with terrible painfulness. Suddenly it occurred to me that if my foot were numb I would not feel the toes being amputated. Only later on, when they began to thaw, would I react to the pain. This insight helped me overcome my reluctance to do what was necessary. In order to prepare for the operation, I crawled to the end of the passage and stuck the injured leg out in the cold. My foot was not long in losing its feeling, and I did not take long either, once I had found the courage and the will, to cut away the frozen, dead bits of flesh. Grotesque stubs of bone remained, the sight of which made me feel strangely queasy, and I had quite a bit of difficulty severing these at the joint. As I had predicted, the operation was painless, but I knew that before long the returning warmth, no matter how gently applied, would have me writhing and screaming in an agony that would not let up.

14

Aftermath

Several days after the great storm I felt strong enough to leave the hut. Scruff, meanwhile, finding the exit open most of the time, took to going out on her own, a habit I encouraged. That she went swimming I could tell by the way little clumps of ice clung to her pelt, and the knowledge relieved me. The last thing I wanted was for Scruff to be restricted because of my disabilities. My leg was too painful for me to exercise more than absolutely necessary. Had I not sprained my ankle I might have taken a walk to the beach, even before repairing the hut, to see if the storm had brought any major changes. In fact, it was a good thing that I could not range too far afield so soon after the disaster, since there was yet another shock in store for me. Two major calamities, following rapidly one after the other without the chance to recoup in the meantime, would no doubt have completely discouraged me if they had not sent me out of my mind altogether. Fortunately, fate has a way of holding her punches at times, long enough for man to recover from one barrage before she blasts him again with body-breaking blows.

I had enough meat and blubber in the hut to keep me going

for a week or so, and rather than drag myself outside to collect ice for water I used the clean snow that had settled inside the hut. Much of the drift had frozen solid against the floor and walls and required chipping off, but I felt too weak to clear it. To a certain extent I was able to come to terms with the perpetual throbbing pain in my foot and leg; other times it seemed unbearable. Most of my hours I spent huddled into my sleeping bag, moving out of it only for essentials—hacking meat off the lump suspended in one corner of the hut for each meal and delving into the blubber store for more fuel. Scruff must have intuitively sensed my suffering and let me rest instead of worrying me to be playful.

Though sleep was fitful, I tried dozing as a way to forget my misery. I would wake from sleep to find myself whimpering and feeling sorry for myself—even to the extent that I wished I would die and end it all. But then Scruff would nuzzle up to me, rubbing her nose against mine and asking to be petted. When I hugged her, she would respond by squirming affectionately and giving me squally "kisses." And in some extraordinary way, these demonstrations of fondness went a long way towards ridding me of my despair and restoring my spirits.

With the disappearance of a spare pair of boots and one or two other items of apparel in the gale, I was obliged to knuckle down to the task of replacing them. I had not counted on the unholy difficulty of sewing skins with hands that were tender and swollen and covered with suppurating blisters. To be any use, the sinew had to be drawn taut, but in my present condition I could take only about fifteen or twenty stitches a day. This meant that I would need days to produce an inner sock of penguin skin and an outside sealskin boot. I compromised on the latter by using a single piece of sealskin with the hair worn inside for warmth. This I folded across the front and tied around the ankle. Worn with the wooden soles that I held in place by thongs threaded through holes gouged round the edge of them, these proved quite serviceable and guarded against stubbing the sore stumps of my toes, which bled easily and were often painful.

Finally, tired of being indoors for so long and feeling an urge to accompany Scruff to the beach to watch her swim, I hobbled out into the pale sunlight. Scruff, sensing my change in morale, was excited and gambolled round, occasionally making a feint as if to pounce, only to check herself at the last minute before bounding away. After she had done this a few times, I caught her and, bowling her over, rolled her from side to side before pelting her with snow. Deliriously excited now, she jumped up, twisting about exuberantly until, by accident rather than by design, she went shooting down a slope on her belly, followed not long after by me on my behind. Seeing her so happy gave me a surge of strength, and I covered the ground to the beach without too much difficulty, much to my surprise.

Once there she raced ahead of me, moving with such a beautiful, galloping, lighthearted motion that I could do nothing but gaze after her admiringly as she disappeared over the rocks towards the farther beach, from where she usually liked to take her swim in the sea. So distracted had I been by her delightful exuberance that it took a while for the significance of the various changes around me to sink in. Lining the beach at its landward extremity was a low rampart of broken icebergs littered with clumps of seaweed and odd bits of driftwood. These were nothing extraordinary in themselves, merely the debris of any tide wrack, but how they had got there, so far inland, nearly one hundred yards beyond the normal reach of the highest tide mark —that was something to stretch the imagination, for it presupposed a gigantic freak wave the dimensions of which I had never seen and never hoped to see either. There was something terrifying about such magnitude, something unearthly, reserved only for those mythical places inhabited by giants or fearsome gods.

I hurried as best I could in the circumstances, aware of a sense of foreboding, and soon saw evidence that confirmed the very worst of my fears. Scattered here and there, where they had been stranded, were penguin corpses, frozen pathetically in their bedraggled state. Beyond them, the caches, which had been so carefully banked around with stones, were empty, and only a few remants of seal meat were left between the remaining rocks. Of the main carcasses I had cached, there was no sign, nor were there any of the skins I had put aside for clothes.

The irony of being devastated by a tidal wave when I had just begun to feel some sense of achievement in logging the extremes and irregularities of the tides was not lost on me, but I had no humour at that moment to enjoy the subtlety. So cruel a joke only served to strengthen my suspicion that the island was indeed possessed of some malignant spirit who toyed with me for his own perverse pleasure, prolonging my agony and uncertainty until he tired of the game, at which time he would decide on some ultimate method for my destruction.

I had little hope that any of my caches on the other beach were intact, and when I was able to make that arduous journey across the peninsula to inspect them, I found that their contents had all been swept away. What was alarming, besides the loss of food, was the destruction of the barrels that had housed my blubber. At least with enough heat we would have an even chance to survive the winter, but with the loss of so much food and fuel the chances were slim that we could come through alive. Some meat and blubber were still cached midway between the two beaches, and I had the sealskin bag half full of blubber in the hut. Even with the strictest economy, however, I could not see how we could last till the wildlife returned in the spring. Shocked as I was by the awful discovery, I did not collapse from it and cower, close to despair. On the contrary, I raged at it, the bitterness spreading through me being in some way revitalizing. It urged me to keep a grip on myself, if only to cheat the devil of his prize.

Obviously, I could not tell how much I would have to ration myself until I had examined the other caches thoroughly and seen what was left. Meanwhile, I could do a rough calculation as to when the wildlife was likely to return. Today was May 13 by my calendar, and the wildlife had been absent, except for a few stragglers, about five or six weeks. Once midwinter passed, which should occur around June 21, I might have, at a guess, ten to twelve weeks before the animals started to come back. Less maybe, if we could rely on a few early arrivals to precede the rest. They, I reflected, were going to be vital to us, starving as we would be by then. By now I felt no sentiment at the thought of killing any animal. Life was teaching me that survival makes

171

its own rules, demanding the sacrifice of the weak to the strong and the innocent to the cunning. A certain stubbornness of will was also beginning to exert itself, almost beyond the level of conscious self, and it considered nothing too ruthless in the struggle against nature.

The journey up to the highlands and across to the other beach was made with great pain and difficulty—not only because of the injury to my leg but because the surface of the terrain had altered so much since the last big storm. Learning from previous mistakes, I had the good sense to take some sealskin roping, which I attached to rocks to pull me along, marking the route at the same time in case the weather should deteriorate before I returned. After spending quite some time locating my inland cache, I decided it would be advisable to ferry it all back to the hut so that I would not have to make the arduous trek again.

If I wanted exercise I could get it near the beach. An interesting new feature of the winter-bound peninsula had been the formation of a causeway around the perimeter of the coast, created by the moisture on the rocks freezing at low tide and being built upon with every fall of tide. A broad strong pathway of ice was thereby formed on which I could easily travel, even with my bad leg, to the previously inaccessible beaches farther round. The sea ice, which now reached several feet of thickness in places, floated in huge heavy slabs on the sea, rising and falling with the tide. The great broken hinge of ice that attached it to the land occasionally groaned and creaked with weird effect.

Rather than carry the food and fuel that had been cached inland, which would have been a strain, I dragged it all the way, soliciting Scruff's help by attaching a rope and a kind of harness to her. Whatever I asked her to do she performed with enthusiasm, and together we managed to shift all of the cache.

I continued to accompany Scruff on her swimming excursions on fine days. While she was swimming, I would try to fish, but my efforts to catch anything were hopeless failures. I wished I could persuade Scruff to hunt for me. Although I still fed her, she was obviously foraging for herself, but there was no way I could tell if she was getting enough. Time no doubt would let me know, but for the present, she seemed wonderfully healthy.

Frequently Scruff swam out of sight. If she was away too long, I would become distressed, thinking she had met with some predator or that she had decided not to come back. I would hang around fretting and angry while getting more and more lonesome and chilled by the cold. When she did return, the look of satisfaction on her face would turn to joyous recognition when she saw me, and I could never bring myself to chide her as I had intended. I would, however, yell to stop her bounding up to me before she had rolled in the snow to absorb the excess moisture.

In this way, we continued without too much change in our lives, even with the start of my rationing. Pleasures were so few that what joys there were I did not want to waste. But then, amidst all the hardship, I would be brought up short by some unexpected aspect of beauty in the most unlikely places, as, for example, in the discovery of ice flowers that could form on new sea ice. These, made up of gorgeous clusters of feathery crystals set amongst delicate needles of ice, were like the symbol of some benevolent presence existing alongside all the lurking evil. As such, they had the power to transform my mood from boredom or frustration to one of wonder and delight.

I shall never forget the beauty of the auroras when, on dark nights, the light split into a thousand gossamer veils that shimmered as they danced and whirled in sinuous motion—pink dissolving into a silver greyness shot through with a luminous and brilliant green. At such moments, nature seemed under the influence of some divine command, and I would be left with such a feeling of rapture that one might have thought I had seen a glimpse of heaven itself.

15

Winter Routine

The weeks till midwinter passed with dreary monotony, storm following storm with very little relief. Cold and wretched, we were confined for long stretches inside the hut without sight of the sun for days on end. Food being of necessity rationed so strictly, the satisfaction of mealtimes was a good deal reduced. In spite of this, meals remained the day's highlight. What was also disheartening was having to ration fuel—the fire being as much a source of cheer as a source of heat in our present circumstances; but cut down I had to on the size of the blaze, and the lamp was a luxury that had to go.

With the hut being as large as it was, the heat from the reduced fire was soon dissipated. I was obliged to gather all my spare skins together to make a kind of tent, which I suspended from one of the rafters in the roof, practically encompassing the fire together with my bunk. While this expedient was successful in conserving the heat, it greatly restricted our movement. The hut became darker still, with the result that I often felt depressed and gloomy, and using skins for this purpose would cut down the amount available for clothing. My sole consolation was that there would be little wear and tear on the suit if I was confined to the hut for what could amount to several weeks.

When it was possible to go outside, I could only bear to remain in the open for a couple of hours at most. The cold was so penetrating that if I breathed deeply my lungs felt on fire. Worse than the cold, however, which I might have got used to, was the wind, which, acting alone or in concert with the cold, seemed to shrivel the very marrow inside my bones. It blew constantly, at varying intensity, shrieking down from the ice dome or along the beach. Occasionally, it hurtled me to leeward; at other times, it stabbed and hacked at me where I stood. Even indoors I could not forget it. It howled down the chimney and shook the ground beneath us as masses of snow or ice nearby avalanched under the fierce pressure of its assault. Often the air was so thick with snow that, beyond a few feet, nothing was visible. Not even Scruff would dare go out into the awful flying greyness that lay beyond.

Lacking any stimulus from outside, Scruff and I, more than ever, were forced to look to each other for entertainment and comfort. Luckily for Scruff, I had a reasonable amount of frozen seal stomachs that I thawed out in the hut before feeding her the mush inside them. I made even her conform to a pattern of reduced meals, fearful lest a prolonged bout of bad weather prevent her from going for a swim and foraging in the sea. I was glad now that I had had the foresight to bring all my food down from the highland cache, for much of the time it would have been inaccessible. Apart from this, such a trip, even in good weather, would have required a lot of energy. The short excursions I made down to the beach and back made me hungry, and I always returned with the very devil of an appetite, which was barely gratified by the lessened amounts I allowed myself.

If, on the one hand, I encouraged myself with the knowledge that once midwinter passed the days would grow lighter, I had forgotten to take into account that they would also be colder. I was obliged to use more fuel than I had allowed in my rationing to get through this most difficult stretch. For a couple of weeks I tried a greatly reduced fire throughout the day and night, but even this proved too much drain on the resource. I was finally obliged to keep the fire going at a minimal level for only a few hours a day. Cooking became nothing more than a mere formality. I would place small portions of meat and snow in the kettle and hang it over the fire to let the ingredients parboil. The soup, if you could call the anemic concoction thus produced by so grand a name, was the only liquid there was to drink. And some of this I shared with Scruff who sucked it up, her tongue being too short for her to lap.

Hacking or sawing away at a large piece of frozen meat for my allotted ration was tiring and difficult. I became increasingly childish and bad-tempered as a result and often ended by putting very much more than I should in the kettle. The gesture had about it a kind of peevish defiance, and I would recklessly guzzle the lot. The satisfaction I got from doing this always seemed well worth the folly at the time. Not only did it bespeak a belly gloriously full, it also provided the sort of victory over circumstances that I needed to sustain me.

On odd days, having nothing to take my mind off my hunger, I gave in to my appetite and allowed myself a real tuck-in feast. I would tell myself that something would turn up before too long which would compensate for the amount I had "stolen." Nothing edible ever did materialize—what's more, I knew in my heart it would not.

I could never have believed there existed such coldness. And I was never so grateful for the warmth of Scruff's body. Without her as my bedfellow I surely would have died. The nights were so cold the air crackled when we breathed. We had to confine ourselves to the sleeping bag, with only the smallest of openings through which to draw a breath. The worst time for me was the start of each morning. My body would shrink from the necessity to leave the bag and face the rigours of yet another day. Scruff, however, always made her escape long before I did and took it upon herself to harass me playfully until I got up. She would invent all manner of physical inducements to remove me from the bag while I tried to resist her tuggings and buffetings, snuggling deeper into the warmth she had vacated. I am sure if she had not insisted that I get up I would have stayed in the bag all day.

Upon my arising, my breath would create a fog in the tent, and I would bite my cracked lips to keep from complaining at the pain in my permanently swollen hands as I fumbled with the tinderbox to light the fire. When this was lighted I would have to knead my boots, which had frozen stiff. The day's routine was pitiful, my chores amounting to collecting the ice or snow that went into the kettle alongside whatever meat was at hand. I pounded the blubber to extract the oil. This ignited more easily than a lump of blubber, and I needed a steady supply of oil to sustain the flame. I chopped Scruff's food to make it easier for her to eat. Everything was an effort because of the condition of my hands. Washing was now completely out of the question. I compromised by scraping the thick layer of soot off my face and clothes. The problem with getting the skins so greasy was that they lost their insulating qualities, and the weather was too cold to allow me to remove my clothes to clean them as I had done earlier in the winter.

If the weather was fine I went to the beach. I got out of breath quickly and had to rest frequently. Every time, I searched intently along the tidemark, hoping for some washed-up morsel or some overlooked scraps from the caches to fill my empty stomach. In spite of my repeated scavenging, not a scrap of food was to be found. The ice cut off all our supply of shrimps; and even when tempests broke up the sea ice in the cove, nothing that resembled food could get through the icy rampart that protected the shore.

Scruff continued to swim, cold as it was. She would race along the frozen causeway and dive into the first pool of water, looking up and almost chittering with pleasure before disappearing out of sight. I was enormously relieved that there was still some open water around for her to swim in, turbulent as it always was. At least this way there was a chance she could find food for herself that I could not provide. Often I would feel too chilled to wait for her to come back and would have to return alone to the hut. Besides, there was nothing I could do to help her should she get into any difficulty in the water, no more than I could muster my former energy for the rough-and-tumble games we used to play as a way of keeping her from freezing when she came in to land.

Returning home, I could do nothing but crawl back into my sleeping bag, hoping to dispel the pangs in my stomach by sleeping the hours away. I had intended to get much done during the winter—observations and a log of the weather, sewing, and even a bit of carving on some elephant seal teeth. These I had dug out of scattered jawbones and cleaned up so they would be ready to be worked on, but I had not foreseen the poor condition of my hands or the dimness of the flickering light from the fire. In any case, the weather and the surroundings did not predispose me to do any work. As an alternative, I tried recalling poems I had learnt and some of the many stories I had read as a youth. My poor brain, however, was incapable of concentrating on anything.

Sleep might have been possible if my bunk had been more comfortable. Since I had been obliged to remove some of the skins that had formed a mattress in order to make up the tent, the moss, which had been a spongy protection from the roughness of the stones, was reduced to a crumble, and I had very little to cushion me other than the skin of the sleeping bag. As a result I spent much of my time tossing and twisting to find some vaguely comfortable place among all the many knobs—an almost hopeless endeavour. My body was covered with so many tender spots and so many patches where my clothing had rubbed against my skin that, between these and the constant pains of hunger, I could not relax.

I had formed the habit each night, as the last formal act before going to sleep, of crossing off my calendar with a mark that represented another day. The calendar was a simple affair—a small piece of planking that doubled as a table top when balanced on my knees. Frequently I forgot to mark the date, or at least I began to suspect that I had forgotten it, and so started adding more notches to the calendar to make up the deficit. Eventually I knew that I had lost all real track of time. I kept telling myself that spring was just round the corner. With the weather so bad, however, I had no definite evidence of the lengthening of the days. Midwinter, I knew definitely, had long passed, even if my calendar showed no special sign to commemorate the importance or significance of that day. Here and there I discovered some strange hieroglyphics that I had no recollection of ever making, nor could I decide whether they were intended to signify the passage of a day or were merely wishful thinking. In fact, judging the passing of the hours was extremely difficult. Time seemed to drag interminably, and the gloom in my den was the same both night and day. I often could not tell whether it was three, four or five days that I had been forced to remain indoors. One consequence was that I could be greatly mistaken about the amounts to which I rationed myself, and I strongly suspected that I would run out of food far sooner than I had originally anticipated.

I depended more and more on Scruff for reassurance. When she was present, the hut was filled with a joyousness that was replaced when she was absent by a frightening and evil presence—an irrational fear of being haunted by the ghosts of the dead men for not having prayed sufficiently over their bodies. Frequently I would be brought up hard, with all my senses alert and suspicious, which reaction suggested that my subconscious was aware of something that my conscious self denied. Often I was sure I heard footsteps crunching on the snow outside, and I would find myself cowering with terror by the time Scruff returned. No sooner was she back, however, than she would go racing round the den, prancing and snuffing into the darkest corners in a way that I took to have much more significance than the mere defining of territory. I believed she too sensed something evil lurking in the corners, and this was her way of telling me of it. Reassured by her actions I would urge her on, at which encouragement she would tumble over herself with sheer exuberance, twisting and balancing her body in all sorts of ecstatic postures as though such unsolicited approval from me was too much to contain. My morbid fears would then retreat to wait for those moments of loneliness before creeping out again to haunt me.

16

The Intruder

As my stocks of food dwindled, I could not believe I had eaten them all myself. Going to my larder to retrieve some particular portion of meat I expected to be there, I would find it missing and would fly into a violent rage, yelling that it had been stolen. Scruff was not the culprit, of that I was certain. What food I had in solid form was not to her liking. No, this had to be some other creature, human or beast, alive or in some spirit form, that was raiding our store. In time I was convinced that I had seen it.

For a long while now, I had been a prey to horrific fantasies. They had begun with noises I could not explain that emanated from all over the peninsula. Strangely animal on occasions, like a moaning or howling, they might turn to squeals and screeches that set my flesh creeping. Judging by the noises I could identify on my own beach, I should have realized these were nothing ominous. Had I not discovered that the sounds of ice under pressure ranged from a creaking and cracking like timber splitting to the yelping of an animal in pain, or yet again a cannon exploding? I told myself the noises had a harmless origin and were simply another example of nature's variety, but I still failed to ease my mind. When the wind blew from certain directions, forcing its way through narrow apertures of my shelter, it sounded to my ears so maniacal and menacing that I was totally unnerved.

I might have got over this fear had not a sense of hostility been transmitted by the surroundings themselves, convincing me I was in mortal danger. I dreaded going outside in the dark, and if I had to fetch in a supply of ice or stores, I would turn on my heel repeatedly or sidestep suddenly to avoid being attacked from behind. I was obsessed with the belief that I was being watched by someone or something big and evil. I kept my knife to hand and sharpened finely to parry any wild attack. And although I might laugh when we returned unharmed to our hut after an excursion, blaming all my fears on an overexcited imagination, the threat remained and grew larger in my mind.

One day, out with Scruff in the half darkness, I was stopped abruptly in my tracks by the sight of a solitary figure lurking in the shadows near the graves. It stopped moving when I stopped and moved again when I moved. I screamed at Scruff to call her off when she began dashing towards it. Terrified, I stood there watching it, and it stood where it was staring back at me—although, in truth, I could not actually see its face, for it was standing in the shadows near the cliffs, no doubt aware that the dark backdrop would disguise it. Finally I summoned my courage to shout at it and struck a threatening posture with the lance I had begun to carry with me, hoping to frighten the creature into running away. It stood its ground, however, appearing the more fearful to me because of its silence until, scared out of my wits, I myself retreated.

For several days afterwards I could hardly bear to leave the hut. I barricaded the entrance and would not let Scruff out lest she be killed or attacked. And listening, more alert than usual, I was sure I could hear the crunch of snow compressed underfoot from some heavy creature prowling around the hut. I was too afraid to go to sleep; and when I did, I was harried by nightmares of the creature. Writhing, I would awake to find Scruff nuzzling up to me as if she knew of such dreams and were trying to comfort me. Worn to a shred of my former self by fear and the debilitating effects of cold and hunger, I would hug and sob over her, relieved and grateful beyond words for her affection.

Even the closest intimates, however, are inadequate in the face of certain forces, and those powerful, dark elements that spread their influence throughout the winter were more than a match for me. Soon not even Scruff could release me from the terror that rampaged through the corridors of my mind day and night. What had begun in dreams had merged into reality. I could no longer tell where the nightmares ended and the reality began.

One day I actually believed that I saw my tormentor raiding my cache. He appeared more and more often, always lurking in the shadow of the rocks near the hut, making it impossible to get a good look at him. Every day there was fresh evidence that he had been at my food store, and I feared that the day was near when all the food would be gone and he would come to the hut to look for me. I was so weak with fright that I was almost too timid to draw a breath in case he would hear me. I dreaded stepping outside and became a prisoner within the walls of my den, starving while he stole, unchallenged, the last remaining morsel of my food.

Goaded by the very devils of hunger, I worked myself into a state of frenzy. Determined to rid myself of the creature once and for all or be killed by him in the struggle, I sharpened my lance to a rapier fineness. More to give myself courage than to frighten my tormentor. I began banging the kettle and screaming the most terrifying cries that a frightened man can utter. When I emerged from the den, I at first caught no sign of him, but as my eyes grew accustomed to the darkness I saw him over by the graves. Fear drove me on—fear that unless I killed this man, I would die the worst death a human being can suffer: I would die with shame and cowardice.

I closed on my tormentor. Screaming in rage and terror I charged, aiming my lance directly at the broad expanse of his chest. The lance struck, shattering the shaft and knocking me backwards with the solidness of the blow. I lay there winded for a minute or two, too horrified to glance at the creature I had attacked. How much longer I would have lain there had Scruff not joined me and started sniffing around I do not know. Her very evident lack of concern finally forced me to open my eyes. Some time elapsed before the full absurdity of what I had done finally registered in my brain. The "creature" that I had attacked with my lance was not any more of a threat to my life than the very ground on which I now lay. What I had struck was a peculiarly wind-fretted boulder of rock.

So fevered had my imagination become that I had created a terrible phantom which, but for my last ounce of self-respect, might well have been the tragic cause of my self-destruction. With my realization of this, my relief was so great that I broke down and wept uncontrollably. Alas, my sense of relief was short-lived. Before my body and mind had recovered, the full and awful significance of my battle with the boulder dawned within me, bringing to light a deeper fear—that I was going insane. My hallucinations were merely the symptoms of a disturbed and unbalanced state of mind. It was not enough that I realized this. The discovery of such a tragic affliction was no guarantee of its cure. I was clearly going out of my mind, and nothing could check my inevitable decline into the mire of black insanity except the food my body needed—and of this food I now had none.

17

Desperation

From the decrease in storms and the vague calculations that my calendar inspired, I judged that winter must soon be over. The ice, though broken up, still blocked the bay, and I had no way of knowing when the animals would return or if, after they did, I would have the strength to slaughter them.

My body was in a pitiable state. My teeth were loose in swollen gums and my arms and legs quite wasted. My ribs could be counted through the thickness of my clothes, and where my belly had once been, there was now only a cavity. All I thought about was food, and all I dreamt about were meals I had eaten in the past or meals I would gorge on in the future. Mercifully I had a greater inclination to sleep these days, which alleviated some of my agony. I frequently awoke to find myself chomping on the coverings.

I was sure the end was near. I had done all I could that was humanly possible to survive and was still faced with a desperate and hopeless situation that only a miracle could solve. The chill of death that had harassed me so long from without was gradually taking hold of my inner core. In the last few days I had thought increasingly of home and of my parents and had come close to tears at the realization of what heartbreak my desertion must have caused them. Grieving for myself and the affection I had lost, my mind would ramble in various directions—clear and lucid or confused and woolly—until some animal impulse would drag me back to thoughts more practical.

Food! My mind searched every possible place for food. I crawled around the hut with the lamp, ransacking every nook and cranny. I spent hours chopping away at the ice that encrusted the lower portion of the hut in the hope of finding even some minute morsel, but I only succeeded in tiring myself out and adding to my depression. I had never known hunger could be so demanding or so indiscriminating. Finding a leather belt amongst my gear, I had it chewed and eaten before I even knew what I was doing, losing two teeth in the process. It satisfied the need to chew something, if not the irrepressible demands of the stomach. It also gave me an idea for my next collation, which was to dig out the old pair of worn boots I had thrown aside long before the start of winter.

The ground was hard—rock solid—with several feet of snow packed firm all around the hut. I had not much to dig with, the pickax I had found on the beach earlier in the season being lost somewhere in a drift when I had carelessly left it outside one night. All I could use was my knife. With this I stabbed the iron crust of snow as I would an animal that deliberately tried to keep from me the bits of sustenance my body craved.

I scratched and scraped, clearing away pitiful handfuls in a frustrating endeavour. In spite of my attempts to husband my strength, resting between each desperate effort, I was quickly exhausted. My overwrought mind nevertheless forced me to resume my search. I scrabbled aimlessly all over the place in a hopeless scramble to explore more ground. Finally, in the middle of the honeycomb I had created, I hacked at the snow in almost maniacal rage.

Returning to the hut, I began gnawing on small bits of sealskin, swallowing handfuls of the stuff between disgorged mouthfuls of hair. Every day for the last two weeks I had vainly searched the beach for shrimps and stood fishing for as long as I could bear through holes in the ice. I had caught nothing, nor had I the slightest indication that there were still fish in the sea to be had. Even the small squids I spotted one day in an upturned piece of ice I could not count as a sign of changing fortune. They so upset my stomach that for hours I lay in an agony of retching that only made me weaker.

I had by now given up the fire and used only the lamp, burning small pieces of blubber, together with the oil that I had extracted from them by pounding. The sight of crisp little slivers was too much for me, and I fished these out and swallowed them before I realized what I was doing, going on to dip small squares of seal hide into the shallow dish to soak up the oil in my despairing need for something to eat. I dreaded the day the lamp should be extinguished, less for the horrors of the darkness than for the fear that it would presage the extinction of my own feeble and flickering life. Scruff evidently suffered no undue hardship in spite of staying indoors with me for days on end with very little food. Obviously nature had adapted her quite well to periods of feast and famine. While thinner after a prolonged period without food, she lost little of her strength.

These days, the weather being very much more tranquil, she took herself off to her haunts beyond the cove from which she would return, refreshed from her swim and no doubt replete from having been able to eat her fill. At first, I was greatly relieved that she could forage, for we had run out of seal stomachs. Then there came a day, I am ashamed to say, when her very exuberance and rude health acted as an affront. I would like to be able to excuse what followed as the natural outcome of all the hardships I had endured. Truly I do believe the unremitting physical demands of the body had affected my mind. Excusable or not, however, I found myself beginning to feel an extraordinary resentment of my seal companion because she could feed herself and had no understanding of how much I, too, needed food. Because she was growing and thriving while I was becoming thinner and weaker, her very joyfulness and vitality became irritating to the point of being unbearable. I was resentful beyond reason. My jealousy and anger grew, and my black feelings finally broke.

Instead of greeting her as I usually did, I ignored her when she
returned to the hut, going so far as to strike her and push her off
when she bounded up on the platform to nuzzle me. I made her
lie on the ground and forbade her to come near me for several
hours. She lay so meekly that I finally relented with a sense of
shame. Calling her to me, I petted her lovingly. She responded to
my peacemaking with a touch of caution before, realizing I was
in earnest, she snuffed and nibbled at me, pushing her face into
my own with unrestrained devotion.

I was to be more cruel the next day when she returned from
her swim. Scruff had been away longer than usual, which put me
on edge as I waited for her return. I hoped she had fed well. I
was plagued with the worst hunger pains I had ever experienced
and had writhed away the night gnawing at the edges of the
skins that still served as a sort of tent.

It being reasonably windless, I left the doorway open to
enable me to see her returning. I did not want her to catch sight
of me before she was inside. I watched breathlessly for her, anxious lest I would have to close up the opening because of the
cold before she appeared.

There she was at last, bounding up towards the hut from the
beach. Hiding in the shadows, I saw her hesitate a few yards
from the hut, perhaps sensing with that special intuition of hers
that something was amiss. She stopped at the entrance, and I
could hear her sniffing. As she came inside the passage, she moved
hesitantly. I had built up the flame of the lamp in order to see her
better, not wanting to be thwarted in my intention. As she stood
there, I was reminded of the gracefulness of her head and neck
and of the sleekness of her body. Her eyes, which for a long time
I had been too indifferent to notice, had grown more beautiful
than ever over the months, heightening her look of intelligence
and gentleness. But I was more callous at that moment then I
had ever been before, and I was not to be stopped by considerations of beauty.

I coaxed her in, talking to her softly while she entered falter-
ingly, trusting and yet unsure, frightened and yet terribly brave
—her fear showing in her eyes and her delicately quivering
whiskers. Before she could change her mind I fell on her, block-

ing her retreat, and dug my fingers savagely into her unprotected flesh.

I cringe now as I think of my cruelty, the roughness with which I manhandled her as she cried out in pain. I was crazed with a hunger that provoked something I had not even known was there in my primitive, savage self. I gripped her violently, shaking her and growing angrier the more she struggled. Her eyes grew wide and rimmed with white as I tightened my grip. I continued to grapple with her roughly in spite of tiring from the effort and trembling. She was stronger than I had imagined.

If I say I was not trying to kill the animal, I speak the truth. And I can swear that it had not been my intention to cause her pain. Admittedly, what I attempted was hurtful and vile outrage upon my companion, but all I was trying was to induce her to regorge what she had eaten, believing in my fevered mind that this was the only way of my obtaining the food without which I could not survive. Thankfully for Scruff, she managed to escape, but not before I had almost choked her by wedging my fingers into her throat.

With a squeal, she fled the hut, leaving me weakened and full of remorse for my vicious behaviour. I crawled into my sleeping bag, suffering from the awful sense of my own despicability and convinced that I was unfit to live another day. I had hurt and frightened a defenseless, innocent animal and had alienated the one creature in the world that was my friend.

That night was the most miserable I have ever endured—the pangs of remorse and shame being even greater than the agony of my hunger. Scruff had abandoned me, and I could not blame the creature. With her long absence I now had no way of keeping at bay the malignant spirits that were always spying on me and waiting for their chance to move in and torture me.

Death was near. I resolved I must prepare to meet it like a man. And yet to die having debased the friendship and trust of the most true and loyal companion that any man could have was a stain on all I had tried to accomplish during my life. I was without hope and I was defeated. Yet amidst all my weaknesses there still glimmered a spark of decency and pride. For the first time in ages I dropped to my knees. "Dear God, spare me this final degradation—let me die decently—not grovelling and scrabbling like a dog. Give me the chance to undo my folly, I beg You—let me make my peace with Scruff before I die." For a moment I believed my prayer would be answered. My strength had gone, however, and I fell forward into blackness.

18

Sacrilege

I came to sometime midmorning of the following day or maybe even of the day after, grim and bitter and with my belly gnawing. Scruff had not returned. I dragged my feeble body to the doorway to scan the beach, but there was no sign of her. I had to shield my eyes because of the unusual brightness of the day. Wretched as I was, I could not help remarking how the sun sparkled off the snow crystals and made them shine like diamonds. A jade-green berg was sailing towards the headland where the ice had opened to reveal a cobalt sea. The day was the first of its kind since the previous summer, and I should have felt exhilarated to be alive. Yet here I was, not much more than a skeleton, sustained only by the automatic impulse that made me breathe.

A viselike grip seized my stomach. Doubling over from the pain, I crawled to my bunk to lie down in the hope that the cramp would ease. Of a sudden I felt angry. Was there to be no letup to my misery? And was I to die with my belly rumbling, my last thoughts given over to nothing more edifying than food? I refused to die in such miserable circumstances. Shouting my intention, I rid my mind of anything remotely alimentary, enjoying the successfulness of my willpower, when once again I was besieged by agonizing thoughts of food.

My mind searched everywhere for something to eat, going over every detail in the hut and exploring every possible place on the peninsula where there might be something edible. The beach, the bird rookeries—I had explored them all countless times without success. Suddenly my attention was loitering near the graves. Without being able to help it, my thoughts returned there again and again. Eventually the picture of myself beside the graves was the only image that filled my mind.

I took a while to realize what the devils of hunger were trying to insinuate. When I did, I shrank from their suggestion as if I had been stung. Horrible thoughts flooded my consciousness. I tried pushing them to the back of my mind, but they recurred again and again. No way could I escape their vile message. If I were to survive, I would have to find some immediate source of food, and since Scruff was the only living creature on the peninsula other than myself and I would rather die than kill her, I was left with no alternative but to eat the flesh of my dead shipmates.

No sooner had I acknowledged this notion than there came a flood of reasons to accept it. What is more, I realized that in spite of only consciously recognizing the idea at this moment, I had been trying to avoid admitting it to my subconscious for over a week.

I fought the grimmest battle with myself that I have ever started, torn between two opposing sides of my nature—one, carrying the voice of conscience—calm and dignified; the other the voice of expedience—rational, ruthless and articulate.

The latter was extraordinarily like conscience, and it talked in the same calm manner that was reassuring. I was persuaded easily that I would be committing no sacrilege. For one thing, it reasoned, the spirit had abandoned the dead long ago. The bodies were no more sacred than the carcasses of any animal. God must have wanted me to live or He would have drowned me with my shipmates. He must have foreseen what dire straits I would be placed in and had therefore washed the bodies ashore that I could survive. Indeed, the arguments were so reasonable and their manner so seducing that I found myself making my way purposefully towards the graves.

I am amazed at how easily the mind can become inured to the most ghastly prospects; perhaps the constant repetition of an unpleasant idea is eventually so blunting to the finer senses that they are no longer able to repress the baser instincts of man. He can become practical, callous or cruel, depending on what is asked of him. On that short walk to the graves, for instance, I indulged a macabre curiosity as to the appearance of the bodies, considering how the flesh was to be cut and from which corpse it was to be taken. Fortunately I found an answer before my more sensitive nature could reassert itself: I would start with one of the seamen that I had not known too well.

The burial mound had been submerged by snowdrifts. I was not too sure where to dig. Because the snow was too hard to shovel, I had to stab at it, and I was close to exhaustion by the time I got down to the stones. These were heavy and iced together, and I had to take my knife and chip away at the edges before I could get a grip on them at all. With this done, I could not move some of them and concluded that the snow had drifted between them and iced them up underneath. The task was so physically demanding that I forgot everything else. Coming upon a slab of stone that was particularly heavy to budge, I hacked at the underside till I had very little strength. If the task continued to be as arduous, I told myself, I should soon be so weak that I would not have any strength to cut up the bodies. Resting, therefore, for a brief time, I decided that I would have to make my meal out of the first bit of flesh I came upon—whoever the owner.

Insensitive as I thought I had become, I have no words to describe the horror I felt as I turned over the slab of stone. In one movement I had laid bare the head of the mate. It was so disfigured by my efforts with the knife to release the covering stone that, in spite of being preserved by the cold, the face looked hideous. It had no nose! A glance at the slab confirmed my suspicion—it had been stuck to the underside of that rock and indeed was still frozen to it! I had also destroyed one eye, leaving the other one glaring balefully. Aghast, I dropped my knife, stumbling over the stones as I tried to step back. For the second time in two days I dropped to my knees. I had committed sacrilege and had no other wish than for the forgiveness of God and an honourable end to my misery.

I must have lapsed into a daze of exhaustion and confused emotion before snapping alert at the squawk of a bird. Since it came so soon after my prayer, my optimism would have been wildly tempted to suggest some coincidence had not a cultivated cynicism rejected the notion. The sound, however, was repeated, and on opening one eye and barely moving my head I saw what looked like a fat white seabird, not unlike a pigeon, perched on the rock on the opposite side of the grave. I had seen many of its kind during the previous summer and had noted them for being scavengers, feeding on eggs and dead chicks and even pecking those that were injured or dying. Often they appeared near the tidemark along the eastern beaches, where shrimps were sometimes to be found mixed in with clumps of seaweed, or washed up in a thick carpet after an easterly gale. For several months these birds had been absent from the beaches, and I saw it now not for the creature it was but for the bellyful of food that was supported on its spindly legs.

Attracted by the uncovered corpse or perhaps merely out of curiosity, it stood on the edge of the circle of stones and eyed the human carrion. I, in turn, was aware of my own eyes lighting up and the saliva beginning to run. Between me and the bird, however, could have been an ocean for all the chance I had of getting my hands on him without some kind of snare or subterfuge. As I tried edging my way towards it it just kept its black bead focused on me and took a few springy steps farther away. Its plumpness, even more, I eyed with greedy anticipation, and I could not prevent the gurgle my impatient stomach made. My suspense and my hopes were to be shattered by Scruff, who, at that very moment, bounded up and made a sudden and playful lunge at the bird, which, with a contemptuous flutter, took off. With it went any subconscious belief I might have had in miracles.

I cursed that seal until I thought my lungs had burst. I fell to crying with frustration, hammering my fists on the ground to prevent myself striking the animal that had twice saved my life

193

and that now in its stupidity had finally destroyed me. Scruff stood quite bewildered. Afraid that she might run away, I knelt and called her to me. She was trailing fronds of kelp, and both she and the kelp were still wet from the sea as I disentangled it from round her neck. Doing so, I caught sight of something that made me snatch up the kelp to examine it. Startling Scruff, I let out a whoop and began scrabbling at the seaweed. There, hidden inside its folds, were plump and succulent-looking shrimps, less than a handful in all. I scooped them out and stuffed them in my mouth, savouring their delicious succulence before hobbling to the beach to search for others. The graves were forgotten. I had even forgotten to cover them. Life was coming back to the island, and I had no more need for the dead.

Near the beach, trails of kelp washed back and forth just out of reach. I would have to wade in if I wanted to get them. I was loath to do this in my weak condition for fear that the cold might kill me. Scruff had watched me gathering the few fronds of the stuff together near the shoreline, and either in fun or in response to her astonishing intuition, she ran up and down, dragging more of the stuff back to me with her mouth. In minutes I had piled up a mound of kelp, which I combed with my fingers for the tiny sea creatures that in their millions serve as food for the whales. I, too, should have needed an enormous amount at that moment to satisfy my hunger. Just as well for me that there were so few; my disordered body would have suffered greatly if I had eaten my fill. Then, remembering the bird, I forced myself to resist the last seven succulent morsels of the precious harvest and resolved I would use them as bait in the hope of catching more substantial fare.

I remembered how the sailors had attached their hook and bait to a length of line, and I made up my mind to try the same technique. A hook gave me no problem, for I had plenty enough of these. The line was not so simple to provide. I had nothing thin enough, unless I painstakingly unravelled a length of hemp and plaited it to the required width. A task such as this might take several hours, and in my present highly excited state two minutes would be one too many. So, instead, I split down the middle the only sealskin line I had remaining, thus making two thin lines—all the others I had devoured at various stages through the winter.

I positioned the baited end with its five shrimps on the one hook near the graves, reasoning that I might still attract the bird. After playing out the line for about ten feet, I covered it with snow and attached the loose end to a rock nearby. Pieces of the other two shrimps I scattered near the bait to act as a lure. This done, I smoothed out the snow all round the baited area with a barrel stave as I moved away in order to leave no footprints.

Dusk had fallen, and the night that followed seemed endless. My hunger was more demanding than ever, and I was sorely tempted to retrieve the bait. I resisted, however, and the next morning was up at first light to inspect my handiwork and make sure it was still there. All morning I waited for the bird's return, my poor stomach screaming complainingly. Two sorties to the beach produced no further shrimps nor very much kelp close to shore. In the hope that I might be able to retrieve some by throwing a line out weighted with a sealing hook, I took that vicious three-pronged hook down to the beach with me on my second visit to the graves.

There, at the sight of the bait, my mouth started watering. My digestive juices were in full flow. I eyed the shrimps, trying to persuade myself that they were more use to me as bait than as food until I could bear it no longer. Overcome, I picked one up and popped it into my mouth. No harm was done, I told myself, if I only sucked it. Alas, in less than a minute every shrimp was gone—leaving nothing at all with which to catch a bird.

As if in punishment for my lack of control, the next moment I heard a harsh cry. Sure enough, not ten yards away sat the bird. It was perched on a rock near the graves and was obviously interested in them, fluttering over and settling on the rock it had been on the day before. My stomach gave a squeeze at the message transmitted to it from my greedy eyes, and my nerves started twitching under the desperate need to get a grip on that bird. Not knowing how to do so without a suitable weapon, I was almost weeping with frustration and the fear that it might fly away. Whichever way I decided to kill it, I would have to get closer. I knew there was no chance of stalking close enough to pounce on it. Somehow or other I would have to stun it from a distance. I did not give much for my chances of being able to hit it with a stone or a piece of ice.

Slowly I crawled to within ten feet of it, trying at the same time to control my nerves and not alarm the bird. I never once took my eyes off the creature, which, surprisingly, sat there, preening itself in an absentminded fashion and occasionally glancing towards me in a casual, uninterested way. What I was to do now that I had got so close, I could not for the life of me fathom. Whatever the action, I would be better off unencumbered by the sealing hook held at my belt. As I was undoing this I could hear Scruff, whom up till now I had forgotten, racing back from the beach in almost exact repetition of her stupidity the day before. The bird turned and saw her, and as she lunged the bird took to the air. It was too much—more than I could bear! To happen a second time was unforgivable. Mad with anger and frustration, I whipped up the line with the sealing hook on the end of it and swung it in a wide circle round my head. I wanted to hurl it as far away from me as it would go—a gesture of disgust and despair, a physical and symbolic casting away of my last hope and last chance of survival. To my utter amazement the hook struck the bird.

A thud followed as the hook hit the ground, and not a squawk came from the bird, which had been impaled by a clean blow through the head. For myself, I could scarcely credit the luck of the strike till I actually held the inert body in my trembling hands. Within seconds, I had bitten the head away from the neck and sucked the still-pulsing stump in order not to lose any of the blood, which tasted more sweet to me than the flesh itself. Stripping away skin and feathers together as if they were a sock, I tore at the body, prizing the flesh away from the bone with the nail of my thumb. This delicious meat I ate immediately, picking off every little scrap. That finished, I chewed the bones till there was no more juice in them, cracking the head open with my teeth to suck out the brain. Finally, I sucked the inside of the

196

skin for the fat that adhered to it, pocketing the feathers when I had finished in case I might find them of some use. Minutes later I was striding back towards the den with Scruff beside me. My belly was full, and for the first time in weeks I was aware of the rush of good blood pumping through my veins. Where the bird had been, there was nothing to show that it had passed that way at all.

19

The Return of Life

The capture of the bird, together with the fact that I had eaten my first fresh meat in months, put me in a scintillating mood, and my spirits rose from then on. I was, however, still reluctant to think of the appearance of the bird as anything more than a natural occurrence that happened to coincide with the lowest point in my life. I realized that but for its timely arrival I might very well have died; miracles, I argued, were strictly the invention of superstitious minds—a way of transferring the responsibility for resolving a hopeless situation from the self to the supernatural. I was not going to fall prey to such irrational ideas. After all, had not the fact that I had stopped relying on luck been the very reason I had survived for so long? Forced to depend solely on myself, I had found hidden resources within me —resources that are the birthright of every human being and only discovered in circumstances of extreme danger or distress.

I could think of all sorts of practical reasons why the bird should have appeared when it did. I did not need to thank God —it was natural! But I do confess, after hours spent straining my eyes across the sea without spotting any further sign of life, I

198

was prepared to concede a principle just this once if only the Almighty would send another fat, juicy, succulent bird in its place.

But no more birds appeared on that day, or indeed for several more. Almost two weeks went by before there were shrimps to be found on the beaches in large enough quantities to provide one moderate-sized meal a day. Nevertheless, the return of hope made me much more resourceful. Remembering the funguslike growth that I had seen on the rocks in the summer, I went in search of that for something additional to eat. There were several varieties on the peninsula near the hut, some of them growing about an inch long in places, and these I scraped off in fistfuls, pushing wads of the stuff into my mouth. It tasted horrible and I found it difficult to swallow but, like the seaweed, it filled a gap. Occasionally a stray chunk of ice was washed up on the beach that must have broken off the underside of a berg that had run aground. Such pieces of ice frequently had sticking to them a variety of creatures such as sponges, starfish and other exotic inhabitants of the ocean floor. I marvelled at their beauty and diversity, reluctant to eat them—an indication, to be sure, that the worst stages of my hunger had passed.

Since there was nothing better to do, I started fishing again. When the weather was calm I would hobble out onto the sea ice in the cove, even to its very edge—from where I began to fish with some success. For hooks I used iron rings that I had found on the northern beach, crudely bent and sharpened to the required shape. These I attached to a length of weighted cordage, employing a jigging sort of movement to impale the fish. I discovered that in spite of the barrenness of the land itself, the sea washing its shores was abundantly rich in a form of life. It was not instantly recognizable as such the first time I saw it, appearing as it did as huge patches of discoloured water, sometimes green or brown or even bloodred. I was curious enough, however, to scoop up a handful of the clouded water and discovered that it contained myriads of minute creatures. With the aid of a scoop made from my old shirt tied round a piece of hooping, I managed to collect a large amount of the stuff and found to my delight that, eaten raw or cooked, it made an interesting and delicately flavoured "mushy" soup.

Eventually a few more vagrant birds visited the peninsula. I put my mind to the construction of snares and slings. The principle of a heavy weight at the end of a length of rope proved ideal in most situations. Sometimes, if a bird took to the air before I was in range, I could actually chase it a few feet before launching the weight and stun or even kill it with a single blow. In this way, with the help of patience and perseverance, I was able to secure enough nourishment to sustain my frail body till such time as the abundance of returning life made it possible for me to feed myself and grow strong again with comfort and ease.

I had not been long in realizing, gratefully, that I had reached a turning point in my life that signified very much more than the mere material improvements in my circumstances. In a sense it was like a breakthrough of the spirit after a long dark winter into a glorious and peaceful spring. This breakthrough confirmed a conviction that I had long suspected—that there was a positive side of nature to balance the negative, a creative side to balance the destructive and, by the same token, a force for goodness that counterbalanced evil. Whether such a dichotomy was represented by two separate supernatural powers or whether the good and evil were two parts of the same god I could not decide.

Whatever its true nature, I drew comfort from my belief in its existence. This positive force—which I still called God with some reluctance—could not be expected to provide miracles; it could only help one to find solutions. The process of solving problems involved a deep effort of will to search within oneself for the logical conclusion. Even when I reached what I believed to be the right answer to my difficulty, the outcome was sometimes unexpected, sometimes even disastrous. If I had done all that was humanly possible and asked for help, the force for good —call it Providence, or God, whatever you prefer—might step in with some timely assistance. But this help had to be earned and nearly always, in my experience, at the expense of unbearable effort.

Strangely, once I had come to terms with this principle, I experienced an extraordinary relief. I had been handicapped till now by a paralyzing dependence on luck to take me through the world; and by relying on luck I had put myself at the mercy of circumstances I could not control. Only by repudiating luck could I learn to master them.

I was to become aware of a wonderful change in the peninsula. Starting simply with a drop of water, suddenly there was a trickle that quickened, and all at once there seemed to be millions of tiny rivulets tumbling and rushing with happy sound beneath the snow. The waters of my land had broken free from their long imprisonment! Icicles formed from the roof and from overhanging rocks and shone gold in the sun like a frieze of inverted crystal candles. The sea ice began to break up and drift away, and bergs of extraordinary beauty and colour sailed past majestically.

Ironically, the improvement in the weather outside was the cause of much discomfort inside the hut. Indeed, the squalid conditions of my hut in the winter were as nothing compared with the squalor of the place once the thaw had really begun! The ice on the walls and ceiling melted, running down in streams or dripping on my head and sleeping bag with all the aggravating discomfort of misplaced rain. Besides, I had no fuel left to dry the skins. After chucking out nearly everything that had begun to perish, I could not get rid of the odour of rot or the pervasive reek of blubber and all the other smells that reminded me of winter and the ordeal I had come through.

20

No Latitude for Error

The first penguin arrived in September. Luckily it timed its approach till after the return of several other birds, or I might well have sacrificed the pleasure of watching it to the demands of a hungry stomach. As it was, having moved my residence that day to a sheltered spot farther along the beach had put me in a good frame of mind, and, having eaten well on fish into the bargain, I was relieved of the necessity of looking for food and free to enjoy its company.

My attention more than ever was focused on the sea as a source of infinite interest. I took pleasure from the sight of seals and birds arriving every day to colonize the peninsula. For a long while I had watched for the penguins, wondering if they would come singly or in the thousands, and I had to laugh at the sight of Johnny Penguin as he arrived, apparently anxious to find a partner. He emerged, plump and bright-eyed, quite unexpectedly from the sea, and came running at a busy, waddling trot up the beach. With his head thrust forward and his flippers stretched out, he looked neither to right nor left, so intent was he on his purpose. Curious to observe the outcome of such serious business, I ambled in his direction. Had I known the effect my interest would have, I should certainly have been more cautious. Spying me, the creature raced over, stood in front of me and, bawling lustily, bowed repeatedly as if to say, "How long it's been since we met, and how nice to see you." Faced with such a greeting, I would have been a churl to ingore it, so I imitated his bowing and squawking to express welcome. My visitor was obviously impressed, if I could judge by his behaviour. He set about building a nest in a mossy clump nearby that, by the size of the hollow he scraped away, looked as if it was intended for the two of us.

I must admit I was amused to be adopted as the mate of our new arrival. Scruff tried to scare Johnny off, finally accepting his presence with a sort of mild indifference. I took my cue from the many pairs of penguins that were coming together to build their nests and presented Johnny from time to time with some small bone or rounded pebble which he used to build up the walls of the nest, like the penguins around him. I concluded that the reason for this procedure was to protect the eggs from rolling away or being swamped and chilled by the melted water, which ran through the various colonies in small streams and runnels.

I expected Johnny sooner or later to find a natural mate. When it was apparent that my camp follower was not going to do so, I began to feel guilty that my mock affection might have been the cause of depriving him of his natural breeding function. If he was frustrated, however, he never seemed distressed. He spent ages trying to tell me something, holding out his flippers and serenading me with his neck stretched gracefully and his head pointed skywards. Such demonstrations made me all the more conscious of my duplicity. In an attempt to redress the wrong, I searched for a stone, roughly egg-shaped, which I put in the nest, which had by now reached gigantic proportions and into which my new friend had vociferously invited me. To my relief, my offering seemed infinitely acceptable, and my feathered friend, content at its appearance, sat on it for days, looking at me with infinite gratitude. Observing as time went by how pairing birds took turns brooding, one returning to the sea in order to eat, while the other stayed in the nest, I had to forcibly eject my feathered partner from the nest and pretend to be taking over. I am sure that if I had not put on an act of doing my share of the egg-warming my partner would have died of starvation, so reluctant was he to desert his post. On his return we went through a charade of penguin noises, bowing and chattering in mutual recognition, much to the disgust of Scruff, who jumped between us. In this way the liaison showed promise of continuing throughout the summer; but unfortunately one day Johnny disappeared completely—the victim, I suspect, of a predator.

I discovered the existence of this predator with some surprise. A solitary animal, it never came ashore but lurked in the shadows of the ice floes, patrolling several beaches for penguins that might dive into the water unaware of its presence. It was a beautiful creature in many ways, sleek and swift. I remember the sealers having talked about the leopard seal, and indeed its silvery grey coat was spotted to some extent like the land animal from which it took its name. Bigger than the fur seal, it had a longer neck and looked quite fierce, with a huge mouth and formidable array of teeth. Once I was aware of its existence, I could detect it floating just awash or see it in the clear water beneath the ice foot where it waited to catch the penguins. Whenever its presence was detected, hordes of penguins would suddenly shoot out of the water onto an ice floe, followed by scores of others, till there was no room left. More would try to get on, however, and sometimes those who were first on were actually pushed off the edge by the weight of numbers jostling behind. A flash of silver would be followed by several streaks of carmine, and small pathetic parcels of skin and feathers would float off before the wind. The animal had a way of grabbing the penguin and shaking it so vigorously that the skin and feathers peeled off intact.

On fine days I would rise early, finding a certain joyfulness in being up and about with the penguins, who stirred at first light. I used to watch them shuffling and yawning as they cast off the dopiness of sleep and never failed to be amused as they moved in their purposeful way towards the beach. A whole concourse would have collected behind the leaders, trotting along in orderly file. At the water's edge they would become a jostling mob, two hundred or more strong, looking for all the world as though the momentous decision to dive in required a determination of which they felt themselves utterly incapable. Their terror, I knew, was entirely justifiable, but somehow the danger never detracted from the humour and pathos of their daily ritual.

Naturally, whenever I saw the leopard seal, I took it as a duty to shout and hurl stones into the water in an effort to frighten it away. I probably did save the lives of some of the penguins, while Scruff unwittingly abetted their predator. Between us we perhaps were responsible for the deaths of as many as we were able to save. Scruff's involvement came strictly out of her love of play. Seeing that the penguins frequently crowded onto the ice floes whether there was a predator about or not, she took pleasure in leaping onto the floe to scatter them, often going so far as to nudge those into the sea that were brave enough to remain. After I realized the implications of her behaviour, I tried to call her off, but she ignored my entreaties. By this time the game had become a habit that she enjoyed tremendously.

As I mentioned before, I had moved my abode, constructing a serviceable shelter with the spare bits of wood retrieved from the wreck of the longboat that had run aground on the headland the previous summer (amongst which was a broken oar that was to be of dramatic significance later). The shelter was intended only as a temporary measure until I could make a tent out of sealskin. When the weather was fine and sunny, I slept in the open, wrapped in my remaining furs, using the shelter only when the wind got up or it was foggy. The weather on the island during the second summer was every bit as intemperate and unpredictable as it had been the first. Nevertheless, I enjoyed it more. Perhaps I had become inured to it, or perhaps I had endured so much in the winter and come so close to dying that life had a sweetness for me now that only those reprieved from death could understand. Physically, with food in plenty, I recuperated quickly. My leg and foot healed dramatically, and I was stronger than I had ever been before. I could stand more extremes of cold than previously, and I could go about with bare head and hands where formerly I would have been well wrapped and still suffering from the cold.

I had plenty to occupy myself. Initially my thoughts were mainly given over to obtaining food. I can remember well the delight of having my first fresh eggs again. Most of the penguins on the peninsula laid at least two large greenish-white eggs, which I had not the slightest qualms in raiding even if to get them I had to submit to many pecks and blows. I retrieved my old pair of worn trousers and tied the legs so that I could carry eggs in them, wearing the garment around my neck to facilitate the transportation. How I rejoiced! For weeks I never ate a meal without those eggs. Fried or boiled, raw or scrambled, they served as a meal in themselves or as an accompaniment to seal or penguin meat in the soup. I collected them by the hundreds, boiling those that I wanted to stash away in cairns against the eggless months ahead and burying others out of the reach of birds for immediate use. Blubber I had in plenty, so the fire was lit constantly, and I made sure that, come what may, be it storms or tidal waves, I would always have stacks of blubber to burn and a continuous source of heat to ignite them.

The winter hut, which I had abandoned as a dwelling because of its awful associations, I cleaned out completely and ventilated, and this also I used as a store for eggs and for the meat and skins that I collected later. Winter was far enough ahead, but I would not let myself forget the lessons I had learned. I salvaged everything washed up and even went to the bother of scraping the pitch off the odd bits of timber I found in case I should have a particular use for them later. There was so much to be done. Slaughtering, butchering, salting and drying, flensing and cleaning—it never stopped. When I ran out of salt, I boiled seawater over a slow heat to obtain the residue left on the bottom of the pan. When not doing any of these things, I had the chores of cooking and collecting water, making clothes and cutting up and storing blubber. I had only three barrels that were intact for this and had therefore to fabricate suitable sealskin containers. These took so long to make that I had no time to brood about the fact that I had been almost a year on the island. A certain period of each day I allowed for exercise, for observing the animal life and writing my journal, and for recreation; but I kept no set routine, suiting the activity to the mood or to the dictates of the weather. I never even thought of home.

About the second week in November, 1819, I was reminded with a shock of the world I had left behind. I had risen to see a particularly disorderly group of penguins gathered near the shoreline as a long, slender object floated nearby on the surf. On casual inspection, I decided it was not a sea creature. Although I could not make out quite what it might be, I was strangely excited. A few days passed before I could confirm what I had begun to suspect during which time several other objects had also started to float back and forth just beyond my reach on the tide. After a particularly blustery night, I discovered wreckage from a ship and was instantly able to ascertain that it was not my own vessel, the wreckage consisting of the anchor stock and spars from a sailing ship whose name I could just make out to be the *San Telmo*.

How disturbing such a discovery was! All of a sudden I was excited by memories I had long suppressed. Hopeful visions of discovery and rescue flooded my mind till I reminded myself that it was the *wreckage* of a ship I was surveying, which in itself suggested a repetition of my own tragedy. There then came upon me the accumulation of all the unease that I had been prey to since leaving home. Here was a link with a world I had almost forgotten yet suddenly realized that I still cherished. I must try to send out some message with my name and whereabouts. I racked my brains to think of something that I could cast adrift that a ship might notice and pick up, or that would be of sufficient interest for the natives of some other land to examine if it washed ashore.

At first I thought of building a miniature vessel that I could turn adrift on the waves, the notice of my exile carved on its deck. I worked hard to make it sturdy and launched it when the weather was not too blustery, only the next day to find it wrecked farther round the coast. Disappointed, I meditated on all the possible other means there might be at my disposal. In truth there was a dearth of materials to aid me in my purpose.

Seals and birds! What raw materials did they provide apart from skins and eggs? And then I had it. Eggs—why not? Maybe I could use the shells to carry messages written on sealskin with the gall of the animal. The pages of my journal were already filled even in the margins or I would have used some of those. If I could stop the opening of the eggs with something waterproof I could make hundreds of them and pitch them from various parts of the coast into the sea. Pitch them! What a fortuitous choice of word! That was the answer. I would use the small amount of pitch I had just salvaged to seal the eggs before tossing them into the sea.

Even though the idea of sending out messages that might effect my rescue occupied my thoughts, I was realistic enough not to become obsessed with this plan and work on it at the expense of everything else. Life must continue normally for me and Scruff if it was to be at all tolerable. In what I convinced myself was my spare time, I began to gather together the materials I would need—starting with several giant petrel's eggs. They were very much larger than penguin eggs—in volume I would guess about twice the size and almost four inches long. They were also much more difficult to acquire, and I received more scratches and bruises during the two days I spent collecting them than I had in the rest of the summer.

My problems, however, had barely begun. Emptying the eggs and drying them out and scraping, cleaning and stretching the sealskins proved to be a most laborious task. Ink had to be obtained and quills to be cut. At first nothing was satisfactory. I used the skins taken from the carcasses of young seals, but I had not made them smooth or supple enough. The ink was inclined to blob, and I had to experiment with feathers of many different kinds before I had made a suitable quill. Eventually I was satisfied with all of the materials and ready to turn my thoughts to what sort of information the message should contain.

Only then did the absurdity of the proposition dawn on me. Quite apart from the doubts I now had about whether the eggs would survive their voyage, the chance was slim that one of them would be picked up by someone who could read what I had written. More to the point, what was I to say in the message? The truth is, I did not know where I was and was not even sure of the date. Without this information the message would not be worth the small piece of skin it was written on.

For the first time since leaving home I had to apply my brain to an intellectual problem. The excitement of this challenge was an indescribable tonic to my soul. For hours on end I paced around muttering, arguing with myself, and scratching diagrams and figures in the wet sand near the water's edge. To find my latitude I required only two pieces of information: the declination of the sun at local noon for any chosen day in the year, and its altitude at that moment in time. But since I had no idea of the date and no almanac, how could I possibly work it out? The problem was intriguing and seemingly without a solution. I almost literally stumbled upon the answer. I recall that moment as one of the most joyful I had ever known. I realized that there were four days in every year for which I knew the sun's declination: the solstices and the equinoxes. The nearest of these to my assumed date was the winter solstice of December 22. On that date the sun would reach its southernmost position—the Tropic of Capricorn. Its declination would then be 23°27' south, which is the same angle as the earth's axis from the perpendicular. Principally because of this angle of the earth's axis we have the seasons of the year, and I well remembered this from geography lessons—one of my favourite subjects at school.

All I needed was to know the date and to find some way of accurately measuring the altitude of the sun at local noon on December 22, when it would have reached its highest point in the sky. If my calendar was right I had almost a month in which to devise a suitable instrument; but I applied my mind first to the problem of finding as precisely as possible the direction of true north. Such a task proved easy enough. I selected a spot some way back from the beach on the highest terrace, where the ground was flat and the surface had been dried out by the sun. Here I planted my sealer's lance, which I had repaired, to serve as a sundial, and over a period of several days I marked on the ground the position of the tip of the lance's shadow. At that moment each day when the shadow was shortest, the time was local noon and the sun was due north.

I put much thought into the various ways of devising some sort of instrument for measuring vertical angles, and I wasted a great deal of time and energy, not to mention materials, on a huge quadrant drawn with painstaking precision on a depilated sealskin that I had stretched over a barrel hoop. I had intended to mount this on the lance, point it due north, and level it by suspending a plumb line from the ninety-degree mark—adjusting it so that the plumb line ran straight down the vertical side of the quadrant. After many hours of applied ingenuity, I failed to find a way of taking accurate readings off the circle. With a sighting stick aimed at the center of the sun, the best I could do was measure an altitude to within two degrees—and such a deviation might translate into an error in my calculated position of as much as one hundred and fifty nautical miles. Nevertheless, this skin quadrant of mine was not without its uses. It proved to be a rough check on the sun's altitude, and it also served as a splendid surface upon which to do my calculations and on which to draw and plot my graphs. I had come up with a simpler and, in theory at least, a more accurate way of solving the question of my latitude.

While comparing the lengths of the shadows cast by the lance, I heard a distant voice from my school days. If I could be certain that the sundial was vertical and the ground receiving its shadow was flat, then I had a right-angled triangle, the lengths of two sides of which I could measure. The fact that I had no "units" accepted as standards by our civilized society did not matter. I could calculate the altitude of the sun by simple trigonometry, using any "units" I chose, providing they were accurately measured. All I needed was to work out the ratio between the perpendicular and the base of my right-angled triangle.

The complication in this was not, however, in the measuring, which I was able, I am proud to say, to achieve with extraordinary precision. The problem was that the ratio between the two sides came out as a natural tangent, and I had no tables with which to convert this into degrees. The sealskin "drum" became the surface upon which I finally solved my problem. Remembering from school days that the tangent of forty-five degrees was one and that ninety degrees was infinity, I was able to calculate two other values by making use of the equilateral triangle and that old schoolboys' favourite, Pythagoras. By drawing a large graph on my drum and plotting the values I knew, I demonstrated to my delight that I could convert any tangent into degrees in the range between thirty and sixty with an accuracy of half a degree.

And so I was all set. The only thing that might now destroy my effort and reduce this ingenuity to a total disaster was if the day of the solstice was overcast. But the supreme irony of all this was that I would not know for certain which day was the solstice until the day that followed it.

The fateful day came after a week during which each noon observation was measured with the attentiveness that was demanded by the fact that my very life might depend on it. I shall never forget the twenty-third of December, 1819. On that day at noon, as the shadow reached my north-south line, I observed it was fractionally longer than the day before! I took that "drum" with my calculations inscribed upon it and beat out a salute to my success marching and leaping along the beach, thumping that ludicrous tambour and rousing every creature with whom I shared that far-flung and desolate spot. I had now confirmed that I was south of every other person on earth! And the animals, if at first alarmed and even confused by my extraordinary behaviour, sensed soon enough the triumph implicit in my demonstration. Excited, they too rejoiced with me until the sound rippling outwards had encompassed the whole of the peninsula with a marvelous trumpeting song of praise.

My calculations indicated that my latitude was 62°27′ south. The accuracy of such an inspired guess was difficult to assess, but I doubted that it could be farther than one degree out, and it might even be within thirty miles—certainly near enough for any rescue ship to get a sight of land, providing I could guess my approximate longitude. No way could I calculate this by observations of the sun, but by racking my memory of our track and drift from the time of leaving South Georgia, I estimated that I was southeast of Cape Horn and probably within about forty miles of longitude 60° west.

Strange how almost unconsciously, having now worked out my position, I should have taken up the idea again of sending out a call to be rescued. I do not believe that in any way this plea for help was a reflection on my state of mind—at that time I was very happy. I can only assume that the desire to send out messages of my whereabouts sprang from a need to let the world outside know that the human race was represented here—that I had come through a terrible ordeal against the most impossible odds and had survived with dignity. Whatever the motives, I returned to the problem of one month earlier with something more to tell.

Needless to say, I could not write much. The messages had to be small enough to fold up neatly inside the shells, and the opening had to be stopped. The task presented no great difficulties, and the job was soon completed. I covered the shells with the pitch. This done, the shells were water-resistant and, I suspect, a good deal stronger than they had been before. Of course, my original estimates of how many shells I would launch fell a long way short of my actual achievements. I launched twenty-one in all—one for every year of my life—and only three were returned with the tides. These I launched a second time, and they were never seen again. Whether any of them would be found or whether they would be destroyed by the sea or whether they would circle the globe forever I cared not. I had performed a duty that I felt I owed to my conscience—and this done, I could at last relax and forget completely about what I had accomplished.

21

Methuselah

Summer was well advanced before I realized just how much of an uproar was created by the intermingling calls and cries of the various creatures. The elephant seals were undoubtedly the rowdiest. Their horrible repertoire covered a variety of sounds from snoring and belching to gargling and retching, with frequent squealings and trumpetings besides. The beach sounded as if it were the scene of some enormous battle. Cries of birds pierced the air, screams came from trampled seal pups, while the bleat of cows mingled with the bulls' incessant roar. As bad as the din was, far worse was the stench of the animals and of the accumulation of years of ordure released from their covering of the winter snows. Accustomed as I had become to smells that would have turned the stomach of most men, I found it hard not to vomit each time I went to the beach and I was obliged to make frequent visits to the elephant seal camps in order to build up a large supply of blubber while I still had the chance.

Ideally, I needed to kill a few good-sized bulls early in the season before they used up all their fat. Each of these would give about three barrels of oil. However, I was still too timid to take on these monstrous creatures, and for the time being at least I was prepared to acknowledge their mastery of the beach. This timidity left me with little alternative but to lie in wait for the younger males as they came out of the shallows. These were simpler to dispatch, although they yielded less blubber and I had to kill more of them to make up my stocks. It would have been far easier for me to have killed the females in pup and easier still when they were suckling, but although I managed to overcome all sorts of scruples during my second summer, that I never did.

Like the fur seals, the elephant seals divided up the beach into harems, over each of which a bull presided. Seen from the cliff tops, these gave the impression of heaps of enormous brown maggots lying around in lethargic clusters. On approaching closer, I saw that, in spite of dozing most of the time, the elephant seals were never completely relaxed. They lay, apparently asleep, belly side up, their bodies twitching and shaking like the victims of the most awful nightmares. They were a mass of itches, and while asleep their fore flippers would be perpetually pawing about—scratching their sides, their heads or even drolly folded across their chests, one flipper scratched by the nails of the other. Whether awake or asleep, they frequently scooped up sand or shingle, which they threw over themselves and their nearest neighbours. Until I had observed some of them closely, I thought many of them had stopped breathing altogether. Lying with nostrils closed for long stretches, they would surprise me by opening just one nostril, which they would spread and close for respiration while keeping the other tightly shut. They were, to my mind, obnoxious animals in every respect. What disturbed me most about them was their indifference to their young.

Naturally, as soon as the pups were born, they wanted to suck. Frequently the mother ignored the pup's entreaty and returned to the water, leaving the pup unattended on the beach to crawl around half blind searching for a willing foster mother. Unlike the fur seals, the elephant seal females would suckle any pup if they felt inclined, but many a calf lay dead that had obviously been unable to find an unoccupied teat. The sight of stray pups wandering around the beach pushing their noses into every stomach as they cried with hunger, was a pathetic one. Too often they got in the way of a lumbering hulk of bull elephant who pinned them beneath his enormous weight, oblivious to the cries of the creature he was crushing to death. The most dangerous time was during the bull elephants' frequent battles, when they could be fatally jostled or pinned against a sharp edge of rock.

I would be wrong to give the impression that none of the female elephant seals showed their pups any tenderness. Those that did so were usually situated on the edges of the colony where it was less crowded, which may have given them more scope to indulge their maternal feelings. Unlike their ugly parents, the youngsters were engagingly pretty. They were born with black fur, which they shed after about a month. I collected the bodies of the dead pups to salvage this fur, which I found ideal for making clothes. Like the adults, the pups too were itchy, and they began scratching almost as soon as they were born. I was amused to watch their contortions as they tried to locate the itch on their backs or heads and I was tempted on occasions to assist them.

The bull elephants by comparison were hideous and bellicose. Habitually, they would rouse themselves from sleep in panic and threaten their neighbours, had they not already been forced to respond to another's challenge. I could not help thinking what unnecessary hardship they imposed on themselves by so much fighting. Their behaviour was all the more incomprehensible when one realized just how much effort it took on the part of the elephant seal to move about on land, where he was hampered by his extraordinary bulk. The only way that he could progress satisfactorily was to rear the front part of his body up and then let it fall forward, bringing his hind parts behind in a sort of humping movement. His weight was too much for him to pull himself along by his fore flippers. Slow and ungainly as he was, he could, in an emergency, move extremely quickly for a short while—his motion looking vaguely like a gallop.

Naturally, because of the size of the bulls and because of the effort involved with every movement, the battles did not last long. But even in a short time, some unfortunate animals had their necks or flanks cut to ribbons. In the light of this, I was obviously loath to take on an adult bull elephant seal. As events turned out, I was obliged to consider doing so in order to end what had become a reign of terror.

By odd coincidence, the first bull among the elephant seals to haul out was old Methuselah, the beast that had nearly succeeded in bringing my hut around my ears during the previous summer. From the moment he arrived, I was aware that he remained a mean character. He roared and assumed a threatening posture whenever I came within ten yards of him, charging and going almost berserk if I approached any closer. I was not sure whether he recognized me for a human or whether the very fact that I moved around in an upright position was menacing. Whatever the reason, he succeeded in annoying me by cutting off my access to my summer dwelling, causing me to make a roundabout approach to it over a stretch of dangerous rocks. If I did attempt to pass through his territory, which after all for a whole winter I had regarded as mine, I would be subjected to mad charges that were as irksome as they were dangerous. I was forced to con-sider either moving my abode or else suffering the inconvenience if I wanted to remain in the same place.

Since I particularly liked the site I had chosen and did not feel inclined to move, I decided I would try using noise to deter Methuselah, noise playing such an important part in the act of intimidation. To my astonishment it did serve to delay a charge, even if I lacked the talent of my intimidator for making loud revolting utterances. The first time I gave a bellow I scared the life out of Scruff. When she emerged moments later from behind the rock where she had hidden, she had such a deprecating look on her face that I felt quite embarrassed. In spite of her initial disgust that I had become so dreadfully common, she grew accustomed to my sounds, and when I took time to practice she would even accompany me with yelpings of her own.

Scruff clearly had a sense of humour. Realizing that Methuse-lah was an object to be teased, she developed her own kind of playful torment. Relying on her nimbleness to keep her out of harm's way, she would run circles around the old bull, nipping him whenever she got the chance. On occasions she would even carry her mischievousness as far as to prevent him from coupling with a cow by nipping the latter just as he was about to mount her. Such treatment upset the cow and the cow then bit the bull. In this way Scruff achieved the maximum disturbance with the least risk to herself.

Methuselah's harem was to one side of the beach, where a large rock effectively served as a barrier to the north side of his territory. This natural boundary cut down the amount of territory he had to defend, but it also left him more time to exercise his pugnacious tendencies on all the seals unfortunate or foolish enough to be on his southern flank.

In appearance, he was a most ugly animal. His nose ran with mucus, and long dribbles always hung from it revoltingly. He was darker than the other male seals, and the flesh of his neck sagged with folds that were covered with the wrinkles and scars of many battles. At what stage in his fighting career he had received those wounds I could not say. In the encounters I witnessed it was clear that no other bull, this season at least, was going to get the better of him, nor did it look as if fate would step in to claim what would in fact have been a death long overdue. This undisputed master of the beach was both the cause of the most awful bloodshed and without question the nastiest and vilest creature I had ever seen.

The extent of the carnage on the boundary of his territory suggested that there was something terrifyingly abnormal in the scale of injury and death he left behind him. I had come to expect a certain amount of natural tragedy. Death was part of the natural cycle over which I had no control and which I told myself I had to accept no matter how horrible. On the other hand, when Methuselah began willfully to crush the baby seals and, completely impervious to their agonized screams, to pin them with his great weight against the sharp rocks, I knew I had to do something to stop him. I had seen him apparently quite insane with rage, charging all over the place and snapping at everything in his path, leaving puzzled fur seals nuzzling their dead young whom minutes before they had been suckling.

At the thought of killing the old bull, my skin began to sweat and prickle. To accomplish it, I would have to arm myself with weapons strong enough to pierce his hide, and such weapons would probably be too unwieldy to be effective. I would have to get closer to this giant of an animal than I had ever dared to approach before, and I would have to guard against slipping on the slimy ground if I did not want to be crushed or mauled to death.

Early on in the summer, I had experimented with various weapons and had provided myself with a fairly comprehensive set of equipment. Nonetheless, a great deal of difference existed between what I had and the kind of weaponry necessary to kill a bull elephant seal. In idle moments I had experimented with a bow that I had lashed together from short strips of whalebone from an old skeleton I had found; the arrows were a problem I had not yet resolved. The answer to Methuselah, I deduced, would be to employ several different types of weapon. My tactics would be to tire the old bull to enable me to get close enough to deliver the fatal blows. The latter would have to be effected from very close quarters with a lance launched with all the weight I could muster if I was to pierce the thick hide to a sufficient depth.

The day before the battle I worked feverishly on a lance that I hoped would be strong enough. It was made from a broken oar that I had found washed up amongst some other gear in a longboat some time previously. At the handle end of this I had lashed my longest knife, which I spent several hours honing until it was as sharp as any knife I had ever seen. As I had expected, this lance was a heavy and unwieldy weapon, but I was confident that it would be strong enough. Realizing how important it was to be rested for the ordeal, I tried to relax, only to find I was extremely nervous and unable to sleep. I got up early and prepared myself a fighter's breakfast of boiled seal and eggs, hoping to build up my strength for the awesome task ahead. What I could not build up was my courage, and what little I had drained from me as the day wore on.

I planned to try and lure the old bull away from his harem. Being more mobile, I would have some advantage, however slight, if I fought him on some open space that was less slippery underfoot. Characteristically, as soon as Methuselah sensed my presence, he dragged his enormous bulk off the ground and reared up, weaving his head from side to side. His eyes bulged as if they would explode with pent-up rage. Opening his mouth wide, he let out a deafening, earth-splitting scream which shattered my nerves like broken glass. Even had that monster made no sound at all, its sheer size would have terrified me. I could no more deter it with my own ineffectual high-pitched squeak than I could throw straight with the stones that I had collected. I had intended to bombard him with them in an attempt to wear him down and tire him. In the event, my aim was erratic, and they were far too small to hurt him. Those that might have done so were too heavy for me to throw.

I fell back on the strategy of dodging about to draw the old bull after me. In no time at all I was sweating profusely and feeling breathless. What I did manage to do was to clear a bit of space by rattling stones in the kettle to frighten some of the nearby seals out of the way. As for Methuselah, if he was tiring, he did not show it. Temporarily exhausted myself, I had to call a halt to my ineffectual prancings while I considered the advisability of rushing him head-on. If I did this with the lance outstretched, the impetus should help me to drive the weapon home. At least, this was what I hoped. I reminded myself that the rush would be the end of me if I could not sidestep quickly enough to get out of his way.

But between the intention and its implementation, a gulf opened that could be bridged only by superhuman courage. After several futile attempts to charge the bull, I was convinced that I was lacking that almost reckless fortitude my plans demanded. Each time I neared the enormous, moving mountain of flesh my resolve weakened, and with each retreat I felt more ashamed and more scared in the pit of my stomach. Strangely, I could not give in. Perhaps my pride drove me on—perhaps the need to prove myself to the spirits of those sealers, my crew mates.

I did make several efforts to lance the animal. If the weapon did not glance off, it only pricked the skin and fell to the ground. Incited thus, my opponent was growing more dangerous with rage every minute. I was about to back off completely when I caught sight of Scruff. Unbelievable as I know it sounds, I swear that seal looked ashamed of me. Mortified, I summoned the very dregs of my courage to approach the bull again. I fixed my arm with lance pointing directly at his chest and tried desperately not to panic as he came within range. I got closer sooner than I had intended, or else he had moved towards me more quickly than I realized. At any rate, suddenly he was there in front of me glowering, his head towering angrily above me some seven or even eight feet above the ground.

I was paralyzed as I stared up at it. Its eyes were bloodshot and bulging murderously. As he threw his head back to trumpet at me, he bared his powerful teeth. His nose had puffed up to horrible proportions, curling over in front of his mouth. The long thick tendrils of mucus that dripped from it swayed as he jerked his head. He was wheezing now, struggling for breath. As his monstrous body shook, thick gobs of feculence were flung off. He gave the impression he was about to explode! Again he wheezed. This time there was a horrible, rattling, puking sound that swelled in volume in his cavernous mouth and was echoed by the cliffs. I was covered with a spray of mucus that almost blinded me and that was followed by a painful and startling fusillade of pebbles that issued straight out of the creature's throat. So powerful had been the force of its exhalation that the stones that seals were wont to swallow had actually been regurgitated by the extraordinary effort of vocalization.

I hurled the lance at his chest. To my horror it bounced off him and fell upon the ground. As I moved away, I slipped and fell, landing heavily on my back in the middle of the deserted harem. Immediately the animal moved towards me. I knew he could rip me wide open with one stroke or burst my body under his weight. Having no time to rise to get out of his way, I hurled myself sideways in the muck.

The ground was a quagmire of filth and feces where the cows had wallowed. The more I floundered, the more it grasped me with its foul, fetid, and glutinous grip. My eyes were smarting

with its noxious stench, and my nose and throat were burning
inside. I was coughing, choking, writhing in that clawing cesspit
to extricate myself when suddenly the bull again came ploughing
through the quagmire towards me. I threw myself out of his way
as he lunged. Again he missed me; but he was driving me in the
direction of his rocky boundary, where he would have me
trapped. Although my nerves screamed at the terror of the anticipated pain, my mind screamed the louder at the vileness of
the setting and the crude indignity of the death that awaited me.

I was defenseless against that wall of rock, the bull blocking
my only route of escape. No way could I avoid him. As he bore
down on me, all I could do was scrabble in the morass of filth
and throw handfuls of the stuff in an attempt to blind him. In
truth I had already given up the fight to save my life and was
trying only, and desperately, to delay by a few more seconds
that tearing pain as his teeth ripped into me. Almost at the very
instant my eyes were closing, something white leapt between us,
and the head that was lowering to strike me shot upwards with
an earsplitting roar of rage and pain.

Scruff, the plucky little creature, had hurled herself at the elephant seal and buried her teeth deep into the flesh of its nose. It
was an incredible sight. Not ten seconds before I had been
screaming with the horror of becoming nothing more than a
mass of mangled carrion, and now, quite miraculously, I had a
chance to escape. Scrambling to my feet, I began to fear for
Scruff. The bull was enraged beyond belief and rampaging about,
lashing his head from side to side and smashing Scruff onto the
soggy ground in an effort to shake her off. With no thought for
myself and no fear at all, I scrambled and slithered past the bull
to retrieve my lance, returned to the rock almost blinded with
anger and with my full weight behind it I rammed it deep into
the chest of the beast as it swung Scruff up in the air.

The blood gushed out like the bursting of a dam as Scruff was
flung off. I heard her fall with a sickening thud some yards
away, obviously hurt. Enraged by her moaning, I grabbed the
oar with the bloodied knife attached to it. Holding it with the
paddle end jammed against the rock, I waited for the wounded

animal to lunge at me. It came with a rush. God, what a sight it was! It impaled itself on that lance right through the heart. I felt the shock of the impact judder through me as the bull's body swallowed up the lance and broke it. I leapt clear as he crashed against the rock, grunting, spluttering and showering me with blood as he gyrated with the broken oar protruding jaggedly from his chest.

I had wounded him mortally, and any second I expected to see him slump. But he was as strong and stubborn as any a creature could be, and though he was in agony, he would not give in. I watched, I must admit, with a reluctant admiration the death throes of that animal struggling to keep his head up and his grip on life. His strength was draining from his nose and mouth. My own strength was fast escaping also. Seeing the possibility of being trapped under the animal if it pitched forward, I jumped for the overhanging rock and clung to it, waiting for him to slump or drop dead. But my fingers were slipping and I knew I must fall any minute. Even when his head began to droop, he tried to make a final stab at me, and I felt a dull thump on my shoulder. The head glanced off me and he folded, dragging me on top of him so that my face was near his as his eyes changed colour, suffused with the bright green light that came over them in death.

Afraid for Scruff, I slithered through the slime to get to her. She was winded and hurt but with no bones broken as far as I could tell. As for my feelings at that moment: the struggle had been so nearly fatal that I could feel no elation at the victory, only a tremendous sense of relief.

I got an enormous amount of blubber off that old bull. Quite by accident, turning over the massive head, I caught a glimpse of a huge boil on one side of his gums where his teeth had rotted. The eruption must have caused him considerable discomfort, and I wondered if this was the reason why he had been so savage. The more I thought about it, the more convinced I became that the animal had been crazed with pain. With the discovery, I started feeling sorry for him. After all, he must have been a great warrior in his prime. In tribute to Methuselah, I returned to the scene of our battle several days later, by which time the scavenging birds had picked clean all the bones, and I collected his jawbone as a memento. Methuselah was not the only bull elephant seal I killed that summer, but no other animal was as memorable as he was or died with as much fight.

22

Killer Whales

There were days in summer, between mists and tempest, when the peninsula was so beautiful and tranquil that I felt intoxicated by the sheer joy of being alive. The sun kept long hours in the heavens, and its delicious heat fired the rocks with such lasting warmth that I could lie for hours on them and enjoy their glow. I liked nothing better on windless days than to shed my garments and stretch naked to let my sun-starved body soak up the sun. My pale skin turned a deep bronze, giving me a feeling of great health. My body was strong and lean, muscular without being gross. I had no lack of subjects to attract my interest, whether it was the wildlife, the sea and its many changing aspects or the interior of the peninsula with its hills, which were still covered with snow. At every turn I saw something new to marvel at, and such wonderful colour, with beautiful contrasts of light and shade.

My senses expanded so fully that I felt an almost mystical fulfillment, becoming one with the world; but one day I became aware of a lack that separated me from the rest of creation and that induced in me moods of black frustration and despair.

The change in my disposition began very simply. I had been watching the fur seals and marvelling at the vitality with which they responded to the urge to mate, when the awareness that I was deprived by my exile of the right to procreate was borne in on me with the most terrible sense of impoverishment. Though I tried to rid myself of the thought, I was surrounded on all sides by such bounteous evidence of the creative act that I began to think of myself as a kind of freak.

I became irritable with Scruff, who had been a most constant and endearing companion—her proximity, of a sudden, was oddly disturbing. On hindsight, I realize that I had found her tantalizing. She had reached an age, not yet mature, when the female in her responded to her obvious awareness of the male in me. Unable to avoid the blatant symbolism in her behaviour, I instinctively shrank from her. Everything became affected by my disquiet. Even the simple pleasure of sunbathing could not be enjoyed without awakening some deep malaise.

What was happening was natural enough, and had I known it I should have been spared much remorse and guilt. My body was reacting to the sun's sensual heat and the general improvement in my circumstances with a reawakening of that sexuality which the months of coldness, starvation and anxiety had repressed. But once I acknowledged this need within me, the sexual urge became so overwhelmingly insistent that even the mere feel of the sun on my body could arouse me and would spread as a warm, deliciously subtle sensation through my system till it reached my loins. There, it would concentrate as a core of fire clamouring for release. I might have taken this for my body's natural adjustment to changing circumstances had not the sudden touch of Scruff, with her careless nuzzling, so excited me on one occasion that my conscience would not be quieted for several days.

Sickened with remorse and terrified by what I imagined must be the ugly and unnatural implications, I banished Scruff from the hut and sentenced myself to rigorous and punishing exercise as an antidote to my condition. Fortunately for my peace of mind, the problem, if it could be described as such, was only temporary. Once the weather worsened again and the mating season was over, my eroticism diminished, and my thoughts turned to other things.

As I have said earlier, the waters around the peninsula were rich in wildlife. I saw whales and even seals and penguins of a different species. These, however, bypassed the peninsula, intent on reaching other locations where conditions for them must have been more favourable. The sight of these animals and my curiosity as to their destination made me wonder more and more about the size and shape and character of the island and gave me a strong urge to discover what were its other features.

I seriously considered climbing up onto the inland ice and making my way across, taking provisions and even a makeshift tent to enable me to stay away several days. Whereas I had been deterred the previous summer from attempting the assault by my lack of clothing and my general ignorance, I was now better equipped both mentally and materially and ready to have a go. As yet the approaches to the inland ice were impassable. Frequent avalanches of snow crashed down from the rocky slopes with a thunderous roar, creating clouds of flying snow and burying everything that lay in their way.

And so Scruff and I contented ourselves with short excursions. In spite of the fact that most of the pack ice had broken up and drifted out to sea, the icy causeway around the perimeter of the shore was still intact. We generally chose to travel east along it, going a little bit farther with every sortie in the hope of exploring a smaller, ice-free peninsula than our own. There was, unfortunately, one problem with this route. For some reason that I could not understand, the ice foot leading on to the next peninsula was worn away for a distance of about thirty yards. I had noticed, however, that the pack ice that swept past the coast when the wind was in a certain direction sometimes jammed up against the shore, forming a bridge in place of the ice causeway. This was safe enough to walk on provided one kept a weather eye open for a change in the drift. Since practically the whole of the coastline was made up of precipitous high cliffs except for the rocky peninsulas, this circuit of the coast was the only way that Scruff and I could indulge our exploratory yearnings.

I had learnt much by the mistakes I had made since first arriving. I always set out with enough food to last several days if I intended to make a long trek. I also always made sure to have my tinderbox and some blubber along with me, together with skins with which I could make some sort of shelter or windbreak. All of this I hauled behind me on a very utilitarian piece of equipment that I am reluctant to call a sledge. It was made of a selection of the bleached whale bones that I had found, which I lashed together to form two rough curved runners and to which I attached several cross bones for a platform. Over this I placed a skin wrapped around my belongings and tied the bundle firmly so it would not fall off. The whole thing was very light, and if not robust enough for rocky terrain, it served very well for the kind of short journey we made along the ice foot.

I carried with me a knife and the sealing hook attached to a length of cordage. The latter served both as a weapon, should I decide to catch a bird, and as a grappling iron for hauling in some piece of driftwood or flotsam that might be out of reach. On several forays I discovered bits of wreckage along the coast, washing in and out just out of reach on the tide, and I was able to retrieve them by throwing the sealing hook over them and dragging them in.

One day, having safely crossed the bridge of pack ice to a beach on the unexplored peninsula, I was distracted by the sight of several tall dorsal fins rising and sinking beneath the surface some distance from the shore. On lengthier examination, I observed that the fins were saberlike, which meant that they could belong to none other than a school of killer whales, the most feared of all predators in the sea. These had themselves no known predator and were considered to be the most cruel and most vindictive of all hunters, killing not as most creatures did, to satisfy the calls of hunger, but from the sheer lust of killing. Not uncommonly, they would maim their prey in the most pitiful manner and play with it till they tired of their sport and abandoned it to wreak further carnage elsewhere. I well recalled my crew mates' tales in which the killer whales were reputed to have deliberately upset boats in order to attack the men in them.

Large baleen whales were terrified of them. The killers hunted in packs, tearing the tongue out of the larger animal and leaving it to bleed to death while the killers indulged themselves with their favourite delicacy. Even as I reminded myself of this, I became aware of a commotion in the waters all around. Hundreds of penguins were shooting out of the sea for the safety of ice floes or dry land. The mass of seal herds that had been bobbing about contentedly till now turned in one accord as the animals made a mad scramble to get ashore. Mother seals called urgently to their young to hurry, while some of these bleated plaintively from the water, either too tired or too frightened to swim any faster. Meanwhile the black fins rose and sank, bringing their sinister owners closer. Here and there odd patches of red showed up where some unfortunate victim had been caught.

I watched transfixed, amazed by the extraordinary spectacle of hundreds of sea creatures overcome by panic and intrigued by the sinister aspect of the killers' approach. They cruised, following the line of the ice edge, while over the water came a loud "snoof" as they exhaled in a long bushy spout. Nearby, a small iceberg, on which were crowded both seals and penguins, had drifted close. Several of the whales took up positions around this, their bodies perpendicular and their heads raised clear of the water. They waited motionless, their small eyes fixed on the animals that had taken refuge.

I heard a piteous bleating. Looking to one side, I saw a baby fur seal flapping its little flippers and trying to scramble up a rock that was too steep for it. The mother leaned down over the rock, calling to it and encouraging it. Although she tried to grasp the youngster by the neck, she could not. The killers were only a few yards away. As they began to close, the mother dived into the water to help the baby. Nuzzling it, she tried to push it to safety. When this failed, she caught it by the neck and tried to lift it. The rock was high and the pup obviously heavy, but the mother balanced against a jut of rock with her fore flippers as she held it. The pup struggled to climb up, clawing at the surface of the rock with its flippers, but the effort was too much, and they both fell backwards. Frantic, the mother tried again to save her pup. This time she came up beneath it, almost as if to give it a heave up on her back so that it could jump to safety. I held my breath, unable to move as I watched the drama. Suddenly a fin cut the water nearby in a rush. There was a flurry and red smother of foaming sea as the mother disappeared completely. Miraculously, the pup had just managed to jump before its support gave way beneath it. It was struggling to keep its balance half over the edge of rock where it had landed, while the head of the killer rose to reach it. I could feel myself cringing with fear for it. When, by the grace of God, it cleared the rock, it still stood dangerously close to the edge, looking over and crying piteously. I was deeply distressed by this incident, and while pondering on the fate of the poor little orphan left all alone, I realized I had lost sight of Scruff, who, I had thought, was beside me.

The next instant my blood froze. I saw that she was in the water not far away, playing with some floating object. Porpoising and splashing, she flipped the small object from place to place, oblivious of the killers nearby. Struck dumb with fright, I could neither shout nor whistle to call her back. I could only watch, hoping desperately she would get bored with the game and return quickly. But she seemed engrossed, pulling the object underneath the water and letting it bob up again in order to pounce on it gleefully. Meanwhile nine fins cruised slowly back and forth with unnerving deliberation, and occasionally all nine fins would point towards her. Why they had not attacked by now I could not fathom. It was as if something unseen was protecting her; otherwise, they would have been upon her, I was sure, with rapacious greed.

Unaware of the danger Scruff continued playing, getting closer all the while to the whales who lay in wait for her. Suddenly finding my voice, I screamed to her, darting out across the ice pack to where she was swimming beyond. Whether in answer to me or not, she turned towards the ice, and the fins began chasing restlessly back and forth, churning the water as they thrashed about. Then, catching sight of me running forwards, Scruff turned away again. In response, the fins changed direction and headed directly for her. I could see a submerged reef separating Scruff from the whales. They came to a halt in line on the other side of it while she frolicked, sometimes near it and then away from it, still engrossed in her game. Sooner or later, I knew she was going to stray beyond the barrier, which, I could tell as I got closer, formed a complete semicircle around where she was playing. Once this happened there would be no saving her from the jaws of death.

I called to Scruff again. Seeing me, she once more darted mischievously towards the reef, clowning about in the water, and looking over to find out if I was watching. I had to stop still lest I cause her to go over the reef. I was becoming desperate, not only because she might stray within reach of the killers but because, a slight freeze had got up and the ice was beginning to creak and grind together. Any minute there was the possibility that it would drift away from land. Sure enough, as I looked at the pool in which Scruff was still gambolling, I could detect that the distance was diminishing between the ice I was on and the reef, which meant that the ice was already drifting out to sea— and as the ice moved seawards, it would force Scruff out of the area of safety. If this happened, she would be dead within seconds.

I took a gamble which was in itself most dangerous. I lay down on the ice so that Scruff could not see me unless she came out of the water onto the floe. By doing this, I hoped to lure her to me. Each second that I waited before she appeared was agony. While I lay there, the ice was constantly moving farther away from land. Then, suddenly, she was beside me, jumping joyfully all over me and allowing me to catch her and hold her close. We would now have to try to find a place where we could safely leap ashore. A wide gap of water already separated us from the cliffs, and the ice was moving ever faster, caught not only by the wind but by a current. I judged that the floe we were on had already passed over the submerged rocks.

I looked towards the sea and saw that the killers were at the edge of the ice, their huge black and yellow heads bobbing up and down to get a look at us. Then suddenly they dived. The next moment I felt the ice cake on which we were standing beginning to tilt. The killers had come up underneath it, banging their heads against it to try to break it up and topple us off. The ice was cracking and splitting all around us, and the huge heads of the killers kept popping up through the gaps between the ice pans to take a look at us before they dived underneath the floe again. Scruff sensed the danger and, staying close at my heels, she jumped with me from one floe to the next. We had drifted at least twenty-five yards from the shore, and the large mass of ice was fracturing and separating into smaller pans under the combined assault of whales and waves. Sooner or later, if we could not reach land or some very much thicker ice floe, we would be pitched into the sea.

I cast my eyes around quickly for some safer piece of ice. All I could see was an iceberg that looked as if it would pass several yards away. I was about to ignore it when I noticed how low its profile was on the near side, low enough for us to clamber onto it if we could only get close. But the chances of doing this were remote, since the current was moving us farther and farther away. It was then that I remembered the sealing hook. If I could throw it onto the berg and it caught on some projection, I could use it to pull our floe closer by hauling in the rope hand over hand.

As the only chance left to us, it was worth a try. I threw the hook, but it did not bite. Feverishly I hauled it in again. The second time it caught. The killers, sensing what we were about, started coming up under the edges of the ice, breaking off pieces and so tipping the floe that we came dangerously close to falling into the sea.

Hauling in the line, I was hot with fear. It had caught amongst some knobbly bits of ice that might easily break with the strain on them. Meanwhile our floe was moving towards the berg at a steady rate. The tension in my arms was almost unbearable as we pulled across the current, and I expected at any moment to be dislodged. For some unaccountable reason the killers held off, contenting themselves by poking their enormous heads out of the water while debating the next move.

The piece of ice, which had been about thirty feet square when we started, was now barely ten feet either way, and a crack already ran through it. Luckily for us, we were only four feet away from the berg when the killers struck again. I was getting ready to jump, having told Scruff to do so first, when the ice rose, lifting me several feet into the air. Aware of the floe shattering into tiny pieces all around me, I threw myself forwards under the impetus of the lift. I was scrambling frantically to climb aboard the berg, nearly toppling backwards into the ice water, when a piece of ice I had grabbed came away in my hand. Clutching and crawling with the strength given only in the direst emergencies, I managed to haul myself onto the ledge of ice just as a furious killer whale sprayed me with what seemed like the tangible evidence of a ferocious roar.

Cold as it was lying on my belly on the ice, for a few minutes I was paralyzed by my narrow escape. The ledge I was on was slippery, and I did not want to jeopardize my safety by moving until I was sure I would not go slithering straight into the sea. Only after I had composed my nerves did I remember Scruff. A second later I knew she had made the jump when my left ear was blasted by a hot, friendly and familiar snort.

Once I had established that I was safe, if only temporarily, I experienced a kind of morbid fascination in observing the whales. In point of fact, they could be described as fairly handsome beasts. They were smaller than most whales, probably averaging about twenty feet, and they were marvellously streamlined, which no doubt enabled them to travel at speed. Their colouring was striking. They were blue-black on top with splashes of yellow behind the eyes and dorsal fins and with a broad expanse of white underneath. The tail fins were proportionately greater than in any other species, but what impressed me most was the length of their dorsal fins, which reached five or even six feet. These cut through the water like enormous scythe blades, making me start back when they came towards the berg for fear they might cut it through. Even more frightening were their large mouths and their formidable array of teeth. The reality of the creatures was every bit as terrifying as any nightmare.

One might have thought that the whales would soon have tired of their vigil, but they seemed unwilling to forget us and let us drift on our way. At one time all nine of them surrounded the berg, rising vertically and holding that position for many seconds, their heads only inches away. If it was their intention to disconcert us, they certainly managed to do so. There was something peculiarly menacing in such intelligent cooperation, just as there had been when they had tried to knock us off the floe.

Our predicament was certainly bizarre. To be marooned on a drifting iceberg was dangerous enough, but add to that the proximity of a pack of man-eating whales and you have a situation which seems too improbable to be true. The berg, moving slowly now, was caught in a current that would take it past the headland of our own peninsula. From there it would probably drift until it broke up somewhere out in the open sea. There was no way that we could survive once we had passed the peninsula. If we were to escape at all, it would have to be soon. Were it not for the killer whales, there would, of course, have been a chance for Scruff to swim ashore at any time; but whatever the circumstances I sensed the little creature would stay with me till the bitter end.

The berg we were on was strong. At its highest point it must have been about thirty feet above the sea. It shelved down from there into various levels that were surrounded by smaller pinnacles that gave on to our small, low, sloping area of hummocky ice. As one would expect, it was a cold place on which to remain for any length of time, uncomfortable to sit on and dangerously slippery if one tried to move about. What is more, it pitched unpleasantly as the wind got up, and every few seconds we were drenched with freezing spray. My teeth were chattering, and I was having a terrible struggle to keep from being washed into the sea. Scruff, who was better suited to bear the inconvenience, nevertheless had become rather subdued. The more I thought about our circumstances, the more they frightened me. The realization that there was nothing I could do to save myself was a small comfort in its own strange way. It meant that for the first time in months I could await whatever destiny had in store without worrying whether more was expected of me.

How long it took to approach the peninsula I could not say. Maybe it was an hour; it may even have been two. Whatever it was, I was by then almost numb from the wet and the cold and the effort of trying not to lose my balance and slip into the sea. In all that time the whales had not let up their uncanny vigil, nor did they seem any less frightening. As we neared the head of the peninsula I scanned the coastline in a frantic search for something that might assist us in our escape. There was nothing that made me feel the least bit confident, nor anything that offered even some small measure of hope. To make matters worse, the berg was increasing its speed and shuddering, caught by a strong and turbulent countercurrent.

The berg began to revolve and rock precariously. My feet went out from under me, and I should have slipped straight off it had I not taken the precaution moments earlier of tying myself to the berg by my wrists against the possibility that my fingers might be too frozen to enable me to do so later. Waves broke over the platform I was on, drenching me through, and the head of a killer broke the surface within inches of my feet. The wide maw opened to catch me as I floundered seawards and snapped shut equally quickly when I retracted my legs. I heard a crunch like the sound of bones cracking. I was convinced my feet had been sundered in spite of feeling no pain. When I had the courage to look along the length of my body as the berg rolled the other way, I saw, thankfully, that my feet still belonged to me, but where they had formerly been resting a crescent-shaped bite had been removed from the berg. Without warning, all hell let loose in the waters around me. The platform juddered mercilessly under the assault of the whales as they butted it in concert with their heads. I dreaded the moment they might break a sizable chunk off. If this happened, the whole berg might capsize before it righted itself, in which case I would be trapped beneath it, tied by the wrists. It would be a mercy then if I drowned before I was cut to pieces by the killer whales. Scruff, sensing that the danger was worse than before, began to make small whimpering sounds, keeping as close to me as possible.

Quite unexpectedly, the berg stabilized and took a course at right angles to its original route. Instead of drifting along a line that would take it past the headland, it was headed on a collision course for the labyrinth of sharp pinnacled rocks that jutted out from the tip of the peninsula into the sea. With the realization of this, I forgot even the whales for the moment while a new problem filled my mind.

I had no doubt that if the berg continued on this way it would soon run aground. What is more, it would probably smash up against the rocks. In spite of the spray being dashed high against them, I could see that they were extremely jagged—some with an almost scalpel fineness to their edges. Ironically, fate had presented us with an opportunity of getting off the berg, yet we would be no better off. We would be stuck on a horrible jagged ridge of rock with fifty yards of seething, reef-strewn water between us and the shore. For Scruff to attempt to swim ashore from there would be dangerous, and I would never have given a thought to the possibility of attempting it myself had not the alternative of falling victim to the killer whales been even more terrifying.

If I were to get ashore, I would have to "hop" from reef to reef, braving fearsomely rough waters in between. The reefs ran in broken parallel lines, forming narrow channels which pointed ashore. The one advantage of this set of circumstances was the fact that the reefs were so close together that the killer whales could not follow us into them. In readiness for action, I cut myself loose, clinging to the berg with my hands.

Scruff, in spite of having the advantage over me, would be at the mercy of the very strong forces of nature on this part of the peninsula, and I was not sure whether she would pull through. Therefore the moment before the berg collided was quite emotional. I hugged and kissed her, fearing I might never see her again, and feeling very tender towards the little creature who had been my companion for so long. I was so deeply grateful to her that I could not hold back my tears at the thought that she too might be about to die.

Deaf to my entreaties to her to swim ashore, Scruff would not leave me. I had to lead the way, balancing precariously along the knife edge of the rocks and within seconds of abandoning the berg, I was hurt when I slipped and fell. Once we had entered the reefs, the killer whales had left us with what sounded like nine snorts of fury, so at least there was no danger from them now. Even though she was aware that the sea was treacherous, Scruff finally decided she would be better off trying her chances in it rather than balancing on the evilly sharp rocks. I travelled as far as I could on the ridge I was on. Then, taking a deep breath, I followed her into the icy foam.

The next instant my heart stopped. I tried to swim, but the cold crippled all movement. Caught up in the maelstrom, I was spun and churned about and finally slammed up against the reefs. My breath exploded from my lungs, and I thought I must drown. I was pulled under again and jerked this way and that, scraping my face and body painfully. Recovering from the shock of cold, I struck out with my arms and clawed for a hold on the rocks that would be long enough for me to snatch a breath. Then down and under I went again.

Several times I was ducked and flung about unmercifully. I might well have drowned had not the force of the water actually thrown me onto a ledge formed inside a huge pinnacle of rock. This unusual feature was tall and broad, with a large hole in the middle of it like a needle's eye. Washed into the eye of the needle, I lay there trying to recover my breath while I reviewed my chances of getting ashore. In some ways I was better off than I had been previously. I had still a fair amount of water to cross, but the rocks close by would allow me to travel along them for several yards closer in to shore. I slipped and fell when I tried this, and very soon my hands were cut and bleeding. Nonetheless, I had only about thirty yards to go when I entered the water again.

The shock of immersion was not as crippling, which was just as well, since I had to use both hands and feet to fend off the shattering impact as I slammed against either side of the narrow channel. Scruff was forgotten, I was so hard put to saving myself. I had a terrible struggle to keep from being swallowed up or pulverized by the raging sea. Although the shore was only thirty yards away, each yard gained signified an exhausting battle. Between bouts of swimming I scrambled onto the rocks to regain some breath and strength for the next bit, but these rests were almost as terrible as being in the sea.

I was exhausted before I had reached the halfway mark, and every muscle in my body ached in spasm. Just when I did not think I could keep up the struggle any longer, I let my eyes rest vacantly on the close but seemingly inaccessible shore. A movement near the beach made me focus reluctantly, and I saw that Scruff had made it. Encouraged, I struck out again. I was so cold and desperately tired that I hardly knew what I was doing, and even to this day I have no recollection of coming ashore.

23

Scruff's Choice

The evening of January 21 the peninsula was magically tranquil. Scavenging birds had disappeared, and the seals dozed contentedly. Even the penguins were mute, mesmerized by the moment's mystery. The occasions were rare when such total peace prevailed and they were always deliciously hypnotic, lulling one into a state of sentience when all blissful fantasies seemed possible. I sat, just idly gazing, where ice here and cloud there contrived spectacular mirages above the horizon.

My imagination played with the sight of icebergs scattered in extraordinary display. I conjured ships from the pillars of ice balanced on the horizon. One I compelled to sail our way till it became a lovely symphony of masts and yards and delicate spidery tracery. The mirage was the most beautiful I had ever seen, and I gazed enchanted. I was marvelling at the extraordinary power of the imagination to give substance to the wildest dreams when something about the vision made me start and strain my eyes. I caught my breath, my heart pounding with excitement.

All at once the image had altered, the contours changing and the parts falling away like mainsails unfurling. It had spun around, making a turn to starboard and begun sailing west, away from us, as could no fantasy. A ship! Could it be true? The thought was too incredible, and yet there she was—a three-masted barque—as sure as I was alive and human. "Ship ahoy! Ahoy there! Ahoy! Ahoy!" I yelled repeatedly. I jumped and pranced about, flapping my arms frantically to attract attention. I hopped and skipped, danced and capered, called lustily and continued to flap my arms. Scruff, who had sprung up with a yap, looking for a cause for my sudden frenzy, flew at the penguins, whom she routed, squawking.

"Aark-aark! Aark-aark!" they screeched persistently while neighbouring penguin colonies started to shrill. The gap lengthened between ship and island, and birds swooped in, splitting the air with their raucous cries. The elephant seals honked and bellowed and the fur seals barked to return their call. The clamour reached a deafening crescendo when the surrounding cliffs bounced back the roar. I had never heard such jarring discord as this simultaneous chorus of wild outcries. I had set the whole peninsula a-panic with my outburst as I watched my chance of rescue fade.

I rushed for blubber to set alight a beacon before realizing it would take hours to fetch and carry enough to make a suitably strong blaze. By then the ship would be leagues away, obscured from the peninsula. But I had to make the effort even if I knew it would be too late. I brought up fuel with difficulty. The night was quickly falling, and blankets of fog encircled me, making the darkness doubly dense. Throughout the night, however, I continued fetching and carrying, stoking the fire repeatedly to increase the blaze.

When morning came, the fog had not lifted, and for the next two days it barely thinned at all. No ship was to be seen when visibility was clear again, and I cursed myself for my negligence in not having been prepared. I could not expel the galling notion that I could have been delivered from my icebound prison if only I had had some foresight. I realized I would now have to construct a chain of coastal beacons. With these I should be able to announce my presence several leagues away should the ship return or should others like her be brought to these waters by some accident or obscure design.

Without delay I set about the task of building cairns and filling them with blubber, which I could ignite quickly. I hardly slept for the next few days. Preparing my signals involved slaughtering more elephant seals to fuel them, and my muscles complained at all the extra work. Wherever I went from then on, I carried a tinderbox with me, together with enough moss and lichen to provide tinder for several fires.

Between times, I started to put my camp in order. In case I had to make a quick departure, I would not leave the place in a disorderly state. The records that I had reduced to the briefest description for want of space in my journal I wrapped together with a map I had made of my location on a piece of depilated, bleached sealskin to take back with me. For the most part my journal described the habits of the wildlife and my observations on the weather written with a quill from a mixture of charcoal and gall. A copy of the map with details of my caches and food and clothing I transcribed onto another piece of depilated seal-skin which I now placed in a small cask (the one I had opened that first Christmas) for the benefit of any future sealing parties or for any unfortunate mariner who might, like me, be marooned without any other sources of help. The records I wanted to keep, not simply as a memento but because they represented a substantial effort on my part. I intended one day to write of my experiences and share the knowledge I had acquired during the last year for the benefit of my fellowmen.

In spite of seeing no more of the ship, I was loath to think that it would not return, and others also, once she reported safely back to port. I knew that the location of rich sealing grounds was a jealously guarded secret and that any skipper coming upon the island would want to suppress the information. But someone would invariably blab about the discovery of new beaches in the taverns when liquor loosened his tongue, and I suspected that the excitement of discovering sealing islands beyond the borders of the previously known world would be too much of a secret to guard for any crew. My isolation was temporary, I had no doubt of it. Only one ship needed to return from these parts with a big cargo of oil and sealskins for others to shadow her every minute of the night and day. If this happened, scores of ships would be arriving in the vicinity; and I was going to be ready for them with a string of lighted beacons that would set afire the very heavens with the fierceness of their blaze.

In the heat of my enthusiasm for my new task I allowed nothing to distract me, hauling heavy stones to the chosen sites with back-breaking dedication and building them into broad, hollow columns which I crammed with blubber. I toiled all day and all night for several days, building and butchering, while the birds of prey stuffed and gorged themselves on the unwanted carcasses. I had neither time nor patience to devote to Scruff.

At first she was content to ignore the slight and keep me company, nosing into the stone constructions with a snort or sniff and generally amusing herself as her mood suggested. When the days went by with no apparent end to my neglect of her or to my time-consuming labours, she became restless and looked for means of attracting my attention. I had to shove her off when her wriggling presence became an obstacle. Instead of deterring her, this rejection only served to encourage her the more to leap and run circles around me with blissfully uncontrolled exuberance. When she was happy, her eyes shone and her mouth parted, giving her a look of uninhibited carefree laughter that I should never have been able to resist had I not been so tired and preoccupied. My mind was set on completing my task, however, and her playfulness was an irritant that left me vexed and testy. When, becoming livelier still, she leapt on the cairn I was constructing, knocking the stones flying, I lashed out with my fist and hit her.

As soon as I had done it, I loathed myself. She yapped, and all joy vanished from her eyes. A look of hurt and bewilderment swept over her pretty face. Unable to bear it, I stopped to hug her, full of remorse for my loss of temper and only then realizing the extent of my neglect of her. I promised I would make amends. She looked at me in understanding, her face softening with forgiveness, and I felt touched and humbled in the presence of such gentleness.

I had just decided to leave the cairn for another time to devote myself to my young companion when I was struck silent with a thought. What was to become of Scruff if I should leave the island? So important was this question that I took several days to resolve it. Initially, my reaction was that she should come back with me to England, but the more I thought about this the less it seemed the right solution, even if I could overcome the obvious impracticalities. To remove her from her true element would make her totally dependent on me. Much as I would love her as a pet—and indeed I could not bear the thought of losing her—she was too intelligent and beautiful to be confined in such a way. Scruff was essentially a wild animal and belonged in her natural habitat.

But if I were to leave the island when the chance arrived, I could not just abandon Scruff to her fate. A partially tamed animal would have little chance of surviving on her own unless she underwent some intensive reconditioning to help her adjust. This would not be easy in Scruff's case. From birth she had led a singularly bizarre existence as the companion of a man whose friendship and land-bound habits she had come to accept in preference to the companionship and pelagic way of life of her own kind. Even now she demanded my affection just as much as she had done when she was a tiny pup. And yet, in spite of this, I knew that, if I could wean her from her attachment to me, life with the other fur seals out at sea, on a continuing basis, must be infinitely richer than anything I or this sterile peninsula could provide.

I did not need to be reminded how much I owed to her. Life would have been unbearable for me alone during the winter, and I was quite sure that without her comforting presence I should have been hard-pressed to find the will to survive. She had several times dragged me back from the brink of madness, and throughout all our misery she had retained an essential joy in being alive. Providence had thrown us together when we were in need of comfort and we had grown strong in each other's company, bearing hardship together which singly neither of us could have coped with. Robust and inured to adversity, we were now better equipped to survive on our own. But Scruff needed liberating from the emotional bond that held her in thrall. She had been born a wild creature and no doubt would still have remained so had not her mother been brutally slaughtered by one of my own kind. By adopting her and looking after her till she was capable of foraging and looking after herself, I had repaid the debt mankind owed to her. If I were to be truly fair, I should now be willing to let her go free.

The arguments were irrefutable. While there was time I would have to naturalize her in the hope that by the end of summer she would be encouraged to go to sea with the other seals. For her to survive, she must learn from them and respond to nature like the other wild pups. The protective intuition with which she had been born must be restored.

But a terrible thought kept nagging me: suppose a ship did not return for me this year? For that matter it could be several years before a ship was seen again, and there was even the possibility that I might never be saved at all. Winter, I reminded myself, had been bad enough with Scruff as my companion. I should be insanely lonely if I were to spend another one without the consolation of her presence. Selfish as such an attitude was, it made me falter and weigh the matter over for several days.

I continued with the task of building beacons, although it had come to give rise to a melancholy I could not shake off. Where previously I had been enthusiastic I was now lagging. The price of freedom was the renunciation of the companionship of the creature who had become dearer to me in my year of isolation than any other life on earth. If the beacons fulfilled their function, I would be destroying a unique relationship with the most beautiful and responsive of animals, and I could replace it with nothing but uncertainty for both myself and Scruff.

No wonder I fretted and balked at making a decision that would have so much power to affect both our lives. I might have gone on in such a manner had not the advanced state of the season forced me to make up my mind. Time was pressing, digging her sharp claws in me. If I did not begin Scruff's reeducation soon, I might be too late to rehabilitate her before the other seals returned to the sea.

I had to avoid the trap of destroying the bond between Scruff and me before I had the chance of replacing it with something as good. The year spent with Scruff had taught me how sensitive were the feelings of the little creature and how very easy it would be to break her heart. Animals, I believed, were as capable of suffering grief as any human.

If I had been allowed plenty of time, the process of alienation could have taken place gradually, and by degrees she could have looked for companionship with others of her kind. But it was already January 28, and there were only six weeks or so before the seals would start to migrate.

During the summer, I had made it a practice to spend all day out of doors when the weather was reasonable, going around the peninsula and erecting weatherproof cairns, which I stocked with enormous quantities of blubber and food. Learning from previous mistakes, I had located these in places well above sea level and out of the line of all possible avalanches. What is more, I aimed to stock them with enough to survive two whole winters lest any unforeseen catastrophe should occur to rob me of part of my stores again. This provisioning and the business of collecting skins had kept me well occupied, but until I saw the ship, I had always found time each day for a ritual hour or so of play with Scruff. She accompanied me everywhere inland and was happy to go swimming and foraging if the work of scraping or stretching skins kept me near the beach.

When I sewed or did other domestic chores that I kept for the bad weather, Scruff would amuse herself in the den with me. A small container filled with stones would entertain her for hours while she listened to and rolled it around. If she became bored, she would steal the garment I was sewing and scamper outside with it, and I would follow in pursuit. She was never happier than when she had me involved in some game.

I told myself I must now cut down on the time I spent playing with her and must even desert her for parts of the day. Only in this way could I gradually break her of her reliance on me and prepare her for her new life. But the practical problem of abandoning Scruff was not that simple. All the places inaccessible to her on the peninsula were even more inaccessible to me unless I fixed ropes at certain points along difficult terrain to give me the necessary haulage and support.

While I had nurtured the desire to climb up the inland ice and explore its periphery, partly for the adventure and partly because I wanted to find out if there were better, less bleak locations in which to live, superficial reconnoiters for a route had indicated that it would be a hard and even dangerous climb and one that would need a lot of preparation. In the circumstances I was content to explore the peninsula, which still contained many beaches that up till now had been too snowbound to visit.

Undertaking Scruff's alienation provided me with the incentive I needed. While she was in the sea, I scaled a rock near the hut that was too precipitous for her to climb. Hiding behind its ample cover on the top allowed me a good view of the beach. When she came out of the water, I could see her register my absence with a look of surprise. She darted around eagerly, relishing what she thought must be a game of hide and seek. She searched in all the usual places for me, and I caught glimpses of how her face would light up each time she approached a hideout with the warm expectancy of discovering me and how her expression dissolved into worry and disbelief when I could not be found. I was distressed to see her so unhappy. She sniffed the air, giving a sort of desolate whimper, before sinking to the ground and crying with the discovery that she was all alone.

This was the first of many such sorties, and their effect on Scruff was enough to wring the heart. How quickly she became miserable! She even hesitated to leave me on the beach while she went into the sea. I could not bear to go any distance and used to spend ages just watching her from nearby where I could not be seen. When she became unhappy, I had a great urge to bound out and comfort her and pretend that it was, in fact, only just another game. But I knew it would be wrong to do so and that it would be much harder the next time for me to resist the engaging quality of her appeal.

When I did force myself to go to the other beaches, I was equally miserable. I could not stop thinking of her, nor could I banish from my mind the tragic wistfulness of her look. I had

little consolation in arguing that my departure was for her benefit. It just made me lonelier to think that some time soon there
was the strong chance we would part. Even a few hours made
me pine for her company, and I started to doubt that I could
bear the thought of losing her.

When I returned, Scruff was always waiting for me. In an
instant her dejection would disappear and a look of relief and
pleasure would sweep her face. As I dropped down the last few
feet of the sheer rock I had climbed, she would throw herself
upon me and shower me with caresses that I knew I did not
deserve. Snuffling and blowing, she would sigh in her delight and
nuzzle me tenderly in the face and neck.

I was not too worried about these rapturous demonstrations of
affection. Scruff had always expressed her devotion to me in a
rather excitable way. But as time went by, I could not help feeling that her puppy love had an element of passion in it which
underlay an insecurity that bordered closely on despair. I worried that it would leave a dangerous void if I were to root out
affection that ran so deep. I alternated periods away with
stretches when we spent hours together, hoping in this way to
accustom Scruff to being without me for short periods, which I
would gradually increase.

We went for walks if it was fine, and I kept close to the water
to encourage her to swim in the sea. But she rarely stayed long
before breaking off to come out and nuzzle me. What is more,
she swam unusually close to the beach instead of exploring farther out as formerly, and she was content to sit by me rather
than play with any of the other seals. I hoped this might be a
temporary reaction, but as time passed and my trips away from
the beach became longer, I noticed that Scruff was no less
attached to me. Now, at least, I did not sneak away while she
was swimming, preferring to go in full view of her rather than to
betray her trust in me. When she tried to follow, I spoke sternly.
Maybe sensing the inexorable quality of my insistence, she
obeyed my wishes and stayed. She could always detect the days
when I was going to leave her. The night before she would
spend hours snuffing and nibbling me in what I believe was a
plea for me not to go. In the morning she would be loath to let

me leave the tent, almost tripping me up in her endeavour to remain close. Were it not all so hopelessly pathetic, I would have found funny the way she gave me such lingering fond looks.

By the time the moult was well advanced I had cached nearly all the stores that I would need. I had seen no other ship to encourage my hopes of rescue and was gradually coming to terms with the possibility that I would have to spend another winter in this latitude. Faced with this, I was tempted to cut short the reeducation of Scruff and continue as we had done before. Then my conscience would intrude with the argument that, having gone so far, I should continue with the program until the time came when Scruff could choose for herself what kind of life she preferred to lead.

I decided I must prolong my absences. Only in this way could I be sure I would not weaken in my resolve. In preparation, I lived a kind of lie to Scruff, with just an occasional lapse towards my true feelings, which my own desolation had to allow. For a start I stopped her sleeping with me, barring the entrance to the tent to prevent her getting in. Those nights, I could not sleep. I was driven nearly to distraction by the sound of her crying, which was as pitiable as the wailing of a child. In the morning she would jump up to greet me when I went outside, and I had to force myself to ignore her, pretending churlish temper by shoving her aside when she tried to approach.

Such constraints on my natural feelings could not be borne without some ill effect. My body showed signs of strain from the suffering that the spirit had to endure. I could not eat. At the mere thought of Scruff and the misery I was causing her, my stomach would seize up with the most acute and lingering pain. A great restlessness spread through my body and made me fidgety and unable to control the muscular spasms I was starting to suffer. Again I was tempted to abandon the project, arguing that it was doing nothing but causing both of us distress; yet conscience would argue even louder that in another year the difficulties of returning her to the wild would be greater.

With my resolve renewed, I made haste to outfit myself for several days away. Scruff sensed, I was sure, a new purpose in my activities. Learning that her demonstrations of devotion were

unacceptable, she toned them down and tried to be less exuber-
ant in her approach. Such consideration was as heartbreaking for
me to see as it was touching. It suggested that my pup was growing up—learning to mask her emotions in a way that signified a
loss of innocence in the awareness of grief.

She prowled restlessly around me while I worked, whining
softly to herself and sighing, her eyes fixed on me for fear I
would disappear if she turned away. I could not bear to face her
squarely, in case I should weaken if I caught her gaze. I had
noted that the light had disappeared from her eyes, leaving them
cloudy and troubled. I could not stay around to witness her
despair. I must go away. Maybe if she knew I was no longer in
the vicinity, she would more easily adapt.

I left the beach that afternoon without a glance at her, too
afraid of succumbing to that lost look of hers that I found so
appealing. What I had not counted on was the effect that the
separation would have on me. I had only reached halfway
towards the beach I had chosen to be my exile when I was overwhelmed by a wave of sadness that quite disabled me. Reluctant
to continue, I retraced my steps, crawling so as not be be
observed by Scruff when I came near enough to watch her. For
the whole of the day she did not move from where she had
posted herself near the foot of the steep cliff that I had climbed.
She remained alert for a long while, nosing the wind and glancing around as if she expected my arrival, but with the passage of
night and the second day, her head lowered and her body
drooped. The second night, too, she remained inert, and I had to
force myself not to rush down to comfort her.

With the arrival of the third morning I became alarmed. She
sat so still that I was afraid she would freeze in an attitude of
abject misery. Anxiously I scrambled down the path that led
to the beach, calling her name loudly to announce my return.
Before I reached her, however, she sprang to life, starting to
bound towards me before checking herself with supreme control
—her body nevertheless squirming with the uncontrollable joy
of seeing me.

I fussed over her, stroking and petting her in the way I had
always done. She wriggled delightedly, stretching her pert head

up repeatedly to make contact with my face. That day we spent together near the beach, sunning ourselves on the rocks out of the wind and enjoying each other's presence. From time to time I walked with her to the water's edge and managed with some difficulty to coax her into the sea, hoping that she would go off and forage. She had barely dived in before she was out again, rubbing up beside me as if it were too much to expect that this time I would not run off.

That night I decided to let Scruff into the tent. I could not bear to upset her again. Stroking her, I spoke aloud of the reason for all the subterfuge and she listened, appearing to understand both what I was saying and the need I had to unburden myself. I was sure she was starving. I knew she had not eaten for several days, and I felt an urge to feed her as I had done when she was a tiny pup. I killed a seal to have fresh meat for myself and turned out the stomach to give Scruff the contents. She ate it gratefully from my hand, massaging my palm with her mouth's gentle pressure as she had done when she was only a few weeks old.

We settled down for the night the way we had slept during a year of her life. As I stroked her I was reminded of all the treasured moments of our previous closeness. Sighing half in desperation and half in contentment, she fell asleep, exhausted, leaving me to brood on the awfulness of having to repress all natural tenderness. I could never have imagined how hard it would be to give up a friend or the extent of the sacrifice it demanded. The sentence I had passed on the two of us was in its own way an experience as bitter as death itself.

Scruff was still asleep when I eased away from her. Recently, any movement awakened her, but days of distress and sleeplessness had taken their toll and she had sunk into a near-coma of exhaustion. It said much for her trust in me that she had allowed herself to succumb to sleep. I would have liked nothing better than to have abandoned my plan, but to have stayed any longer with her would have destroyed my decision to desert her. Fighting my own fatigue, I sneaked away to make what I had decided must be the final break.

I made direct for one of the more distant beaches on the other

side of the peninsula. Getting there involved a difficult climb followed by a descent too steep for Scruff to follow. I planned to
remain away at least two weeks in order to give my plan the
final test. By the end of that time most of the seals would have
left the island, and only a few stragglers would remain. Camping
on this beach required little preparation. I had discovered a horizontal cleft in the cliff face that would serve as a shelter, reaching it along a hazardously narrow ledge forty feet above a sheer
drop to the sea. Here I could creep in to sleep or shelter during
bad weather, warmed by a blubber fire and stretched out on several skins to take off the chill. Lying down in this den was more
comfortable than sitting stooped under the low roof. I had
plenty of sewing to do. I needed clothes for travelling and for
the winter, but I could not bring myself to concentrate. I could
only think constantly of Scruff. From the den I looked out over
the cove where I had first come ashore and the island near where
we had anchored. To my north stretched the jagged western
coastline of the peninsula, which contrasted sharply with the ice
cliffs that flanked me on the south.

The seals had already begun to leave when I arrived on the far
beach. I could see where they had been lying and each day
noticed the numbers dwindling. The animals would also be
migrating from Half-Moon Beach, and I wondered how long it
would be before Scruff followed their example. But would she
go, or would she wait, lonely and patient, in the hope that I
would return? I missed her very much.

After a week the loneliness of my exile was almost unbearable.
I forced myself to remain, trailing along the beach aimlessly and
vowing that if Scruff were still there when I returned I should
keep her with me forever and never let her out of my sight. By
the ninth day the separation had become like a nagging, crippling ache, and by the twelfth day it had become a raging agony.
What is more, a new element had begun to creep into my conscience which contested the theory that by abandoning Scruff I
was doing her good. What if she had died while I had been
away? What if she had pined, brokenhearted? After all, for the
whole of her young existence she had adapted her life to mine.
For all I knew, this contact with man might have created an

unbridgeable gulf between her and nature. What if my efforts had been misguided? I suddenly questioned both my judgment and my methods, and my mind filled with accusations of cruelty and neglect. I could stand the isolation no longer. I would return immediately to Half-Moon Beach. Try as I might, I could no longer deny how much Scruff meant to me. I would let life take its natural course without forcing events, and I would let fate make the decisions.

With this vow, a weight lifted off my heart, and for the first time in weeks I felt elated. Before I knew it, I was hurrying to leave the beach, aware of a great urgency. Half crawling and slipping, I scrambled up the steep ascent, twisting my ankle in my feverish haste. I ignored the pain, limping and stumbling across the the high rough ground of the peninsula. One thought only engrossed my mind: to reach Scruff as quickly as I could and to reaffirm my affection for her. From now on I would never deny it. I must get to her before she became a casualty of grief or a dispossessed, unwilling migrant. Twelve days was a long time to be away—long enough for all sorts of things to happen—and I began to pray to allay the fears that crowded in on me.

My crippled foot impeded my rush to reach our familiar trails, with all their associated memories. Thick snow was falling as I hobbled along them, making the going heavy. I took the shortest and steepest route, hurtling down the last few yards in the face of the flying snow that drove my shouts for Scruff back down my throat. A thick layer of white carpeted the beach, covering even the few seals that remained, making it impossible to tell which was Scruff unless I went right up to them. Only after a cursory search showed no sign of my friend did I remember that she had never lain out in the open and that I had always encouraged her to keep to the more sheltered areas of the beach where we could get some protection. Realizing it was more than likely that she would be in those places where she had been accustomed to lie, I hastened to explore them. The weather had worsened to a storm. I would not take shelter for fear that if she were sleeping somewhere I might miss her. The wind had risen to a screaming pitch, drowning my calls. I had to rely on the possibility of stumbling upon Scruff, since it was unlikely she would hear me. Finally I was forced by the wind to stop and seek shelter, and having seen no sign of Scruff, I was beginning to worry.

As soon as the weather cleared, I was out again, searching and calling. I looked everywhere, not only on my own beach but on others we had both frequented. I searched those places amongst the rocks where I had often found dead seal pups, approaching them reluctantly in case I found her dead. Her disappearance had made me fear the worst, but I had no evidence to support these fears.

Within the next few days the last of the seals had gone, leaving me all alone except for a few birds that were late in migrating. In the face of the obvious conclusion, my mind was a good while accepting the fact that Scruff had actually departed. Ironically, although all that I had been working towards in the last seven weeks had been achieved, there was a poignancy in the victory. When I did recognize the fact that Scruff must have returned to the wild, I wept unashamedly with a sorrow that knew no suppressing. My grief was accompanied by the remorse that came from knowing I had been cruel to the silky white seal that for a year had been my constant and devoted companion. I could not easily come to terms with the part I had played in severing the friendship. Drawn frequently to the headland, I would stand gazing out to sea, hoping she would return. "Dear Scruff, forgive me!" The words were wrung from my heart. "I loved you, and I miss you beyond all understanding."

Time can heal the most hurtful wound, and this case was no exception. After a while I realized that I had made the right decision on behalf of Scruff, and I felt this with a deep conviction. As to how she would fare in the wild, I would hazard a guess that her chances were as good as those of any other fur seal. She was intelligent and she was strong and she could forage. Beyond that, destiny would affect her life as it would mine—and I was about to enter a whole new era.

24

The Ice Cap

I had resisted the urge to explore while Scruff was with me; but with my companion gone and my caches filled, there was nothing to delay me further. Although I had tried hard to forget Scruff, reminders of her were everywhere and practically every square foot of the place stirred some sad memory. When the last of the animal life had departed, the silence was unbearable; and I made up my mind to leave, if only for a short time, in order to refresh my spirits.

Apart from the challenge of contending with difficulties and the satisfaction of pitting one's wits against the forces of nature, I would also have the thrill of seeing spectacles never before viewed by human eyes. In addition, I would look for a more sheltered site to set up home, since my peninsula, jutting northwards, bore the full brunt of the frequent easterly and northwesterly gales. I suspected that I would find more protected areas on the southern side of the island. There might even be a cave suitable enough to live in, which would save the effort of building. Moving residence would pose the difficult question, however, of how to transport my food and fuel. Presumably all animal life would have departed from the southern beaches this late in the season, which would mean that I would have missed my opportunity of settling there this year. What did it matter, however? For the moment, there would be enough satisfaction in simply exploring as far as I could.

I intended to be away twenty days. Any longer journey would require an enormous weight to be hauled; food and fuel as well as the bulk of spare clothes and a tent. The latter would have to be strong enough to survive the severest weather, for already the winter storms were setting in. In theory, the more food I carried the greater distance I should be able to travel; in fact, the more weight I hauled the harder I would have to work, and the more I would have to eat to replace lost energy.

I had no idea when I started how complicated and lengthy the preparations would become. By far the greatest problem was the sledge. Not only would I have to find enough materials to construct a suitably large and strong one, but the design itself required much thought. I had an assortment of timber and seal and whalebone, and I immersed the last in water to make it easier to shape. Basically, I needed enough materials to make two strong runners, curved at the ends, which would be separated by several cross pieces for the load. Simple, one might think, but several models had to be scrapped after futile tests.

I held the trials on the inland ice. After a steep ascent to the ice dome, which involved hacking a zigzag route up a rise of hard-packed snow, I got my first taste of the wavelike irregularities in the snow crust that were to cause me so much misery and frustration on the trip itself. Even empty, the sledge was difficult to maneuver through this frozen, sealike surface, and when it was loaded, it would capsize into the troughs. I fell repeatedly, slipping on the smooth surfaces and banging myself on the jagged ridges. I had to make several modifications to the sledge before I was satisfied that I had a design that might do.

I was surprised to discover how many factors affected one's draught power. I had always assumed that the only influence was the weight, but the condition of the sledge runners and the type of travelling surface had an equally important effect. Other questions involved the way the sledge was loaded, the width of the load and the length of the sledge itself. I proved that a rigid structure was liable to break, and I was obliged to experiment with lashing the joints in different styles to make them strong and yet flexible enough to offer the most play on rough and uneven surfaces without jeopardizing their capacity to carry a load.

I had always imagined snow and ice to be very much the same from one place to another. As a sledge traveller, I found a world of difference between floundering knee-deep through soft, powdered snow and trying to keep a footing on snow that was so hard and compact and wind-polished that I could have skated on it. Equally, the experience of trudging for miles over a monotonous flat plain of snow bore no resemblance to the back-breaking and sledge-breaking effort of crossing the wind-scoured areas with their wavelike surfaces. But either condition put a strain on some part of the body. Add to that the frequent falls and the effort and weight of sledge hauling, and you have a good idea of a few of the problems that confronted me on my first essays.

When it came to making a suitable tent, the consideration of weight had to be set off against the need for enough size and durability to protect me from the onslaught of the most intemperate storm. I eventually contrived a simple, ridged structure that I could erect over the sledge, supported by a couple of vertical poles which I anchored at either end. Over the lot I draped a covering of crudely shaped sealskin that had a flap that could be tied to act as entrance and exit. The whole thing had to be anchored by staves at ground level and then banked up with snow around the edges to exclude as much draught and drift as possible. The tent was serviceable, with a small opening near the top to act as an air vent, but it was extremely heavy and cumbersome to erect.

I had thought of carrying a permanent fire with me and racked my brains to devise a safe method of transporting lighted blubber, but I failed in this respect. I finally had to take my tinderbox with plenty of spare tinder and oil to light the blubber lamp. Needless to say, the weight was beginning to mount up. On top of the food and the spare clothing which I carried in case what I was wearing got torn or wet, there were a sleeping bag, cooking pot, shovel, pickax, spare rope and various odds and ends. The load looked so enormous when it was gathered together that I wondered if I would ever manage to haul the sledge at all.

I made a harness of sealskin to pass across my waist and chest. It had a broad band reaching from it over each shoulder and crossing over the back. When I saw how numerous and camouflaged were the crevasses in the snow, I had to come up with some method of tying the trace, so that if I slipped or fell, the sledge would not tip in after me but would be carried across the opening of the gap. I concluded that this effect could be achieved only by tying the trace to the middle rung of the sledge, although doing this made the sledge swing on its axis and extremely difficult to guide.

Having discovered on my trial runs that many crevasses had a span of over seven feet, I was obliged to lengthen the runners to about nine feet as a safety precaution. Not surprisingly, in the light of all the problems I faced, a good three weeks passed before I was ready to entertain the thought of departure. Even then, I felt I was taking a gamble on the effectiveness of my equipment to do its job.

I left the peninsula on a fine day in late April, and I was excited as I lashed up the sledge. In spite of the struggle to get the full load even to the start of the incline that led to the ice cap, I was not discouraged, reasoning that it was only natural for things to be an effort until I found my stride. I had shod the runners, which had been spliced together to form the required shape, with pieces of barrel hooping for easier traction and had honed them smooth; but they were badly scratched by the rocks on the way to the inland ice and I had to go over their surface again before I began the climb.

I do not know how many times I made an attempt on the slope—getting partway and then slipping back down—but the sun had passed a whole quarter before I was eventually at the top. My clothes were wet through with sweat, and every fiber of my body ached. Still, I felt good at having passed the first obstacle, and after a brief rest I did not want to delay. Looking back at the place that had been my home for over a year, I had an

uncanny feeling that I might not be seeing it again. I had no fore-
bodings at the thought, maybe even a sense of contentment and
relief. I had spent the last night tidying up the winter hut and
the area around it, more for my own benefit than from any
expectation of a visit. I reasoned that I would be feeling lonely
on my return without my old companion to welcome me and
that a tidy place was much cheerier to come back to than a slum.
I could not restrain a twinge of nostalgia when I finally turned
away from the settlement.

In spite of the good weather, I had not travelled far before the
cold currents of the higher slopes, circulating around me and
freezing the sweat, made my body chill. Unlike the previous
trials, when I had travelled a good distance onto the ice cap, the
going was hard for me with the fully loaded sledge, and I was
soon gasping for breath. Although the straps of the harness were
broad enough not to cut me, they felt as if they were eating into
my flesh. I got such a pain across my chest after a while that
there was nothing to do except rest. I was a bit disappointed not
to have gone farther—I must have travelled only about half a
mile, but I reasoned that no more was to be expected, in view of
the weight of the load, my inexperience in handling it and the
fact that I was pulling uphill most of the time. A meal and a
couple of hours' rest would put me in good shape to carry on,
and I wanted to travel as far as possible before night came or the
weather broke.

It was an extraordinary thrill to stand on the ice cap and
survey the landscape. A blue sea, flecked with icebergs of varying size, sparkled to the north. To the northeast was the island
where our ship first found refuge, and beyond were smaller
islands and the distant point of my own landmass. Although I
had lost sight of my encampment, the whole peninsula stretched
below me, revealing parts I had never seen before. Westwards, I
could see the island where the longboat had been taken ashore
with a handful of the crew to hunt seal. Suddenly the whole of
that forgotten episode flooded my mind, along with all its conse-
quences. What an eternity had passed between then and now,
and had any group of people less idea of what fate held in store?
Sitting on the sledge, chewing a piece of blubber, I reflected on

what had happened during my sixteen months of exile and chuckled at the difference between the helpless youth who had arrived here and the resourceful man I had become. Was it not surprising how quickly man could adapt himself to adversity? And was it not remarkable how much he could achieve with guts and determination when, on the face of it, there seemed no possible way he could survive? What was that mysterious force that drives men to overreach themselves, I wondered—that force that makes a man want to transcend the boundaries of his mortal self? Could it possibly be a particle of the Divine in every human that sought to be reunited with the Greater Whole? For a good while I could not move because of the intensity of these thoughts. When I did set off again, I had shed all remnants of the loneliness I had suffered since Scruff had left. My heart was full with the knowledge that I was a pioneer—one of nature's privileged—and I turned my face inland with an urgent desire to explore.

I had intended to follow the coast westwards, pass the ice cliffs that abutted the peninsula, to the southern beaches; but during my sledge trials, I had discovered a treacherous belt of ice running along the periphery and I had therefore decided to go up onto the main ice mass. This alternate route forced me to cross a dangerously crevassed stretch to reach the safer ice. I had tested it a few days before to mark out a route and was fairly confident I could pick my way through. I was grateful for fair weather. It would have been easy to make a mistake in poor light and to stumble into a yawning abyss. Some of the crevasses were obvious; others were perfectly concealed by a thin bridge of snow. I had taken the precaution of carrying a pike to probe possibly dangerous areas. Although this testing made progress painfully slow, I was loath to hurry for fear of an accident. Indeed I got a nasty shock on one steep section when the sledge slewed sideways and a corner of it broke through the crust. As I tried to maneuver it back to safety, more of the snow crust fell away, revealing a deep chasm into which the sledge leaned at a precarious angle, threatening to plunge heavily into it with me following at the end of my trace. I could not release the harness without loosing the sledge. Somehow I would have to transfer the weight before the pull of the load became too strong. I was leaning forward, almost parallel to the surface, and were it not for the slight knobbiness of the terrain, I would have slipped downhill on my belly and plunged over the edge.

Where I had stopped, the snow cover was thin, and there was no way I could dig the pike I had made into the blue ice beneath. If there had been even a thin crack nearby I could have wedged the pike in it and belayed a line to this, attached to the harness; but any such fissures were too far for me to reach. Meanwhile I could hear the creak of the sledge as the load shifted, and I knew I must think of something before it was too late.

I do not know what made me chip away at the ice in front of me. Call it intuition, or impulse, or the desperation that makes a drowning man clutch at air; at any rate, I chipped out a U-shaped tunnel in an ice span of about six inches. This done, I fumbled at my belt to release the few feet of sail line I had slung there for just such an emergency. With fingers that seemed twice their normal thickness from cold and fright, I tried to thread the line through the tunnel after tying it to the harness. My breath was coming short now and my shoulders were aching, and at any moment I might be jerked in a wide trajectory down into the chasm. The creaking grew ominously urgent behind me. I could not thread the line through the tunnel. Why is it that anxiety makes one so clumsy? Even when I had threaded the line, bending it to the required knot took an age. I had hardly finished when there was a loud groaning noise, and I could visualize the crust collapsing beneath the strain of the sledge. The next second I was jerked almost upright. For a second I teetered, and then my knees crumpled and I was pinned to the ground in an extraordinary crouch. After another couple of seconds, I realized that the line I had just attached was taut and holding perfectly without any sign that the tunnel of ice I had made might break. I do not know how much weight I had on it, but it held as strong as if it had been made of iron.

Getting out of the harness without tipping the sledge further was a difficulty I solved before trying to tackle the load. I then had to crawl towards the sledge and undo some of the seal line that was lashed on the top. Running a line from the sledge at an angle to the trace, I could pull it clear. Had I hauled on the trace, the sledge might have slewed even farther round and dropped over the edge, in which case I would surely not have had the strength to drag it free. By attaching a second line, which I anchored like the first, I could pull on the sledge from a different direction and at the same time prevent it from slipping deeper. By taking turns in attaching the slack from each line as I heaved hand over fist, I had the full load safe on firm snow again.

When late afternoon arrived, I had extended my distance in a direct line only another half mile. I had come a tortuous route through a maze of crevasses. With the promise of a gently sloping rise ahead of me, I reasoned it would be safe enough for me to camp. I was hungry and weary but strangely satisfied. As I set about making camp, I was treated to a spectacular celestial display. The atmosphere was full of minute ice crystals that sparkled with rainbow colours in the sun's rays. The sky looked like a beautiful wine glass, tinted by warm golden tones; as I gazed, it appeared to shatter, raining delicate fragments and droplets which shone iridescent across the face of the sun. From the horizon a fine shaft of silver leaped upwards through the core of the sun, followed by another shaft, equally luminous, that transected it horizontally to form a perfect cross. Then miniature suns, coloured green and yellow, became visible simultaneously, one on the end of either arm. I was transfixed with a sense of infinite majesty, as if the Trinity itself had miraculously appeared. I had seen many beautiful examples of these extraordinary phenomena—they were called mock suns—but I can remember none as lovely or as intensely moving. The spectacle slowly dissolved, leaving me almost mystically contented. I fell asleep in the tent that night with the ease of a man who has been drugged.

I woke, at I do not know what time, with the sensation of being hammered on the head. For a minute or two I could not place my whereabouts. I soon remembered, and I realized that outside a violent storm was blowing. The wall of the tent nearest me flapped with a trouncing motion, and I had to try to lean away from it to avoid its vicious assault. The tent was too small to allow much room to maneuver.

Part of me was buffeted for as long as the storm raged, and the rest of me grew cramped from having to hold itself at such an awkward angle. The tempest lasted a good twenty-four hours. By the time the wind had ceased I was suffering from what I thought would be a permanent pain in the head.

I received no comfort when I looked outside at the weather. Gone was the radiantly clear atmosphere of the start of my journey. In its place was the milky obscurity of the all-too-familiar fog. For the next two days I was confined to the tent, except for one or two daylight hours when the fog would clear long enough for me to break camp and shuffle forward a mile or so across the desolate, gently undulating desert towards the south. Haste was impossible and dangerous. The effect of the fog was to distort all proportion, making hills out of hummocks and small hollows out of bone-juddering dips. Other hazards were disguised by dissipating shadows. I had no idea the third night out that I had made camp on the very edge of a deep crevasse. Never have I been so blissfully unaware of danger as I lay in my sleeping bag on top of the sledge. I shall never forget the shock of crawling out of the tent in the morning to find myself poised perilously over the brim. Blue ice walls, encrusted with beautiful branching growths of ice crystals, fell away to indigo depth. A false step the night before as I fixed the tent and I would have gone over, and there would have been no possible way that I could have climbed out.

I promised myself to be extra cautious. Even without the dangers of unexpected chasms or crevasses, the cold gave me plenty to think about. So bitter was it at times that my lungs were savaged with every breathful. The cold blistered exposed skin like a burn, and my nose and cheeks were soon raw and sore from its continuous scourging. Worse, when the wind blew, drifting snow grated against the skin like grains of sand. Snow and ice accumulated on the tent and sleeping bag, making them stiff as boards and awkward to handle, besides increasing their weight. With all the hard work, my hands suffered. Although they had become hardened over the last year, they split at the fingertips and around the nails, and I was worried lest I get frostbite. At least I had learned to recognize the sharp stinging sensation in the flesh that warned of this condition and took great care not to get too cold. However, my sweat still froze on me, and the inside of my garments became lined with ice. By loosening my clothes I could shake this out, but my body temperature would drop alarmingly after a few hours on the march.

On very cold days I stopped and put up the tent, lighting the blubber lamp I had brought. I ate meat raw or parboiled depending on the time I had or on my hunger. Travelling the way I did made me thirsty; and since eating snow was chilling and unsatisfactory, I devised a method of melting it while on the march. I put some in a small pouch I had made out of seal flipper and wore under my clothing against my skin. This I filled with fresh snow when I had drunk what was in it, and by such means I saved myself the bother of always having to light the lamp to get a drink.

If I were to describe all the storms I weathered and every discomfort I suffered, my journey would appear a catalogue of unmitigated woe. Although hardly one obstacle was overcome before some fresh one made its appearance, I prefer to remember those moments of elation when the pervading fog lifted and some grand scenic spectacle burst into view. I could not help gasping at the wild beauty of distant mountains suddenly revealed to the east. Ice floes and snow corries, blade ridges and lofty peaks appeared to be cast in substance not unlike alabaster, deepening into purple in the distance from their nearby delicate blush of pink. I had the conviction that I was on the threshold of a world of infinite splendour, the likes of which no man had ever dreamed of. And in the knowledge that I was witness to a scene denied to all others, I felt an exhilaration beyond any previous joyousness. I speculated on the mysteries I would yet behold if I could only find a way of sustaining myself by replenishing my food stocks along the way.

I had been gone from the peninsula ten days and had travelled about fifteen miles. Most of the journey had been spent plodding upwards towards the dome of the inland ice. Wind erosion had made the surface jagged, with deep troughs rising to such steep ridges that I had been forced to hack my way through them. From an elevation rising above the broad expanse of icy highway, I could make out foothills and snowfields and glaciers not far off, but how much energy and food I would use before getting close enough to explore them was a question that I would have to consider carefully. To travel any farther away from the peninsula would soon be to court disaster. The season was rapidly advancing, and I knew only too well how dangerous it could be to get caught out with insufficient food and fuel. Yet I could not think of returning now without being overcome by a sense of failure. By going on half rations or even quarter rations I could extend the number of days' travel; if by doing so I might put my life in the balance, I was convinced that the beauty of discovery must outweigh the risk.

What was life worth, I asked myself, if it lacked endeavour? What joy would it be to return now without the satisfaction of having reached some definite goal? True, I had no certain idea of what goal I was aiming for; but I felt that a natural turning point lay ahead that would limit this first foray of mine. It was essential to my spirit to reach it. Prudence suggested I set myself a limit of five more days. If at the end of that time nothing of any significance was discovered, or I had found no more attractive area to live, I should have to be satisfied with the journey for its own sake. With this decision made, I became extremely satisfied and, gaining strength from my determination to succeed, I pressed forward, drawn by the desire for discovery.

The following day I had the hardest travelling since setting out. The morning began misty, with sky and land merging into the same horrible dull grey. The surface was alternately hard and soft, with the hard places so slippery that my falls were frequent and jarring. On the soft surface, the sledge runners sank into the loose snow, and it required the greatest effort just to move the sledge an inch. On one steep incline, as I let the sledge descend on its own before me, it slewed sideways and slammed into a jut of rock. Several struts broke, and by the time I had the sledge repaired and reloaded I was frozen to the core, and a biting wind had risen. While the wind cleared the mist, it made little difference to my progress, merely adding a further hardship to the strain of the march. Hungry without being able to indulge my hunger, cold and exhausted, I took little comfort in telling myself that each footstep was a fresh conquest of the great unknown. Only by a repetition of the thought that things would be better tomorrow could I get my numbed limbs to move at all.

During the next two days, fate succeeded in thwarting my advance by sending a storm of such ferociousness that I feared my tent would be ripped apart if it was not blown clean off the plateau with me and the sledge. I collapsed it to the lowest possible level to decrease the sail area and lay almost flat for nearly the whole of the two days. Any fire was out of the question, and I could not even alleviate the discomfort with a decent meal. Instead, I tried to sleep as much as possible.

I got a fright when I eventually tried to rise. A deep layer of snow had frozen solid and formed a hard casing around me and the tent. I was forced to cut through my sleeping bag and stab hard at the crust several times before it would break. Even when I managed to prize the sledge out, a gravelike mound was left in its place. Setting out on an almost empty stomach without a hot drink to warm me was horrible, and worse was the condition of my clothes. They were stiff, with frozen clumps of snow and ice clinging to them, and they crackled and rubbed hard against me. I had the steepest climb of all that day and camped just short of the summit of the dome after a gruelling march.

That night was cold and miserable, and I shivered in the tent until I thought my teeth would drop out. When morning showed another misty day ahead, I feared it was already too late in the season to be travelling at all. Not only would continuing any farther be hazardous, but I might not even be able to make my way back. Reluctantly, I decided to postpone any further exploration unless I achieved some positive advance by evening.

At midday the sky had cleared, and when I reached the dome of the plateau I saw that the surface in front of me sloped gradually downwards. In the distance was a narrow sound with a rugged island beyond it. My view of the intervening country was obscured by a rocky rampart some four miles or so away. Between this and my present position it looked easy going for once; and after I had got into my stride, I found myself racing on the hard, polished snow. A couple of times I feared I had become too hasty. I broke through several layers of seemingly bottomless crust up to my waist, but overall I maintained a steady rate and covered three miles in as many hours. With the improvement in my progress, my spirits rose.

That night I felt convinced that I was on the verge of some wonderful discovery. With all the dangers surrounding me, I could not help experiencing a sense of achievement at what I had come through. Admittedly, I was still in a crevassed area, but I prided myself that I had developed an eye for even the most camouflaged of crevasses and could detect them without the probe.

I had camped by the side of a rugged glacier whose surface was such a twisted jumble of huge, irregular ridges that it left one awestruck at the thought of the pressure that could cause such a disturbance. The tops of the ridges were knife-sharp, and between the folds were deep crevasses. I would obviously have to try to find a place to cross farther along. Opposite my camp a gap in the rocky rampart offered a prospect of some fascinating snow-free country that could prove to be a sizable peninsula, but a complete view was obscured by the angle of the pass. I could not wait till the morning to explore further.

I ate a good breakfast in preparation for what I believed would be a long travelling day. The sky was clear and cloudless, promising fine steady weather. Deciding on a reconnoiter before hitching up the sledge, I discovered that, lower down, the glacier formed a natural hollow in which a honeycomb of holes had been drilled by the sun. At the height of summer the comb must have murmured with the traffic of subglacial streams, although now it was quiet—frozen into silence by the advanced state of the season. In one of the passages a shaft branched off in the direction of the coast, which at this point was only about a mile away, and I could imagine a whole network of underground tunnels snaking their way to the sea. Thinking that if I was careful I might be able to cross the glacier at this location, I hurried back to hitch up the sledge.

To begin with, I had to thread my way around a maze of forbidding, bottomless funnels that were quite awesome and frightening. After a while they seemed more widely dispersed and easier to get by. Some of the holes were filled with snow which looked firm and solid enough to tread on; but I still did not take a chance on them, preferring to go around. Although the diameter of most of them was about three feet, a few were large enough to swallow a whole sledge. The glacier itself was only about one hundred yards in width where I started out, but it would take me at least an hour to negotiate the tricky obstacle.

I was three quarters the way across when I broke through a hummock of ice. Before I knew it, my breath was knocked out of me and my harness tightened with a sudden jolt, as painful as an iron bar across my chest. I was suspended in a narrow shaft barely wider than my own body. As I had intended when I attached the trace to the inner rung of the sledge, it held me so that I would not fall farther; but instead of acting as a bridge, the sledge now acted as a lid, completely covering the opening and making it impossible for me to see anything. All around I could feel the chill of icy walls, whose smoothness allowed no foothold. Ice fragments showered down on me from the rim, and I was seized by an indescribable terror at the thought of the awful nothingness below. I groped about on every side to find some projection that I might use to lever myself up the shaft, but I could feel nothing except the slippery smooth wall. For a while I thought I would have to dangle there till I became embalmed. Then it occurred to me that, if I was careful, I could climb the trace and maybe wedge myself at the top of the shaft before pushing the sledge out of the way.

It was one thing to propose climbing the trace and another thing to do it. Maneuvering in such a tight space was extremely difficult, especially in my bulky clothing, and my hands kept slipping on the icy trace. The chill from the surrounding shaft soon attacked my body, making me stiff and clumsy, and because I was afraid that my struggles would put a strain on the sledge strut and break it, I was further inhibited from doing my best. It took several attempts to climb the trace, and I was left exhausted. I had enough to do bracing myself against the front and back walls without the added effort of trying to force the sledge out of the way. To my dismay, the sledge had jammed, or else it was heavier than I realized. At any rate, after an excruciating and unsuccessful struggle to budge it, I found myself slithering down the shaft again. As before, my descent was stopped by a sickening jolt that left me dazed and debilitated—too demoralized to try the ascent again.

Hanging limply with my head bent, I wriggled my toes and fingers, being careful at the same time not to slip out of my harness. The movement made my body rotate slightly, and I caught sight of what seemed to be the palest hint of brightness several feet below me in the shaft. My heart and pulse began to beat rapidly. Using my hands against the walls to hold me still, I searched for what I dared hardly hope. Yes, although it was too dim for me to be absolutely certain, there appeared to be a shaft leading off horizontally from the funnel in the direction of the sea. I had no way of knowing how long the shaft would be, how wide, or even if it would meet up with others or come to a dead end. Yet if there was not a reasonable chance that it could lead right beneath the glacier to the coast, how else had the water disappeared from the various melt holes?

The discovery made my mind work fast. It had to if I were not soon to succumb to the cold. Obviously I must try climbing the trace again and moving the sledge; but if this was unsuccessful, would it not be better to drop out of my harness and try exploring the shaft? I could get an approximate sense of its depth by dropping something and counting how long it took to strike the bottom. If I could hear it when it struck and if it did not seem too deep, I could perhaps take the chance of dropping to the bottom myself. The alternative was to hang helplessly where I was.

My next attempt to climb the trace was as crippling as the last and as unsuccessful. I did manage to slash the underside of the skin that covered the load so that I could reach in and retrieve some items. As I was doing this, some other items dropped past my head. While I had no thought of counting how long they took to reach the bottom of the shaft, I was aware that they landed fairly soon. Whatever I could lay hands on that was small or edible I stuffed inside my jacket, along with my journal, which I was afraid to lose. Coming upon a spare rope, I had just time to tie one end of it around two of the sledge struts before I fell for the third time. This time it took me much longer to recover my wind, but I was less afraid than formerly and quite eager to explore the adjoining shaft. By attaching the second line to the sledge I had extended my depth into the funnel. Slipping out of the harness, I shinned down to the edge of the second rope, from where I could see the bottom.

There was a drop of about six feet, which I completed without hurting myself. At the base the shaft opened out into a much wider bowl. A horizontal opening just wider than my shoulders did lead off it, and I could see a bright bluish light at the end. Daunting as was the thought of getting trapped so far below ground, I was at the same time intensely curious. Within seconds I was half slipping and half crawling along the extraordinary ice passage. Midway, it became so suddenly steep that I feared it would end in some vast underground lake or cavern from which there would be no escaping. Nonetheless, I inched forward, drawn by a desire to discover what it was that created the bluish light. A little farther on several other tunnels converged with the one I was in, forming one fairly large subglacial gallery in which it was possible to stand erect. What was equally pleasing was the fact that light filtered through several of the other tunnels and that I could now see the sky. The sensation was extraordinary. There I was in a great subterranean network yet able to look up at the sky. The light I had seen was, in fact, the greenish-blue ice of the glacier itself, which the sunlight, filtering downwards through the honeycomb of melt holes, had invested with a wonderful gemlike hue. Here and there icicles hung in glorious clusters that sparkled with brilliant crystals. I wondered whether nature would ever cease to surprise me with the wonderful mysteries she kept out of sight.

Cheered by the view of sky, I found the subglacial passageway much less threatening, even when it again steepened sharply, forcing me to continue on my behind. From the way the floor grew suddenly uneven, I could tell that a strong fast river had flowed along it in summer and worn grooves in the surface. Once my body was in motion there was no stopping it. I was soon slipping and bouncing along the crystal chute at a tremendous speed. One moment I was on my back, and the next I had bounced two feet in the air before landing painfully and continuing helplessly on my side. I could feel the sealskin of my clothes being scorched off me as my body hurtled over the ice. I was moving so fast that I could see nothing except a bluish blur. A roar in my ears grew thunderously ominous, and a brilliant burst of brightness coincided with a touch of salty moisture in the air. The next moment spray and sunshine leapt upon me with the sound of the ocean's mighty roar. After a series of jolting and scraping collisions, I rolled over several times and came to an abrupt halt.

A few minutes passed before I regained my senses. Winded, I was too bruised and dazed to move. I had landed within yards of the sea, sprawled against a wall of debris whose jumbled rocks had been deposited by glaciers over hundreds of years. I examined the space around me. The long broad tongue of the glacier showed furrowed and blue-green alongside the cavernous exit of the subglacial river, flecked with patches of grit and sand. Dragging myself to my feet, I gazed around spellbound. I had come out into an extraordinary stretch of countryside, totally different from the rest of the island. Where the peninsula I had been living on was rugged and windswept, sharp-featured and inhospitable, the land here was gentle and undulating—an oasis of tranquility in a world of strife. Even the most fleeting glance revealed that it supported an abundance of wildlife during the summer and that its sheltered location would afford an excellent sanctuary to set up a winter home. Although good sense directed that I try to find a way of retrieving the sledge while the weather was fine, I could not resist the tremendous urge to go and explore.

25

The Last Decision

There had been many occasions on the island when I had thrilled to the discovery of some new revelation of nature; I doubt if any of them induced as much excitement as I felt that day. For the first time since I had left South Georgia over a year ago I saw grass growing—some of it almost a foot high. A coarse variety, sprouting in tussocky clumps, it was in sharp contrast to the remains of delicate miniature flowers that had bloomed earlier here and there when the sun was at its warmest. Hardly a step passed without there being some new aspect to delight the eye or some new wonder at which to gaze. So much was there to see and marvel at, I am at a loss to find the words to record it faithfully. When I try, images crowd my mind so profusely that I am bound to miss some of them in my haste.

I had one terrifying moment amidst all the joy. Leaning over a lake, of which there were many in this peninsula, to see if it contained fresh water, I was brought face to face with a savage of such wild, unkempt appearance that I fell back in terror—until it dawned on me that the reflection I saw was of myself. Long matted hair, joining an outcrop of facial growth, gave a truly

ferocious aspect to my countenance, which my animal-skin clothing did nothing to subdue. I needed several minutes to get over
the shock of the specter before I could go on to explore elsewhere. The water was fresh but tainted, and I suspected that
seals had been at the lake from the tracks round the edge.

The pleasure bubbling and spilling out of me made me laugh
aloud in sheer delight. Ice caves that sparkled with a million bril-
liants; rock caves where I could make a home for myself; vistas
of mountains and islets of striking splendour were just some of
the wonders I exulted in that day. I came across fossils of trees
and plants that must have existed many millions of years earlier,
as well as the mummified bodies of seals preserved in absolutely
perfect form.

The peninsula spread westwards. Although most of its northern shore was rocky and inaccessible from the sea, beautiful wide
stretches of beach with claylike soil extended to a gently rising
interior of rounded hillocks. Following the beach round the
northwest coast towards the more southern, calmer sea
approaches, I came upon a collection of various animal bones and
the gigantic skeleton of a whale. It was bleached white, almost
stone-solid after years of exposure in the open. When I stood
close, its huge ribs formed an arch that towered above me.
Gazing up at this wondrous specimen, I could not help feeling I
had strayed into the very workshop of creation, in which the
fossils and other stuff of life scattered about where the proto-
types from which all else was made. Letting my gaze travel over
the vast, beautifully constructed skeleton of the marvellous
animal laid out before me, I understood how insignificant was
my own self in the whole concept of creation. Overcome by an
intense feeling of humility and awe, I explored the rest of the
peninsula as though I were treading on hallowed ground, my
heart full of wonder and inspired reverence.

By evening I had looked at the peninsula from every angle,
and I was enchanted. The sky was the most beautiful I had ever
seen. Streamers of every shade and hue interweaving and changing colour in the opal heavens hinted at a divine artist testing colours for some spectacular display. Intoxicated by the unearthly
splendour of my surroundings, I had no urge to eat or sleep. I

mused that nature reserved her special mysteries for distant, dangerous places and wondered who could begrudge her any sacrifice for the privilege of witnessing them. I sat gazing southwards beyond the two islands in the near distance well into the night and must have dozed off, finally exhausted. I came to in the early hours of the next morning, sitting in the same place, after being awaked by an almighty sneeze.

An unaccountable touch of sulphur was in the air, and I thought the heavens themselves had exploded. The sky was dense with clouds of smoke billowing high into the zenith. They had their base in one of the islands to my south, which had erupted all along its length into an almost continuous line of fire. As I watched, fresh bursts billowed upwards, and I concluded that many small volcanic eruptions were taking place close to the shore. An occasional splash or ripple in the water indicated the presence of fish or even some other form of marine life, and I saw what looked like a seal, although quite different from either of the two species on the other peninsula. This was indeed exciting, even if the the seal was in the process of migrating northwards. I might yet have a chance of obtaining fresh food, maybe even enough to last the winter. Observing some fish close to the water's edge, I put a few morsels of blubber in the water to see if they would bite. To my amazement I succeeded in scooping several of them out with my hand without even a hook or line.

I remained near the beach, exploring the caves for a suitable dwelling and feeding on the fish, which I ate raw. The waters were teeming, and I wondered if the disturbance on the nearby island had caused the marine life to come this way. I had intended to try to recover my sledge from the ice cap before the weather broke. My catches had put me in a sparkling mood, however, and I was prepared to take a chance on remaining where I was for today at least, since I had fish in plenty to last me several days. If they remained till the sea froze over and if I could get some seal—and they were still about—I could possibly winter in the peninsula without having to return for supplies. By good chance a carcass of a seal in a cave provided me with some blubber, but the day was so calm I decided not to bother trying to light a fire.

The prospect of my own bleak peninsula was totally unappealing, and I urged myself not to think about it. By nightfall I had found a cave that would be perfect for a residence, choosing a different one to spend the night in so that I might observe the volcano. Although the fires had lessened considerably, sporadic explosions still sent a mass of smoke and debris skywards in a singularly high cloud.

Well into the following morning I was jolted into wakefulness. Stiff and a little chill without a covering, I had barely wiped the sleep from my eyes before I involuntarily started up. I thought my imagination was playing tricks on me; but no—there was the unmistakable sound of human voices. Had a ship seen the volcano and come this way to identify the phenomenon? While the island had stopped its eruptions, there was still some sign of the volcano's smoke. Again I heard what I was convinced was the sound of men talking. What should I do? You might have thought I would rush forward to the beach to investigate and make myself known. Far from it. Faced with the possibility of men arriving on this island, which had for a whole year and more been home for me, I was thrown into a state near to panic. Taking care not to show myself, I crept to the cave entrance to look out. What I saw set my heart racing. Not thirty yards away was a boatload of strangely dressed mariners talking excitedly as they pulled into the shallows. I could not hear what they were saying, but I knew they were foreign. The volcanic island seemed the subject of their attention in spite of their obvious excitement about the peninsula. They were not dressed like sealers; nevertheless, they seemed much interested in the various skeletons of seal strewing the beach.

All the time they chatted and moved about, they cast glances towards the inland ice mass. I hid, fearing they might come in my direction. Strange as it may seem, after months of longing to be rescued, I now dreaded the imminence of the possibility. I had become used to a savage sort of existence; and the renewal of contact with human beings, however peaceful they were, was abhorrent, involving complexities and rituals of behaviour that I sensed were far beyond me and to which I doubted I would ever readjust. Besides, I had found a part of the island well suited to my needs, one which would offer a commodious way of life once I was organized.

How contrary fate can be in certain circumstances! When I had begged for deliverance, she had denied it. Now that I sought to avoid the instruments of rescue, she had them come to me. It was a young boy who discovered the cave. I had seen him approach and had retreated deep inside it, hoping he would go past. As if drawn by some compulsion he could not resist, he came directly for it, stopping at the entrance to peer in. He stood quite motionless, and would not go away. I hardly breathed lest I make a noise that would alarm him and bring in the others. Strangely, he, too, became alert and tense, probably instinctively warned of another presence. He remained in silhouette, ready to spring back should some specter emerge from the cave's blackness. I shrank from this human being as though we were not of the same species.

More confused than alarmed by the unexpected appearance of men on these shores, I wanted time to think before being confronted. There is a sadness at the passing of every phase, and a natural reluctance to end a meaningful chapter of one's life. My last sixteen months had been unique. The island on which I had been marooned was no ordinary one. Neither had it been an ordinary achievement to have survived on it for so long. Desolate and situated beyond the boundaries of the known world, the island had required a superhuman effort to remain alive. As compensation I had had the privilege of being the first man to live on it and had seen phenomena that no other human had ever witnessed. As a pioneer and an explorer I had been initiated into the most sacred mysteries of the universe.

What had the outside world to offer except barbarism and greed? True, life here could also be cruel. That was the way of nature, and as such was part of an order that we could not change. The cruelty of man to his fellow, on the other hand, was something that could be altered if only there were enough well-meaning people to care sufficiently to try.

A voice inside me argued that I had a debt still to pay to mankind, a duty to try to do what I could to improve the lot of my fellows. Besides, what was the use of discovering an island if those who came afterwards returned home without me to make their own claim? Not only would my discovery belong to strangers but those strangers were from a foreign country. Why had I taken such time and trouble to log the weather and the habits of the wild animals if not to pass on this information?

I was still undecided what to do when a man called, and the boy slightly turned his head. As he did so, his face was revealed in a shaft of light. Distracted temporarily from his intense curiosity and his awe of the cave, his face had about it a look that was open and friendly. My fears vanished, and I felt inclined to speak. I had just made up my mind that I should try to break the silence gently when another call from the beach made the boy turn immediately and walk away.

I was left staring at the blinding brightness of the cave entrance. A chill passed through my body and a heaviness settled on my heart. If the mariners returned to their ship, I would be alone again. I thought of what would happen when I got back to England. My parents would be overjoyed to see me safe. I could imagine their astonishment as I told them of all my adventures. And then what, after the excitement of my return had worn off? Previously I had been no more than a boy, a callow youth. Now I was a man whose experienced had taught him that nothing worthwhile, whether it be climbing the rigging in a howling gale or surviving in a frozen waste, can be achieved without a long apprenticeship. Whatever my calling, I reasoned I had earned my place among my fellowmen.

I desperately wanted to approach the strangers but was unable to move. And then something happened that snapped the bonds that held me in thrall. I heard laughter, not mean or malicious laughter but the laughter that comes only from a fullness and goodness of heart. It was loud and lingering and infinitely mellow—the kind that scatters fear and puts the Devil to flight. Before I knew it, I had left my hiding place. The sound of that laughter had evoked a response in me that my human nature could not deny.